# JOSEPH FINDER

# HOUSE ON FIRE

HEAD of ZEUS

First published in the UK in 2020 by Head of Zeus Ltd
This paperback edition first published in 2020 by Head of Zeus Ltd

9 7 5 3 1 2 4 6 8

A catalogue record for this book is available from
the British Library.

ISBN (PB): 9781838930554
ISBN (E): 9781838930516

Printed and bound in Great Britain by
CPI Group (UK) Ltd, Croydon CR0 4YY

Head of Zeus Ltd
First Floor East
5–8 Hardwick Street
London EC1R 4RG

WWW.HEADOFZEUS.COM

for
H.D.F.
and
E.J.S.F.

# HOUSE ON
# FIRE

*Not for the first time, he puzzled over the curious nature of families—that family bonds tended to keep together people who had little in common.*

*He would never have chosen the members of his family as friends.*

—Lydia Davis, *Sketches for a Life of Wassilly*

# 1

S o how are you going to do it?" the guy asked me.

"'Do it'?"

He paused, glanced around—there was no one else in my office—and muttered, barely audible, the words he didn't want to say aloud. "Kill him. How are you going to kill him?"

"The less you know," I said, "the better. For both of us. You don't have a problem with that, do you?"

He didn't answer me. "It has to look like an accident," he said. "Or a random . . . whatever."

I gave him a long, direct look, blinked once. He'd told me that three times already.

Mort Vallison was sixty, but he looked ten years older. He was a once-handsome man under a lifetime of stress. He had short gray hair, neatly parted, and sincere brown eyes, but they were haunted. Hollow. He wore an expensive-looking navy-blue blazer and pricy shoes. He was not born to wealth, which was probably why he always dressed expensively.

He looked away. Vallison had insisted on coming to my office rather than have me come to his company headquarters. My firm, Heller Associates, is located in an old brick building in Boston's financial district, a renovated nineteenth-century lead-pipe factory with a steampunk look to it: the bare brick walls, the exposed ductwork, the big factory windows. The office used to belong to a dot-com that sailed high and crashed and left behind their Humanscale chairs.

"He's embezzling," he said. "But we haven't been able to catch him at it."

Vallison was the co-owner of a chain of excellent restaurants in Boston and down the East Coast, Neptune Seafood, a Boston institution. He was a wealthy man, with an impressive home in Chestnut Hill. He was convinced that his partner, Herb Martz, was cheating him out of millions of dollars. But he wasn't able to prove it. This on top of animosity that had accrued over the years had driven him to extreme measures. He wanted me to arrange Martz's death, and do it undetectably. He was offering a lot of money for the job.

"I don't need to know," I said. "The less contact we have, the better. And I'm going to need you to pay me in cryptocurrency—bitcoin, Ethereum, or whatever. The last thing we need is a money trail." He didn't seem to understand, so I explained it to him. He was a restaurateur, not a tech guy.


Herb Martz, his partner, kept to a routine. He lived with his wife in a condo in the Four Seasons. He saw a personal trainer three times a week, early in the morning. He went into work at ten, to their offices on the waterfront. He usually had lunch at one of the Neptunes around the city: a hamburger, most of the time. I guess he was tired of seafood.

The next day, late morning, I followed him from the Neptune Seafood at the Prudential Center to a sketchy hotel in Kenmore Square not too far from Fenway Park. I took my gray Toyota Camry. I have two cars; the other one is a truck, a Land Rover Defender in Coniston green. But that's a distinctive-looking vehicle. Whereas the Camry is so anonymous it's nearly invisible in traffic. That's the superpower of an ordinary car.

Martz parked his black Mercedes S-Class in a garage next to the hotel, and I pulled into the garage a few cars behind him. I followed him out of the garage and into the lobby. The guy at the desk asked him if he had luggage, and he said no. He checked into the hotel and checked out half an hour later.

He was, I assumed, seeing a mistress. And given how quick the assignation was, I figured it had been going on for some time. They knew each other, so they could get right down to business. Skip the preliminaries.

I followed him out of the hotel and back to his car. I took the stairs and got there before he did. From a distance, I watched him return to the Mercedes. Then I came around to the passenger's side and got in.

Stunned, he whipped around to look at me. Martz was a rough-looking, pot-bellied guy in his sixties with gin blossoms on his cheeks and tobacco-stained teeth. He wore a blue down vest over his dress shirt. "What the hell?" he said. "Jesus. You scared the shit out of me."

I said nothing. I took out my iPhone and hit play.

*So how are you going to do it?*

*"Do it"?*

*Kill him. How are you going to kill him?*

"Motherfucker," Martz said. "Like I told you. He has some bullshit excuse about how—"

"So what do you want to do?" I interrupted. "I'll go through some of our options."

"Did he pay you already?"

"Half."

"You planning on keeping that payment?"

"Nah, it's forensic evidence. Connects him to the cyber wallet." Everyone thinks cyber currency keeps you anonymous. But there are tricks you have to do to hide your identity, and neither of these guys knew them. "So come on, how do you want to play this?"

Martz was staring off into space, like he was thinking. "How much more would it cost if you finished the job?"

"I have no idea what you're talking about," I said. "You want to bring in law enforcement, right?"

"Finish the job. As in finish him. Take the bastard out."

I wasn't surprised, frankly, and I played it cool. "That's not on the menu."

"Don't bullshit me," Martz said. "You think I didn't do my due diligence? I know your reputation. You're ex–Special Forces. You've killed guys for a living. You're trained for this."

"Yeah, we were more about winning hearts and minds."

"You've confirmed that I've got a problem. Nice work. Now make my problem go away. I'll pay you another forty thousand. Make it worth your time. Call it a happy ending."

"I think I'll take a pass."

"I'm a paying customer, Heller. You ever hear the expression 'The customer is always right'?"

"Thing is, Herb, you're not the customer."

"The client, then."

"Yeah, you're not the client either."

"What the hell are you talking about?"

I couldn't keep a little grin from my face. I pointed out the window, where six state troopers were surrounding the car, ready to arrest Martz.

"The hell—?"

"See, you're the target. First rule in my trade: always know who you're working for, and always know the play. Yep, I did my due diligence too. And I found another play."

The car door on the driver's side opened, and one of the troopers said, "Step out of the car, Mr. Martz."

# 2

Originally, Herb Martz had come to see me to get proof his partner, Mort Vallison, was trying to kill him. The brake lines on his Mercedes had been cut, he said. He wanted me to get the proof on tape so he could go to the police and get his partner put away.

It took me almost a week to get to Mort, because it had to be done subtly. Eventually I ran into him in Oak Long Bar in the Copley Plaza, where Herb told me he hung out sometimes, managed to bump into him as we both stood at one end of the crowded bar.

Soon we'd struck up a conversation about my military days and how the world would just be better off with some people taken out, wouldn't it? I let him know, as subtly as I could, that once in a while I did favors for friends along those lines. And sure enough, he was intrigued. He asked for my business card.

I gave him one.

A week later, Mort came to my office to discuss business. I assured him the office was a safe place to talk. He wanted me to get rid of his partner. Not that I asked, but he gave a reason that almost held up: his partner was embezzling profits from the company, had been doing so for decades.

You'd be surprised how often I get asked to kill people, to do "hits." I have to explain that it's not in my list of client services. But something about Herb Martz didn't smell right.

So I agreed to take on the job.

Right away I got in touch with my friend Major Liz Rodriguez from the state police's Special Investigations Unit, and she liked my idea of setting up a sting.

My instincts proved correct. It turned out that both Mort and Herb had been illegally diverting cash from Neptune Seafood for years, cheating the government out of tens of millions of dollars in taxes. And both of them were under investigation by the IRS.

Herb was afraid Mort would weaken and rat them out to the IRS, turn state's evidence, expose their long-running scam. Mort was a man who was constantly honored for his philanthropy, and he simply couldn't cope with the disgrace of going to prison. He would try to make a deal.

The two men deserved each other.

Right about now the two of them were probably in separate interview rooms at state police headquarters in Framingham. I was guessing that each of them was trying hard to make a deal.

Neither one of them would escape prison now.

The only downside in this? I wasn't going to get paid.


I didn't get to the office until early afternoon. I waved hello to the scowling Mr. Derderian, who was in the doorway of his high-end oriental carpet shop next door. The sign on my second-floor office door reads HELLER ASSOCIATES—ACTUARIAL CONSULTING SERVICES, which cuts down on foot traffic. I keep a very low profile. In my line of work, the less my face and name are known, the better.

My receptionist and office manager, Jillian Alperin, was eating a late lunch at her desk. Jillian, covered with tattoos and piercings, had turned out to be quite bright. She was still a little intimidated by me, though, which was fine.

"A couple of messages for you already, Nick," she said after taking a large swallow of her—what was it again?—tempeh.

6

"Thanks. Dorothy?"

"In the break room, I think."

Dorothy Duval, my forensic data tech and researcher, was making a fresh pot of coffee, even though that was really Jillian's job. She just liked doing things for herself because she liked them done right.

Dorothy had a style all her own. Her head was close-shaven, and she normally wore very large earrings. But today she was dressed more conservatively than usual, in a black pencil skirt and blue blazer over a white blouse, and normal-size earrings.

She noticed me checking her out and said, "I had a meeting." Her coffee mug was at the ready. It read *Jesus Saves, I spend.* She was a devoted churchgoer with a sense of humor about the Lord.

"Business meeting?"

"Personal." Then she took a breath. "Well, I'm not going to hide it from you, because I need your help. I was just interviewed this morning by the chairman of the co-op board of a building I want to buy into."

"*Co-op* board? Isn't that a very New York thing?"

"We've got a few in Boston," she said impatiently. "This one's called the Kenway Tower on Comm. Ave. In Kenmore Square."

"What kind of questions did he ask?"

"That's the thing, Nick. On the phone he was as friendly as can be. Really talkative, about how great the building is, and the neighborhood. He wanted to ask me about the NSA, and I think he really dug all the secrecy, the stuff I couldn't talk about."

Dorothy used to work at the National Security Agency but apparently hadn't been a good personality fit. So she got a job at a private intelligence firm in DC, Stoddard Associates, where I also used to work before I went off on my own. Later I asked her to join me at Heller Associates. My first and most important hire.

She went on. "So I was expecting the third degree when I came in this morning, and instead they could barely get me out of there fast enough. I mean, the dude's face fell when he saw me."

7

"Uh-oh." The board of a co-op association has the power to determine who gets to buy into the building.

"Yeah, that's what I was thinking too, uh-oh. They didn't know I was black until they met me. Then it was like, 'Later, dude.'"

I thought about mentioning the fact that, with her shaved head and her extreme ear piercings, the hedgerow of silver hoops outlining the curving helix of each ear, she could look a little fierce. But it didn't seem like the right time to say it. And she was making her bow to conventionality by wearing a blue blazer and, I noticed, high-heeled shoes.

She continued. "He said he had some concerns about my income and my credit history."

"Meaning your income's not enough to afford—"

"No, it *is* enough. I mean, I could always use a raise, to make it easier, but the numbers work, and I've saved up a lot. I've had years of decent, steady income."

"So what was his problem?"

"He said he's worried about *you*. He said private investigators work close to the bone and often have to lay off their employees. Could you write the board a letter assuring them I've got steady employment for the foreseeable future?"

I shrugged. "Sure. Write it up for me and I'll sign whatever. What's wrong with your credit history?"

"Nothing. I pay on time. I don't know what he's talking about. Anyway, how'd it go today?"

I gave her a quick download on the Neptune Seafood partners, Mort Vallison and Herb Martz, and how the two of them got arrested.

She said, "This Liz Rodriguez from the Staties?"

"That's the one."

"So you won't get paid for any of the work. You're just doing a good deed. Being a good citizen."

"Something like that."

"Maybe this isn't the best time to ask, but . . . are we financially solvent?"

"Sure. As long as I don't need to hire anybody else, we're doing okay." Could we have been doing a little better? Sure. But I still refused to handle things like divorce cases, and maybe it was time to get over that particular exception. Matrimonial jobs could be lucrative, but they always made me feel grubby. I did private intelligence work. That did not include putting a GPS tracker on a straying spouse's car.

I had standards. Or so I told myself.

On the way to my desk, my intercom sounded. "It's Patty Lenehan," Jillian announced over the speaker. "She's calling from a Cape Cod number."

"I'll take it," I said.

If it was Patty Lenehan, I knew it was important.

Patty was married to Sean Lenehan, who'd been a member of my Special Forces A-team. He saved my life once, in Afghanistan, and you don't easily forget something like that. I was the godfather to one of his kids. I was their uncle Nick.

Sean came back from Afghanistan and Iraq four tours after I left and soon thereafter developed a drug problem. Like millions of Americans, he became addicted to opioids. The epidemic is particularly bad on Cape Cod. But the Department of Veterans Affairs there proved to be no help. And he didn't have any money. So I paid for an expensive course of treatment at a pricy rehab center in Falmouth called Fresh Beginnings or something.

Getting him to agree to rehab—that had been the hard part. It was a macho, Special Forces thing: never admit to any chinks in your armor. So I spent a fair amount of time in Westham, trying to convince him. Along the way, I got to know his kids. Finally he consented, and three months in rehab really seemed to do the trick. The past year, I thought he'd remained clean. I just hoped he hadn't backslid.

I answered the call. "Patty, is everything okay?"

"Nick? Please. How soon can you get here?"

"How soon do you need me?" I mentally ran through the list of client meetings and phone calls I'd scheduled. Which ones I could reschedule and which ones I couldn't.

Her voice had gotten high and small. I barely heard what she said and almost asked her to repeat it, until it sank in.

"He's—dead," she said. "Overdose."

# 3

I thought he was clean."

"So did I."

"The kids—never mind. I'm going to leave Boston now. I'll be there in a couple of hours."

"Thank you, Nick," Patty said. "The kids really need to see you. Stay at our place. The guest room's free."


An hour later I was in my Land Rover Defender 90, driving along the Southeast Expressway toward Cape Cod and Sean's house.

I was shocked yet not shocked to hear that Sean had died. I thought he'd successfully gotten free of an insidious opioid addiction. But he'd died from an overdose. It was easy to relapse.

His death wasn't just heartbreaking, it was infuriating.

I liked him a lot. Most people did. He was a natural extrovert, very friendly, very funny, very smart. I used to imagine him running for office, becoming a state rep or a congressman or something. He had the right personality for it.

Sean was stocky, and strong, and short. Like a lot of the guys in the Special Forces. He had a baby face, and it took forever for his beard to become visible. When it came in, it was a scraggly, patchy mess.

He and I joined the army at the same time, in what's called the 18 X-ray program, which was then sort of a new thing. It was an accelerated path into the elite Special Forces. You used to have to join the army and make the grade of E-4 before you could even apply to join it. Instead, in the 18X program, if you'd done some college, you could apply to try out for the Green Berets. The army was recruiting scholar-athletes—the ideal being the PhD who could win a bar fight, or so the joke went. Smart kids who also played football or ran track. That didn't quite describe me, since I was a pretty mediocre student. But I was a dropout from Yale, which must have intrigued the recruitment office. I was nineteen.

You went through basic training at Fort Benning plus advanced individual training in one seventeen-week course. Then to jump school for a few weeks—five static-line jumps—and then you're shipped to Fort Bragg in North Carolina, where you go through the unique torture that is Special Forces training.

Those of you who are left in the program, that is. More than sixty percent of the candidates drop out along the way. You went on long rucksack marches. You went slogging through the swamp. You were constantly wet and cold and exhausted and desperate for sleep. The process weeded out the weak of body and spirit. Sean endured the whole drill without complaining. He always seemed happy despite it all. He'd make jokes to jolly everyone else up.

I'd been so surprised, at first, that someone that strong could succumb to pain pills.

After we qualified for the Special Forces, Sean and I were assigned to the same A-team. I was the junior weapons sergeant for some reason—I guess I demonstrated competency in weapons handling, though I was and am no gun nut. (Later I went through the training and became the intel sergeant, which seemed a more natural fit.)

Sean was the junior engineer, which meant he worked with demolitions. He was our breacher: he blew up doors and walls so we could go in.

All those years of working closely with explosives must have done damage to his brain. At least, that's the theory. It's called breacher syndrome. Repeated exposure to low-level blasts can cause traumatic brain injury. He came back with terrible headaches, shooting pain in his forehead. He also started getting regular migraines. A doctor at the VA hospital prescribed Oxydone, a nasal inhaler that dispenses a powerful opiate quickly, and just like that, Sean was hooked.

I should have checked in with Patty weeks ago. I guess I was figuring that if he was back on drugs, she'd let me know. I obviously figured wrong. I was angry at myself for not staying more closely in touch.

He saved my life once; I should have been able to save his.

# 4

I drove past Sidney's Clam Shack (*Voted best fried clams on the Cape!*), a few motels with VACANCY signs, and competing beach-toy stores on either side of the road that were both shuttered now that summer had passed. I drove carefully and at exactly forty miles an hour. Westham was a famous speed trap, crawling with cops waiting to ticket summer visitors for driving two miles an hour over the speed limit. This was the off-season, but the Westham cops would probably be even more aggressive than usual given the scarcity of prey.

When I rang the doorbell, Patty flung open the screen door and hugged me, hard. She was a small, compact brunette, a former high school cheerleader who ran almost every day. She was a nurse at Cape Cod Hospital and worked long hours, and she seemed to have an infinite supply of energy. Like a lot of military wives whose husbands were gone so much, she ran the house; she had no choice.

But now you could see she was depleted, her eyelids heavy, her eyes swollen. Her mascara was smeared. She was still in her hospital scrubs. Her kids were swarming and bickering behind her.

"Thank you, Nick," she said.

"For what?"

"For being here."

"Come on," I said.

Brendan was ten, and the oldest. He was a cool, smart kid whose dad had been deployed for much of his childhood. And when Sean got back, he soon became an opioid addict. So for much of Brendan's life, his father was absent, in one way or another. I was Brendan's godfather and his surrogate dad. I was sort of a surrogate dad to his brother, Andrew, and his sister, Molly, too.

I know I'm never going to have children—I don't want them, thanks—but I admit to getting a paternal glow from helping these kids out. My nephew, Gabe, is the closest I'll ever come to having my own. I love him dearly, but he's an odd one.

I felt terrible for Brendan and his siblings. Normally, when I came by their house, Brendan would come running. Not like when he was four or five, literally racing through the house to fling himself at me. But still, he hustled and beamed. This time he was hanging back. His eyes looked bruised. He was mournful and distant, just like his mother. Brendan was often called on to be the man of the family with Dad gone a lot, and he took it seriously.

I stepped into the room and hugged Brendan and then Molly, who was eight and just as tall and played soccer. "Where'd Andrew go?" I said. I could see Andrew, six, hiding behind the La-Z-Boy recliner. "He just disappeared."

Andrew burst out laughing. He didn't seem to be sad at all. I wondered if he was too young, if he just didn't get the enormity of what had happened to him.

"Andrew's being annoying," Brendan said.

Andrew ran over to me and hugged me around the legs. "When's Daddy coming back?" he said, his words muffled.

Oh, he understood something.

"Baby," Patty said, "Daddy's not coming back. He's in Heaven, honey."

"No!" Andrew said, correcting her as if it were obvious. "He's coming back. Daddy always goes away, and he always comes back."

"Dad's dead," Brendan snapped, stunning everyone into silence.

"Hey, Bren," I said. "How's the coin collection?"

He turned to me. "I got the new proof set—you wanna see?"

"I would."

We went to his room, where he pulled out from a desk drawer the latest additions to his coin collection and made sure I understood their importance. How all the proof coins bore the "S" mark of the U.S. Mint at San Francisco. The special-edition Lincoln penny struck with the "W" mark of the West Point Mint. When he finally fell silent, I said, "I know how hard it must be to lose your daddy."

"But isn't your dad still alive?"

"He is," I admitted.

"What about your mom?"

"She's alive too. Lives outside of Boston."

There was a pause. "Isn't your dad in prison?"

"Yep."

"Was he in prison when you were growing up?"

"Part of it. When I was a teenager he fled the country, went into hiding. Left us with nothing. Eventually the good guys caught up with him in Switzerland."

"'The good guys'?" Brendan smiled. "Was your dad a bad guy?"

"Very much."

"But he's alive."

"Yes."

"Oh. Did Mom tell you how Dad died?"

I hesitated. Had she told Brendan? I wondered. He kept talking. "It was an overdose. He was back on the drugs. I knew it. I knew he was. I could always tell when he was using."

I nodded.

"He'd get all sad and really angry, and him and Mom used to fight all the time. I don't—I don't understand, Uncle Nick. Why'd he do it?"

"Because he was an addict, and it's really hard to quit some of those drugs."

"No. Why'd he go and . . . kill himself?"

"I'm not so sure he did."

"He took an overdose."

"But it's really easy to do that by accident. Even if he didn't mean to."

"But we really *needed* him! Why did he do it?"

"He couldn't help it." A long moment passed, and then I said, "He was really proud of you, you know that?"

Brendan's face had gone red. He'd begun to weep silently. Tears were dripping off his cheeks. He shook his head.

I went on. "He was. He was always telling his friends stories about you. Like how you insisted on carving the Thanksgiving turkey? And your mom didn't want you to use the big sharp knife? But you did it anyway and you did it perfectly. Didn't even cut yourself. He was so proud of you."

Brendan clamped his hands over his face. "He showed . . . He showed . . ." He was choking out the words and finally got out: "He showed it in a great way, huh?" he said with bitter sarcasm.

I went back downstairs to the family room with Patty. It was a cozy, crowded place with a fireplace, an orange shag carpet, a big TV.

"'He always comes back,'" Patty said, quoting her younger son. "Do you know what Andrew means? He's talking about the Oxy. He's talking about how even when his dad was here, he was gone."

"So he knows?"

"He's seen the light go out in his father's eyes. The way he'd disappear for days at a time. Then come back. But he just doesn't know that this time, Daddy's not coming back."

"Patty, I talked to Sean three weeks ago and he seemed fine. He was off the pills. He said the rehab worked."

"Yeah, but you know how precarious addiction and recovery can be. He wasn't strong enough. He gave in to it. Went back to it. Then got fired. From the construction crew."

"You mean, laid off?" Cape Cod contractors worked a seasonal, cyclical business.

"Fired. Couple days ago. He'd gone back to using, and his boss could see it." She paused, turned away, and suddenly broke down in tears. I put my arms around her. It seemed like the right thing to do.

There had always been a spark between Patty and me, but neither one of us ever acknowledged it or acted upon it. That would have been the ultimate betrayal of my comrade, off fighting the war after I'd come back, and that was unthinkable. Still, she had lively eyes and an irresistible smile, and her daily running kept her in great shape.

She said, her words muffled against my shirt, "I found him passed out on the bathroom floor. Overdosed on an Oxydone inhaler."

"Did the kids see him?"

She sniffed, pulled away. Shook her head. "They were at school, thank God. He'd bought the Oxy off another vet whose doctor prescribed him twice as much as he needed."

I nodded. I didn't know what to say.

"I just have to hold it together for the kids. When you have kids, you don't get to fall apart."

"I know."

"You're not a parent; you can't really know."

"Fair enough. But I think I understand."

"You understood *Sean*, that's the thing. Sometimes I felt you knew him better than I did. What you two went through together."

I nodded, attempted a smile.

"It's gonna take all the energy I have just to get up in the morning and get through the day," she said.

I nodded again.

She'd moved over to a corner of the family room where a small writing desk was stacked with envelopes and staplers and a

18

Scotch-tape dispenser and a calculator. She picked up one stack and waved it.

"The funeral home wants twenty thousand bucks. That's twenty thousand bucks I don't have. He used up all our savings on drugs."

"Twenty *thousand*? For what?"

"Well, eighteen, to be exact. A couple years ago Sean saw a flier somewhere advertising free burial for vets in the national cemetery in Bourne. *You may now prequalify!* it said. He wanted to plan for the future. So the funeral home sold him what they called a pre-need funeral contract. I guess he didn't really look at the fine print. So now I have to come up with eighteen thousand bucks on top of whatever Brendan's braces are going to cost."

"I'm happy to loan you whatever you need," I said. Though I wasn't sure how liquid I was these days. Business had been slow.

I took the top envelope from the stack she'd been waving. Haddad Funeral Home. I opened up the bill and read it over.

"I'm not taking a loan from you, Nick," she said.

"Interesting," I said, slipping the statement back into the envelope. I took note of Haddad Funeral Home's address in Orleans, Massachusetts. "Mind if I borrow this?"

"No, you're not paying them a visit. It's my problem, not yours."

I gave her the envelope back. "Okay. Hey, I'm keeping you from your kids, aren't I?"

"More like protecting me from them. Nick, do you think Sean always had this . . . weakness? Was he always like this?"

She meant the drugs.

"People change, Patty."

"You think?"

"When he came back the last time, he was different. All that breaching, all those explosives, all those years—I think it did something to him."

"And the stress of what you guys went through."

19

"Maybe. But, man, he could do anything. I remember when the Humvee broke down and we were waiting hours for the mechanics, he finally got out and got under the thing and got the hoses unkinked or whatever it was, got it running again. Sean was the engine whisperer. There was nothing he couldn't fix."

"Yeah," she said sadly. "Except himself."

# 5

Sean Lenehan's funeral was at Our Lady of Grace church in Westham. It was a long Catholic ceremony, and it was better attended
than the wake. Most of Patty's family was there: her dad and two of her
brothers were lobstermen in town and had a lot of friends in the business. They mostly wore Windbreakers and Carhartt work jackets and
Patriots jackets—not a lot of suits or blazers for the men—and drove
pickup trucks with lobster traps in the back. Whereas Sean's family all
lived in South Carolina and weren't that close, and I think his parents
were dead.

I was one of the pallbearers, along with one of Patty's brothers and
a couple of nephews and the only other guy there from our Special
Forces A-team, a guy we called Merlin. His real name was Walter Mc-
George. He had been our communications sergeant. After he left
the service, he'd become an expert in technical surveillance
countermeasures—finding bugs and such. Merlin lived in Maryland,
where he was a serious sport fisherman and kept a boat on the Chesapeake Bay. He looked the same as always—a small, compact guy who
could have been a jockey. He'd shaved his mustache and was wearing
a black suit and well-shined shoes. He didn't give Patty a hug but extended his hand to shake. He was always formal, to the point of uncomfortable, around women. He wore a green blazer with a regimental tie,
because he was a member of the Special Forces Association. I didn't

belong. I just wore a black suit. Patty asked me to say a few words, and so I did, about how he'd saved my life.

Then everyone drove to the veterans' cemetery in the town of Bourne, half an hour away. It was a lushly landscaped nature preserve. There, they gave Sean a military burial. Four young army soldiers, in their dress blues, draped Sean's casket with an American flag. As we carried the casket to the grave site, a few among the gathering saluted. Vets, they had to be.

One woman stood out from the other mourners. She was a hippieish woman in her thirties, wearing a busily colored fringed, crochet-knit shawl over a black dress. I'd noticed her before, at the church, sitting off by herself. I remembered the shawl. Now she was standing alone in the third ring of mourners around the grave. She didn't look like she came from here. I couldn't figure her out. My first thought was that she was a journalist, but then I ruled that out—she was dressed too nicely. I also had the strong feeling she'd been looking at me.

The brief burial service began, led by their local priest, who had silver hair and wire-rimmed glasses. Two servicemen, dressed in blues, took the flag off Sean's casket and proceeded to fold it crisply and carefully. Each fold represented something. When they were finished, only the stars showed. One member of the honor guard presented the flag to Patty. He spoke the memorized line: "On behalf of the President of the United States, the United States Army, and a grateful nation, please accept this flag as a symbol of our appreciation for your loved one's honorable and faithful service."

Her eyes pooled with tears, which streamed down her face as she accepted the flag.

They fired three shots in the air. Then one of them pulled out a bugle and put it to his mouth. Taps issued from a boom box while he pretended to play the tune. Merlin and I and a couple of other guys saluted as the casket was lowered into the grave. I gave Patty a hug and then her kids, and then I backed away to let others greet her.

People drifted away. Merlin put a hand on my shoulder. "I thought he was in rehab."

"He was for a while."

Merlin fidgeted, then looked over at the grave site, where the casket had just been lowered into the ground. "What a great guy he was. Just—I mean, he never settled for the easy way out, did he? Always volunteered for the hard schools, wanted to be on point. The lead climber. The jumpmaster."

"That was Sean," I said. He'd always gravitated to the more dangerous jobs in training. Always volunteered to run the rifle range, which is a lousy job. When we did training jumps from the C-130, he was the guy who inspected the parachutes and the helmets and tugged at the straps before anyone could jump. It was a serious responsibility. Nobody wanted to do it but Sean.

"Sort of a badge-hunter," Merlin said, "but he always wanted to be the number one guy in the stack."

I nodded. In close-quarters battle, you didn't want to be the first guy in.

The first guy in the stack was the one who got shot, if it was going to happen. When you're walking through the mountains of Afghanistan, the first guy in line is the one who's going to trigger a land mine. But Sean always volunteered to do it.

"Not to mention he saved my life," I said.

"Yeah, there's that."

I sensed someone approaching, and I turned to see the hippie woman come up to me. "I liked what you said earlier," she said.

"Are you a relative?" I asked. "I don't think we've met. I'm Nick Heller."

"Not a relative. And yeah, I know who you are."

Up close her attire seemed less hippie, more boho—artsy, funky. Her shawl looked expensive. Designer, maybe. I noticed her unlined features, the irises that seemed to flicker between gray and brown. "Oh, yeah?" I said.

She gave me a long, measuring look as if she was making a decision. Finally, she said, "Can we talk?"

# 6

Montanaro's was a large, roomy restaurant on Route 6 that was known to the locals for its excellent Italian food, its homemade pasta and fresh-baked bread, and the best pizza outside of New Haven, Connecticut. It was dismissed by summer visitors, who preferred the seafood shacks, which they considered more authentic, like outsider art. That was just fine with the locals.

We met in the parking lot. The day was chilly and raw, and it felt good to walk into the humid warmth of the restaurant. The place was deserted. It was in between lunch and dinner, but they were willing to let us just order soft drinks. After we were seated, I glanced at the menu, changed my mind, and ordered some fried calamari and rigatoni with vodka sauce. When she ordered a garden salad, I figured she'd stop at that, but she went on to add the lasagna al forno. So we were having lunch, this mystery woman and I. She had dark brown hair cut in a sort of shag, just touching her shoulders. She had a sharp nose and lively brown eyes, but she just missed being pretty. A slight rearrangement of her refined features and she would have been.

She took off her shawl. Underneath she was wearing a black crepe gathered midi dress. The heavy crepe material looked very high-end, like it was cut to fit her. She wore dark opaque stockings and black suede booties with chunky wooden heels. Diamond stud earrings and a single diamond pendant around her neck. The whole outfit looked Parisian, very free-spirited. I pay close attention to what women wear, not because I care about fashion but because I think women tell you a lot with what they choose to wear, much more than men do. This woman was artistically inclined, and wealthy, and unconventional.

"Okay," she said, folding her hands on the table. Her nails were painted the color of a bruise. "My name is Susan Kimball. You've probably heard of my father, Conrad Kimball."

"As in the Kimball Gallery at Harvard?"

"And the Kimball Wing of the National Gallery, and the Kimball School of Medicine, and on and on."

"And Kimball Pharma."

She arched her brows. "Exactly."

The Kimball name was on countless buildings around the world and wings of museums. Conrad Kimball was a great philanthropist. He was also known to be a rapacious entrepreneur. I knew only the basics about the guy. The company he'd founded, Kimball Pharmaceutical, made the opioid drug Oxydone, the drug that Sean Lenehan had overdosed on.

The waitress brought a steaming loaf of crusty bread impaled by a steak knife. I cut a few pieces and offered the basket to Susan. She took a piece, and then I did.

"You didn't know Sean, and you're not related to him," I said. "Nobody here knows you. So why *are* you here?"

"Because I knew you'd be here."

I paused a moment, considered asking her how. Decided not to. "You could have emailed me."

"You don't have a website."

"That's true."

"You're also not listed anywhere. Neither is Heller Associates."

"Also true." My clients all get to me through word of mouth. I prefer that to advertising on the World Wide Web and putting a big target out there for bad guys to try to hack.

26

"You're not on Facebook or Twitter, at least not under your name. But I heard about you. So I hired someone to find you."

Another private investigator, no doubt. Well, I wasn't in hiding either, so finding me wasn't that impressive an achievement. "Well done," I said. "What can I do for you, Susan?"

"You're a, what? Private intelligence agent?"

"Something like that."

"So, not a private investigator?"

"Not just." I reached for another piece of bread. "So you showed up at the burial of someone you don't know—is that, maybe, a little strange, considering where your family's fortune comes from?"

"Or maybe it's totally appropriate," she said defiantly, her nostrils flaring.

"Do you know how Sean Lenehan died?"

"Overdose of Oxydone. A hundred and thirty people die from an opioid overdose every day. Nearly fifty thousand every year. And then there's the two million people who are addicted and desperate."

I looked at her with surprise.

"The drug is fiendishly addictive," she said. "And it made Daddy a billionaire many times over."

"Are you on the outs with him?"

She shook her head. "Though I'm sure he considers me a disappointment."

The waitress placed a dish of fried calamari in front of me.

"You like squid?" I said.

"Love it. Thank you. I'm famished." She took a piece with a lot of tentacles on it. The squid was crisp and delicious and not too oily.

"Were you cut out of the will or something?"

She shook her head again. "Not that I know of. Though he's not above doing it. May I call you Nick?"

"Sure."

27

"Call me Sukie."

"Sukie," I said. "What do you do, Sukie?"

"I'm a documentary filmmaker. As Susan Garber, which is my mother's maiden name."

"Do you go to a lot of funerals like this?"

"As a matter of fact, I do. This is, let's see, the twenty-seventh opioid-related funeral I've attended in the last two months."

"All people you don't know."

"One I knew, actually. A friend of mine OD'd on heroin. She'd started with Oxydone in the hospital. You get addicted and then your prescription runs out, and it turns out heroin is a lot cheaper than pills and gives you the same high. But no, I don't know most of these people."

I nodded, chewed. "How do you find them?"

"The funerals?"

"The Oxydone-related deaths."

"I told you, I hire people who find me names. Lots to choose from."

"When you go to all these funerals, do they know who you are?"

"No."

"Do you introduce yourself?"

"Oh, God no." She carefully selected another tentacle piece. "I'd be tarred and feathered." She held the piece up in the air at the end of her fork. "I'd be deep fried."

"So what's the point?"

"Why do I do it? Because I think *some* member of my family ought to bear witness to the victims of the drug that made us all rich. Since we sold them all the poison that killed them. Does that make sense?"

"Sure, I guess so."

"Come face-to-face with what the poison is doing. I looked at that widow today, I saw her weeping, and her three young kids, and I just thought—I just can't live with that. Our family business isn't about curing pain. It's about causing it."

"But you still haven't told me what you want."

"Very simple. I want you to find—and steal—a document."

"A document."

"Let me give you the short version. It's a clinical trial, a study that was done on Oxydone while it was being developed. It was a bombshell study. It showed how dangerously addictive Oxydone was. If the government, the FDA, had found out about that study, they'd have killed Oxydone instantly. Considered it a threat to public safety. The drug would never have been allowed to go on the market."

"So the government never found out about the study?"

"Somehow they buried it. My dad must have arranged to make it disappear. I don't know, exactly. I just know the rumors. He knew what a huge moneymaker Oxydone could be. How it could transform Kimball Pharma. And he didn't want anything to get in its way."

"So you want me to find a copy of this clinical trial. Which would be like, what? A couple of thick file folders' worth of paper? Or a computer file?"

"Hard copy. My dad's old-school. He's eighty years old. Prefers paper. Always has."

"How long ago was the study done?"

"Probably twenty years ago."

"Then there's almost certainly a digital copy of it. A PDF file. That's the first thing I'd look for. And let me save you some money. You don't need to hire me for this." Rich people love bargains more than anyone. "Hire a hacker to break into the Kimball Pharma network. If you hired me, that's what I'd do—I'd go out and hire a hacker myself, probably. So why not cut out the middleman?"

"Because all the digital copies have been purged from the company's network. I've hired people to look for me. All evidence of that trial has been deleted from the digital archives."

"Maybe. But every company keeps corporate archives. Hard copy. It's your dad's company—do you know where Kimball Pharma stores its paper files?"

"There's a central filing facility at the headquarters building in Purchase, but I've checked it already. That file is missing."

"There have to be backup files at some place like Iron Mountain." That was a company that stored corporate records, physical and electronic, in underground vaults and warehouses. They did what they called "information management," a great vague phrase. They also shredded sensitive files, which they call "secure destruction."

"Maybe," she said. "But I know there's a copy somewhere."

"Unless all copies have been destroyed."

"You don't know my father. He throws nothing away. The original packrat. In his office at home he keeps all the most sensitive company and personal files, in locked file cabinets. Understand, this is a man who reads newspapers and books only in print. He totally distrusts the cloud. He thinks people who trust the cloud are naive and will regret it, and soon."

"Which home? I'm sure your father has more than one."

"I'm talking about the house in Katonah, New York. The house where we all grew up."

"Have you looked there?"

"Are you kidding? My dad always keeps his office locked when he's not there. He's a very suspicious man."

"Sukie, why do you want this document?"

She tipped her chin to one side. "I have my reasons."

"That's not good enough," I said. "Are you in some kind of trouble?"

"No," she said. "I'm about to *cause* trouble. A lot of it."

# 7

I'm guessing if a document like that were made public, it would be financially devastating to Kimball Pharma," I said.

"More than that. We could well end up with criminal indictments against the top officers at Kimball—starting with my father."

"So if you made it public, you'd be putting him in prison."

"He'd have put himself there. Look, this is the right thing to do. The moral thing to do. Because Oxydone is dangerously addictive, and they should be forced to admit it. They should be made to pay for their deception."

"But I assume you'd pay too. As an heir. You okay with that?"

"Okay with that? I want that, desperately. It's the only way anything changes. This is a business that feeds off addiction like a vampire drinks blood. You think another Facebook group, another devastatingly barbed tweet, another strongly worded op-ed in the *New York Times* is going to make a difference?" She shook her head. "People are dying, Nick. Every goddamn day."

"What turned you?"

"In what way?"

"Something radicalized you. Caused you to start questioning your family's role. What happened?"

She stirred Splenda into her coffee, which was lightened with half-and-half. "It was what happened to a college friend of mine. Woman named Charlotte, on the college women's squash team. She was great at everything—Chaucer to football. Great athlete. Four years ago, something happened to her. She threw out her back, then had spinal surgery, and was put on painkillers. Oxydone, of course. Her parents had just died in an auto crash; she'd just gone through a messy breakup with her boyfriend. I don't know what else. What I do know is she quickly became addicted to Oxy. And one day she OD'd. Was it deliberate? Was it an accident? I have no idea. But they found a couple of empty Oxydone inhalers in her bathroom and she died in the shower." She spoke not very loudly but fervently. "And I thought, my God, *we* did it, *we* poisoned her. And before long I started to realize that this was happening all over the place. Do you know every year we lose more veterans to opiates than we lost to the Iraqis? Or ISIS?"

I nodded. Sean's was just one death. She was seeing opiate-related deaths on a wholesale level. "I understand," I said. "It's just—"

"You think I'm crazy."

"No, it's not that. I'm not clear on what you're trying to accomplish. What you're trying to do."

"I want leverage. I want blackmail."

"For what? Not—for money?"

"Nothing for me. I want to force my father to set up a network of clinics around the world to take care of the people he's addicted."

"Think he'd do that?"

"It's that or I hand the study to a reporter for the *Times* or the *Washington Post*. His choice."

"What would happen then?"

"Kimball Pharma would be hit with massive fines—I'm talking billions of dollars—and he'd go to jail. Believe me, he doesn't want this file made public."

"Seriously, billions?"

"When GlaxoSmithKline got caught burying studies that showed their drug Paxil, their antidepressant, was ineffective, they were charged with health-care fraud and fined three *billion* dollars."

"Jesus."

"And this fraud is of a whole different order. So I'll be making my father an offer he can't refuse."

"And what do your brothers and sisters think of what you're doing?"

"They don't know, and they can't."

"How do you think they're going to react?"

"With surprise. That meek and mild Sukie, the middle child no one pays attention to, could do anything so unexpected."

I thought that was interesting. "But wouldn't you just be harming yourself by making such a document public? I assume your wealth is mostly tied up in Kimball Pharma stock."

"I'm already rich enough for several lifetimes. Look, I'm talking about people I love. Let's be clear. I know that. But I've got a chance to pull the brake cord. And I will not be able to live with myself if I don't do it."

"I just wonder if you know the risks here."

"The risks? The big risk is that I do nothing."

"Things don't always turn out like you plan. Big companies don't go down easy."

"Oh, yeah? So what would you have me do instead—get another hot-stone spa treatment? Put cucumber slices over my eyes and call it a day? Buy a yacht? I've already seen too much. It just gets worse and worse by the day. We're running out of time. And if you don't get that, we probably shouldn't be working together."

Our eyes met, and neither of us looked away.

"I've still got a lot of questions, Sukie."

"And I've got just one." She took a deep, unsteady breath. "Can I trust you?"

# 8

The waitress brought Sukie's salad and lasagna and my rigatoni. We both ate for a while. Then Sukie said, "Wasn't your father Victor Heller?"

I smiled. "Still is." That was a matter of public record. And it was a problem for some potential clients, by the way. Victor Heller became symbolic of all that was scuzzy about Wall Street. Would you want to hire that guy's son?

"I once met your dad. I guess he's a friend of my father's. A great big brain, a tiny shriveled heart. A dangerous combination, you know?"

"How'd you meet him?"

"I was doing research for a documentary about white-collar crime."

"He's a guy you want to talk to."

"He told me about you. He's the reason I'm here."

"I doubt he recommended me."

"No," she admitted. "But I figured you knew something about my world. You grew up with money, didn't you?"

"Until Dad was arrested."

Dad was serving a thirty-year sentence in a prison in upstate New York, for wire fraud, racketeering, securities fraud, and income tax evasion. After his arrest, when he fled the country, he abandoned us, left us impoverished. All the property and bank accounts were seized. My mom had to start over, with two young kids, moving in with her mother in Malden, Massachusetts.

"That's unfortunate for his family."

"Life is a garden of forking paths," I said. "I had a happy childhood."

"Well, we were like that family in that Visconti film, *The Damned*?"

I shook my head. I hadn't seen it.

"The rich, doomed industrialist family who were doing business with the Nazis?"

"Okay." I was being interviewed, and it felt like it. I had to remind myself that she made documentaries. She was probably used to doing deep research and interviews.

"Isn't your brother in prison too?"

"True."

"Two brothers and a dad. One of these things is not like the other."

"I was the family rebel," I said.

"Your brother carried on the family business?"

"It's more that my brother bonded with my father in a way I never did. He revered him. They were cut from the same cloth. Is it my turn to ask questions?"

"Go ahead."

"How am I supposed to get into your father's home office? Or is that my problem?" I could foresee all sorts of challenges to getting into Conrad Kimball's inner sanctum undetected. But there was always a way.

"I can get you into the house. You'll have to get into his office yourself."

"Will your father be gone?"

"Are you kidding? He's the star of the show. The center of the party."

"Party?"

"It's a party for my father, who's turning eighty."

"A retirement party?"

"You obviously don't know my father. Men like him don't retire. They can't."

"The party's in the Katonah house?"

She nodded. "I think you'll clean up nicely. Unlike most private investigators I've interviewed for this job. Didn't you go to Yale?"

"Never graduated. I dropped out."

"You worked for McKinsey, the management consulting company."

"A couple of summers. It didn't take. So you'll get me invited as a guest?"

"I'm going to bring you in as my date, actually. You're plausible enough. Anyone who asks, you're a consultant. With McKinsey. They'll be too polite to inquire further—at least, overtly."

"When's the party?"

"Tomorrow."

# 9

One of Patty's friends had brought over a large tray of homemade stuffed shells and chicken fricassee, so Sean's family and I had it for dinner along with a salad. The two brothers bickered throughout the meal.

After dinner, I took the kids out for ice cream at our favorite soft-serve place, to give Patty a little break. When I got back and the kids allegedly prepared for bedtime, Patty and I sat in the kitchen. She poured us each a Scotch on the rocks.

"You know," she said, absently wiping her hand along the Formica countertop, "for the longest time I thought Sean was weak. Resorting to this painkiller to basically get high. It never occurred to me that he might really be addicted, that he might have been powerless over the drug."

"He wasn't weak," I said, taking a long swig.

"And then I realized there are all these people out there, I mean doctors and lawyers and businessmen and moms, and they're all hooked on Oxydone, or Oxycontin, or whatever. Sean got addicted because his doctor wrote him a prescription and told him to take it. Take Oxydone, he said. But he didn't say, Be careful, you might get addicted. Why is that not malpractice?"

"Sean was an incredibly strong person. It wasn't his fault he got addicted to Oxydone."

"Then who do you blame?"

I didn't have an answer.

# 10

The next day I flew from Logan Airport in Boston to the much smaller Westchester County Airport, where I was met by a uniformed driver outside baggage claim holding an iPad sign: MR. HELLER.

"Any luggage, sir?" the driver said.

"Just my backpack," I said, which was light and on my right shoulder. He gestured for it, but I shook my head. My backpack contained overnight stuff like toothpaste and a toothbrush, a razor and some shaving cream. I had a carry-on garment bag that held my suit.

Dorothy had prepared for me a dossier, a dump file on the Conrad Kimball family and fortune, which I read late into the evening and finished on the flight.

Conrad Kimball was a self-made man who rose through sheer will. He was the most determined man most anyone had ever met.

His father had been a high school football star in a hardscrabble part of West Texas, and Conrad was determined to be like Dad. Problem was, he wasn't much of an athlete. When he wasn't picked for his high school team, he trained for hours on his own until he finally made it through sheer stubbornness.

After he got into a small college in Texas, something clicked. Instead of doing what Dad did, why not be something Dad could respect? And what was more respectable than being a doctor? So medical school it was. Suddenly he was on the dean's list every semester. No more football.

His family couldn't afford medical school, so he took a job as a pharmaceutical salesman to pay for it and quickly became the most successful salesman ever to work for Roche. He was as responsible as anybody for putting Valium on the map in the early sixties. *Mother's little helper.* That was his genius—convincing doctors to prescribe a sedative. Especially once he became a doctor too. Shortly after he got his MD, he invested some of his Roche bonus money and acquired a small pharmaceutical company that made eye drops and laxatives. Because the penny had dropped. The big money wasn't being made by the sales guys anymore. The big money was being raked in, by the hundreds of millions, by the companies that made the product.

So now he was in business too, and he had an idea.

He'd become interested in synthetic morphine as a painkiller. Way back in 1900, the German company Bayer Chemical invented a drug called heroin, a synthetic form of opium twice as powerful as morphine. They made a ton of money selling heroin over the counter for years until it was outlawed. Now opioids were sold only by prescription, but there was a lot of money to be made in it, Conrad thought.

So he bought another company that was developing a nasal inhaler that dispensed synthetic morphine. This became his star drug, Oxydone. It was found to be effective in treating migraine headaches. Of course, Oxydone was nothing new, nothing more than a novel way to dispense nature's oldest drug, opium. A new delivery system. But he knew that if he marketed it right, he could create out of it a pharmaceutical empire. An inhaled opiate.

The real breakthrough, the real secret to the swift and explosive growth of Kimball Pharma, wasn't the drug they were selling to doctors. It was the *way* they sold it to doctors. Conrad Kimball completely rethought his company's sales strategy. Target the people who write the prescriptions. *Enlist* them. Target their sense of compassion. Appeal to their ethical side. Kimball launched an army of sales reps who'd been trained to tell their customers, their doctors, that prescribing Oxydone to their patients in pain was the compassionate, moral thing to do.

This message was delivered to doctors poolside at pain-management seminars in Hawaii. Turned out that doctors who went on these free, all-expenses-paid trips to resorts in Hawaii or Las Vegas, Scottsdale, or Palm Beach, prescribed Oxydone twice as often as those who didn't. And some of the doctors who'd been on these junkets did studies that showed the drug was safe, that it wasn't addictive.

Kimball Pharma paid for the studies. That helped.

Now the Kimball family was number twelve on the *Forbes* "America's Richest Families" list. The family's wealth was calculated at fourteen billion dollars. There were six members of the Kimball family, *Forbes* said. Conrad Kimball and his five kids. If you divided that evenly, each Kimball family member was worth 2.3 billion dollars. Of course, it didn't work that way. Conrad, as the patriarch and founder, was worth most of that, but he was believed to have passed much on to his kids in the form of trusts.

Conrad Kimball had been married three times and was currently engaged to one Natalya Alexandrovna Aksyonova, about whom little was known other than that she was a Russian national, she was a former fashion model, and she was almost forty years his junior.

I looked up and saw that we were pulling up to a handsome white clapboard, seven-room luxury inn. The Inn at Katonah was a Relais & Châteaux property that my research told me was quietly owned by the Kimball family.

Idling next to us was a black town car.

The driver switched off the engine. He came around and opened the door for me. "Ms. Kimball is waiting for you," he said.

# 11

G oing like that?" Sukie Kimball said with a tart smile.

She meant my tattered jeans and sneakers.

"Think your father will mind if I change at his house?"

"There's thirty-seven rooms in my father's house. I'm sure we can find one to use."

She had on a pair of black leather pants and a lacy white top. She raised her voice. "Hey, Keith, why don't you take a smoke break," she called to the driver.

"Yes, ma'am."

As soon as the driver had left the car, she pulled out a folded sheet of paper and handed it to me. I unfolded it. It was a photocopy of an architectural drawing. She'd already emailed me the drawings the day before.

"Mind if we go over this again?" she said. "This is the first floor of the house. I've marked the study."

"The files are in his study?"

"Somewhere in there."

"What does that mean, 'somewhere'? You don't know where he keeps his files?"

"It's more complicated than that. He has file drawers for family and personal matters. But then he keeps the most sensitive, secret files . . . somewhere. He won't talk about it. I just know they're somewhere in his home office."

"So you're not even sure the file in question is in there somewhere?"

"Oh, it's in there somewhere. That I'm sure of. Something that explosive, that secret—he's going to hide a copy in his personal files. I know him."

"And I'm supposed to wander off to use the bathroom and end up in his study?"

"During the party or after."

We'd arranged for me to stay in the house, in a separate guest bedroom—Sukie said she was just being respectful to her dad, who insisted that unmarried couples could not cohabitate under his roof—but we hadn't made any specific plans beyond that. The when and the how of it were up to me.

"He gives some big parties, for an eighty-year-old man."

"It's not like he's rolling out the phyllo dough for the appetizers himself."

"Who's the social arbiter in the marriage—him or his Russian fiancée? Or is she wife by now?"

"Natalya's not his wife. Not yet. But it'll happen soon enough. She's been glued to him practically since the day they met on Russian Beauties Dot Com."

"Is that how they met, for real?"

"Or one of those websites." She attempted a mock Russian accent: "'Do you vant real love, romance, or marriage with stunning Russian lady?'" She wasn't bad.

"Where'd we meet, you and I?" I said.

"A party in TriBeCa."

"I can make that work. I live in Boston, work for McKinsey and Company as a consultant, and beyond that you stopped asking. That's all you know."

"That's enough."

"Is there security I should be aware of?"

"People or electronic?"

"Either. Both."

"There's always someone. Like Dad's security chief, Fritz Heston. He might be there."

"What about electronic security? I'm thinking specifically of his office."

"Only when he's out of the house. Other times, he usually keeps it turned off."

I nodded, poring over the architectural drawings.

"Where are the bedrooms?"

She handed me another folded drawing. The second floor of the house. I saw a room labeled MAP ROOM and a bunch of bedrooms.

"Where am I staying?"

"The one nearest my bedroom, and yes, my father's bedroom is in the same wing. And he's a light sleeper."

We pulled up beside a guard booth, slowed to a brief stop, just a few seconds, long enough to lower the window on the left side of the passenger's compartment. The guard took a quick look and waved us through. I wasn't impressed by the security protocol. The guard barely looked at me. Sloppy.

"That was too easy," I said.

"Fair enough," she said. "So far no one has tried to target Daddy's house. But there have been protests against us. Like the one at MoMA."

I remembered hearing about that—on a busy Saturday afternoon, a large group came into the Museum of Modern Art and went up to the Kimball Gallery and lay down on the floor. It was a "die-in." They had scattered empty prescription spray bottles of Oxydone all over the place.

"Only a matter of time before people start protesting outside the

43

gates of the house," I said. "I'd get a lot more serious about the security."

We approached a brick Georgian house, handsome but surprisingly modest. For a moment I marveled at how simple and unpretentious the Kimball family house turned out to be.

Until I realized that it was a gatehouse we'd just passed. Where the gardeners or the gatekeepers were probably lodged. The main house was another half mile down a silky-smooth paved road banked by mature oaks.

This house was impressive. It was built in a Tudor Revival style, and it reminded me of the neo-Gothic mansion I grew up in, before my father disappeared and we were broke. It too was immense and rambling. Most of the rooms were furnished but never used, dusted regularly by the housekeeping staff.

This one was originally built in 1924 as a summer home by one of the so-called robber barons, a shipping magnate whose ancestors had gotten rich off the importation of Chinese opium a century earlier, I kid you not. I wondered if Conrad Kimball knew that when he bought the estate decades earlier.

It was surrounded by 250 acres, which included a large natural forest. We passed the tennis courts and a pool and pool house and manicured gardens, as we approached the house. On the other side of the house were gardens and acres of pristine forestland.

"Welcome to Kimball Hall," she said with a twist of a smile.

Of course it had a name.

# 12

In a sitting room that looked and smelled like it was rarely used—oil paintings on the wall, uncomfortable Edwardian furniture, the cool tang of lemon-oil furniture polish—I changed into a suit that I liked for occasions like this because it had a number of well-concealed pockets.

I looked around for visible security cameras, didn't see any, but I hadn't expected to. I pulled out the architectural plans and scanned them again, familiarizing myself with the layout. Then I refolded them and slipped them into an inner pocket on the suit coat. I put my street clothes in the garment bag, left it on a chair, and went out to find Sukie. If I was going to pretend to be her date for the evening, I had to stay pretty much by her side. I'd be an outsider in this family gathering and would thus be scrutinized especially closely. I had to be ready for that.

When I emerged, I could see that the guests had started arriving in the spacious entry foyer. Maybe a dozen people were gathered at the foot of the mighty stone staircase, the sort of grand feature that was probably used for weddings and other ceremonial occasions when you wanted to make a dramatic entrance.

I glanced at the small crowd. They were all members of the Kimball family, whether by birth or by marriage. Heirs to the Kimball Pharma fortune. Gathered here at the estate of Dr. Conrad Kimball, the patriarch, the doctor turned pharmaceutical tycoon, to celebrate his eightieth birthday.

And I was here—I reminded myself—as Sukie Kimball's date. I was not Nick Heller. I was a guy she met at a party in TriBeCa. I worked for McKinsey and Company in Boston. I was a consultant named Nick Brown.

It was a light cover. I had a counterfeit Massachusetts driver's license in the name of Nicholas Brown and a fictional address on Beacon Hill. If someone checked with McKinsey, my cover would probably be blown. Unless someone actually named Nick Brown worked for them, which was totally possible. But I had no reason, at that point, to expect anyone to challenge me. This was a family birthday party I was invited to. I wasn't infiltrating a meeting of the politburo.

I also had more on my mind than just getting by. I'd been given a rare opportunity to penetrate the Kimball family, to interact among them as an equal. A temporary insider. So I needed to do some social engineering.

Because if for some reason I failed at getting to the old man's secret files, I might have to come back again, to some other family function at the estate. And the more comfortable the siblings were with me, the more they'd share. In my experience, people like to talk if you know how to listen. There were more secrets to be found, I was sure. And the secret you think you're looking for may not be the one you really need to know.

As I approached, I thought I recognized a few of the arrivals, but at that distance I couldn't be sure. A couple of small blond boys in blue blazers, making a ruckus. They had to be the sons of Megan Kimball, forty-five, the second-oldest child of Conrad Kimball. I thought of her as the corporate one. She was the only family member in the family business, a vice president. There were also a couple of awkward teenage boys in blue blazers, hers, who looked like they'd much rather be playing *Fortnite*.

Then there were the servants bustling in and out, carrying silver trays. They all looked tense. From what I'd read, Dr. Conrad Kimball, that self-made man, wasn't good with staff. He went through people at a fast clip.

Looking up, I noticed a few discreet CCTV cameras hidden in the carved walnut ceiling molding. It was important to remember that Dr. Kimball was a highly suspicious man. He had reason to be. His family was under assault.

I heard a laugh that sounded like Sukie's and turned to see her— shaggy brown hair, brown eyes, sharp nose—smiling at a tall woman a few years younger with a short boyish haircut and that same prominent blade of a nose. Her younger sister. Hayden Kimball, the Broadway impresario, was wearing a neatly pressed denim shirt and black jeans and boots.

Sukie broke off to say to me, "Nick, sweetie, meet my sister Hayden."

"Nice to meet you," I said. "Nick Brown."

She nodded, smiled remotely, didn't extend a hand.

"You've produced some terrific plays," I said.

"Oh, yeah?" Her face colored. "Thank you." She seemed to be loosening up a bit. I obviously knew who she was. She was president and majority owner of the Kimball Theater Group, which owned five Broadway theaters and produced some successful Broadway plays and musicals. She was famous, in a small world.

"You said you're Nick Browne, with an *e*?"

"No *e*." Last I looked, Nick Browne yielded nineteen million search results on Google; drop the *e* and you're up to seven hundred million. Far more anonymous.

"And you, uh—how do you know my sister?"

"We met at a party in TriBeCa," Sukie said.

I waited for Hayden to ask, "Whose party?" but instead she said, "Are you in the arts?"

"Just the dark arts of McKinsey and Company."

"McKinsey," she said. "The consulting firm."

I nodded.

"Huh."

She looked like she was mulling a follow-up question. Maybe she knew somebody who worked there. So I quickly changed the subject. "I'm looking forward to your all-Asian version of *Suddenly Last Summer*," I said. I'd read in a profile in the *New York Times* that she was partial to Tennessee Williams.

She seemed to loosen up even more. With a tilt of her head, she said, "Yes, that's shaping up to be a powerful piece."

At that moment, a waitress appeared with a tray of miniature hamburgers. I took a slider. Sukie drew close to me for a moment and muttered under her breath, "Uh-oh. Danger, Will Robinson."

# 13

Another woman was approaching: a tall, broad-shouldered woman. Megan, the second-oldest, was blond, her hair parted at the center and going down to her shoulders, cool gray eyes like her father's. And the sharp Kimball nose, a family emblem.

A graduate of Princeton and Stanford Business School, Megan had started at Kimball Pharma as an assistant in the marketing department. Therefore she was most likely to succeed her father as CEO. She was divorced and had four sons, who were clearly the ones in the blazers. She was wearing a gray pantsuit and a white blouse and could not have looked more corporate-generic. Not fashionable at all. Everything I'd read painted her as ferociously ambitious, intimidatingly smart, and a cold fish.

She extended her hand toward me and offered a controlled smile. She shook firmly, almost bone-crushingly, and said, "You're the only one here I don't recognize. Megan Kimball." Her voice was surprisingly deep.

"Nick Brown," I said. I noticed Megan hadn't greeted her sister Hayden and was standing at a distance from her.

"Did I hear you say something about McKinsey? I have ears like a bat."

"I work there."

"McKinsey New York?"

"Boston."

"Oh, you must know Chuck Neely!"

Chuck *who*? My brain raced.

I paused for a long moment and then said, "Plugs or rugs? What's your money on?"

She arched her brow, smiled genuinely this time, said, "I'm sorry?"

"C'mon. The only guy I know whose hairline *advances* as he ages."

She laughed. "To be honest, I haven't seen him in, like, ten years. But I know what you mean."

I let out a silent breath. It had taken a moment to call Chuck Neely's photo and details to mind. "Anyway, Chuck's no longer in charge of the Boston office." That was true. I'd done my homework. "It's now Jim French."

"I don't know him."

Neither did I, and I sighed relief inwardly. The two moppet-headed child terrorists began tugging on Megan's arms and nagging, "When do we get to eat? When do we get to eat?" and "I don't like those *sliders*. Those are yucky." These kids could have starred in a social media campaign for vasectomies. Their older brothers, the teenage boys, were off to one side laughing raucously, looking at something on one of the kids' phones.

"Grandpa's coming down right now, and as soon as he gets here, we'll sit down to dinner," Megan said to her boys. "That's how it always works. There he is." She pointed. An ancient elevator off the foyer, which I hadn't noticed before, opened, and Conrad Kimball emerged, with a much younger woman in a white suit on his arm. He walked slowly but erect and with assurance. In his photographs he looked frail. In person, in motion, he looked far more powerful.

# 14

Time had not bent Conrad Kimball. He had a bristly white mustache and sparse white hair, but he was mostly bald on top. A dark, heavy brow. A long, sharp nose. He was wearing a blue button-down shirt and, over it, a navy cardigan sweater, unbuttoned. He looked like he'd just gotten up from his afternoon nap. Tufts of stray white hairs stuck out on either side of his head like wires.

Back in the day, Kimball was known for his plainspoken manner, I'd read, but as he aged, he grew more intimidating. Now he was short with business associates, always blunt.

The woman on his arm was wasp-waisted and elegant and blond and looked to be about forty. At a distance she could have been Grace Kelly. An Hermès scarf was tied around her neck. That had to be Natalya, the fiancée. She looked like she was arriving at an awards ceremony where she was the featured nominee. She also looked like she'd recently had her lips filled.

"Happy birthday, Daddy!" Megan called out, and the rest of the crowd responded in kind, wishing him happy birthday in a ragged torrent of voices.

"Where the hell are my sons?" Conrad said. "I see my sweet girls are here, but what the hell happened to Paul and Cameron, those lousy bums?"

Sukie said, "Paul's on his way, and Cameron—Cameron is Cameron."

51

A couple of people chuckled knowingly. Someone's cell phone rang. One of the moppet-headed kids said, "Can we eat?" and Conrad said, "Hell yeah, we can eat!"

He put out his arms as he walked toward the younger kids and then enfolded both of them at once. I wondered if they were fraternal twins. One was taller and thinner than the other, but they looked otherwise alike. Meanwhile, the teenage boys appeared to be tussling over ownership of a phone.

Alone, at the edge of the crowd, stood Natalya, smiling cryptically. No one was greeting her. She was the proverbial skunk at the garden party. A frightened-looking waitress came by with a glass of red wine on a tray, and as she stepped forward to hand it to Natalya, the waitress must have tripped on the carpet, because she lost her balance and upended the wineglass. The spill missed Natalya, but dark red wine splashed onto the arm of the pale yellow sofa, staining it at once.

The waitress's face crumpled, and she began to weep as she righted the wineglass. Natalya swiftly untied her scarf from her neck and let it flutter over the wine stain on the arm of the sofa. The scarf covered the stain entirely.

She smiled at the waitress and winked. "Conrad does not have to know," she murmured.

Meanwhile, Conrad, busy with the kids, was braying, "Someday that kid is going to get himself killed." I assumed he was talking about his youngest, Cameron, twenty-two, who was known to be a hard-core party dude.

His daughters were lining up to hug him. None of them currently had a husband, I noted. Conrad probably wasn't a good male role model. Megan had an ex who didn't seem to be here. There was a big gap in age between her teenage sons and the moppet-headed terrorists, who looked to be around eight.

After she hugged her father, Sukie introduced me as her friend Nick. Conrad turned to me with squinty, suspicious eyes. He gave me his hand, which was as cool and dry as an old broken-in leather baseball mitt. With his left hand he was holding on to the edge of a table. He was probably in need of a walker or at least a cane, but he was too vain to use one. Didn't want to appear infirm.

"Nick Brown," I said.

"You an artist too, Mr. Brown?" he said pleasantly. "A filmmaker, like Sukie?"

"No, sorry, I'm boring. Just a businessman. A consultant for Mc-Kinsey."

"Oh, is that right?" Conrad said with a slight tilt of his head and a glinting smile. His teeth were either bad veneers or dentures. "I was expecting another one of those strange weedy anarchists. You don't seem Sukie's type."

"You'd be surprised," Sukie cut in flatly.

He looked at his daughter. His eyes twinkled, became playful for an instant. "So you're no longer with . . . *Gregg?*" he said. You could see he was toying with her and taking pleasure in her annoyance.

"That's been over for months."

He turned back to me. "So is there any consulting wisdom you can give me, Mr. Brown? How's the world looking to you?"

"I don't know about wisdom," I said, "but if *I* were running Kimball Pharma, I'd shut down my Budapest operation immediately, before that Hungarian autocrat seizes it on behalf of the government. Which he's about to do. Any day now." I'd come prepared.

His genial smile faded. "That right?"

I gazed at the old man directly. "Maybe he'll leave Kimball Pharma alone, but I know for a fact he's targeting Merck."

His eyes lasered in on mine, all fierce concentration. "You know this how?"

53

"I travel a lot."

He put a hand on Sukie's right shoulder. "You got hold of an interesting one this time, Susan," he said.

Then he turned back to me, and I saw he wasn't smiling. His slate-gray eyes had gone hard. In a low voice, he said, "But I don't think you're the man you pretend to be."

My stomach did a flip, and I saw the color drain from Sukie's face. I held her gaze a moment, partly to compose myself before responding to Conrad. But when I turned to face him, he'd turned away.

"Not sure I understand," I replied blandly.

He turned back. "You're far too interesting to be one of those stamped-from-a-mold McKinsey kids."

A butler approached the old man.

"Oh, it takes all types," I said, relieved.

"Will you excuse me, sir," the butler said to Kimball, "but we're ready to serve whenever you'd like."

"Well, hell, let's eat now," Kimball announced. "To be continued," he said to me with a wag of a finger.

# 15

The old man, steadied by the statuesque Natalya, made his way slowly into the dining room. Most of the rest of the crowd hung back, except for the kids, who ran ahead. I noticed they had their own table, for which I was grateful.

I lingered behind with the rest of them, eavesdropping while pretending to look around at the decor.

I heard one of the smaller kids say, "Is Grandpa gonna marry that lady?"

"Yes, sweetie, he is," Megan replied. "Her name is Natalya."

I went back to Sukie's side. She and her sister Hayden were conversing quietly. I feigned distraction and overheard Sukie say, "I don't like the way that woman looks at me."

Hayden replied, "Hey, I've seen *Gold Diggers of 1933*. I don't need to live through it. And what's the deal with her lips? She's looking more and more like the Joker, don't you think? I mean, talk about duck lips."

The room we entered wasn't the huge formal dining room I'd passed walking in. This one's walls were lacquered in oxblood with marble busts in low-lit niches every few feet. A long table, covered in a pleated white tablecloth, set for close to a dozen people. Around it, gold-painted bamboo chairs. The table was next to a huge stone fireplace, but no fire was lit; it wasn't cold enough.

The four grandkids sat at their own table next to the far end of the main one, far from where Conrad Kimball and Natalya were seated. My place card read *Susan Kimball Guest* in fancy script. I was seated not far from Conrad, with Megan on my right. Which was exactly who I didn't want to be seated next to for the entirety of dinner. Megan seemed to know too much about what "Nick Brown" did. I looked to my left and saw a card that read *Paul Kimball*. That was the absent eldest son. Sukie was on the other side of the table from me, fairly distant. We could wave at each other, that's all.

Then a stoop-shouldered, gray-haired guy came into the room, apologizing noisily. I recognized him as Paul, the oldest Kimball child, mid-fifties. On his arm was a tall woman I recognized as a superstar MIT professor, a Moroccan-born artist and architect and designer. It would be sexist of me to mention that she was also fashion-model-beautiful and had pouty red lips and a wild head of curly brown hair, so I won't. She was known to be extremely smart.

"So sorry, Dad. I was stuck in revision hell." Paul went up to Conrad and kissed him on top of the head. Conrad responded by patting his son awkwardly on the shoulder. Paul handed him a gift-wrapped book.

"I said no gifts!" the old man barked.

But he tore off the paper anyway. I was close enough to see that it was a hardcover by someone named Yuval Noah Harari, titled *Habitus*. It meant nothing to me.

For some reason there was an eruption of squabbling at the kids' table, and then the two moppet-headed terrorists ran to Megan, who turned around and said something quietly that made them race out of the room.

The two of them returned a minute later, together lugging a big set of Titleist golf clubs festooned in red ribbon with a big bow on top. They brought it to the head of the table. Conrad wagged his finger at Megan and said, "I see what you're doing here. You're having the kiddies do it so I won't yell!"

"Guilty as charged," Megan said with a smile. "You know me too well."

To the boys Conrad said, "How did you know I wanted new clubs?"

"You always want new clubs, Grandpa," one of them said.

"Well, you got the kind I like and everything."

A couple of servants were dishing out dinner, which looked like whole racks of barbecue pork ribs and greens and cornbread and something else. A woman was pouring iced tea. It was a Texas barbecue on Wedgwood china.

Then a man entered the room, a bland-looking man in his forties with rimless glasses and hair that was either blond or gray-white, it was hard to tell. Hard blue-gray eyes. I wondered if that was his head of security, Fritz Heston, who was said to be sort of his consigliere. He went up to Conrad and began whispering, his head bowed. Conrad's rheumy eyes widened, and he turned his head to look directly, and unambiguously, at me.

As if they were talking about me. I caught the old man's eyes. As he listened and nodded, he squinted and blinked a few times, staring at me the whole while.

I couldn't suppress a little wriggle of anxiety.

# 16

Just then there came a loud, blatting noise from outside, like a car with a hole in its muffler.

"Well, let me guess," Megan said to me, and shook her head, scowling. A little louder she said, "Nice of him to show up."

There was muted laughter up and down the table.

"In one of his jalopies," said her father.

I took out my phone and fired off a quick text message, then set it down on the table.

Paul Kimball sat down next to me, while his brilliant girlfriend sat across the table from us. He introduced himself. "You're with Sukie?" he said.

I nodded, shook hands. "Nick Brown."

He took the napkin off the table, placed it in his lap, and smiled at one of the servants who came right over with a tray of food.

"Thank you, Andrea," he said. "I'm starved."

After he was served his ribs and cornbread, he turned to me and leaned his head in confidingly. "Be careful with that one, please," he said as he nodded at Sukie.

"She's in good hands," I reassured him.

"Not worried about her," he said. "Worried about you. She's a tricky one. Complicated."

"Complicated?"

"Like no one you ever met."

Then he turned away.

I noticed the pale-haired security chief had left the table and was now lurking in the doorway to the hall, looking in.

I excused myself, got up from the table, left the phone there. At the entrance to the room, Fritz Heston looked at me.

"Excuse me," I said quietly, as if he were a servant, "where would I find the bathroom?"

He pointed, didn't reply. Up close I could see he had white hair and was probably around sixty.

I found the small guest bathroom right off the foyer, all black and white tiles and nickel fixtures, like a restroom in a men's club from the 1920s. Took my time in there. When I came back, I could see at a distance Fritz walking away from the table.

I returned to the table, picked up my phone, and glanced at it. On its screen, and visible to anyone, were a couple of texts. One was from a Mark_Foster@mckinsey.com, its subject "quick wins." Another one from Kerry_Granville@mckinsey.com, subject "MECE analysis." I slipped it back into my breast pocket. I had no doubt that Fritz Heston had taken a peek at my phone. He couldn't resist. Then I sneaked a glance and saw that he had left the room. Maybe the ruse had worked.

Suddenly a slight blond man in his early twenties burst into the room. He had on ripped jeans and Chuck Taylors and a wrinkled tuxedo jacket worn ironically. "Happy birthday, Dad," he sang out. "Sorry I'm late. Car trouble." He laughed delightedly. Cameron was weaving slightly as he approached the head of the table. Accompanying him was a woman I at first saw only from the side, but I recognized her gait before I knew for sure who she was.

I felt my blood jump.

*It can't be.*

"The prodigal son arrives at last," said Conrad, extending his arms. He wasn't smiling.

I kept staring at Cameron's date. Everything else fell away.

"The gang's all here," Cameron said. "Saving the best for last."

As the couple came up to Conrad, I could finally see the woman's face. I startled, jerked my head like a cartoon character.

*It is* her.

Megan must have noticed me gaping like an idiot, because she said, "Wait, you know her?"

At least I recovered quickly. I shook my head. "No. She just looks like someone I used to know," I said.

# 17

*Seven years ago*

I was still recovering from a gunshot wound I'd gotten in Afghanistan, working on Joint Base Anacostia-Bolling in southwest DC for a covert unit of the Defense Intelligence Agency, when I got an email with an order to report to something called DCIS, the Defense Criminal Investigative Service. No explanation, of course. DCIS was based not in the Pentagon but in a generic office building in Alexandria. They uncovered fraud and corruption within the Pentagon and in the defense procurement system. That sounded cool to me.

Anyway, I went where I was told. When I got there, I went to a conference room, where I was met by a very stern-faced woman around my age who acted a lot older. Major Margret C. Benson looked over my service jacket for a while before launching into a no-bullshit briefing on the operation I was joining. She was running it. The target was a civilian procurement officer in the Pentagon named Harkins who was rumored to be corrupt. Harkins was meeting someone for dinner at the Capital Grille who he believed worked for a big defense contractor. The whole dinner was being choreographed, audiotaped and videotaped, and I was to be one of the lowly techs who sat in a white panel van during dinner, making sure the feed was good, standing by to replace any defective component if need be.

Major Benson was small and lithe, almost wiry. Her uniform

always seemed a size too big. She was cute but serious as all hell, never cracked a smile. She thanked the DIA for providing much-needed manpower. Then she drilled us on how the op was going to proceed.

When she was finished, I made an attempt to get out of tech duty. I suggested that I could, instead, play the defense contractor executive. After all, I'd just served a couple of combat deployments, yet no one knew who I was. I could talk armaments knowledgeably. It was a ballsy suggestion, for a neophyte, and she cut me right off. "I got dibs on that, Sergeant Heller," she said with a slight smile. I reminded her I was no longer "sergeant," since I was now a civilian, but that didn't stop her from calling me Sergeant Heller.

A few hours later, I was sitting in the van watching our target, Harkins, the greedy procurement officer, sip his water and gnaw at his bread, waiting. The broadcast quality was excellent.

Then a big, blowsy woman came up to the table, all big hair and French manicure and copious makeup. She spoke in a strong Texan twang, ordered a Cosmo, and soon they were laughing and drinking and making deals. He was drinking bourbon, and she was inhaling Cosmos. Her accent dripped sugar syrup. I wondered about this woman. Either she really was Marjorie Cairns of Irving, Texas, or she was Meryl Streep.

"Who the hell is that?" I asked one of the other techs in the van.

"You don't know? That's Major Benson."

"That's Maggie Benson? Underneath the big shoulders and all that hair?"

"Yeah."

"Man, she's good," I said.

"Oh, you have no idea."

# 18

Now the slight blond man in the dinner jacket and his date were standing before me. He offered his palm, a touch and a slide, barely a handshake at all.

"Cameron," he said to me.

The woman had copper-red hair and blue eyes, and she was dressed in a black, off-the-shoulder sheath. Her eyes gazed directly, defiantly at me. "I'm Hildy," she said, almost daring me to acknowledge her.

"Nice to meet you, Hildy," I said, "I'm Nicholas Brown."

"Nicholas." She smiled politely but barely glanced at me, as if she didn't know me. Well played.

I played it the same way. Whatever she was up to, I wasn't going to derail it. Nor did I want her to mess up my cover.

But what the hell was she doing?

Cameron said, "You with somebody?"

"Sukie," I said.

From across the table, Sukie flapped a hand. "Nice of you to make it," she said to Cameron.

He grinned, cocked an eyebrow. He looked at Sukie, then back at me. "Huh," he said after another beat. "Huh. Well, enjoy. Welcome." He half-sauntered, half-stumbled his way down the table to his place at the far end near the kids.

Maggie Benson went around to the other side. She was far enough away that I couldn't talk with her, yet close enough that I could watch her interact with Cameron and the others. She was either a little drunk herself or plausibly acting that way. She took a sip of wine.

Maggie was wearing a reddish wig and probably contact lenses. I hadn't seen her in seven years, and she was even more beautiful than she was back then. She also had to be a dozen years older than Cameron, though she didn't look it.

But my thoughts were interrupted by Megan, on my right. "So how long have you and Sukie been together?" she said.

"Just a couple weeks," I said, gnawing on a rib, and I came right back: "So you're the senior VP for Europe, right?" Most people like talking about themselves.

"Right," she said.

I glanced at Maggie and saw her take another sip of wine, though the level in her glass didn't seem to be dropping.

Then I turned back to Megan. "It's surprising, if you don't mind my saying so, that you haven't been made CEO already. I mean, with your smarts and experience? I'd think a lot of companies would feel very comfortable with you in the cockpit. So what am I missing?"

I could see her flush a little before she replied, smoothly, "My father's sharp as a tack. And as long as he stays that way, we're in the best possible hands."

Conrad Kimball was not in listening range, and besides, he was busy berating the waitress who kept refilling his coffee. "I get the god-damned cream and coffee proportions just perfect and you come along and splash more in and screw it up," he was scolding the terrified young woman.

Lowering my voice a bit, I said to Megan, "The man's eighty years old. How long is this arrangement going to last?"

A sort of giggle escaped her. "Could be forever." Hastily she added, to cover her slip, "If we're lucky. My day will come."

Maggie took another sip from her wineglass and laughed whoopingly about something.

While our dinner plates were being cleared away, someone started clinking a glass with a spoon or something, and the table quieted down except for loud whispering from the kids' table.

"And now," Conrad Kimball said, "as is our custom, we move to the library for coffee, cake, and champagne!"

The kiddie end of the table erupted in cheers. Chairs scraped against the stone floor.

Conrad and his fiancée got up from the table.

I got up and came around to join Sukie. We trundled through an arched doorway into a warm, amber-lit room lined with books, antique leather-bound volumes in sets, all color coordinated. More marble busts here, posing in spotlit niches, every ten or twelve feet. Several waiters and waitresses were holding aloft trays of champagne flutes, all full. The kids were given what looked like apple juice in champagne flutes. One of them said something to Sukie that made her laugh, then pulled her over to the other kids.

Everyone gathered around a table on which was a big cake in the shape of Texas. In the northern part of the state was a big red square that I assumed represented the Kimball Ranch, all five hundred acres, where he'd grown up. In the middle of the red square a single candle had been placed. Everyone sang "Happy Birthday," and Conrad Kimball blew out the candle. A waitress began slicing the cake while Conrad held up a flute of champagne.

He cleared his throat, and the room hushed.

"Everyone has a drink who drinks?" he said. "I'd like to make a toast. Not to myself, but to my family. To all of you. Because right now there's all kinds of bad things being said about us out there. All sorts of lies. Blaming us for society's problems. It's unbelievable." His champagne glass trembled a bit in his hand. "We have our enemies, no question about it. But you know, a wise man once said, when there's no enemy within, the enemies outside can't hurt us. A house divided against itself cannot stand. But we're not divided, and we don't have enemies inside the family. We're all rowing in the same direction. I know it. I know my boys and girls, and we all share a polestar. Because the strength of a family, like an army, is in its loyalty to each other. And thank the Lord, we have ourselves one loving family." He lifted his glass even higher. "To family."

Megan said, "Happy birthday, Daddy."

"Happy birthday," the crowd raggedly said.

I took a sip of champagne and felt someone grab me by the biceps. I turned. It was Natalya. She caressed my arm.

"Your name is Nicholas?" she said.

Up close I could see that she was a beautiful woman with too much makeup on.

"Nick Brown. Nice to meet you."

"Have we met before?" She had a thick Russian accent.

"Haven't had the pleasure."

"And you and Susan, you have been together long time?"

"No, just met a few weeks ago."

A waiter handed her a slice of cake along with a fork, then gave me one too. It was an unusual-looking cake, made up of countless thin layers. Natalya forked some cake into her mouth. "Try," she said. "It's very special cake. Like a mille-feuille. A thousand layers."

I tried some. It melted in the mouth. "Very nice," I said.

"They make this from twenty paper-thin crepes, and in between is pastry cream. Delicious, no?"

"Delicious. I—I saw what you did earlier. With your scarf. That was awfully nice."

She smiled. "I'm sure Conrad's children think I am expert at covering things up. Are you?"

"Am I what?"

"You and Susan—you can't keep hands off each other."

I smiled. She was being sarcastic.

"Yes," she said. "I can see chemistry between you two. Please."

"Excuse me?"

"You are not who you are pretending to be," she said. Her tone was playful. "You are here for another reason. Did Sukie bring you to investigate me?"

"What's to investigate?" I said.

"I have always been outsider, all my life," she said. "One thing people like me very good at is spotting other one."

"Very good," I said. "I'd consider myself an outsider too."

She held up the plate of cake. "You are like this Napoleon cake. Many layers."

"Thank you," I said.

She patted me on the arm again as she turned away. "Maybe I will peel back some layers, Nicholas."

# 19

Well, I'd been warned. The family was instinctually suspicious of me. I was like a virus invading the bloodstream, and they were sending out their antibodies. I felt sure I'd neutralized the security guy with my fake McKinsey texts. He'd be thinking his source at McKinsey had made a mistake. Not that I was an impostor.

But Natalya surprised me. How suspicious she was. She knew how unpopular she was with Kimball's kids and what lengths they might go to to expose her if possible. So she was right to suspect me, an outsider. She clearly was a survivor and wasn't going to take any chances. She was someone to keep an eye on.

Which made me wonder whether Maggie was going to cause me problems. What she was here for. Whether she was trying to get into Dr. Kimball's private files as well. Or maybe she had some other agenda, some other reason for being here undercover. I wondered whether Sukie had any idea her brother had hired a private investigator too.

Fortunately, cake and coffee and champagne were over fairly quickly, and the old man went back to his elevator with his young Natalya. The security chief left. The kids were racing around the room, and one of them broke a plate. Someone hit someone else. Tears were shed. This was so clearly not a house designed for kids. It was like living in a museum.

I was expecting some sort of after party with the siblings, drinks in the game room or whatever, and more opportunities to schmooze with—interact with—the adult Kimball children. Also greater opportunity for my cover to be blown. But the party broke up shortly after the old man departed. Megan left with her brood to go home. She also lived in Westchester County, in a normal, ten-million-dollar house in Chappaqua about a fifteen-minute drive away.

That left us, Hayden, Paul and his brilliant girlfriend, and Cameron—and Maggie.

Now I had two missions, which was not good for focus. I had to get into the old man's home office files; that was what I'd been hired to do. But now I also wanted to talk to Maggie. I wanted to find out why she was here undercover too, what she was after. I wondered if she was looking for the same thing I was.

And I wondered what had happened to her these last seven years.

But Paul and his MIT girlfriend went up to their room, or rooms, followed by Maggie and Cameron, who seemed bleary and about to collapse after pounding all that booze.

I put my arm around Sukie's waist and walked with her up the staircase. I thought it was important to keep up appearances. In case anyone was watching. In my other hand I carried my garment bag with my street clothes.

She led me down the hallway to my bedroom, pointing out the rooms on the way. She silently pointed at a bedroom door that I assumed was her father's suite. Outside my room I gave her a kiss on the lips, the way real lovers would. She didn't exactly respond, but she didn't bat me away either. I think she was surprised. But at the same time she was making it clear that I was to stay within the boundaries we'd agreed on. Keep it strictly professional. Yes, I was playing her boyfriend, but Dr. Kimball didn't believe in cohabitation before marriage. So it was separate bedrooms.

Mine was a blue-painted guest room with a four-poster bed. On the wall, an antique tapestry. A dresser with folded towels on top.

The next part was hard: waiting until the house was asleep, which

I'd worked out with Sukie would be by around two o'clock in the morning. I was too tense to nap. I was as tight as a bowstring. So I lay on the bed and read my email on my phone, then read the news, and thought. I kept checking my watch. The minutes crept by. I thought about Maggie.

I heard nothing from any of the adjoining rooms. Attribute that to top-notch work by artisan stonemasons imported from Italy and their early-twentieth-century craftsmanship. When labor was cheap, and good stone and fine wood were plentiful.

Then I retrieved my tools from the pockets of my suit and placed them in my leather dopp kit, my shaving kit. I changed into sweats and a T-shirt. Lay back down on the bed and waited.

Finally, it was two in the morning.

# 20

I stood up, grabbed my shaving kit, and quietly went out into the hall, passing Conrad's bedroom suite as if in search of the hall bathroom. The floor, fortunately, was covered in a long oriental runner that must have been custom woven for the original owner a century ago. It also muffled my footfalls, which was great. I was barefoot and knew how to move stealthily in a silent house, but creaky old wooden floors were often a problem in grand houses. The house where I spent my childhood had creaky floors.

The hallway was dark. But I had studied the blueprints, and I knew where I was going.

Conrad Kimball's study was on the first floor in the other wing of the house. I reached the stone staircase I'd climbed a few hours before. A skylight filtered faint moonlight. I descended the carpeted stairs.

Were there servants around and awake? Maybe, but if so, they were unlikely to question a houseguest, even one roaming the house at two in the morning.

I walked on, my bare feet touching the cold stone of the tiled foyer. The old man's study was around the corner, the first door on the left, off a small alcove. Across the hall was a swinging door that led into the kitchen. I knew this from the blueprints.

The study door was closed. It was a heavy, medieval-looking door made out of carved wood, of the sort you might see in *Game of Thrones*.

But mounted on the right side of the door was a modern contraption, a small steel number pad with a bright red pinpoint LED light.

Which meant, of course, that the office was alarmed. That I hadn't expected. Not when his family was in residence.

Shit.

That wasn't the end of the road, though. I took note of the alarm manufacturer, conveniently right there on the control pad. It was a newly installed system, and it was wireless. There were ways to defeat—jam—wireless systems. I'd be better prepared the next time I visited.

So there would have to be a next time.

Conrad Kimball was an extremely suspicious man. That wasn't surprising after all. Kimball Pharma was a company under fire these days, and so was the Kimball family.

I turned to go. And then I heard footsteps, someone advancing along the hall very quietly. Very slowly.

# 21

Someone was coming around the corner. I immediately backed up against the doorway, flattening myself so I was momentarily out of his line of sight. For a few seconds.

A whisper: "Heller? What the hell?"

Maggie. In jeans and a white T-shirt and white sneakers. She still had her coppery wig on. At least I assumed it was a wig. A big purse was slung over her shoulder.

"Mags? I was going to ask you the same thing."

She moved in close, and then she kissed me, to my surprise. Then backed up a few inches. "I got dibs, Heller," she whispered.

"On what?"

"On the *files* is what, and you know it."

I nodded. "The alarm is on."

"What'd you expect? You have any idea how paranoid the man is? A couple of months ago, he brought in some high-end security contractors to protect his home files. Now he always sets the alarm. Lets his housekeeping staff in to clean but only when he's there. He's protecting something."

"Probably all his company's dirty secrets. Do you have the alarm code?"

"He doesn't trust his own kids, Heller. No, I don't. But I don't think I'm going to need it. Not as long as I have this." She pulled out a hand-held device with four antennas on it like teeth of a comb.

"Wi-Fi jammer?"

She smiled. This little gimmick blocked the signal between the control panel and the alarm sensors, temporarily disabling the alarm. I saw the red LED light go dark. She leaned forward and inserted a key in the lock. She turned the key, then pulled open the door. No alarm sounded, no noise.

It was pitch-black inside.

"We have two hours," she said.

"How do you know that?"

"If the sensor doesn't receive a signal in a hundred twenty minutes, the alarm goes off. It's a countermeasure."

"Anything else to worry about inside? Motion sensor?"

"Not in his home office."

"Pressure pads?"

"Highly doubt it."

She followed close behind me as I entered, then closed the door after us. She stood her Wi-Fi jammer on the floor right next to the door.

I exhaled. I could hear her breathe too, could smell her perfume. Something different from what she used to use. Brassier. A perfume called Opium, I decided. Part of her disguise. In the old days she wore patchouli. I closed my eyes and opened them again, letting my eyes get used to the dark. It wasn't pitch-black after all. Faint mottled moonlight came in through the leaded-glass diamond-pane windows.

"What are you after?" I asked.

"The files."

"Which ones?"

She paused. "Not gonna say."

"Who hired you?"

"Can't say. You?"

"Same. Where'd you get the key?"

She shrugged. "Can't say."

"You have any idea where the files are?"

"Not exactly. Could be anywhere. But I'm interested in the fact that he had a safe room put in a few months back. With a concealed entrance."

"For the files, you think?"

"Dunno. Maybe it's only for Natalya's jewelry. So I plan to search the whole office." She pulled out a tiny LED flashlight and swept it back and forth across the room. I could make out some shadowy details, including a large, ornately carved desk. Books lined the walls. A Chesterfield-style leather sofa, with matching hulking leather Chesterfield chairs facing it on the other side of a coffee table.

Nothing that looked like a filing cabinet.

I glanced back at the desk drawers. Possible. I took out my own little Maglite and approached the desk, tugging at the top right drawer. It slid open. No lock.

I smelled lemon-oil furniture polish and cigars. I focused the light. A Scotch-tape dispenser, a checkbook, a couple of pens and sharpened pencils, a pair of scissors.

The next drawer down was taller and more likely to contain files. That one came right open as well, revealing a stack of individually wrapped reams of computer paper. Nothing else. Conrad Kimball's files weren't in his desk.

I turned around to see Maggie, meanwhile, inspecting the bookshelves closely with her flashlight. She'd mentioned a safe room with a concealed entrance. A safe room, also known as a panic room, is a hardened shelter installed in a private residence that can be used by the homeowners to hide in order to stay safe during home invasions. Some of them, like the civil defense shelters of the early sixties, were big enough, with enough supplies, to live in for a few weeks. It would also make a logical place to hide something valuable.

My flashlight beam raked the walls of the study, the bookshelves, looking for cleverly built-in cabinetry. Lines in the wood that looked wrong. Seams. But I found nothing. Just books. The floor was covered in an antique-looking Aubusson carpet. The windows had recently been fitted with alarm contacts.

I noticed a door that I remembered from the plans led to a bathroom. That was worth checking out. I opened the door, saw a narrow space. An old-fashioned toilet with a pull-chain water closet above, black and white tiles on the floor, subway tiles on the walls. An old pedestal sink. All probably original to the house.

And it had windows that opened to the outside. I entered the bathroom, inspected the windows, saw no alarm contacts. They hadn't bothered to alarm the bathroom window. Had I known this, I could have sneaked in that way, from outside, avoiding the alarm entirely.

Then a faint sound came from the hallway.

The sound of a door closing.

# 22

Maggie and I looked at each other. We couldn't really see each other's eyes, but we both knew what to do. We immediately dropped to the floor, scuttled across the carpet, and squatted down behind the biggest pieces of furniture we could find—the bulky Chesterfield armchairs—flattening ourselves on the floor. Staying out of sight lines in case someone entered the study.

Breathing slowly, I calmed myself and waited for the study door to open.

Conrad Kimball was a light sleeper. Maybe he was a night owl. If he entered the room and switched on the lights, we were both well and truly screwed.

Maybe he was looking for something. Maybe he forgot something.

Maybe Maggie's intel was bad and a pressure-sensitive silent alarm under the Aubusson had alerted him.

Breathing through my nostrils, I once again managed to steady my pulse. I waited to be discovered.

After all, I was staging a break-in from within the target's house. The target being a highly suspicious man. Who had at least three outsiders as houseguests: Maggie, me, and Paul's brilliant Moroccan girlfriend.

I found myself staring at the carpet, at the wooden baseboard. Once my eyes had acclimated to the dark, I could see an odd, misplaced seam in the polished cherrywood baseboard molding. I shone the flashlight on it, pulsed it on and off, and confirmed that there was a vertical seam where—given the high-end craftsmanship that went into building this house, the uninterrupted length of the boards—there shouldn't be.

A repair? Possibly, but not likely.

So while I listened for the door to open, I crawled across the carpet on my hands and knees and drew closer to the errant seam. I felt it, touched the baseboard, hoping for something like a spring-loaded touch-latch that would open some hidden compartment in the book-case. I was thinking of a kick panel that might unlock a hidden door. But nothing clicked or moved. I looked more closely, searching for telltale traces of dust that might indicate an air leak from an adjoining room, due to temperature differentials or pressure changes. But I saw none.

I waited for a few more seconds, perfectly still. The door to the study didn't open.

No one walked in or walked by.

A false alarm. A servant using the bathroom, maybe. No one was coming.

I caught Maggie's eye and decided to stand. I saw nobody. I thought about the blueprints of the study I'd examined. I distinctly remembered seeing a large closet in the plans, but there didn't appear to be one here anymore.

So I took out a tiny infrared thermal camera and attached it to my cell phone. I focused on the bookshelves and saw a spill of blue at the baseboard molding, about two or three feet wide.

The blue indicated cold air.

That told me that behind the wall of books was an unheated space; the closet that used to be here had been walled over.

Or converted into a safe room but covered with a bookcase to conceal its entrance. I began testing each shelf, pressing here and there, looking for a spring latch. Maggie got to her feet, saw what I was doing, and started testing the risers, the vertical boards that comprised the bookcases, while I tested the horizontal boards. But nothing clicked. Nothing moved.

Maybe you had to pull a certain book. I'd seen that trick before. Mostly in movies, but occasionally in real life, inspired by the movies. But nothing popped open.

Until Maggie touched the edge of a lower shelf a few inches off the ground and something gave way. A thud, and then a section of shelves jutted open. The shelves were bolted to a metal door. I grasped the edge of the heavy door—heavy because of all the books, plus it was steel—and pulled it open.

The safe room.

Lined with filing cabinets.

She smiled at me. "We're in," she said.

# 23

We were standing in a small white-painted steel room with a steel floor and rows of gray steel filing cabinets lining two of the walls, narrowing the space where you could stand. Overhead lighting had come on as soon as we entered. I could tell this safe room had been assembled from prefab steel panels, built to a standard size. This one was probably eight by ten. On the back wall were a few shelves. I saw jewelry boxes with pearl necklaces and diamond brooches and other costly items like that, laid out on black velvet. On display like a jewelry store. Natalya's stash, no doubt.

"Jesus," she breathed.

But Maggie wasn't looking at the jewelry. She was focused on the file cabinets.

I pulled the bookshelf-door behind us closed. It clicked shut. Somewhere a ventilation fan began to whirr faintly. I'm not claustrophobic, but this was a small space. It was built to house files and jewelry, not really as a panic room, where the family could hide out in case of an intrusion. It was too cramped to hold more than a couple of people, and there were no visible supplies.

"Leave the door open," Maggie said.

"Why?"

"I want to hear noises."

"Fair enough," I said, and pushed the door open. The vent fan went off.

I said in a low voice, "We're probably looking for different things. But we can help each other. So what *are* you looking for?"

This time she didn't hold back. "His new will. The kids are afraid they're getting written out and Natalya's getting written in. They think she's manipulating Conrad, that she's all about the Benjamins. What about you?"

"There was a drug trial done on Oxydone years ago. Found that the drug was dangerously addictive in humans and warned against marketing it. That trial was buried, but the files on it are probably somewhere in here."

"Always thought that was just a rumor."

"What?"

"That they had proof how addictive it was but somehow the FDA got paid off or something."

"All I know is there's a file, and it's here somewhere."

She tugged at a steel cabinet labeled LEGAL, but the drawers were locked. I pulled at the one right in front of me, marked FAMILY, and that too was locked.

Then I found a cabinet labeled OXYDONE: EARLY DEVELOPMENT.

"You got a pick set?" she said.

"Of course."

I took out my leather shaving kit and removed a flat pick with a hook on it. I did the gentlemanly thing and turned to the Legal cabinet first, the one Maggie was interested in. It was a four-pin file cabinet lock. It couldn't have been easier. I pushed in, then pushed down, and the lock popped out. She pulled at the top drawer, and it opened.

"You're good," she said. "I forgot how good."

"Learned from the best." I had no doubt she knew how to pick locks too—she'd probably taken the government course "Defense Against Methods of Entry," a series of classes on how to break into places. I'd taken such a course, though by then I already knew how to pick locks, courtesy of a repo man I once met at Norman Lang Motors

81

in Malden, Mass. That's where I used to hang out a lot with my friend whose dad owned it.

Then I turned back around and found the Oxydone file cabinet and picked its lock. I'd gotten it down to five seconds, which wasn't bad.

"Estate plans," she muttered. "We're in the right area code. Thank you."

"How much time do we have on the clock?" I asked her.

"Hour and a half. Being conservative." She took out an iPhone.

For the next few minutes there was just silence, broken only by the rustling of paper files, the occasional camera-lens-click from her phone. It was starting to get hot in there.

A lot of what I do is routine. Scut work. It's not dramatic, it's not cinematic, but it's a major part of my job. I pored over as many files as I could.

I was able to pick each cabinet open in less than five seconds. In the Family cabinet I found a section labeled PSYCHIATRIC INVENTORIES/ CONFIDENTIAL. There, I found psychiatric evaluations of each of his five children. One folder was marked "Susan Kimball." I pulled it out, feeling a little guilty. Skimmed it. Read phrases like "Subject is a bright, intense individual who is somewhat naive for her age." And "used to being bullied by her powerful father." And "likely to be a follower rather than a leader . . . Fear of being taken advantage of . . . Particularly vulnerable to humiliation."

Then I skimmed the one marked "Cameron Kimball." Various phrases jumped out at me—"motor vehicle homicide" and "sealed juvenile record." These files represented nearly fifty years, beginning with when Conrad Kimball started his medical practice and soon thereafter acquired the small pharmaceutical company, Cedar Laboratories, that later became Kimball Pharma.

"Bingo," Maggie said abruptly, startling me. She pulled a thick file from the top drawer. "His kids will not be happy. But Natalya's gonna be one rich widow." She closed the file drawer. "Revised ten days ago. And that's . . . as long as I'm staying in this claustrophobic box."

"Excuse me?"

"I'm out of here. And, Heller, you should get out of here soon too. We can't risk staying longer."

"Soon as I find my file. Wanna help me?"

"Just for a minute or two, but then we should leave. I'll start with the bottom drawer. Wait." She put up a hand and cocked her head. I listened too. I heard nothing.

She shook her head. "Okay, sorry."

She pulled out the bottom drawer of the Oxydone cabinet and knelt on the floor as she flicked through the files.

I was not having any luck. I found a section on Development, but it was just a lot of chemical formulas and back-and-forth between scientists. A section on Investors. One drawer did contain just drug trial results. But here there appeared to be a gap, missing files about an inch thick.

As I searched the files on either side of the gap, Maggie got to her feet. A few seconds later, she whispered, "Heller?"

I turned, looked.

"You see this?"

She was pointing at a safe bolted onto the floor at the back of the little steel room.

"Check this out."

There it was. There had to be a safe somewhere in his office. Probably others, elsewhere in the house, too. I'd come prepared for this, at least.

I stopped what I was doing, sidled over to the safe, squatted down. It was made of dull gray steel. A round digital keypad in the center of the front face, attached to a handle. This was the sort of inexpensive safe you might pick up at Home Depot. A lot of rich people are cheap when it comes to home security. This one had an electronic lock, pry-resistant hinges, one-inch-thick bolts to keep the door in place, and you could drop it from fifteen feet, no problem. But the manufacturers had put a cheap nickel solenoid in the locking mechanism.

Its Achilles' heel.

"I'll do the honors," she said. She punched in four digits—"the month and date Conrad met Natalya," she said—and it beeped without unlocking.

"As I remember, this brand uses five digits, not four."

She punched in several other numbers. I let her try, while I pulled something out of my shaving kit. It looked like a white tube sock with something round and heavy in it.

"Keep your phone away," I said. "This thing will wipe it clean."

"What is it?"

"It's a rare-earth magnet."

These things were extremely powerful. They wiped out phones and credit cards and computer hard drives instantly.

"What do you—" she began. But then she fell silent, watching me position the magnet, in the white sock, against the top of the safe, just above the keypad. The magnet clamped right on, through the sock. I twisted the leg of the sock, fashioning a sort of handle. The magnet did as expected; then I jerked the handle and the safe came right open.

"Heller!" she whispered in astonishment.

I pulled at the sock and managed to slide the magnet off the front of the safe. That's what the sock is for; otherwise, it's fiendishly difficult to pull the magnet off.

I don't know what I expected to find: More jewelry? Computer disks? Inside was just a thick Kraft-paper envelope, the old-fashioned kind that closes with a button and string.

She slipped her hand in and pulled out the envelope. Now I saw what she'd just seen. On the front of the envelope were two strips of white label tape with black lettering, all caps. They read:

**TO BE DESTROYED**
**UPON MY DEATH**

"Huh," I said.
"I got dibs, Heller," she said.

# 24

I don't think so," I replied. "We wouldn't have these if it weren't for me and my magnet. You came here to find his will, and you got it."

"We wouldn't be in this office if it weren't for me shutting off that alarm."

"True," I admitted. "Where'd you get the key to the study?"

"From my client. Who thought the alarm would be off."

"Who's your client?"

She shrugged. She wasn't going to tell me. "Let me take this first," she said, "take some pictures, hand it back to you."

"What's inside?" I said, ignoring her suggestion.

She was already unwinding the string from the paper button on the back of the envelope. Then she pulled out a small pile of brown folders, maybe an inch thick.

"That's it?" I said. "Just paper?"

"Some photographs. Who's Eric Sidney Tucker?"

"Megan's ex-husband."

"If Eric Sidney Tucker has a mustache, this must be photos of him in bed with some woman. Who is clearly not his wife, Megan Kimball."

*Kompromat*, I thought. The Russians were famously great at collecting blackmail on people and exerting it to get their way. So was Conrad Kimball.

"He must not want his daughter to know he hired a PI on her husband," I said. "That he has evidence against him."

"But Megan's divorced. Maybe she knows already."

"Maybe, maybe not. What else is there?"

"Here's a folder on Cameron Kimball."

I took a look. "Jesus," I whispered. I scanned through the folder, saw the police report, the court documents. But that wasn't what I was looking for. "What else?"

"You mean something like this?"

She held up a thick brown file folder. Its label, in a clear plastic tab, typewritten, read, OXYDONE/PHOENICIA. That referred to the contract research organization that had done the tests whose explosive results they had buried. Phoenicia Health Sciences.

"I'll take that one."

"How about you let me have it until breakfast? Which is when this birthday party is over, right? That's when I'm leaving."

"How about you take your pictures right here?"

"You don't trust me?"

"Of course I trust you. It's a matter of speed."

"The light will be better in the room I'm staying in."

"Okay," I said reluctantly. "But let me take a quick look." She handed it to me, and I flipped through the file. Correspondence, but I didn't find any clinical trial. I handed it back to her.

Then we both heard a high-pitched beeping, three beeps in a row, coming from the study. The alarm. We looked at each other. If the door to the safe room had been closed, we wouldn't have heard it.

"Shit, Heller," she said.

"Did it just rearm?"

"The batteries in my jammer must have died."

"We're stuck," I said.

Not necessarily in the file room, but in the study. It was now alarmed. We couldn't open the study door from the inside without setting off the alarm.

She bowed her head, which was what she always did when she

87

wanted to think hard. Then she said, "No motion sensor inside the study. But we can't open the door."

"Right," I said, impatiently.

"Windows are all alarmed."

"Not all," I said, thinking of the narrow bathroom window. "We can get out through the bathroom," I said.

"How do you know?"

"No contacts on the windows. I noticed earlier."

"Fantastic, Heller."

Envelope in hand, she left the safe room and went to retrieve her dead Wi-Fi jammer from where she'd left it standing, on the wooden floor by the door to the hallway. The room was still mostly dark. I could smell the faint cigar, the lemon oil. The highly polished surface of his desk now gleamed in the moonlight. It was a few minutes after three in the morning. I pushed the safe room door closed. It clicked smoothly into place. A fairly recent installation, I thought, very high-end. That he hadn't cheaped out on.

Maggie opened the bathroom door, saw the narrow window I was talking about. "I can fit through it no problem, but you're a big guy, Heller."

"But lithe," I pointed out. Which was an overstatement. She opened the window—double-hung and heavy—and swung her feet around, and in a neat maneuver she slid through the open window and thumped onto the grass outside.

I followed, though it took an extra bit of maneuvering, given the tight space between the toilet and the sink. But a moment later I landed on the grass below. It was chilly fall weather out there, with a strong breeze and a few drops of rain.

Maggie put a finger to her lips. I nodded, and I followed her across the lawn until we reached a manicured chess garden enclosed almost entirely by tall hedges. From here you couldn't see the house, which made it a good place to talk.

88

In the center of the garden was a gazebo, and inside that was a small stone table topped with a black marble chessboard.

"Nick Heller saves the day again," she said, shaking her head.

"Just lucky I noticed the window," I said.

"Man, I really fucked up. I should have put that jammer through a field test. Good thing Nick Heller was here."

It was sort of strange, the way she kept using my full name, like I was a brand, or maybe a superhero. She'd called me Heller when we were seeing each other, so I was used to her just saying my last name. But full name? That was new.

"You're not actually *with* Sukie Kimball, are you?" she said as I sat down.

"No. Hired by her. You were hired by Cameron?"

She paused, looked at me. "Can I trust you?"

"What do you think?" I said.

She nodded. We had to trust each other, and she knew it. She was grateful to me for pointing out the unalarmed bathroom window. "I was hired by Megan, but Cameron's cooperating."

"Megan wanted to see her father's latest will?"

"That's part of it. They're all afraid Natalya's going to cheat them out of their inheritance. They have reason to believe Daddy revised his will again, but he'll never talk about it. So she didn't just want the will. She wanted to find out where he stashes his secret assets. So I was also looking for records on shell companies, that sort of thing."

"How long have you been private?"

"Four years."

"You're out of the army?"

"Seven years. Since—us."

"What have you been doing?"

"You mean, have I been dating?"

"No, that's not what I said."

"Isn't it? Anyway, I've been staying busy, got a lot of work, building this private-eye business. Staying in trouble." She grinned.

"Am I forgiven?" I said after a pause.

She was silent for a long time. "You know, what happened before, we don't need to get into that, Heller."

"Maybe we should."

"The way we left things between us maybe was a good place to leave things."

"Now I get it," I said. "It took me a long time, I'll admit. But I understand now why you were so angry."

"Why are women always described as angry?"

I didn't want to get into it with her. "Remember when you made that bouncer at the bar in Fort Bragg back down?"

She laughed. I'd forgotten how much I loved this woman's laugh.

"You scared the shit out of him," I went on. She laughed even more. "Talk about female anger."

She took my hand in hers. "You could always make me laugh, Heller."

"Okay," I said. "You have to get back to your room and take some pictures. Then get the envelope back to me by eight, okay? Put it in a bag so it's not recognizable. Break's over."

# 25

The mansion was completely dark. Dawn would come soon. The wind still whipped, but it didn't rain, just spattered a bit. We made our way back to the house. Her room was in the other wing, and we decided it made the most sense for her to enter at the back door.

"Remember, I'm Hildy," she said.

Turned out that we both knew the code to the main house alarm— it was the month, day, and year that Conrad Kimball had first met his Natalya. That code his kids knew. The alarm was still on by the time I got to the front door, which just meant that I'd beat Maggie to it. I punched in the code, and it instantly disarmed.

The grand stone staircase was right before me. I padded up the staircase to the second floor, to the wing where I was staying. In the dark hall someone passed by quickly. I saw that it was Cameron, presumably going into his own room. Maybe he was too drunk to recognize me. I hoped so.

I located my bedroom and collapsed on the bed. I was exhausted. I glanced at my watch. Four in the morning.

I'd catch a few hours of sleep. My alarm clock would be Maggie Benson knocking on my door at eight A.M.

I dozed fitfully, had troubled dreams.

I still dream about things that happened to me in Iraq and

Afghanistan. You can't avoid it. If you don't dream it, something's wrong; you're suppressing bad stuff. Sometimes I'll dream about people dying. Friends dying. Or I'm exposed in a combat situation and suddenly my rifle jams. Regular people have anxiety dreams about, like, discovering they're about to take a final exam in a course they forgot they had signed up for.

But if they've served in combat, they might dream that they're ten shots into a guy, an enemy, and he won't go down, he just keeps advancing.

I dream, sometimes, of combat situations I've been in. Probably because on some level my brain needs to keep processing these moments of high anxiety, to keep me sane. That's my theory, anyway.

That night I dreamed of the time Sean Lenehan saved my life.

We were based in Asadabad, in Kunar province, in the northeastern part of Afghanistan. Our mission was to advise three hundred or so soldiers in an Afghan National Army *kandak*, which is their word for battalion.

One day one of our two interpreters, Abdul Rahim, rushed in to the team house and told us that the other interpreter, Khalid, had been kidnapped by the Taliban. He was being held in a house in a village in the Pech Valley, one of the most violent and dangerous areas in Afghanistan.

Abdul Rahim said he'd received a desperate call from a member of Khalid's family. He wasn't being held for ransom. They were going to lop off his head in the village square in the morning, to make an example of him.

Khalid was a slight man in his twenties who stammered a little in English but was a super-fast interpreter and a dear person. Everyone liked him. We needed him. There was no debate about whether to attempt a hostage rescue to get Khalid back. We all loved the guy and wanted to try to save him. We were all in agreement.

Our team leader, Captain McShane, called the company commander at Jalalabad and secured permission for a limited rescue operation. But how to carry it off? Normally we'd have a few days for mission prep, a few days to gather intelligence by whatever means possible. Then a day or two to rehearse. But if we were going to save Khalid's life, we had to move that very night.

All we knew was that he was being held hostage in some compound in this small village. If we were going to move at midnight, we had maybe twelve hours to gather all available intel on the house where Khalid was imprisoned.

And since I was the intel sergeant, that was my job.

I begged Jalalabad to lend us a drone, a UAV, to fly and circle over the village for five hours and collect whatever info we could. We needed to develop a pattern of life, as it's called. The company commander said okay.

That allowed us to locate the right house. It turned out to be fairly obvious: the only house in the village that kept a sentry on the roof. I estimated there were six to eight men inside the house.

The team leaders and I met in the Op Cen, the team conference room, sitting in metal folding chairs around a four-by-eight plywood table. It was a chilly afternoon. People don't know how cold it can get in the mountains of eastern Afghanistan. It snowed several inches every week.

When it was my turn to speak, I let everyone on the team know that this was going to be riskier than normal. There were far too many unknowns.

"So noted," said Captain McShane, and everyone fell quiet for an uncomfortable few seconds. "Moving on."

We came up with our CONOPS, or concept of the operation. Then all the fallback plans, the PACE plans—the primary plan, the alternate, the contingency, and the emergency. (The military loves its acronyms.) Our ops sergeant had put in a call to his higher-ups at Jalalabad for permission to use a couple of Black Hawks. He decided we'd infil via helicopter a few terrain features away. This would reduce the sound of the choppers.

Then we'd move on foot to the target area. Once we'd set up the observation and support positions, the stack would move toward the compound and position itself for entry through the front door.

Meanwhile, I got to work on the operational preparation of the battlefield, the OPE. That meant I checked on the weather, terrain, enemy situation, and so on. It was a cold, dry night, which was good. I requested overhead imagery. I did a terrain study using maps and photos, to help determine the infil and exfil routes. And where the choppers should land.

This was all on me, which just jacked up my stress level.

We rehearsed the mission a few times. Did a few walk-throughs. The warrant officer announced that I was going to be the first guy in the stack, since I was most familiar with Khalid. Sean was fourth. The hostage rescue was scheduled for midnight. Zero hundred hours.

And I had a bad feeling about this mission.

Partly that was because of the odds. You can only go through so many gunfights and not get shot. That was one thing. The odds said it was my turn to get shot. But partly too it was because I was number one in the stack. The lead guy's the one who sets off the IEDs or gets shot. Someone's got to be the lead, though, and plenty of times I had volunteered for it. But that day my Spidey-sense told me something was going to go wrong, so I didn't volunteer—and got chosen all the same.

Over the course of the evening, while we waited for zero hundred hours, we all tried to decompress in our different ways.

Some of us worked out. Most of us hung out in our barracks. Some guys played online games; some listened to music. You often used to hear a 3 Doors Down song playing, "When I'm Gone" ("Love me when I'm gone, when I'm gone"). Merlin did Sudoku, super-advanced, black-belt stuff.

Some guys put on headphones and blasted music so loud you

could hear it clearly in the barracks. A lot of the guys Skyped with their families, just to say hi. You weren't allowed to tell them that in a few hours you were going on a hazardous mission in which you might be killed. Instead, you were "just checking in." It was always the dangerous missions that inspired people to make one last phone call. Sean called Patty, and she immediately figured out something was looming, but that was just Patty.

Everyone was nervous. Your stomach gets tight. The adrenaline is pumping. I checked the fit of my helmet, made sure it was on right. Did a comms check to make sure my handheld communications device was working. I found if I spent some time before a mission doing all my pre-op checks, it kept my anxiety at a manageable level.

I read a book by Lee Child. I like the Jack Reacher stories. And I waited. I thought a lot. We didn't know how many guys were in the house or what kind of arms they had. Nor could we tell how many might be lying in wait in neighboring houses. It had occurred to me— and I'd told the entire team my theory—that the Taliban had kidnapped Khalid as a way to lure us into an ambush.

Any of us could be shot or KIA that night.

There were too many unknowns.


At just before midnight, we gathered on the airfield near the two Black Hawks. It was our detachment of twelve, plus Abdul Rahim, the other interpreter, and what's called a JTAC, an Air Force special tactics airman. That made fourteen of us. Seven in each chopper.

We checked our communications devices, the MBITRs. We checked and checked again: Did we have our tear gas grenades? Protective eyewear? Fragmentation grenades? It's always the little things that go wrong, so you obsessively look at every detail. We examined our M9 Beretta pistols, our M4s, the magazine pouches for the M4s. Put on our earmuffs that plugged into our MBITRs, which protected our hearing but also let us all stay in communication. Made sure we had the gloves to avoid burns. Checked our NODs, our night observation devices—that's night-vision goggles to you. One of our slogans used to be "We Own the Night." In part, that's because the enemy didn't have night-vision equipment. We could see in the darkness, and they, at that time, could not. Maybe by now that's changed.

We were all wearing body armor plates front and back. Hanging from the plate carrier was a bunch of equipment, including the medical kit.

That one you didn't want to forget.

We all strapped into our harnesses in the helicopter and took off quickly. The doors remained open, despite the cold night. It wasn't a long trip, maybe thirty klicks. On our headphones "When I'm Gone" was playing, like a soundtrack to our infiltration. It was intended to pump everyone up, get everyone hyped up and ready. To me, that night, it sounded a little morbid.

We landed in a small river valley, pulled off our seatbelt harnesses, and jumped out of the chopper. I could feel the icy river water through my boots. We were completely exposed.

We made our stealthy approach into the village, clutching our M4 rifles, and over to an observation point where we could see the compound where Khalid was being held. Sure enough, through our NODs, we could see there was one sentry on the roof, as the drone had spotted. One of our team members was watching the drone's feed on a small screen and confirmed that the house was exactly as anticipated.

No one was standing guard outside. Earlier in the day someone had been there. Now, nobody. I didn't like that.

Our four-man stack quietly moved in closer. A team sniper/ observer found a position from which he could see the back of the house. Ready to shoot any squirter, which is what we called someone who sneaks out the back door or window, running away from the attack.

The front door wasn't terribly substantial, so we rammed it in instead of breaching it with an explosive charge. As we four entered the house, we tossed flash-bangs. There was dust everywhere, the smell of gunpowder.

And through our NODs we could see that the house was swarming with enemy soldiers. Were they expecting us? Had we just stepped into the middle of an ambush? Maybe we'd been betrayed by one of the Afghan soldiers we'd been training. Maybe one of them had placed a call on their mobile phone.

Or maybe it was something much simpler. Maybe they had simply heard the sound of the choppers and grabbed their weapons.

The air exploded with gunfire. Everyone, it seemed, was firing at us at once.

As the first one in, I was the first one shot. A couple of times. It felt like my left leg had been pierced by a flaming arrow. An explosion of pain. I crumpled to the floor. Later, I learned that the first round had broken my femur. The second one had pierced my femoral artery. It's hard to describe the magnitude of the pain, but it took over my body, disoriented me. I saw blood spewing from my leg. I thought about the very real possibility that I might die in a matter of minutes. I struggled to get up but suddenly didn't have the strength. This, I thought, was my time. It had finally come.

Suddenly I was being dragged across the room and out of the house. Sean, who was the fourth guy in the stack, had run into the house, exposing himself to the enemy, in order to grab me by a shoulder strap of my body armor. He pulled me across the floor, out the door, and then outside along the ground until he got me safely behind a high stone wall.

I managed to croak out, "Thank you."

"Not done yet," I heard Sean say as if from a distance.

Meanwhile, George Devlin, our communications sergeant, was on the radio, calling in a 9 line for a medevac helicopter. Sean got a tourniquet off my kit and applied it to my leg to stop the bleeding. He also put gauze and a bandage on the wounds.

Blood was everywhere. I was in shock, so my memory of everything afterward is hazy. I heard Sean muttering, and I asked him to repeat it.

"You know, there's an ancient Chinese proverb," he said. "If you save a man's life, you're responsible for it."

My brain was operating just barely enough to allow me to rasp, "Having second thoughts?"

A Black Hawk medevac bird arrived moments later, and I was lifted into it on a stretcher. A medic on the chopper checked my airway, assessed me for shock, took my blood pressure, looked worried, and gave me a fentanyl lollipop. I licked it a few times. I don't remember much beyond that until I woke up hours later in a surgical tent in Jalalabad.

I muttered, "How's Khalid?"

Silence around me. A little louder, I said, "The hostage? How is he?"

"The hostage didn't make it," someone said.

Khalid had been executed minutes before we got there.

We never figured out whether we were betrayed by one of the *kandak* or if they were just alerted by the chopper sound.

Sometimes you just don't know. Combat is iffy. Sometimes it just goes bad.

# 26

Around nine I found myself awake and a little annoyed that Maggie was taking so long photographing the "destroy upon my death" files. Why hadn't she come by yet?

I took a shower, brushed my teeth, got dressed, and went in search of Sukie's room. I knocked, but there was no answer. She was probably already downstairs.

By the time I got to the staircase I could hear voices and laughter coming from below. Maybe Maggie was down there and had some reason why she hadn't been able to return the files yet. *Hildy*, I reminded myself. I descended the stairs, and as I drew closer the voices became more distinct.

I passed through the entry foyer to the swinging door that led to the kitchen. But instead of entering, I stood outside and listened for a moment. There are all sorts of devices you can use to amplify distant conversations, including "bionic ears" and such, which let you hear a whisper from three hundred feet away. But I didn't have any with me, and I wouldn't have used them if I did. Too unsubtle. I didn't want to be caught with any incriminating equipment.

I stood there against the wall, smelling coffee and bacon frying.

A male voice was saying, ". . . but once she gets keys to the car, she'll drive it off a bridge and screw us out of everything."

"Dad wouldn't make that mistake," a woman said.

"He's changed. We can't be sure of anything. And she's got a leash on Cameron like he's her puppy."

"The kind that's never quite house-trained."

A few laughs. Who was the "she" they were talking about—Natalya, the Russian fiancée? One of the sisters? Obviously Cameron wasn't in the kitchen. They were talking about him. Probably Maggie wasn't either. So the male voice had to be Paul, the older brother.

Paul's voice from inside the kitchen said, ". . . see what she was wearing?"

A mumble.

A woman: "Surgically augmented figure." Who was speaking? Sukie? Hayden? Megan was gone, and there were two women in the room, who had to be Sukie and Hayden.

A second woman, maybe Sukie: "She was a flight attendant, I swear."

"Definitely mail order," Paul said. "Or whatever the internet equivalent of mail order is."

The first woman again, maybe Hayden, said, "Why don't you just ask him?"

"Where's the fun in that?"

"I did ask him, 'What do you like about her?' and he said, 'I enjoy having a conversation with an intellectual equal,'" Sukie, I was now sure it was Sukie, said.

The three roared with laughter.

The longer I waited outside the kitchen, the greater the chance someone would walk by, or come out the swinging doors, and discover me. So I stood there poised to move at any moment.

Maybe Hayden was saying, ". . . changed his will a thousand times." But the next few lines were obscured by a clatter of pots or pans.

Then a man said, "He's gonna screw over Barb and your mom too for this bimbo, and I'm not going to put up with it."

A murmur and then a female voice: ". . . controls him now. He does whatever Natalya wants."

I decided then it was risky to stay out here any longer, eavesdropping, so I pushed open the kitchen door and entered.

Three of the adult Kimball kids were sitting around a long metal-topped worktable on stools, mugs of coffee in their hands. No Maggie.

"You remember her at all?" Paul was saying. "She was the nightmare nanny."

"The Irish one?" said Sukie.

"Maureen, the bad-tempered one from Dublin," said Paul. "I eventually got her fired. I was quite proud of that. Well, hello there. I forgot your name." He looked uncomfortable, like he was wondering how much I'd heard.

"Nick. Good morning." I leaned over and gave Sukie a kiss on the lips. Somewhere a dishwasher was going. The air was warm and humid.

"Morning," she said. She was in gym shorts and a T-shirt. "Coffee?" She waved at a glass carafe of coffee in the middle of the dented metal tabletop.

"Sure. Black, thanks."

She retrieved a big white mug from the counter behind her. Pouring a full mug of coffee from the glass carafe, she handed it to me, and as she did, she looked me straight in the eye. Arched her brow. As if asking, *Well? How'd it go?*

I just nodded, once, and said, "Thanks."

# 27

You're the first of the guests to come down," Paul said. "You're all late sleepers. Layla is still trying to adjust from Hong Kong time. She should be down in an hour or so. And Cameron—"

"Cameron is Cameron," said Hayden, like an old joke. A rueful laugh.

"And I imagine his girlfriend got just as pissed as he did," said Paul. "They seemed compatible. What was her name again?"

"Hildy," said Hayden, in sweatpants and Wesleyan sweatshirt.

"Pissed?" said Sukie. "In the British sense?"

"Of course. Blotted. Legless." Paul shook his head. He was wearing blue striped pajamas and looked, with his gray cowlick, like an overgrown child. He was sitting at the head of the table as if he'd called a meeting. He had a sad little potbelly.

I looked around for a moment. This was a huge commercial-grade kitchen, with a couple of ten-burner stainless-steel Vulcan gas ranges and ovens, steel hoods, two huge True refrigerators. Exposed brick walls, brown tile floors. Nothing fancy in here. This wasn't a kitchen built for show. It was used mostly by professional cooks, who could prepare a lot of meals here; it looked recently updated. Pot racks mounted on the ceiling. A giant KitchenAid mixer. A Bunn commercial coffeemaker.

"Your dad a late sleeper?" I asked.

"Not him. He's having his morning massage."

"You know, Rosa's dying," said Hayden. "We all have to visit her. She's still in Queens."

"I'd heard she wasn't well, but I had no idea she was dying," said Sukie.

"Stage-four cancer," said Hayden.

"Rosa took care of us younger kids," Sukie explained. "We all loved her."

The kitchen door swung open, and I turned around to see if it was Maggie.

But it was Conrad Kimball, wearing jeans and a plaid flannel shirt with an unbuttoned gray cardigan over it, reading glasses on a chain around his neck. He was smiling.

I could feel the mood shift. Everyone was suddenly less relaxed.

"Morning, Dad," they called out, nearly in unison. "Morning."

"Good morning," he proclaimed. "Where is my beloved? She's not back yet?"

"Natalya?" said Sukie. "She's not catching up on her beauty sleep?" She said it in an innocent way, but I knew it was a jab.

"No, she's an early riser," Conrad replied. "Ever since Young Pioneer camp. She went for a walk in the woods. On the trails. She said it reminds her of the forests outside of Moscow. Well, she's bound to get hungry sometime soon."

"Wasn't it raining earlier?" asked Hayden.

"It cleared up nicely," said Paul.

Sukie poured her father a mug of coffee and handed it to him. "You're in a good mood this morning," she said to him.

"A good massage always puts me in a good frame of mind. Almost makes me forget the call I got yesterday from the director of the Whitney."

"Let me guess," said Paul. "They want you to give another gallery."

"He was asking, in the most delicate way possible, whether I'd be agreeable to changing the name of the Kimball Gallery."

"Changing it to what?" said Hayden.

"Just . . . taking down the name. They've had a lot of protests against us. All those crazies out there, the nutjobs, the sob sisters."

"What did you tell him?" asked Sukie. She pulled out a chair for him, not a stool.

"I said, 'What do you think Gertrude Vanderbilt Whitney would say if you asked her the same thing?'"

"Daddy, there's a lot of anger out there," Sukie said.

"And you're not helping," he said. "Going to all these funerals. Only a matter of time before the *Wall Street Journal* does a story about you, and it's the rats are deserting the sinking ship. It's goddamn disloyal to the family." He said it like a slap.

"People are OD'ing by the thousands every year, Daddy. They're snorting Oxydone like cocaine. Hundreds of—"

"You know what mistake I made with you?" Conrad said, raising a stubby index finger. "Letting you go to Oberlin."

"What's wrong with Oberlin?" said Hayden.

"Oberlin was great," Sukie said.

"It's where she got indoctrinated with all her high ideals," said Conrad. Then he smiled, as if to brush it off.

"Did you tell Dad about Sundance?" said Hayden.

"What's this?" said Conrad.

"Her new documentary just got accepted to Sundance. Isn't that fantastic?"

"Hey, congrats, Sukie," said Paul.

"Yeah, isn't that great?" Sukie said.

"Sundance," said Conrad. "That's one of those little festivals in some cutesy town where people go to watch documentaries like yours, right?"

"Well, yeah," said Sukie.

He shook his head, smiled in amusement. "Like a drug that never makes it out of trials. How's your book?" Now he was talking to Paul.

"So I've got a bit of good news too," Paul replied. "Finally."

"Oh, yeah, what's that?" said Hayden.

"So an editor at Dodd Merriwether really loves my book proposal, and I think they're going to make an offer."

"What's your book?" I asked. Someone nearby was knocking on a door.

"It's a social history. A cultural history. Basically, it's about how we got to be so ass-backward and upside down. As a culture, right?"

"Uh-huh," I said. I could see his sisters' eyes starting to glaze over.

"At first it was going to start with the sixties. But then I realized the fifties are really the sixties, you know? Ginsberg, the Beats, Transcendental Meditation, all that shit."

The knocking on the kitchen door continued.

"The fifties. Postwar era. Except, actually, you know, wrong war. It's after the *First* World War that you see this whole—well, a culture of nihilism, really. Like, we've just burned down Western civilization, and we're okay with it. So long as we've got our gas masks."

"Okay, Paul, he gets it," Sukie interrupted.

The knocking continued, but no one got up.

"Sounds like a great idea for a book," I lied. Paul had gone to Harvard, then spent ten years in grad school in art history. He never finished his dissertation. For a while he was a teaching fellow at Harvard, then he taught expository writing there.

But Paul wasn't done yet. "I'm thinking like *All That Is Solid Melts into Air* or *The Culture of Narcissism*—I mean, we're talking a *big* book." He mentioned the titles of the books as if everyone should know them.

"What kind of an offer are we talking about?" asked Conrad.

"Someone's at the door," said Hayden.

"Natalya wouldn't knock," said Conrad.

Sukie got up to answer it.

"Maybe six figures," said Paul.

"I guess it helped that I played a couple rounds of golf with that fat German guy who owns the joint."

"Dodd Merriwether is owned by a German holding company," Paul explained to his siblings.

"A privately held publishing company. Been in Dieter's family for five generations. Used to publish hymnals, he told me."

"I don't want your help, Dad," said Paul.

I could hear Hayden talking to whoever was at the door. I heard Spanish being spoken, a male voice.

"Too late," said Conrad. "I always do what I can to help my children. I can't avoid it. Ask Hayden how she came by—"

"Paul, you speak Spanish fluently, right?" said Hayden, coming from across the room. By her side was a gnarled older Hispanic-looking guy in jeans and boots and a twill work shirt, clutching a battered straw hat to his torso.

"*Buenos días, Santiago,*" Conrad said. "*¿Pasa algo?*"

The old man bowed his head toward Conrad and then the others. He was younger than Conrad by at least twenty years, but a life of hard work in the sun had knotted and aged him.

"*Buenos días, patrón,*" he said. "*No—bueno, pos sí, patrón, encontramos un cadáver. Tábamos tirando la hojarasca en el bosque y vimos una mujer. Muerta.*" He craned his neck in a funny direction, and I realized he was doing an imitation.

Paul said, "They found a woman's body. In the woods."

106

# 28

Paul stood up and said to the gardener, "*¿Dónde exactamente?*" Where was this, exactly?

"*Mero abajito de 'onde está la pared de piedra, ¿sí me entiende? Como que se cayó. Un accidente.*" Just below where that stone wall is, you know? Like maybe someone fell. An accident.

"Oh, my God," said Sukie. "It looks like someone fell. *¿Joven, vieja? ¿Le viste la cara?*" Young? Old? Did you see her face?

"*Jovencita,*" the man replied. A young woman.

I had a bad feeling. I stood up and walked over to the gardener. "*Muéstrame.*" Show me.

Conrad said, "Now, hold on a minute here, Santiago. You stay right there." He took out his phone and looked at it for a moment. He swiped and dabbed.

"Fritz," he said into the phone, "I need you." He wandered off, still talking, through another swinging door that probably led to the main dining room.

"I mean, who's not here?" said Paul. "Where's Natalya? I know Layla's in bed, I saw her."

I said, "*Llévame a donde encontraste el cuerpo, por favor.*" Show me where you found the body.

The gardener shrugged, shook his head. As if he didn't understand or couldn't disobey the boss.

The kitchen door from the outside opened, and everyone turned, and then Natalya entered. She was wearing a hunting jacket from Burberry or some such and a scarf around her head like a babushka. A babushka who liked to go fox hunting. As she took off the scarf, she said, "They found a body."

At that point my mind was racing. I had a sickening feeling that I now knew why Maggie never came by my room. I wanted to race out right that second and make sure it wasn't her. I'd last seen her at the side of the house at nearly four in the morning. She was going around to the back of the house, to her room.

"Shouldn't we call the police?" said Sukie.

"Yes," I said. I was still standing there with the reluctant gardener. I didn't want to go back to the table. I wanted nothing more at that point than to see the dead woman and make sure it wasn't Maggie.

"Someone should call the police," said Natalya.

Conrad returned to the kitchen then and declared, "Okay, Fritz is calling the cops. He's on his way over. Everybody just stay calm. *Gracias, Santiago. La policía viene en camino.*"

"*Vamos,*" I said to the gardener quietly. "*Muéstrame antes de que llegue la policía.*" Show me now before the police get here.

There was something about the way I spoke to him that made him respect me. Maybe it was the time in the military. He looked at Conrad, then back at me, and when he heard no objections from his boss, he looked at me again and began walking to the door. No one stopped him. I followed him outside.

We were at the back of the house. This was the first time I'd seen the property in the daytime. It was amazing. A rolling lawn and then gardens—I could see tall hedges. In that direction was the chess garden Maggie had taken me to.

"*Es un buen tramo,*" he said. "*Sígame.*" It's a long walk. Follow me.

He walked slowly and carefully and said nothing. That was all right with me. My mind felt numb, dreading what he might be leading me to. I thought, hopefully, *This probably has nothing to do with Maggie.*

Anyone could get into the forest that Conrad Kimball owned. This was some poor unfortunate girl from the town of Katonah.

I hoped. Maggie was upstairs at the house, asleep in her room, I told myself.

I was wishing death upon someone I didn't know, which was strange.

We arrived at a series of beautifully manicured, hedged-in gardens. We passed a rose garden, another one that looked wilder, less tended, and then we came to an old, low stone wall on the ridge of a ravine. By that time I'd finally talked myself out of my darker theories about Maggie being the victim I was about to see.

Santiago looked at me, then waved me closer to the wall. It looked like it had been laid when the house was built. It was crumbling in places. It marked the end of the tended property. After this was acres of undisturbed forest.

He pointed at the top of the wall and mimed someone walking, until he remembered that I understood Spanish well enough. *"Aquí merito. A lo mejor andaba caminando por aquí, trepada a la pared, y a lo mejor 'taba borracha y se cayó."*

Maybe she was walking here, on the wall, and she was drunk, and she fell.

*"¿Dónde?"* I said. Where?

He pointed at the ravine. I stood at the edge of the wall and looked down to where he was pointing.

I saw a body, its head twisted in the wrong direction. I couldn't see the face, but I could see the jeans and the white sneakers.

109

# 29

*Seven years ago*

I was surprised when Major Margret Benson, a.k.a. Maggie, called me in to her shoebox-size office the next morning.

I'd been assigned to pore over records of orders processed through Harkins's office. That was the guy she'd had dinner with the night before as the blowsy Texan. She'd completely snowed him. But now, instead of making an immediate arrest, she wanted to do a complete assessment of the extent of his possible criminality. There was a lot more, she was convinced.

"Sergeant Heller, you've driven Humvees, right?"

"In Afghanistan and Iraq, yes, ma'am."

"I want you to go over these shipping records." She indicated a mountain of banker's boxes stacked four high. "Humvee parts. Check for anomalies."

"Such as?"

"I don't know, whatever you can find. I need someone who's familiar with the Humvee, inside and out."

I wouldn't have considered myself an expert on Humvees, or military vehicles in general, but I didn't object, because I couldn't. Also I'd begun to figure out that after four years in the Special Forces, I'd actually learned a lot. And maybe I wanted to impress Maggie Benson. That could have been part of it.

"Okay," I said.

She cocked her head, looked at me aslant, and smiled. "I just handed you the baton, sergeant. Your only job is to run like hell and bring it home."

It was tedious work, scanning thousands upon thousands of pages of paper records. After two days I'd made no breakthroughs. She left me alone, didn't check up on me. She expected a status update, and probably soon.

That night I stayed late. I was the only one in the office. The Pentagon never shuts down, but my section at the generic office building was quiet, all the other lights off.

At around ten o'clock something clicked in my head. I got up from the table of boxes and went over to my cubicle, signed into my email, and sent Major Benson a quick note telling her the good news.

Then I went back to my boxes of printouts and continued making notes on a legal pad. About half an hour later, Major Benson walked in. No more uniform. She was wearing a black leather jacket and jeans and a T-shirt, and she looked incredible. It was ten thirty at night, and she looked like she'd been out on the town. She smelled like patchouli and cigarette smoke even though I knew she wasn't a smoker. Like she'd been hanging out with smokers outside a bar.

"Tell me, Sergeant Heller."

"It's pretty clever, actually. The invoice prices they charge for the parts are all reasonably standard. A little high, maybe, but this is the Pentagon we're talking about."

"So where's the padding?"

"Check this out," I said, pulling out a file folder. "LED headlights for the Humvee, right? Around two hundred bucks a pop. You can get them for half that on eBay, but this is still within the realm of normal. But it's the *shipping* that's inflated, and hugely. A crate of ten headlights weigh almost a thousand pounds? I don't think so. More like ten pounds. They're padding the shipping. A lot. That's where they're making the money."

She inspected the pages I showed her. "All these shipments, from a company in Indiana, use the same less-than-truckload carrier Red-Line Ball Shipping."

She was taking notes on one of the yellow pads she always used. I could see REDLINE BALL SHIPPING underlined and circled. LED HEAD-LIGHTS underlined three times.

"Right," I went on. "RedLine Ball is in on it with Harkins, I'll guarantee that."

"Hot damn, Heller! You found it!" She dropped her yellow pad on her desk.

"It was just a lot of grunt work," I said, attempting modesty, which is not one of my strengths.

"You brought the baton home," she said.

She left the room and came back a minute later with a bottle of Jack Daniel's and two plastic cups. She splashed some into each cup and handed me one.

"Thank you, Major Benson."

"After hours I'm Maggie, Heller," she said.

"And I'm Nick. But I prefer Heller."

"So it'll be Heller, then. Heller, do you ever leave this place? You ever get dinner?"

Was she asking me out? "Once in a while, yeah."

"How about tomorrow night?"

# 30

Devastated, I followed Santiago along the low stone wall for a few hundred feet until the wall ended. Ahead, a path led steeply down to the gulley.

I was in a state of shock, or close to it. At the same time, I felt queasy. Maggie had been on her way into the house; how could she have been diverted back to the yard and the adjacent property? It didn't make sense.

"*Por aquí. Empujé la carretilla pa' acá pa' tirar la hojarasca del jardín. Y entonces me topé con . . . esto.*" He'd rolled his wheelbarrow down here to dump the leaves from the yard and then he saw the body down below.

Soon we were clambering over the low stone wall and down the steep hill. Santiago was like a mountain goat, steady on his feet, grabbing branches to steady himself. I followed his lead. It was steep enough that you could lose your footing and tumble headlong. But I held on to brush and vines and branches and rock faces. I stepped carefully, finally turned around to face the hillside. Then I climbed down using my hands and legs, like it was some climbing wall in a fancy gym.

I saw the body again and scrambled through the woods toward it.

Maggie Benson lay on the ground, her white T-shirt soiled, her legs and arms splayed oddly. Her copper wig was astray. I knelt beside her. From this angle I could see her face. Her eyes were open, staring. It looked like her neck was broken.

There was no question she was dead; I didn't need to feel her pulse.

No envelope, no file on the ground near her, but I didn't expect there would be.

*"No lo toque,"* the gardener warned me as he approached. *"No toque al muerto."* Don't touch the body.

He waggled his index finger. He knew something about American police work.

# 31

As we scrabbled up the steep hillside, I could see red and blue lights flashing faintly in the sky. Emergency vehicles, the police, had arrived. Their lights bounced against the clouds on the other side of the mansion.

The blood was hot in my veins. My heart was racing, and not from the exertion of climbing. I was in another place. I prickled with anger. Someone had killed Maggie for some reason. She wasn't drunk, and she hadn't just fallen. I couldn't get the image of Maggie's broken neck and staring eyes out of my mind.

Anger can be a great motivator, and I was angry as I'd never been before. But anger can also cause you to act irrationally. I reminded myself that the best chance of getting to the truth was to maintain my cover. Which meant putting my anger in a deep freeze with a thick layer of pond ice over it.

In battle there was no time to grieve for your fallen comrades; you had to remain focused and tactical. So it was here. I couldn't let anyone know that I knew the victim, that we had a connection, that she wasn't who everybody else thought she was, except Cameron and Megan. And neither was I.

When we reached the stone wall, Santiago excused himself and returned to his work. I told him the police would want to talk with him, and he said he already expected that.

As I approached the house, the kitchen door was flung open and Kimball's security director, Fritz Heston, came out. "Excuse me, sir," Heston said to me. He was wearing a blue Patagonia fleece over a collared white shirt. "Mr. Brown. Did you see the body?"

I told him I did.

"Was it one of our guests?"

"Yes," I said. "Cameron's date, I've forgotten her name."

"Oh, dear God. What happened, can you tell?"

"Her neck is broken," I said. "It could have been any number of things."

"The woman was pretty intoxicated last night, last I saw her. She must have gone out into the woods for some reason. And fallen. That's probably what happened."

"Could be," I said with a grunt.

"How far into the woods was it?"

"In the ravine right below the stone wall."

A man in a suit was approaching from around the side of the house. "I'm looking for Mr. Heston," the man said. He was middle-aged and overweight and balding and had a short gray beard.

"Yeah, that's me," Heston said.

"Mr. Heston, I'm Detective-Sergeant Goldman from the Town of Bedford homicide squad. I understand you're the gentleman to talk to."

"That's right."

"Did you see the victim?"

Heston pointed at me. "He just did."

"Sir," Detective Goldman said, looking at me, "did you get close enough to the body to see any signs of life?"

"I did, and the woman is dead." It was sickening just to say the words. I fairly successfully feigned an expression of nonchalance, but my heart was revving.

"Who found her?"

"One of the gardeners. He's working near the pool." I'd seen Santiago wrapping burlap bags over the scraggly sticks of a hydrangea bush, protecting it from the coming winter.

Detective Goldman took out a small pad of paper and made a note.

Heston said to the policeman, "The woman was a guest of one of Dr. Kimball's sons, and I think you should know that she was seriously intoxicated last night."

"She was?" said the detective, looking to me for confirmation.

I said nothing.

"That's right," Heston went on. "I mean, it's tragic, certainly, but I think it's clear what happened. She must have taken a tumble while intoxicated. A terrible thing. But not a homicide. Let's be clear on that."

"Well, sir, we'll have to investigate and make sure," Detective Goldman said to Heston. "Standard procedure. Tell me something. This was a birthday party for Dr. Kimball, and several of his dinner guests spent the night here, is that right?"

"Right," Heston said.

"How many?"

"Well." He counted on his fingers. "Dr. Kimball and his fiancée, four of his children, and their three guests. Including Miss Andersen."

"Andersen, with an *e*?"

"Right. Hildy Andersen. She was a guest of Cameron's."

He took another note. "We're going to need to talk to all of your guests and all family members and any employees in the residence."

Heston shook his head. "I'm afraid that's not possible. The guests are all about to leave."

"Not anymore, they're not," Goldman said.

"Dr. Kimball's houseguests are not prisoners. How about you collect names and phone numbers and you can follow up with each person if you need to? If you have any questions. But let his guests go now. Because this is so obviously a tragic accident. That's all."

Detective Goldman was not going to be big-footed by some corporate security director. "I'll tell you what, Mr. Heston. I'm going to order up a small bus to transport everyone in the house to the police station, where we can interview everybody separately, one at a time."

"What? There's no need for that! Fine. You can talk to everyone here. There are plenty of rooms."

Detective Goldman smiled graciously. I liked this guy right away. He was clever. "Would that be all right with Dr. Kimball?"

"Let me ask, but I'm sure that would be fine."

"Thank you. Your guests can leave as soon as we've talked to them." Goldman asked us to all go into the house. On my way in, I passed a team of EMTs carrying a stretcher.

Sukie, standing outside vaping something, grabbed me as I passed. "Is it—was it—Cameron's date?"

I nodded.

"Is she . . . ?"

I kept nodding.

"What was she doing in the woods? What happened?"

"I don't know," I said.

She looked around before saying, "Did you get it?" She didn't seem to be concerned that a woman had been killed.

"I didn't succeed in getting the file," I said, keeping it ambiguous. I couldn't tell her about Maggie, who she really was and what she was up to.

"Shit."

"But there's a lot of interesting stuff there."

"What happened?"

"I don't think we should be talking about this now."

She fell silent, nodded. Took another puff on her electronic cigarette. "Nick, are the police going to find out your real name?"

"Probably."

"Oh, God. When it gets out, my family's going to go ballistic."

"I'll handle it. Don't worry about it."

I had a lot more on my mind than that.

118

# 32

When I got back to the kitchen, I saw Cameron huddling with his sister Megan at the metal-topped worktable. He'd finally awakened. He was wearing a purplish paisley dressing gown over a white T-shirt, and slippers. His hair was all messed up. She was wearing a blouse and skirt and black pumps and looked like she was on her way to work.

They both glanced up as I entered.

"Did you see the body?" Megan said, at the same time Cameron said, "Was it her? Was it—Hildy?" They kept talking at once. "Does it look like an accident?" said Cameron, his voice high-pitched. "Who is it?"

"I'm very sorry," I said. "It *is* Hildy." I wondered if either of them knew her real name. Probably. If not, they would soon.

"Oh, my God," Cameron said. "I didn't even know she'd gone outside. When did this happen?" They were sleeping in separate rooms, I remembered. At the same time, Megan said, "What happened to her?"

I answered Megan. "I can't tell, but it looks like she fell and broke her neck," I said. "*If* she fell. In any case, her neck is broken." I said it dispassionately, just the facts. "Maybe she was pushed."

In a low voice, through clenched teeth, Cameron muttered something to Megan. She gave him a fierce look, then glanced at me. She replied crisply, "You'll tell them the truth. That she's a friend of a friend and you don't know her well. Didn't know her well. That she—"

She stopped talking, seeing a couple of uniformed policemen approaching. "Are you Cameron Kimball?" one of them asked. "We'd like to talk to you. Can you follow me?"

The entry hall had been turned into a kind of informal ops center, with uniformed and nonuniformed cops gathered, conferring, radios squawking. Conrad was talking to Detective Goldman, who was clearly running the crime scene. I heard Conrad say, "You do your job, boys. What a terrible, terrible accident."

A young plainclothes detective came up to me and asked my name. Without hesitation, I told him "Nicholas Brown." He wrote that down on a small pad. He asked me to follow him.

"Excuse me," I said. "I'm going to need to talk to Detective Goldman."

He looked at me for a moment. "Do you know him?"

"No," I admitted. "But he'll want to talk to me."

He didn't know what to do. He looked away, looked back at me, said, "Wait here." Then he went up to the detective-sergeant. I couldn't hear what they were saying, but Goldman looked at me curiously. He said something definitive to the younger detective. A moment later the young detective was back.

"Come with me," he said.

I followed him out of the foyer, into the hall, and then into a room I'd never been in before. It was furnished like another sitting room, with a huge oriental carpet, a couple of couches, an arrangement of chairs and tables. It looked like another room no one ever went in. We had rooms like that in the house I grew up in.

"Mr. Brown, if you could just take a seat in here, please."

I sat on a hard, uncomfortable sofa. The detective left the room and closed the door, and I sat in silence for a good long time, a quarter of an hour or so.

Until there was a quick, loud knock on the door, and it immediately opened.

Detective Goldman entered the room and closed the door. "Mr. Brown, you wanted to talk to me, did I hear that right?"

"You did," I said.

"I'm all ears."

"First of all, my name is Nick Heller, not Nick Brown, and I'm a licensed private investigator in Boston." I pulled out my Massachusetts driver's license and my PI license.

Goldman took it from me and looked at it and said, "Aha. And what are you doing here, Mr. Heller?"

"I was hired by a family member, Susan Kimball. Also known as Sukie. She arranged for me to come to the dinner with her, as her date. Under light cover."

"To what end?"

Here I fudged some. "She wanted me to do due diligence on Kimball Pharma and find out if there was any truth to the worst allegations that were making the rounds."

He shook his head. "What are we talking about here?"

"You've heard of Kimball Pharma?"

"I'm not a Wall Street guy, Mr. Heller, but yeah, I heard of them. Dr. Kimball's company." He continued standing while I was sitting, a show of dominance.

"They make the opioid drug Oxydone."

"That I've heard of. Oh, I see. Huh." He shifted his weight from foot to foot. "They have a lot of enemies."

"They do."

"Huh."

"I'd appreciate it if you'd help me maintain my cover with the family."

He shrugged. "We'll see. First, I have a few questions. Were you in law enforcement, Mr. Heller?"

121

"The military," I said. "Why?"

"I just like to know who I'm dealing with. Did you know the deceased, Hildy Andersen?"

"Yes."

He looked at me. "You did?"

"Yes. But that's not her name."

He furrowed his brow at that.

I said, "That's the cover name she was using. Her real name is Margret Benson." I spelled it for him.

Now he sat down on a chair next to the couch where I was sitting and pulled out a small black notebook. "Why was *she* using an alias?"

"She was hired by another member of the family."

"Which one?"

"Megan, I believe."

"Miss Benson told you this?"

"Yes."

"Hired for what? Same reason? 'Due diligence,' whatever that means?"

"I don't know."

"Was Ms. Benson intoxicated at dinner?"

"No. She was acting that way, though."

"Why?"

I shrugged. "Part of her cover. But she wasn't drunk."

"You know this how?"

I paused. "We exchanged a few words after dinner."

"Did she tell you what she was here to do?"

I instinctively held back. "Just that she was working for Megan."

"Was she afraid for her life, Mr. Heller?"

"I don't know. But I know she was killed."

"You know this how?"

"Because she had no reason to go outside, especially beyond the gardens. And because Dr. Kimball is a very private man and Kimball Pharma is a very suspicious company. So she was careful."

"And I'm a very simple man, and not very bright, so maybe you can explain to me how Kimball Pharma being a 'suspicious company,' as you put it, has anything to do with homicide."

"Maybe she found something they didn't want found."

"'They'?"

I shrugged again. "Have you had a chance to talk to Mr. Heston?"

"Mr. Heston was the one who called this in. He was nineteen miles away."

"He may know something," I said. I didn't want to push too hard. "I would pay some attention to Fritz Heston."

He gave me a long, penetrating look. "Thank you, Mr. Heller," he said. I couldn't quite read his tone, but I had a feeling he knew more than he was letting on. "And where were you last night? In bed?"

# 33

I had to be careful how I answered that.

I was fairly certain my image was captured on the CCTVs in the front foyer, coming into the house. It was probably an always-on system, ever recording and recording over. Once they saw me coming into the house, I'd automatically become a suspect in Maggie's murder. But in the normal course of events, it would be a few days before he got access to the security system's recordings.

If I told him the truth, I'd be a suspect in her murder. That could tangle me up for quite some time. Plus, my DNA might be on her. We'd kissed.

So telling the truth seemed like a bad idea at that time. "I was here, sleeping in my bedroom in the east wing."

"You said you spoke with Ms., uh, Benson? When was this?"

"Right after dinner. After Megan and her kids left, the remaining couples were standing around in the foyer."

He nodded, like he'd just figured something out. "You and Ms. Benson couldn't let anybody know that you knew each other, isn't that right?"

"Right."

"So how were you able to talk openly with her?"

He had me there, of course. "In a low voice. At a moment when no one was paying us any attention."

"How do you know Ms. Benson?"

The wrong answer: *We were lovers once.*

"We both worked in the Pentagon at the same time."

"Not good enough," Goldman said. "There are, what, hundreds of thousands of people working in the Pentagon. A decent-size city. How'd you know her?"

I shrugged. "Friend of a friend. Army friends."

He seemed to accept this. He pulled out a tan box that I recognized as a police footwear impression system. "Are you wearing the shoes you wore last night?"

"Yes."

He had me stand on a piece of paper, which made an impression of the soles of each of my shoes.

"Can I have your cell phone number, Mr. Heller? Email, address, home phone number? In case I need to reach you?"

I gave him all my contact information. I had no doubt I'd be hearing from him again in a couple of days.

He said, "And when was the last time you'd seen Miss Benson?"


*Seven years ago*


Dinner with Maggie Benson was great. After one glass of wine, she loosened up a little, and the stern Major Benson relaxed into a funny, sexy woman. She had an amazing gift for accents. I asked her to do Marjorie Cairns, the defense contractor she'd pretended to be the other night. Her Texas accent was perfect. She'd done a lot of plays in high school and once wanted to be an actress, but that was before she'd enlisted. Now she hunted for corruption in the procurement process within the Pentagon. She said she was a happy warrior.

But there was something sad in her eyes. Her effervescent personality hid it most of the time, but I could see it was there.

After dinner she invited me back to her apartment. She poured us liqueur, Poire Williams, which I don't like but I didn't tell her so. Her apartment, in Crystal City, was small but neat. Her bookshelves were full of college books, including the collected Zora Neale Hurston. Her coffee table was covered with hardcover novels by Jodi Picoult, Lisa Gardner, Tess Gerritsen, all broken-backed and obviously read. I noticed a couple of wigs on wig holders, which I assumed she used for work. She had short reddish-brown hair, a pixie cut, not a standard military cut.

We sat together on the couch and talked about her search for Harkins and why she wanted to get the son of a bitch. Then there was a long pause, and to my surprise she leaned over and kissed me.

I kissed her back, tasted the liqueur.

And then suddenly she pulled back. She hugged herself, started breathing deeply. It looked like she was in the throes of a full-fledged panic attack.

I put my arms around her and said, "Are you okay?"

"I don't know, Heller."

"Hey, it's not a problem," I said. "We work together. I totally understand."

"No, actually, you don't," she replied. "There's something we should talk about."

# 34

I went to find Sukie and say goodbye. I found her sitting in the game room in the basement, with some of her siblings. The room was painted deep green and was crowded with toys—a pool table, a dartboard, a foosball table, an air hockey table. The air was hazy. Cameron was smoking a cigarette, and Sukie was vaping. She was still wearing a bathrobe over her nightgown. And a pair of suede sandals, which looked too dressy, until I realized she was wearing the shoes for the footwear impressions the cops wanted.

"Why the hell are the cops wasting our time with this?" Cameron was saying. He looked angry. No longer the fun-loving drunk. He was almost pouting. "It was so obviously an accident."

"They have to do their job," Megan said. "Rule out homicide."

"For God's sake, she was drunk as a skunk. She was a hazard. Couldn't handle her liquor." Did he not know she was faking it?

"Don't use that word, 'hazard,'" Megan said. "That makes us liable."

"Well, I was asleep," Sukie said through a haze of vapor.

"Me too," said Cameron. I remembered seeing him in the hallway at around four in the morning, dressed, coming in from somewhere. I knew he was lying.

I said, "I wonder if the security cameras were on."

Cameron's face quickly flushed. He winced.

"Oh no," Paul said. "Oh, shit, you didn't. A booty call at the Hole in the Wall? It even rhymes."

Sukie turned to me. "Cam has a relationship with Big Boobs Betty, the barmaid at our local Irish pub."

"She goes by Beth these days," said Cameron. "I guess she's my alibi, then."

Megan said, "What did you tell the police? Did you tell them you were asleep upstairs?"

"I forgot about the cameras," her brother said.

"You have to be honest with these people," said Megan.

"Go back and amend your statement," said Sukie. "Tell them the truth."

"The goddamned cameras," he said. "I totally forgot about them."

"You were embarrassed," Megan said. "You wanted to protect Beth. That's why you didn't give them a full account the first time. Like that. Which is about the size of it, right?"

"The point is," Paul said, "this woman was intoxicated and for some reason decided to walk the property, and she must have fallen to her death. It's as simple as that."

I made a let's-get-out-of-here gesture with my head, and Sukie followed me out of the room and into the hallway. I walked a distance down the hall, away from the game room, so we couldn't be overheard.

"It's handled," I said. "The detective is going to make some calls. If I check out, he'll keep it quiet."

"Sort of professional courtesy?"

"Something like that. But now I need to get out of here. Either we go for a drive or I'll get an Uber."

Sukie called for her car and announced to her siblings that she was going back to the city. She tracked down her father and said goodbye. Ten minutes later we were sitting in the back of the town car.

I didn't talk much in the car, because I'm a suspicious type myself and have been burned by limo drivers before who listen for pay. But when we got to the Westchester Airport, where she was dropping me

128

off, we both got out and stood outside the terminal in the cold air while her car waited in the lot.

"Look," I told her, "the reason I didn't get any files is that I let Maggie take them first."

"Maggie."

"The real name of the woman who was killed."

"And you know this how?"

"Because we were friends. We worked together in the Pentagon, and she later became a private investigator."

"She was a PI too?"

I nodded.

"Cameron brought her in? *Cameron?*"

"Well, Megan hired her."

"For what?"

"Megan wanted to see your father's latest will. To see how much he's leaving to Natalya. And find out who was left out." I told her briefly about our breaking into Conrad's study and my finding the safe room. And the safe. And the envelope of photos and documents Conrad Kimball wanted destroyed upon his death. But the Phoenicia study seemed to be missing.

When she'd heard enough, she said, "Oh, dear God, she was killed. The woman was murdered."

"I think so."

"By whom?"

"Somebody working for your father, I assume."

"Fritz?"

"He'd be at the top of my list of suspects."

"Oh, *God*. They could be coming after me! If they figure out that I'm trying to get this clinical trial— Jesus, Nick, I could be a target."

"You're a member of the family, let me remind you. You're safe. And no one knows what I was doing. They don't know I got into your father's study. As long as no one knows—"

"I want you to stop. The job is completed."

"I haven't gotten the documents."

"I don't care. You tried, you came close, we're done."

I looked at her. "Do you know why I took the job in the first place?" I said.

"Because I asked you."

"No," I said. "Because of a man named Sean Lenehan, whose funeral you attended. A man who saved my life."

She fell silent, looked down. Played with the rings on her fingers. "I understand," she finally said. "But I want you to stop. You're done."

I nodded, looked away. In fact, I wasn't going to stop now. Sean and Maggie both were killed, in different ways and for different reasons, because of the same drug.

No, I wasn't done.

# 35

*Seven years ago*

S omebody hurt you," I said to Maggie.

A long, long silence during which my mind revved.

"I was raped." She said it in an oddly affectless, far-away-sounding voice.

"My God."

"It's the kind of thing that can mess with your mind."

I put my arm around her. "Of course it is. Talk to me. How long ago did it happen?"

"Five months ago."

"Did you report it?"

"He—he's a four-star."

"Who?"

She shook her head.

"Why don't you want to tell me who it was?"

"Is it okay if we don't talk about this?"

"I don't know, is it really okay? Because, Maggie—maybe you should talk to someone."

She remained silent.

"What happened to the guy?" I said.

"Nothing."

Over the next half hour it came out. She hadn't filed any reports.

She finally told me the name of her attacker. General Garrett Moore. Of course I'd heard of him.

"He called me and asked me to come to a meeting in his hotel room. This was in Vienna."

"Don't tell me he was in a bathrobe."

She nodded. Attempted a smile. "Almost. Just a pair of gym shorts and an erection. I thought I was there for a business meeting. Silly me." She lowered her voice to a murmur. "He said he'd been thinking of me a lot. He—wouldn't stop. He physically restrained me—he wouldn't stop."

"Jesus."

She sobbed silently, convulsively. I held her. After a while I said, "Are you in his chain of command?"

She shook her head.

"Pretty . . . ballsy to go after an investigator like you."

"He didn't think it was rape."

"What?"

"He said he was just doing what I ultimately wanted. What he knew I wanted. Thing is, he's done this with other women. I've heard the rumors."

"You've told people?"

"You're the only one I've ever told. Promise me you won't do anything," she said.

"You haven't said anything to anyone? Why not?"

"Because—Heller, I like what I do, okay? I don't want to be the girl who brought down General Garrett Moore. That would turn into my entire identity. You know how many enlisted guys would take a goddamned *bullet* for General Moore?"

"But couldn't you file a restricted report?"

"And then you think it's prosecuted? It's ignored, and I'm ostracized. Do you know how powerful a general is? He can influence promotions, assignments, fitness reports, investigations, all sorts of things."

"I know."

"You file a charge against a general and you're teasing a snake."

"If he raped you—if it comes out—"

"It'll be my word against his. He'll deny it, of course. Oh, sure, if I insisted, we could move forward with a legal claim. And it would blow up my life here. I'd be radioactive. So, yeah, after the rape I made a decision. I didn't want to be that girl. I just wanted to put it behind me."

"Maggie," I said softly, "this is not behind you."

# 36

At the JetBlue counter at the Westchester Airport, I bought a ticket to Albany, New York. Then I called my father's lawyer and arranged to visit him in prison.

"He has a condition," the lawyer told me.

"You mean senile dementia? That again?"

At one time he was pretending to have some kind of unspecified senility and was asking for compassionate release. But he couldn't keep up the ruse. He got tired of acting demented.

"That's not what I mean," the lawyer said.

"What kind of condition?"

"He'll tell you. He may not talk to you unless you agree to his condition."

The lawyer wouldn't explain beyond that, and I didn't push it. I got on my flight, and by the afternoon I had arrived, in a rented car, at the grimy Victorian Gothic redbrick prison, the medium-security Altamont Correctional Facility.

It had once been a hospital for the criminally insane, the Altamont Lunatic Asylum, and it was still a forbidding place. I went through the security procedures, the metal detector and the ion scan and two metal cages, until I got to the visitors' room, which smelled, as always, of ammonia and sweat. Its floor was green linoleum, its walls beige, a large mural painted on the visitors' side.

Victor Heller, the Dark Prince of Wall Street, was serving thirty years. He had thirteen years left. I often wondered whether he would die in prison. It wouldn't bother me if he did.

Victor was waiting for me. He was the only one sitting at the long counter on the prisoners' side. I was the only visitor.

I rarely visited my father, but every time I saw him, he got smaller. He wore a dark green shirt and pants and had a great white beard, like some Old Testament prophet, and eyebrows like fat white caterpillars. His cheeks and forehead were peeling, shedding flakes of skin. His psoriasis had gotten bad. They say it's exacerbated by stress.

He gave me a rheumy stare and did not smile. I sat down on the molded plastic chair. "I think we have a little business to transact first," he said.

"Your condition."

He nodded. "Very simple and quite reasonable. For some reason my daughter-in-law will not permit her son to visit me in prison. I want to see him. He's my only grandchild."

My nephew, Gabe, lived in Cambridge, across the river from my office. He'd graduated from high school and had decided he wasn't going to college. Which mortified his parents, my brother, Roger, and his wife, Lauren. But Roger was in prison himself and therefore in no position to pass judgment. Gabe was working at a record store in Central Square, and living with a lot of roommates, with whom he didn't get along.

Lauren, who hated Victor, refused to let Gabe visit him. Theoretically, Gabe could do what he wanted, but he disliked going against his mother's wishes. So he had never been to Altamont, and that rankled Victor.

"I'm not his dad," I said. "He's not going to listen to me."

"He listens to you plenty. He idolizes you. He'll do what you tell him. And what I want you to tell him is that he needs to visit his grandfather in prison. That I want him to come as soon as possible. If we agree on that, Nicholas, I'm willing to spend time with you today."

I almost burst out laughing. The man was in prison, probably desperate for visitors, yet he'd be "willing to *spend time*" with me. How comically arrogant. But he had me over a barrel. I needed to talk to him.

I pursed my lips and said, "Agreed."

"You'll tell Gabe to visit me?"

"I can't order him to, but I'll suggest it. It's not going to be easy for him to get here. He's too young to rent a car in Massachusetts. I think you have to be twenty-five. Plus, he has a job."

"I'm sure you can figure out a way for him to get here. I want to see my only grandchild."

"Deal."

"I want his mobile phone number."

"Deal." I gave it to him. I was surprised when Victor took out a regular roller-ball pen from the pocket of his trousers and took a note. "They let you have stuff like that in prison?" I asked.

"Haven't you learned yet, Nicholas? You have to know the right people. Now, for you to come all the way here from Boston, you must want something pretty badly."

"You were a friend of Conrad Kimball, isn't that right?"

"The Oxydone king? I wouldn't call him a friend. Though at one point I took a private equity position in Kimball Pharma. So I got to know him and his company well. Well enough, anyway. Why?"

I told him what had happened. I was rarely this candid with him, but I needed him to know the details.

"Oh, it's delicious, is it not?" my father said.

"What is?"

"All the sensitive *artistes* protesting Conrad Kimball's 'tainted' money, as if there was any other kind. Where do you think the Medici fortune came from? In part, at least, from their poisoning their rivals."

136

"I think the point is that Kimball has become a billion-dollar company by profiting on human weakness."

"Oh, for God's sake," Victor said. "Human weakness is the greatest business opportunity there ever was. Always has been. People have a sweet tooth, and entrepreneurs make a fortune producing sugar and feeding the addiction. The Delano dynasty—as in Franklin *Delano* Roosevelt—was in the opium trade. Merck got huge off heroin. Mallinckrodt began in the cocaine business. Smart suppliers create their own demand. People say I was greedy? Wrong. I made money off *other* people's greed."

I shrugged. He was not an easy man to argue with.

"And let me tell you something about Kimball Pharma. If Conrad is smart, he's in the process of changing the company's mission dramatically. He won't be alive to see it, but in ten years, Kimball will be an entirely different company."

"Why do you say that?"

"*'If we want things to stay as they are, things will have to change.'* Since you're not particularly well read, that's a line from Lampedusa's *The Leopard.*"

"Wasn't on the reading list in college."

"Motorola used to make car radios. Now they make phones and computer chips. IBM used to make supercomputers. Now they're a service company. In order to survive, companies must evolve. Chesterton has a wonderful metaphor. If you leave a white fence post alone, it will soon be a black post. So if you want to keep it white, you always have to be painting it again. If you want the old white post, you have to have a new white post."

"I see."

"If I know Conrad, he's in the process of making some big changes."

"All right," I said. "The fact is, a woman was killed."

He looked at me for a long time. He had been making a point, and I had cut him off. Then he said, "Killed by whom?"

"Maybe a contractor working for Kimball Pharma's security department. Or the security director himself."

"Why?"

"Because of what she took. An envelope of documents. Some of which I need, but they're all gone now."

"You want this murder solved, I take it."

"You take it right."

"Which documents did she find?"

"His latest will, for one. Whereas I was looking for proof they buried a human subject trial."

"Who did the trial in question?"

"A company called Phoenicia Health Sciences."

"And you don't think *they* have a copy of their own work somewhere?"

"The trick would be getting inside."

"I'm sure you can figure that out. Being the *gumshoe* that you are." He said it with a twist of his mouth, a kind of sneer of contempt. Like I was a noir cliché. Everything about the direction of my career— dropping out of Yale to join the army Special Forces, working as a civilian in the Pentagon, then quitting to become a private spy—mystified him. To him, I was a man who had made one disastrous career move after another.

Then again, he was the one sitting in prison. Not me.

I nodded. "There's always a way."

"Find out what happened to it. Falsifying drug trials opens up a company to legal liability that can bring it to bankruptcy. You can bankrupt Kimball single-handedly by proving they falsified a drug trial. So go get that weapon. Once you have that weapon, you have the power. Do you remember *The Thirty-Six Stratagems*?"

"Vaguely." He was referring to a book he had read in prison and become fond of. It was an ancient Chinese work that discussed a series of schemes to be used in war and politics.

138

*"Loot a burning house,"* he said. "When a country is plagued by internal conflicts and crime and famine and disease—when the house is burning—this is the optimal time to attack. To loot. And Kimball Pharma is a company besieged from without. This is the time to attack from within."

"What am I looting?"

"Get the damned proof that Kimball lied about a drug trial. Get that, and you get motive."

I nodded. "But how?"

"No man is a hero to his own valet."

"Companies don't have valets."

"They have *vendors*. Your valet does the stuff you don't want to do. Vendors do the stuff a company doesn't want to do or can't manage. And it's harder to erase their memories."

"Contractors," I said.

"Outsiders. Exactly." He blinked steadily, lizard-like.

"All right," I said. "Lovely to see you as always."

"I expect to see Gabe within a week."

"I'll do my best," I said.

# 37

*Seven years ago*

After Maggie told me about her rape, I became laser-focused. I made it my business to learn everything I could about the man who raped her, General Garrett Moore. For a while I even staked him out.

There were seven four-star generals in the army, and apparently it's a pretty cushy gig. General Moore had a chef, a personal valet, and four enlisted guys tending his lawn. He lived like a pasha. But even for a four-star, he pushed the envelope. And it turned out, he had made a few enemies in his rise to the top.

After a while I found an estranged former military aide to the general who told me to look into the general's GTCC, his government travel charge card. I might find something interesting there. When I pushed for details, the aide revealed that General Moore used his travel card in strip clubs overseas. The more I dug, the more great stuff I found. Moore had gone to the Boom Boom Room in Rome and spent almost two thousand dollars. He'd gone to the Kit Kat Klub in Seoul, South Korea, and paid three thousand.

But he wasn't just paying for overpriced champagne and big tips. He was using his card to pay for massages with happy endings. Then he made the mistake of disputing the charges with Citibank— declaring, in writing, that the charges were fraudulent.

A couple of months after Maggie and I began seeing each other, I had had enough. It took a lot of self-restraint to keep from telling her, along the way, what I'd found out about General Moore.

I tried to make an appointment with the general's office to see him. I asked for five minutes of the general's tightly scheduled time. I said it was personal business. But because I wouldn't reveal my agenda in advance, he wouldn't see me.

So one Friday night I trailed him to his weekend cabin in Delaware. My intel told me that his wife didn't like the cabin and rarely went, and that was where he had the occasional assignation. When I got out of my vehicle, I called out to him.

"Who the hell are you?" he said.

I gave him my name, told him my former rank.

"I don't know what you think you're up to, but I suggest you get the hell out of here before I make a call."

"I will, sure. I just want five minutes of your time. In *r* .vate."

"You want to talk to me? We can talk right h⸱ .

"You'll want this to be in private. I can .ssure you of that."

Looking more aggrieved than curious, he went to his car, opened the door, and said to his driver, "Don't go anywhere."

Then he walked to the front door of his cabin and unlocked it. The cabin smelled strongly of burnt wood. He switched on a light and folded his arms. "Now, what the hell do you want, sergeant?"

I told him what I'd found. "I don't think your wife knows about the Boom Boom Room," I pointed out.

"You trying to blackmail me? You really think you'll get away with that?"

"Depends on how we handle this. Just know that your bogus statement to Citibank violates Article 107 of the Uniform Code of Military Justice. Oh, and my favorite, Article 133. Conduct unbecoming an officer and a gentleman."

His face turned red, and he spoke slowly, baring his teeth like

141

fangs. "You're not doing this through channels, sergeant. You want to go after me, go after me. But go through the chain of command."

"Really? Because I was thinking I might not submit any report at all."

"How much do you want?"

"Not a cent," I said. "Just your resignation."

"Oh, really? This gets buried. You'll see. You've got a lot to learn about how the world works, Sergeant . . . Sergeant, what's your name again?"

"Heller," I said. "Nicholas Heller."

"Sergeant, you're making the mistake of your life. I've got friends."

"Today, as a four-star general in good standing, sure. But as the subject of a disciplinary probe? Suddenly your calls aren't returned. The conversation switches from what a good guy you are to who gets what you've got. Your car, your driver, your epaulets? They're not yours. You're just renting them. And there's a hundred people who think they can put them to better use than you can."

I enjoyed seeing him deflate like a blow-up doll in a nail factory. I returned home and made some calls. I knew people too. Some of the newer compliance officers in the Pentagon, some of them younger and female. They weren't going to bury this, I knew. Times had changed.

# 38

I caught an evening flight out of the Albany International Airport and was back in Boston by midnight. I dozed on the short flight, but I remained on edge.

What would happen when Detective Goldman viewed the CCTV video? He'd see me creeping in and out of the Kimball place and know that I'd been lying to him. I had to be ready for that.

I was up early the next day, out of my loft and over to my office by seven. I had a lot to puzzle on, and this may be the part of my work I like best.

I had a tough problem to solve. How the hell was I going to get inside Phoenicia Health Sciences? I knew nothing about the company, so I did a bit of basic research. Pharmaceutical companies contract out to what are called CROs, contract research organizations, which do testing and human trials and commercial research for the drug companies. Phoenicia was one of these CROs. It turned out to be headquartered in Waltham, Massachusetts, not far from Boston.

I called an old friend of mine—we'd been McKinsey interns together, before I joined the military—who was now a senior VP at Novartis, another big pharmaceutical company. I remember Kim Trepanier had set her sights on pharma from the outset. She was going to run a Merck or a Novartis or an AstraZeneca someday. I always believed it. She was also an excellent poker player. She was a triathlete, a slender woman with short blond hair in a Dorothy Hamill cut.

We'd gone out a few times but never really clicked. We were friends anyway.

"I have a strange question for you," I said.

"*Okay.*"

"How easy is it to bury a clinical trial?"

"What do you mean, 'bury it'?"

"You've got a new drug and you test it and you get back some bad results. Like it's super-addictive and hard to quit. But you don't want the FDA to know about it. What do you do?"

"You're supposed to register all clinical trials with the US government in an online database. You're obliged to report the results, and the government goes after you if you don't."

"And does what?"

"Your drug doesn't get approved. Plus you get a big fine."

"What if you did the study abroad?"

"Western Europe has the same requirements. But you do a trial in Asia or Africa or Eastern Europe, you can do whatever you want."

"Really?"

"Oh, yeah. So there was this French company developing a drug, an antidepressant, and it turns out that if you inject it into your veins, it gives you a buzz, right? But if you don't dissolve it properly, it starts to eat away at your flesh. Of course they never reported that. I've seen videos from Russia of people with their fingers necrosed, eaten away at the tips. I've seen people with the flesh on their arms eaten away, exposing the bone. Just horrible. And all because of a buried study."

"Where'd they do the study?"

"Eastern Europe. Estonia."

"They deep-sixed it?"

"Right. You can do that in Estonia."

"But who? Who can bury it?"

"The CRO. You know what that is?"

144

"Yeah. Contract research organization." *Outsiders,* my father had said. *Vendors. It's harder to erase their memories.*

"Exactly. All it takes is someone complicit in the company. Money talks."

"Is that the sort of thing Conrad Kimball might do?"

She laughed but didn't answer.

"What's your take on the old man?"

"Smart guy and a great marketer."

"Dishonest?"

She hesitated. "I'd say the word is ruthless. Relentless. Apparently he still runs the company at eighty. I think I know what you're talking about."

"Oh, yeah?"

"Oxydone. Was there a study done on Oxydone that Kimball had buried? There've long been rumors."

"I've heard the rumors too."

"Is this a case you're working on?"

"An interest of mine," I said. "Sort of a side hustle." I'd already said way too much. "I gotta run."

I sent Gabe a text but didn't hear back; he was probably asleep. The record store opened at eleven; he might not start work till noon.

Dorothy, meanwhile, was building my alias, the fake background of the fake McKinsey consultant named Nicholas Brown.

I'd started at the Kimball house under a notional cover, which wasn't expected to withstand heavy scrutiny. But now Dorothy was working on creating a deeper, more durable cover.

A cover, in the intelligence business, is the collection of lies and false companies and such you've created to make a fictional entity—in my case, "Nick Brown"—checkable. We call it backstopping. I got in touch with the new head of the Boston office of McKinsey, who turned out to be a friend of a friend, and I asked him to backstop me

145

if and when a call came. We set up a phone line. Turned out there were already several Nick Browns working for the firm. Now you called and someone answered and said I was traveling.

In the old days, the CIA hired forgers to create ID cards and driver's licenses and birth certificates and school records. And fake passports, fake plane tickets, all that stuff.

But it's not so easy these days. Not in the age of Facebook and Google and LinkedIn. Now you've got to be able to survive a Google search. Anyone checking up on you, if they can't find your digital vapor trail, they know you're a fraud. You have to create a credit history. Dorothy set up my LinkedIn account so it looked like it had been up for seven years. It couldn't look like it just went up yesterday. She even put up a convincing Facebook page that looked like it had been around for five years or so. There were tricks to the trade, and Dorothy knew a lot of them.

Usually those tricks are enough, but not always.

# 39

"ho was it you want me to write a letter to?" I asked Dorothy. "Some guy on a co-op board, right?" She was wearing an earth-toned silk blouse and a brown skirt and looked unusually professional once again.

She gave me the name and an email address. I jotted it down on my little black pocket notebook. She wanted a letter—an email would do—affirming that she would be employed by Heller Associates for the foreseeable future.

I didn't plan to write such a letter, though, but she didn't need to know that. I had other plans.

A couple of emails had come in from the City of Boston with attachments.

They concerned John Warren, the chairman of the co-op board at the Kenway Tower in Boston. The man who was giving Dorothy a hard time and who had "concerns" about her income and credit history. I knew if I bore down I'd find some dirt. You almost always do.

Was the guy a racist? Was he trying to keep her out because she was black? Possibly. Maybe even probably, but sometimes it's hard to prove bias.

Well, I wasn't trying to make a case. I just wanted to help Dorothy.

And I'd figured out a way. I'd gotten a copy of the assessed value of the guy's apartment, and like I suspected it would be, the figure was ridiculously low, way below the value of a high-floor apartment in a tower in the city of Boston. I punched out the phone number for Mr. Warren, and while it rang, I quickly rehearsed what I was going to do. *I'm no real estate guy,* I'd say, *but I can see the assessed value of your co-op is less than half what it should be. If a concerned citizen, say, were to make a phone call to the city tax authorities, your property taxes will double. And I'd hate for that to happen.*

Yeah, I could do that. I could probably make the guy fold instantly. He'd let Dorothy buy in, once his finances were challenged. No matter what color her skin was, his self-interest would prevail.

I could do that. But then I was thinking of Maggie and something that happened with her years ago.

I hung up.

Instead, I put the printouts in a file folder and walked them over to Dorothy's cubicle. I dropped the thick folder on her desk.

"Do with it what you want," I said.

"What's this?"

"Check out John Warren's property taxes. How low they are."

"That asshole John Warren from the co-op board?"

"The very one. I almost set up a meeting with him. But it's your fight. Not mine."

"Thank you," she said.


I decided it was a good time to pay a visit to Phoenicia Health Sciences, just as the morning rush hour was beginning. Do a little surveillance while people were arriving at work. I threw on a suit jacket and headed out the door.

I retrieved the Defender from the garage where I parked it to protect it from the Boston snow and salt. I took the Mass. Turnpike out to I-95 into Waltham. The tree-lined road—the leaves were russet and gold—gave way to a sleek, futuristic seven-story chrome-and-glass building surrounded by cedar trees, with a couple of connected parking lots on the back side, nicely set in the landscape.

This gleaming structure was the world headquarters of Phoenicia Health Sciences. I guess there was a lot of money to be made from testing drugs. I drove around the lots. There was reserved parking for certain executives. Part of a lot was reserved for clinical study patients. The rest were unmarked.

I didn't want to enter the building yet. I was beginning to formulate a plan, which meant I'd have to come back, and I didn't want to be recognized on a return visit. On the way home I placed a couple of calls. One was to my old friend George Devlin, who'd been on my Special Forces A-team, a communications sergeant. Devlin now made his living as a TSCM guy, which stands for technical surveillance countermeasures. Helping companies protect against being spied on. He called himself a hacker, a label he was proud of.

I told him what I wanted to do and arranged for him to come by my office later in the week. That didn't mean he'd actually come into my office. He lived in an immense RV, a combo home and office, and rarely emerged from it. He was terribly mutilated, from an IED. I would meet with him inside his vehicle.

When I got back to my office, Dorothy rose from her desk and said, "I've been doing some more digging into Kimball Pharma, and I found something interesting. I found a scientist who was fired from Kimball a couple of years ago after complaining about Oxydone. About the company's role in pushing millions of prescriptions. Kind of a whistle-blower. But after he got fired, he stopped talking. Maybe he'll talk to you. You might want to give him a call."

"You think? Hell, yeah. Great. Now, I'm going to need blueprints of the Phoenicia headquarters building in Waltham. You know, the architect's plans."

"Why not just call the city of Waltham's building department, see if they have building plans?"

149

"Because it's a small town and people talk, and I don't want someone there calling over to the CEO's office at Phoenicia and saying, hey, someone was asking for the plans for your headquarters."

"I doubt that would happen."

"Maybe not. But I don't want to take the chance," I said. "I think I have a better idea." I explained it to her. "But first, do you think you can find the whistle-blower's phone number?"

Dorothy rarely disappointed. In one of her many databases she quickly found a home phone number for the man, whose name was Dr. William Sossong. She also emailed me a couple of articles about him. Pieces from the *Washington Post* and the *New York Times* and *The Guardian* that called him the "Kimball Pharma whistle-blower." They were all from around five years ago. He had been Kimball's principal scientist and lived in Port Chester, New York.

I pulled up a piece about him from the *New York Times*.

## ORIGINS OF AN EPIDEMIC: KIMBALL PHARMA KNEW ITS OPIOIDS WERE WIDELY ABUSED

**Former Lead Scientist Claims Company Ignored Reports.**

Kimball Pharmaceuticals, the company that helped plant the seeds of the opioid epidemic through its aggressive marketing of its Oxydone inhalers, has always claimed to be unaware of abuse of the powerful opioid painkiller until years after it went on the market.

But the former top medical officer at Kimball claims that the company has known of "widespread" abuse of Oxydone for years. "These officers knew that people were snorting Oxydone and getting addicted, but they continued to tell doctors that it was less addictive than OxyCon-

150

tin," said Dr. William Sossong, who was recently fired by the company. "Yet they claim they were unaware it was being abused. And they concealed it. I mean, we got reports about how people were stealing it from pharmacies, and some doctors were selling prescriptions."

Over 200,000 people have died from opioid overdoses, much of it attributable to Kimball Pharma's widely prescribed Oxydone inhaler. A spokesman for Kimball Pharma, however, said—

There had been dozens of articles quoting Dr. Sossong, calling him a whistle-blower.

And then five years ago he stopped doing interviews.

Normally I much prefer talking to people in person, and not on the phone. But I didn't have time to get to him.

I dialed his number. A woman answered the phone and then put it down and called his name. A minute later, a man got on the line. "This is Bill Sossong," he said. "Who's this?"

I gave him the name Ben Ellison and told him I was writing a book about Kimball Pharma. He cut me off right away. "I can't talk to you. I signed an NDA."

As I figured.

"I can assure you right now I will protect your name and not quote a word of what you say."

"What kind of book are you writing about Kimball?"

"It's about the opioid epidemic and Kimball Pharma," I said, plunging right into it, figuring the direct approach would work best with him. Most whistle-blowers risk their jobs and their livelihoods out of a sense of moral outrage. Dr. Sossong seemed to be one of those people. A guy who did the right thing and got fired for it.

"Yeah, well, I can't discuss it."

"No one at Kimball is willing to talk," I said.

"I wish I could help you."

"Let me tell you what I'm mostly interested in. There are reports that Kimball Pharma knew how powerfully addictive its blockbuster drug was, but hid the evidence."

He exhaled loudly into the phone. "I've said all I'm gonna say on that subject. They got all kinds of reports on how people were abusing Oxydone. They knew."

"I see."

The man who couldn't talk went on. "I mean, these sons of bitches knew that people were snorting Oxydone and getting addicted, but they continued telling doctors that it was less addictive than OxyContin. People were stealing it from pharmacies. Doctors were selling prescriptions. I told them about internet chat rooms I visited where drug users were talking about snorting it recreationally. But Conrad Kimball ignored it."

"I've heard there was a clinical trial that Kimball somehow buried."

"True. The FDA would never have approved Oxydone if they'd seen that study."

"And I'm trying to find it. Apparently the study was done by a CRO called Phoenicia Health Sciences."

"You'll never get that out of them. Conrad Kimball wanted it to disappear, and Phoenicia obliged."

"You think a bribe was involved?"

"Oh, for sure."

"Did you ever see that study?"

"No. I just remember hearing it was done in Eastern Europe somewhere."

"You think Phoenicia has a copy?"

"Absolutely."

"Where?"

"Damned if I know."

"What about people there who might have saved a copy? The CEO, do you think?"

"Maybe, maybe not. You know who's likely to have a copy is a guy named Dr. Arthur Scavolini. He's been there forever. But if he does, he's going to keep it under lock and key."

I asked him to spell the name. He said, "He's their CSO, their chief scientific officer."

"You think he got bribed?"

"Wouldn't surprise me. He's got the juice to make the study disappear. But you can't quote me on any of this. You hear me? I cannot be connected in any way."

I thanked him and quickly got off the phone. I had a lot to do that afternoon.

# 40

At a few minutes after one o'clock I pulled up to the used record store on Mass. Ave. in Central Square. The place was cluttered with signs advertising vinyl new and used, current records, reissues, CDs, VHS, eight-tracks. Everything retro except Victrolas. Albums in the display window by Black Sabbath and Pure Prairie League. Otis Redding was on the loudspeaker, sittin' on the dock of the bay.

I walked in, past milk crates full of one-dollar LPs, a wall of used cassette tapes. In the back of the shop, I found Gabe opening a box of LPs.

He spun when he saw me. "Hey, Uncle Nick, everything okay?"

"Can you take lunch?"

"Let me ask my boss." Gabe, who was seventeen, had gotten tall and scrawny, with a mop of black curly hair. For the last year he'd been living in the third floor of a three-decker on Putnam Avenue in a part of the city called Cambridgeport. He went off to talk to a chubby, bearded, and bespectacled guy about ten years older. Then he came back and said, "Half an hour long enough?"

"Let's do it." Together we walked out of the store.

The Chinese place next door where we liked to go was closed for renovations, so Gabe said, "You mind going to a vegan place?"

"No problem." I'd felt like having a hamburger, but I had a feeling I would end up having a tempeh burger. "How goes the writing?" Gabe was a terrifically talented graphic artist and novelist. He wanted to make a living writing graphic novels but realized it wasn't easy, so he worked uncomplainingly at the record store to support himself. College, he had decided, was not for him.

His mother wasn't supporting him. I think she wanted him to try to support himself, fail at it, and return home, realizing how hard the world was out there. And then, she probably figured, he'd beg to go to college.

"I'm almost done with a book," he said.

"When do I get to see it?"

"When I'm ready to send it to publishers. Not before."

I remembered his mother nagging him for spending too much time on his graphic novel work. Once he'd gotten into trouble at his private boys' school in DC for some graphic novel he'd written and illustrated that made fun of teachers and administrators. He was really good.

He was wearing a black-and-white ringer T-shirt for the Blinders, with red barbed wire around the name. "What happened to Slipknot?" Slipknot was a heavy metal band that Gabe used to love when he was in high school.

"Nothing happened to Slipknot. I'm just into these guys more."

"Are they heavy metal too?"

He scoffed. "They're British. Political punk rock. They're awesome."

"Okay."

We ended up at Veggie Annex, which featured acai bowls and carioca smoothies. Not my kind of place, but we barely had time to eat anyway, so I didn't. "Uncle Nick," Gabe said, scarfing down his acai bowl, "I need to make more money somehow. Rent in Cambridge is insane."

"Why don't you live with Nana?" His grandmother, my mother, had a condo in Newton.

"Nah. I'd just get in the way."

"You wouldn't. She loves you, you know that."

"I know. It's just . . . living with your grandmother, you know?"

I didn't pursue it any further. "You need money?" His mother would be furious if she knew I'd offered him a loan.

"Yeah, but not from you."

I respected that. "Could you take a second job?" I hoped he wasn't asking to work for me. He and Dorothy for some reason didn't get along. Having him around my office could be a problem.

"Yeah, I was thinking about how you're doing work for some big pharmaceutical company, and I decided I want to be a human guinea pig," he announced. I'd told him over the phone what case I was working, but with Gabe you never knew what penetrated.

"What does that mean?"

"Like, one of the guys in the shop was telling me that the Harvard Business School has lab-based studies in human behavior, and they pay you for it. Or there's research studies at Harvard Med that pay you thousands of dollars for spending a couple of weeks in a hospital taking some drug or some placebo or something. For, like, getting endoscopies or colonoscopies."

"You would voluntarily have a colonoscopy?"

"If I got paid enough, yeah, sure."

I shook my head. Then I told him about my conversation with my father, his grandfather, how Victor Heller wanted to see him.

"I'd kinda like to see him, but Mom won't let me."

"Do you want me to talk to your mother about it?"

He nodded. "She's already so weird about me not living at home in DC. Yeah, could you?"

"I will."

"Thanks. She listens to you."

"No problem."

"Where's the jail, like upstate New York somewhere?"

"Near Albany. About three hours and change from Boston. You can drive, right?"

156

"Yeah, but I don't have a car."

"You can borrow one of mine."

"Really?"

"Sure."

"The Defender?"

"You don't want to drive the Defender for six hours on the highway going sixty or seventy. It's gonna be awfully loud inside."

I walked Gabe back to the record store after half an hour, my head somewhere else. He'd given me an idea, and I needed to get back to the office right away to act on it.

# 41

Maggie Benson was killed by someone working for Kimball Pharma, I suspected, maybe because they thought she was threatening to uncover some kind of corporate wrongdoing. Maybe they knew she had broken into the file room in Conrad's home study. Probably they assumed she'd found something explosive. If it wasn't Fritz Heston himself who did it, it was someone else connected with the company who killed her, because of what she'd found.

They did it to protect Conrad Kimball. So I wanted to find whoever killed Maggie, and in the process, I vowed, I was going to take this company down by whatever means possible.

It was already personal. Now it bordered on obsession. Sukie had fired me, but I was unfiring myself.

Everything started with Phoenicia Health Sciences, the company that did the addiction study and then buried it. I had to get into Phoenicia somehow. And Gabe had given me an idea.

On the Phoenicia website was a link that read, *Volunteer for a study.* I clicked it, and it took me to a page with a very long list of human clinical trials that you could volunteer for. All for different drugs. They wanted people with high LDL cholesterol or Parkinson's disease. Or smokers. People with major depressive disorder. That sort of thing. But some asked just for healthy volunteers between the ages of eighteen and sixty-five.

What caught my eye was the compensation. They were offering

five and six thousand dollars, even over eight thousand dollars in some cases. The higher-paid ones were longer studies—you had to live in a corporate facility, basically, for several weeks or even months. There was probably some area within the company's headquarters where they had pastel colors on the wall and offices that had been turned into bedrooms where they could watch you on video. I couldn't imagine wanting to do that. But I guess the money was pretty good.

And you could feel good about doing it too. There was a lot of pretty language. "When you take part in paid clinical trials," it read in big type, "you are helping to advance the human journey to new discoveries that will vastly improve lives worldwide for decades to come."

Maybe some people did it for altruistic reasons. Most did it for money.

I thought about what Gabe had said about human guinea pigs. I did some Googling. These were people whose entire job was being a medical drug research subject. They did study after study; they lived in hospitals and office suites converted into sort-of bedrooms and had their blood pressure measured and their blood drawn and endured colonoscopies and bronchoscopies and all that sort of thing. It was a full-time job, and it paid okay.

I just wanted to find a study that required one or more overnight stays at Phoenicia headquarters and required healthy volunteers.

I found one that was studying "brain changes and people's responses to painful stimuli," where you got three MRIs. No thanks. I found one study for a drug that required two overnight stays. It didn't say what the drug was, but I filled out the online form and clicked Submit.


Meanwhile, Dorothy was doing a deep dive on Phoenicia. After considerable searching, she discovered that the company's CFO was on vacation, in Costa Rica. "At least, according to his Facebook page. Man, people are so indiscreet on social media."

"Excellent. What's their accounting firm?"

"They use Deloitte." That was one of the big four accounting companies. "Anything else?"

"Do you have the name of the CFO's admin?"

She nodded. "I'll send it to you right now."

She drifted out of my office, and a minute later a box popped up on my computer screen with a name and phone number. I called it.

When Jennifer Talalay, the CFO's admin, answered, I said, "Jen? This is Tom Rogin over at Deloitte, and we've got a problem I was hoping you could take care of."

"Problem?"

"Yeah, and I really don't want to bother Bob in Costa Rica."

"Sure, tell me what I can do." She was reassured by the fact that I knew her name and that I knew Bob Newell's vacation plans. She had no reason to wonder whether I really was an accountant.

"Here's the thing," I said. "The city assessor is saying that your square footage for personnel is three thousand square feet more than what we've stated. This puts us in a different tax bracket, which we don't want."

She chuckled. "No, sir."

"So we're pushing back, and to that end, I'm going to need a set of building plans or drawings ASAP for the audit."

"Drawings?"

"Bob said if anyone can find the plans, it's you."

She asked for an email address. I gave her the fake one, at DeloitteUS.com, that Dorothy had set up for me. It would auto-forward to me. I don't even think DeloitteUS.com was a real domain name, but five minutes later she had emailed me the building plans for Phoenicia's world headquarters.

Then my phone rang again.

"Mr. Heller? This is Catherine from Phoenicia Health Sciences. You're interested in participating in a clinical trial?"

"Yes, that's right." I settled back in my chair.

The woman's voice over the phone was businesslike but friendly. She had a great Boston accent. "This is a clinical trial that requires taking an investigational drug or a placebo."

"Okay."

"Mr. Heller, this study will involve a blood draw or an IV as well as an ultrasound and an overnight stay."

"I understand."

She then asked me a series of questions—race, ethnicity, height and weight, blood pressure, did I smoke, how many alcoholic drinks did I have per week . . . Did I know where Phoenicia was located. The study, she told me, started next Wednesday. That was too far off.

"There's nothing sooner?"

"That's when this study begins. Why, is that—"

"I know I probably should have gotten to this earlier, but my week off started yesterday, and I wanted to make some money as soon as I can. I was hoping to get into a study tonight."

"Tonight?"

"Not possible?"

She hummed to herself, loudly tapped at keys. "We actually have a cancellation in a study that begins in three days. I guess the volunteer took sick. This study requires a healthy donor. You're not a smoker, are you?"

"No."

"Does that work?"

"I think I can make it work," I said, smiling. I thanked her and hung up.

There was a knock at my office door, and Gabe entered. He was wearing his black leather jacket. I said, "Hey."

"Hey, Uncle Nick, can I borrow a car?"

"You already heard from your grandfather?"

He nodded. "I'm going to drive out there tomorrow morning. I got the day off from the record shop."

I thought a moment. "Not the Defender. I need it. Plus, like I said, you don't want it on the Mass. Turnpike. It's loud."

"That's okay."

"You can take my Toyota. But be careful."

"Cool. I will. Not a scratch."

I was only a little worried about my car, but I let it go, because my intercom was buzzing again.

"Nick, it's Patty Lenehan."

I picked right up. "Patty?"

Her voice was raspy. "Nick, I'm so sorry, but I really need you back here."

"Everything okay?"

"I can't—I just can't—it's Brendan. He's angry all the time, and he's taking it out on me. He's been breaking things, and he refuses to do anything I ask him to do. He says he hates me. I just can't get to him. He needs you. *I* need you."

I hung up and tossed Gabe, my other surrogate son, the keys to the Toyota.

# 42

*Seven years ago*

When news of General Garrett Moore's sudden and unexpected early retirement came out, Maggie's reaction stunned me. She was livid.

"You gave me your word, Heller!" she yelled. Her eyes were wild. "You promised me you wouldn't do anything about it."

For a moment I didn't know how to respond. "You think I could have this guy walking around with impunity after what he did to you? With power over other people? That was unacceptable."

"Oh, unacceptable? Nick, this was never about you and what you think is acceptable or not. No, you don't get to do that. This was my fight, and you wanted to make it yours—and you don't get to do that."

I stared in disbelief.

"What happens when people find out? They'll think you took revenge on him because I had eyes for him. For the general."

"Well, that's bullshit."

"How easy do you think it is for me to continue in my job after this? For you this is just one battle. For me—for any woman in my position—it's a war. It's something we deal with day in and day out."

"I'm sorry," I said.

"Men always know better," she said hotly, "right?"

That evening ended our relationship. My apologies did nothing. She was furious at me, and, though it took me a while to get it, I eventually came to understand. It wasn't my battle to fight. It was hers.

I've always taken on other people's battles, even when I shouldn't. It's a lesson I still haven't really learned.

# 43

Early the next morning I gassed up the Defender—the hundred miles or so from Boston to Westham would use more than half of the Defender's tank, and the fuel tank held fifteen gallons. I headed out through rush-hour traffic down the Southeast Expressway, that terrible, always-choked highway out of Boston. Patty Lenehan had sounded like she was at her wits' end but said she could wait until today.

My mobile phone rang, and I glanced at it. A 914 area code, which meant Westchester County. I knew it wasn't Sukie, because her cell started with 917. I didn't recognize this number.

"Is this Mr. Heller?" A gruff male voice.

"Speaking." I changed lanes and headed toward Route 3.

"This is Detective Goldman from the Town of Bedford Police."

"Oh, yes," I said.

"Remember I said I might have some additional questions regarding the death of Margret Benson? So a couple of things have come up, and I wonder, are you available to talk for a few minutes?"

I suppose I could have told him that I was driving and call him later, but I was far too curious about what he was calling for. Because I had a pretty good idea where this was going. He'd seen me on the surveillance video at Kimball's house. What else could it be?

"Sure," I said, my stomach tight.

"A couple of loose ends came up. When we talked at the Kimball residence, you told me that you spent the night sleeping in your bed-room in the east wing, does that sound right?" Cars were starting to pass me. The Defender engine roars loudly when you step on the gas, so I was instead easing up, trying to keep the noise level down. I moved to the right lane.

"That's right."

"Which parts of the house did you visit when you stayed there?"

"Let me see. Besides my bedroom on the second floor, I saw the rooms everyone else saw—the smaller dining room, the library, the kitchen. . . . Let's see, the room where you questioned me in the morning . . ."

"No other rooms in the house?"

"The game room in the basement."

"Any other rooms?"

"It's possible, but not that I can recall right now."

"I see."

He was silent for long enough that I thought the call might have gotten cut off.

"Hello?"

"Yes, Mr. Heller. Would there be any reason why we might find any information that said you were in a room that you say you weren't in?"

A carefully worded question. And an accusation. *We have informa-tion proving you were in parts of the house you're not telling us about. You're a liar.*

"Sure, it's possible. I forget what-all I saw. I was a guest of Sukie's and I went where she went."

He wasn't happy with that answer. "You said you slept through the night, is that right?"

"I don't think I said that."

"You said, 'I was here, sleeping in my bedroom in the east wing.'"

"I don't think I said I slept through the night. I never sleep through the night."

In fact, I usually do sleep through the night, most nights. I'm untroubled, usually, by insomnia. And to be indelicate, I usually don't have to get up to pee in the middle of the night like a lot of guys.

"So you didn't sleep through the night? The night you stayed at the Kimball house?"

"I got up a few times, as I recall. To use the bathroom."

The problem was, I couldn't be sure whether he'd actually seen the video—nor how much it showed him, if he had. I didn't know where cameras might have been concealed in the house. Where else besides the entry foyer? Was he even talking about the surveillance video?

"Was the bathroom next to your bedroom? Like, en suite?"

"Yes. But I might have taken a stroll around the house. I was curious."

The Heller house wasn't as big as Kimball Hall, but that's like comparing yachts. Big is big.

"A 'stroll around the house'? What time was that?"

"Not sure. I didn't look at my watch. Two, three in the morning, maybe?"

"Were you snooping?"

I paused. "You could call it that. Healthy curiosity. 'Snoop' is a matter of opinion, and of course I didn't have permission."

"What if we found information that you were creeping through the home as if stealthily looking for someone? What would you say to that?"

So he'd seen the video. "I'd say I wasn't stealthily looking for anyone. I simply went for a walk because I couldn't sleep."

A long pause. I thought, *Does he have me and Maggie on video?* Was there a time when the two of us walked together through the foyer?

I didn't think so.

"Mr. Heller, you travel a great deal. Do you have any plans to leave the country in the foreseeable future?"

"Is this where you tell me not to leave the country without letting you know?"

"No, I just want to make sure I can reach you in the next day or two. If I need to."

"You've got my number," I said. "Is that it?"

"That's it."

"Thanks," I said, and I hung up.

It suddenly occurred to me: He didn't ask whether I went *outside* the house. He didn't talk about the time Maggie and I spent in the backyard and the property beyond the yard.

Was it possible there were no video cameras at the back of the house?

He knew more than he was telling me, and that made lying to him a dangerous undertaking.

My phone rang again, and this time I recognized the caller.

"Dorothy," I said. "What've you got?"

"Just wanted to say thank you."

"Yeah?"

"I went through that file you left me? On the tax assessment? For the asshole?"

"Yeah? Talk to him yet? Let him know what you know?"

"You know what, Nick? John Warren is not only a tax cheat, but he's a racist. And maybe I don't want to live in a building where the head of the co-op board is a racist. Maybe I'm too good for these assholes."

I smiled as I ended the call.

I picked up the phone and called Major Liz Rodriguez of the Massachusetts State Police.

168

# 44

Patty was waiting for me, behind the screen door. She opened it as I approached and gave me a kiss. She'd just come back from a run, I could tell. She was still wearing her shorts and colorful running shoes and a wicking T-shirt, and she smelled of perspiration and something floral, maybe a shampoo or conditioner. Patty looked a lot better than she had just a few days earlier, though still visibly tired.

"Thank you so much for coming."

"Of course. Kids at school?"

She shook her head. "He's upstairs. He refuses to go to school. And I can't make him, Nick. Though I try. Maybe you can."

I nodded.

"I took him to a therapist and he wouldn't talk. Nick, he hates me. He actually says that. And he's saying stuff like, 'My dad was just a junkie, he wasn't a hero.'"

"Okay," I said. "Let me try to talk to him. How are Molly and Andrew doing?"

"They're in school. Andrew seems the most normal, like nothing happened, and I really worry about that. Molly is sad, sometimes oppositional, but she's coping. She's going to school, and her friends have been great. We've talked a lot. But Brendan—Brendan used to be the easy one."

"Okay. I'll go upstairs."

"I have to get to work," she said. "And, Nick? Thank you."

I found the kid lying on his bed playing with his phone. He barely looked up when I entered, which surprised me. "Hey, Uncle Nick," he said flatly. His eyes still had that bruised look.

His room was crowded with posters—for *Minecraft* and *Fortnite*, for Marvel superheroes, for the Boston Red Sox and the New England Patriots and the Boston Bruins. And old soccer and baseball trophies. He was an outgoing, popular kid, like his late father had been. A happy kid, most of the time. Or he used to be.

"Hey, Brendan, what're you up to?"

"Nothing."

"Your mom wants me to get you to go to school, but I have a better idea. Let's play hooky."

"Hooky?"

"Skip it. Skip school."

He looked at me now, as if to determine whether I was messing with him. He saw I wasn't.

"Okay," he said uncertainly.

"Come on, get out of your PJs and get dressed and come with me. I have an idea."

I left him to it and went back downstairs. Patty was in the shower.

Brendan came downstairs twenty minutes later. He was taking his time. He got into the Defender without saying anything. Instead of trying to cajole a conversation out of him, I followed his lead and said nothing. So we drove in silence. I turned off my phone so when it rang it didn't disturb us.

"Where're we going?" he finally said.

"The beach."

He just nodded. It wasn't beach season; it was the fall, and no one went swimming in the ocean without a wetsuit this time of year. But he knew which beach I was talking about. It was the secluded beach he and I always went to when I visited in the summer.

I drove down a long, narrow tree-lined road that ended in a gulley and a serious-looking NO PARKING sign and a dirt path through the woods. Since there was no parking, the only way to get to the beach was to walk nearly a quarter of a mile through the woods. As a result, this nameless ocean beach was almost always deserted.

I parked, expecting to get a ticket, considered it the price of convenience. We got out wordlessly and headed down the dirt path.

We walked in absolute silence through the dense, twilit woods. I could hear the cracking of twigs and the tweeting of birds and the chiggering of insects.

Finally the woods began to grow light and then bright and the trees became sparse and we came to a big sand dune, and there was the Atlantic Ocean spread out before us, blue-gray and glistening, lapping loudly on the shore. A sunny blue sky, a postcard.

We took off our shoes. I took a left, and he went with me. I walked beside him on the smooth wet sand. And I waited for him to say something.

And waited.

Finally, after another ten minutes of silence, I put up the white flag of surrender. "Remember the first time I brought you here?" I said. I kept walking.

He glanced at me but didn't answer, kept walking. About half a minute later I saw his face redden and he started to cry, silently.

"I hate him," he said. "I hate that he did this to us."

"Sometimes I hate him too," I said. "But he was my friend, and I loved him. And you know he saved my life." I'd told him the story too many times. "He made some really bad choices, and that hurt a lot of people I love, like you."

"So why did he do it?" he near-shouted.

"He had an illness, and sometimes that's stronger than love. It can take someone over. Addiction to Oxydone or any of those other opioid drugs is incredibly powerful. Too powerful for most human beings, even strong, great men like your dad."

He cried, still silently, and he stopped walking. Then he cried a little louder and put his hand over his red face. After another minute he put his hand down and said, "It's not fair. I can't do it all."

"Do what all?"

"Everybody says now I'm the man in the family. I gotta be the man in the family."

"No," I said. "No, you don't. You're a kid. Who's hurting because you've lost your dad. Look, you know I'm not going to take your father's place, but I'm a grown-up, and right now the grown-ups need to be in charge. And you get to be a kid."

Now his sobbing became convulsive. He sank to the sand, nearly collapsing, and I sat down and held him. I sort of rocked him, let him be a baby.

"You know I'm there for you, Bren," I said. "Whatever you need."

He just sobbed.

"You're going to get through this," I said. "I know it doesn't feel like you will. It feels like the hurt will never go away. But it will." I was quiet for a long time. "And let me tell you something else. Your dad was a hero."

# 45

When we returned to the Lenehans' house, Brendan went back upstairs and I checked my phone.

Seven calls, a couple of messages.

Dorothy had called; nothing urgent. Another call came from a different clinical supervisor at Phoenicia Health Sciences with instructions for the upcoming clinical trial.

Gabe had called four times, finally leaving a message: Was it okay if he kept the car a little longer so he could spend the night with a camp friend from Albany?

I made a quick call to his mom, and she was okay with that. I called him back and said it was fine.

The seventh call was from that same Westchester County phone number: Detective Goldman. He wanted me to call as soon as I could.

I did.

"Mr. Heller, I got a call from a Liz Rodriguez of the Massachusetts State Police, vouching for you."

"Good."

"Liz says you're a trained investigator."

"Right."

"And that you've been very helpful to law enforcement."

"Okay."

"Same class at St. John's, Liz and me."

"Ah."

173

"So if she trusts you, so do I."

"Thank you."

"So I wanted to tell you, the medical examiner has just determined that the victim, Ms. Benson, was a homicide."

"Cause of death?"

"She broke her neck in a fall from a height. There appears to have been a struggle, a scuffle."

"I see."

"So I'm hoping you can help me."

"Happy to. Let me ask you a question."

"Actually, I was thinking I'd ask the questions, Mr. Heller."

"Allow me one."

A pause. "Go."

"You've seen the security camera footage, right?"

"Yeah?"

"Were the cameras all off at the back of the house?"

A pause. "How'd you know?"

"Because of what you *don't* know. Maggie and I met in the back of the house in the middle of the night. To talk. And you didn't ask me about that. Which means you didn't see it. We would have been picked up by the exterior cameras."

"You're right. All the cameras on the back of the house were off. So why were you meeting outside in the middle of the night?"

"Because we wanted to talk. We hadn't seen each other in years, and I wanted to know what she was doing. She wanted to know what I was doing. This was the only way for us to talk further without everyone else in the house knowing that we knew each other. Why were the cameras off?"

"Excellent question. So Ms. Benson told you what she was doing?"

"She said she was interested in some documents that she suspected were in storage in the house there. Old-fashioned hard-copy documents."

"Did she ever find them?"

"Yes."

"Really? And where were they in storage? Did she tell you?"

I paused a long moment. "In the old man's study."

"You think that might have something to do with her being killed?"

"Yes," I said. "I do."

"Was she afraid for her life?"

I exhaled, long and hard. He'd asked that before. "No," I said. "Not when I talked with her."

"You're pretty sure of that?"

"Yes."

"And you still like Frederick Heston for this?"

"That's Fritz? Yes, I do."

"Here's the problem," Goldman said. "Everyone saw him leave after dinner, right? He lives twenty miles away, in Scarsdale. And only one vehicle pulled up to the front of the house in the middle of the night, a Camaro belonging to Cameron Kimball. Not Fritz Heston's. Meaning he didn't return to the house. Plus his wife confirms he was at home after midnight. And he says he has time-stamped security footage at his home backing all this up."

"Huh."

"Meanwhile, anyone who spent the night in the house could theoretically have done it. Gone out the back door and killed Margret Benson."

"So you have a houseful of suspects, is that it?"

"A regular Agatha Christie–type deal. But there's also the possibility that someone was lurking in the woods behind the house, maybe even for a couple of days."

"Maybe so. But why would Maggie have gone all the way back there in the dark? Makes no sense."

"To meet someone, I figure."

"Could have been one of the houseguests."

"Coulda. Did you happen to notice whether Ms. Benson had a phone with her?"

"She did."

"I figured. But that's missing. Our crime scene guys searched the woods in case it fell out of her pocket, but they found nothing. You know, it's also possible that she fell. As for now it's classified as a possible homicide."

"You have her blood alcohol level, I'm sure. From the autopsy."

"She wasn't drunk. Not even close."

"Like I said."


Patty Lenehan and I took her kids out to Montanaro's for pizza. My treat. Patty drove the family Jeep Cherokee, which was old and dented and smelled a little funky, like something electrical was burnt. The three kids sat in the back seat, surprisingly quiet. I expected them to all be fighting over something. Brendan looked somber, and you could see he'd been crying. I was glad we'd had that talk and wondered what he'd be like, whether his behavior would be any different. Mostly he seemed quieter than usual.

I ordered a white-clam pizza, which nobody wanted to share. Their loss. It was excellent. Patty ordered a mushroom pizza for her and her family, and some pasta with butter and cheese for six-year-old Andrew, who kept singing "The Wheels on the Bus Go Round and Round" over and over. Brendan said to him, "You're being annoying," and I had to agree.

When the pizzas arrived, he scowled. "I don't want mushroom," he said. "I hate mushroom."

"What are you talking about?" Patty said. "You love mushroom pizza."

"You don't know me at all," he spat back. "I hate it. Why do you have to get the one thing you know I hate?"

I was surprised to see Patty's face redden and tears well up. She covered her eyes with her left hand.

His sister, the eight-year-old, said, "Why do you have to spoil everything, Brendan?" She got out of her chair and went to her mom and hugged her. "It's okay, Mom," she said, glaring at Brendan.

Meanwhile, the wheels on the bus went round and round.

When the kids were in bed, or allegedly in bed, Patty and I shared some Buffalo Trace, the bourbon Sean preferred. We drank it out of chipped blue water glasses, sitting at the Formica-topped kitchen table.

"Thanks for dinner," she said.

"Sure."

"Sorry it was so awful. I don't know what to do about Brendan. He's angry at Sean for what he put us through. And who can blame him? You think I'm not angry at Sean, at what he did?"

"We all are."

"Not Molly. Not Andrew."

"They're just dealing with their father's death differently."

"But why the hell is he angry at *me*?"

"He's angry at you for not protecting him."

"That doesn't make any sense!"

"Of course not," I said. "But it's natural. He's overwhelmed. He's thinking he has to step into his father's role. People keep telling him he's now the man of the family. That it's his job to take care of his siblings and you. You gotta let him know he can be a kid."

"Yeah," she said, but it didn't sound like agreement, and I'm not a therapist. She finished her bourbon and splashed some more into her glass. She tipped the bottle at me, and I shook my head. I was still working on my first.

"Oh, Nick, I've been approached on this huge class-action lawsuit against Kimball Pharma and the Kimball family."

"What kind of lawsuit?"

"Supposed to be the biggest class-action lawsuit since tobacco, twenty years ago. The lawyer told me that Kimball knew how addictive Oxydone was."

"Are you going to do it?"

"I think so. I need to make money any way I can."

I was sorely tempted to tell her what I'd seen and what I was on the hunt for. What if I could deliver to her lawyers the very proof they were seeking? But I didn't want her talking, possibly endangering herself—how did I know? So I kept silent. She stood up and said it was late, and I stood up too.

Suddenly she was kissing me, urgently at first. Her mouth was hot on mine, and I could taste the bourbon. I kissed back. Patty was so sexy, and I'm human. I'd always found her attractive. She held my face with her hands. Her tongue, cold from the bourbon, probed my mouth.

Then I pulled away. Her eyes were large. "What?"

I whispered, because sound carried far in that small house. "Look, you know I'm attracted to you, Patty, that's obvious. Maybe a little too obvious."

"So what are you—?"

"You're a little drunk."

"I have the right to get drunk. I just buried my husband, for God's sake."

"Of course you do. But I think maybe this is too soon."

*It feels like a betrayal,* I thought, but didn't want to say it.

Patty was looking for comfort, that was all, and I had just denied it to her. It felt like the right thing to do, but that didn't mean it felt good.

# 46

Breakfast was a little awkward. Not on my part, but Patty seemed embarrassed around me. Brendan was much more communicative than he'd been the day before. I left before Patty and the kids had to head out the door—she to the hospital, they all to school—because I had to get to the office as soon as I could. We all hugged goodbye, and I kissed Patty on the cheek.

I texted Dorothy and asked her if we could meet first thing.

She was there before me. I'd run into some bad rush-hour traffic around Braintree. Dorothy handed me a mug of black coffee as I entered my office. She was wearing jeans and a black sleeveless top.

"Whoever killed Maggie Benson also took her phone," I said.

"And you want to locate that phone."

"That's an interesting idea. I'll call the detective who's on the homicide. But I had a different thought. I saw her taking pictures of Kimball's documents on her phone. Won't they be backed up to her iCloud account? Won't they be on some Apple server somewhere?"

She shrugged. "The detective can serve a warrant on Apple. Maybe he did already."

"I'll ask."

"And then they get in line. It's a long line—takes a couple days. Apple gets a lot of warrants. Unless it's a missing person's case, say. Those, Apple will give them within minutes. People think they have some right to privacy—wrong, they do not. Cloud storage falls under their terms of service, which basically says, 'We cooperate with law enforcement.'"

"So how can *I* get it?"

"Without knowing her Apple ID and password, you're stuck. You can't."

"Shit." I picked up one of my Blackwing pencils and drummed its eraser on the desktop, making a rhythmic tattoo.

"Plus, Nick, you don't know the pics ever got backed up to the cloud."

"We don't?"

"Only if her phone was set to automatically sync with iCloud. But there's different settings. I set mine to sync only when it's plugged in. I do that to save battery."

"So the pictures might not even have been backed up."

She nodded. She seemed to be about to say something. I said, "What?"

"What are you doing?"

"Doing?"

"This case. You said the client wants the investigation shut down."

"She does."

"So what, we're going to work for free? For a woman who's *loaded*? My God."

"This is about Maggie now," I said. I didn't explain.

My mobile phone rang. It was George Devlin.

His big white RV, bristling with antennas, was parked outside on the street. I knocked on the exterior to let him know I was there, then opened the door and got in.

Inside the light was dim, and it took my eyes a while to adjust.

George Devlin did not go out in public, not since he returned from the war. He lived in dim light because he didn't want to be seen. When he joined my Special Forces A-Team, he was a happy, upbeat, and very handsome guy. A chick magnet. Someone on the team dubbed him Romeo, and it stuck.

Until the day that an IED nearly killed him. He survived, but most of his face was gone. Now it was a welter of scar tissue. He had nostrils but no nose, a jagged slash of a mouth. Some might have called him a monster.

George was sitting on a stool in the darkness, in front of a slim counter that held electronic equipment, secured to the walls of the RV. He spoke in a raspy whisper, because his vocal cords were badly damaged. "Do you have any drawings?"

"Blueprints," I said, and handed him the sheaf of papers on which the drawings had been printed.

He moved his head close to the pages and looked them over in silence.

"You targeting the executive suite?"

"Right."

"Seventh floor. What's the company?"

"Phoenicia Health Sciences?"

"Sounds like a government cat's paw." He loathed the government and considered all law enforcement agencies to be the enemy.

"It's not. It's a CRO—a company that does tests for pharmaceutical companies."

"What does this have to do with Sean Lenehan?"

I explained quickly about Sukie Kimball and how she wanted proof that her family's company had buried the evidence that Oxydone was dangerously addictive. After a slight pause, I told him about Maggie's murder. He didn't know her, of course, but I wanted him to understand that for me, this was personal.

"Well, I want to tell you something," he said, and he swiveled on his stool to look at me directly through his one eye. Pulled out a small white inhaler and breathed in through it. "I am constantly in pain,

Heller." His mouth made a clicking sound. "And only Oxydone gets me through."

I nodded. Said nothing. It sounded like an advertisement. *Only Oxydone gets me through.* The man had to live his life not only terribly disfigured but in physical agony.

He went on. "Is Oxydone addictive? Of course it's addictive. I'm an addict. But I can't imagine life without it."

I didn't know what to say. He didn't mind being an addict. As long as he kept getting a prescription, and he was somehow able to function, who was I to say it was wrong? But that didn't diminish one bit my determination to find proof of the goddamned study. Because for everyone like Devlin there was someone else—maybe ten people— who were helpless under the drug's spell.

And because of what had happened to Maggie.

"I assume Phoenicia's employees use RFID cards like everyone else, right?"

"Right."

"Are you looking to clone one card or multiple?"

"Multiple. And choose whoever has the highest access level."

"Have you used this toy before?" He slid across the counter what looked like a laptop computer in its case. "It's called the Boscloner. It captures and clones RFID cards."

I shook my head. "What's the read range?"

"Three feet."

"Really? That's fantastic." He showed me how to use it, how to control it with my iPhone, how to clone a lot of ID cards and not just one.

"Once you get into the target's office, what do you want to do?"

"Steal the entire contents of his computer hard drive. Everything."

"If they have even rudimentary security, their network's gonna be password protected."

"For sure."

"You don't have the guy's password, I assume, right?"

"No."

"All right, so you need two separate payloads."

"If you say so."

"Here we go. This is what you need." He handed me a little black device with a USB plug at the end of it. Maybe a couple of inches long, half an inch thick. "This is called the Bash Bunny."

"Cute name."

"From the folks who brought you the Rubber Ducky and the Pineapple. Notice the switch on the side?"

I nodded.

"Up for payload one. Down for payload two. Then you plug it in to a USB port."

"Okay."

"Now, we're going to need to copy all the files to something, and we've got a choice. This guy or this guy?"

One device he held up was a five-inch oblong, three inches wide, fairly thick. The other looked like a black credit card. It said *Sandisk* on it.

I took the credit card. "That holds two terabytes of data," Devlin said, "as opposed to four terabytes on the other guy. But two terabytes will surely be enough."

"If you say so."

"I should warn you the one you're holding is a lot more expensive."

"I have a rich client." Who'd asked that the investigation be discontinued. But I had a feeling she'd eventually pay.

"What antivirus program does Phoenicia use, do you know?"

"How the hell would I know?"

"Huh," he said. He swiveled on his stool and hunched his shoulders. Tapped at a keyboard. A flat-screen came to life. He tapped some more. "All right, let's see. I'm on the Phoenicia Health Sciences website. Help wanted. Positions available. Here we go. Requires familiarity with Office, LANDesk, and McAfee ePO."

"Translation?"

He shook his head. "These corporations are so stupid. They tell you right there on their website what antivirus software they use. What kinda security is that? All right. Well, good for us."

Devlin spent a few more minutes programming the little black device, and then I left with my collection of toys.

I also thought it might be useful to do some basic social media research on Dr. Arthur Scavolini. I don't know of a better invention for eliminating privacy than social media. People post everything about themselves—pictures of their kids, their families, pictures of themselves doing adventure travel, pictures of themselves with more famous people. Where and when they did whatever. All kinds of personal stuff.

So I knew he'd gone to Rush Medical College in Chicago and trained in Chicago and at Duke. He seemed to have no hobbies. He had three kids and worked a lot of hours. Overall he seemed extremely nerdy, but that just made him a perfect fit for the job. He seemed to be well-off, seemed to have come into wealth a few years back. He and his wife, Linda, had gone on a high-end cruise in the Mediterranean a couple of years ago and had posted lots of photos of Morocco.

But the task still remained: I had to figure out how to get into his office. That was going to be the hard part.

# 47

At four thirty that afternoon, cars were streaming out of the Phoenicia Health Sciences parking lot. I was headed in the opposite direction. I found a space in the visitors' lot, grabbed my trusty metal clipboard and the Boscloner device, in its laptop bag.

I was wearing a suit and no tie—I'd noticed on my last visit that ties were rare at Phoenicia—and a pair of heavy black-framed glasses. The clipboard was key. It made you look official, like you belonged wherever you were.

I approached the silvery, modernistic building. I passed through a revolving door into a marble-walled lobby, saw the long marble reception desk, saw turnstiles, people hustling through them and exiting the building, leaving for the day. I looped around the lobby, at one point taking a picture of the big Phoenicia logo behind the reception desk (but actually capturing an image of the security guard in his gray uniform).

I stood by the revolving doors, examining my clipboard, generally standing in the way.

And letting the Boscloner do its thing. Stealing the creds, as the expression goes—the credentials. Every time anyone with a Phoenicia Health Sciences security badge passed within three feet of me, it was recording a long series of numbers associated with their badge. All the metadata. I'd turned off the notification sounds on my phone, so it was doing it silently.

I stood there as long as I dared, recording badge numbers and observing security. It seemed fairly tight. No one could just come in and enter the building. You had to either have an RFID card or be issued a temporary one, as a visitor. After about five minutes, it seemed long enough. If everything was working right, I had captured the data off several dozen badges. Any one of them would get me past the turnstiles and into the building itself. But beyond that, I had no idea what level of access they'd get me. How close to the executive suites.

With a final glance at my clipboard, I turned around and entered one of the revolving doors and left the building.

Then I walked around the building all the way to the back, where the loading dock was located.

Sure enough, there was an outdoor smoking area next to it. Smokers, in our censorious times, are often relegated to undesirable locations, like next to a loading dock.

A couple of smokers stood far apart from each other on a freshly paved asphalt square, near a parking area for trucks, on either side of the loading dock. The dock was still operating; the doors were open. I glanced at my watch. Twenty minutes before five o'clock. Still early in the evening rush hour.

The two smokers were a man and a woman, apparently unconnected to each other. They could have been executives, or lab techs, or administrative assistants. You couldn't tell from the way they were dressed. I took out a pack of Marlboros, shook one out. Put it in my mouth. Made a show of feeling my pockets, looking for a match or a lighter. Then I approached the woman, who looked to be in her forties. I took the cigarette out of my mouth and said, "Could I bum a light?"

She said, "I think I can do that," in a heavy smoker's rasp, pulled out a cheap Bic lighter, and handed it to me.

While my Boscloner captured the data off her ID badge, I looked at it, clipped to her purse over her left shoulder, and mentally recorded its appearance. Light blue with Phoenicia Health Sciences' logo and her last name in big letters on top—O'GRADY—and her first name on the bottom: DARLENE.

"Thanks," I said.

"No problem," she replied with a pleasant smile.

We stood, smoking for a while in companionable silence. If I needed any intel about the company, now would be the right time to strike up a casual conversation. But all I needed was her badge data.

A white van pulled up nearby, and a number of navy-blue-uniformed men and women got out. One of them opened the van's rear doors and began taking out mops and buckets and distributing them. The cleaners were here for their evening shift, just as people were vacating their offices.

I walked over to the van and, while my device was capturing their ID card data, I asked one of them, a small woman of indeterminate age, how to get to Route 95 South.

Depending on the company, and the security precautions it takes, cleaners of office buildings often have wide access. Their RFID badges could be particularly valuable.

"Pardon?" she said.

"Ninety-five south," I repeated, gesturing toward the exit.

She shrugged and kept wheeling her mop-and-bucket. She joined a line of blue-uniformed employees, all pushing carts or pulling buckets behind them.

I had what I needed now. I'd stolen enough creds.

I drifted away from the loading dock and headed back to my car.

# 48

That handy device that Devlin had lent me, the Boscloner, could generate its own blank keys, but because I wanted it to look as close to a real badge as possible, I preferred to use the ID card printer I'd bought for around a thousand bucks.

Dorothy figured out how to operate it, and back at the office she made me one that looked a lot like the real thing. A medium blue PVC card key with the Phoenicia logo on it. The name "GRANT James." Meanwhile, my receptionist, Jillian Alperin, was hunting down for me the simple gray uniform that Phoenicia's security staff wore. I had a small collection of uniforms, but not that.

At seven in the morning, I arrived at the silvery cube that was Phoenicia Health Sciences' headquarters in Waltham. Very few cars in the parking lot; several in the CLINIC and CLINICAL PATIENTS spaces. There was a separate entrance to the research clinic at the back of the building, by a row of manicured cedars, just for people taking part in medical studies here.

A very nice receptionist guided me to a waiting room, where a very nice nurse greeted me and handed me a bunch of forms to fill out. All the chairs and couches in the waiting room looked brand-new. There were just a few other people there, two small, dark-haired young women, who seemed to know each other, and a heavyset guy of around thirty with long, greasy blond hair.

I found myself filling out a consent form that indemnified the company in case of all types of possible calamities, including "mutilation or death." I didn't like the sound of that one. And there were all kinds of other forms that protected Phoenicia from being sued.

Within a couple of minutes the waiting room had filled up with twelve visitors. The head nurse led us all into the adjoining room and made us watch a short video that was basically propaganda about all the good we were doing for science and humanity. The guy with the greasy blond hair turned around and said, "I've seen this one, like, ten times already," and he chuckled. He sounded like a regular.

Another woman came out, a research coordinator. She was tall and broad and clearly comfortable being in charge. She explained to us how the study was going to work. Nothing very complicated. They were testing a new acid-suppression medicine. They'd give us a pill, give us three meals, and measure our stomach acid throughout the day and night.

She didn't explain how.

She gave a little wave to the guy with the greasy blond hair. "Hi, Winston," she said. "Welcome back." By now I was starting to get hungry. They required you eat nothing after midnight the night before. I could drink water; that was all. Don't take any antacids.

A few minutes later my name was called and I was shown to a curtained-off area full of medical machinery, like blood pressure monitors and such. A sprightly redheaded nurse named Denise measured my blood pressure and drew blood. She gave me a cup, asked me to fill it with urine. I went to the nearby bathroom and did it.

Meanwhile, I was looking around at the layout, the floor plan in my head. Looking for cameras. Making mental notes of where the exits were located and how visible they were.

Denise left and came back a few minutes later with a coil of thin plastic tubing sealed in a ziplock bag. She didn't explain what it was. "You haven't eaten anything since midnight, is that right?"

"Right. What's that?"

"The pH probe."

"I see. And where does it go?"

"Into your stomach."

"How?"

"Through your nose, down your esophagus, into your stomach."

"That tube goes down my nose?"

"That's right."

"Okay," I said.

I had endured far worse. But I hadn't counted on this little complication.

She unwrapped a long syringe, filled it with a topical anesthetic, and stuck the thing in my nose. She squeezed out some cold viscous liquid into my right nostril. Then she refilled her syringe and asked me to open my mouth and squeezed some more of the liquid onto the back of my throat. My nose went numb, and so did my throat. The stuff tasted nasty. She gave me a cup of water with a straw.

Then she wiped some kind of goop on the thin plastic tube and inserted it into my left nostril, which felt weird. She kept pushing it in, threading it down, and asked me to take a sip of water and swallow, to help move the tube down my throat. I almost gagged. My eyes watered.

"Sip and swallow," she said.

I took another sip. It slid down farther. I could feel it slithering down my throat and I almost gagged again. She taped the probe to my nose and then connected the probe to a small plastic computer-looking box, which she said was the data recorder.

I sneezed. Then I asked, "I have to carry this thing around?"

"This can just be clipped to your belt during the day."

"What about at night?"

"You can put it on your beside table," she said.

Then she gave me a large red pill and asked me to swallow it. She told me that this was the medication they were testing, that it was supposed to suppress stomach acid for twenty-four hours. I swallowed, and the tube pulled at my nose from the inside.

She showed me to my bedroom. It looked like a college dorm, with a bunk bed. My roommate was already there. The heavyset guy with the greasy blond hair. He was sitting on the bottom bunk. The tube was already in his nose and taped to his face.

"Hi, I'm Winston," he said.

"Nick."

We shook hands.

"Breakfast is coming," Denise said as she left.

So I didn't have my own room. That could be a problem. I didn't plan to stay in my room all night.

"You've done this kind of thing before?" I asked.

"Not with the nasal probe. But I do clinical studies all the time."

"Pay good?"

"Better than working at Dunkin' Donuts."

"I guess."

"I mean, I don't mind getting paid to piss in a bucket, you know what I mean? So I'm a human lab rat, man."

"Okay."

"Why are *you* doing this?"

"To advance medicine and help humanity."

"And the money."

I shrugged. "I won't turn it away." It paid a few hundred dollars.

"The overnight studies is where you make the real money," he said. "I did a bedrest study for NASA. I basically lay in bed for ninety days and got paid fifteen thousand bucks. I mean, fifteen thousand bucks to watch TV and play video games? I'm there."

I nodded. "That's three months of lying in bed?"

"Fifteen thousand bucks. What do you do, Nick?"

"I'm an actuary," I said. That's usually a conversation-killer. Most people don't know what that is and won't ask.

191

"Uh-huh. Anyway, I did one study where I got twenty-five hundred bucks for doing painkillers and drinking booze!"

"You're not worried about doing damage to yourself?"

"I did hear about one study where a guy died. Had a bad drug reaction. But that doesn't happen very often."

"Huh."

"I oughta move to Austin, man. That's where all the clinical trials are."

Then breakfast was brought in on two trays. Scrambled eggs, toast, fruit cup. Institutional and perfectly okay.

Then they left us alone for a while. Winston asked me if I wanted to play pool, and I demurred. He went in search of the inevitable video games, and I made calls and used their Wi-Fi.


The day passed slowly. I made a lot of phone calls and read old magazines.

At two in the morning, I got up—I hadn't been sleeping; I was lying there mentally going over my next moves. I used the ladder to get out of the top bunk, moving quietly. I didn't want to wake Winston, who was snoring pretty loudly.

The first thing I did was to tug the long tube out of my stomach, out of my esophagus, and out of my nose. It made me feel queasy again, but that feeling passed quickly. It was a relief to have the thing out. I left the probe and the data recorder on a wooden dresser. Then I changed into my security-company uniform, or at least as close to a uniform as Jillian was able to assemble. It was a pair of gray pants and a gray shirt. Unfortunately, the gray shirt was just a generic gray shirt from Target; it was missing the stitched-on logo of the security company. I took out my metal clipboard. My forged Phoenicia ID badge hung around my neck on a lanyard. It was a good forgery.

Winston kept snoring.

I slung a small nylon messenger bag over my shoulder. It contained a few small pieces of equipment. My bag of toys.

I opened the bedroom door slowly and quietly and looked to either side to see if anyone was out there.

No one.

I slipped out, closing the door gently behind me. All was quiet, just the rhythmic *pheep pheep pheep* from some machine.

The lights were on out here, but I didn't see anyone awake and working. Maybe there was a skeleton night staff. No one saw me. No CCTV camera globes in this part of the clinic. In a place like this, they'd be obvious, not concealed.

I found a door marked simply EXIT. I was fairly sure this was the right door, based on the floor plan I'd memorized. There were several. For reasons having to do with the fire code, it didn't require an ID. You just pushed the door open. Coming back in you'd need an ID badge. Which, of course, I had.

It opened onto the concrete apron of a large, dark loading dock. It was cold and smelled of gasoline. It was dimly lit by just the low-power emergency lights. I could just barely make out a row of large plastic trash bins, some of them marked with a biohazard symbol. This was where the clinic's rubbish was dumped and stored. I looked up and saw a video camera mounted high on the wall. Just where it should be on the loading dock. Presumably there was at least one more, on the other side.

I had to assume the camera was being monitored. Probably by a couple of guys sitting in a room somewhere in the building that had a lot of screens on the wall. But that was okay. I looked like a member of their security force.

There was no one in the loading dock. Not at 2:05 in the morning. Walking like I belonged, I made my way to the freight elevator that I knew was there, from the floor plans. Pressed the button, and it opened right away.

I got in. There was a camera in the elevator, which didn't surprise me. Management didn't trust the guys who worked the loading dock.

Right away I took out my phone and put it to my ear. "What's up?" I said to no one. Phone in my ear, clipboard in my hand, I looked like a busy supervisor.

I hit the button for the seventh floor, where the executive suite was located. Including the office of the chief scientific officer.

The elevator didn't move. I put my ID badge near the card reader, and the elevator started moving, up.

I'd studied the seventh-floor drawings particularly closely, so I had a pretty good idea where the executive offices were. But the drawings were original, done before the headquarters building was constructed, and the company could have done all kinds of renovation since then. I'd have to explore.

As the elevator rose, I continued talking into my phone, making inane conversation. "Yeah, Jack, I'll check it out. Sure, if you say so. So far so good."

There was a video cam mounted at the ceiling of the elevator. It probably didn't capture sound as well. But if anyone was watching the monitors, they'd see my mouth moving. They'd see me talking on the phone and looking like I knew what I was doing. I was going about my security business.

My fake Phoenicia badge was a clone of one of the maintenance workers' badges. So it would probably get me anywhere in the building. I'd chosen that one because it had the widest privileges of any of the ID badges I captured.

In a minute the elevator's doors opened on what I assumed was the seventh floor. It was a dark corridor. The floor was carpeted with squares of some cheap indoor-outdoor fabric. Straight ahead of me was a door, and next to the jamb was a wall-mounted RFID reader. It was highly unlikely there was a camera here, but I kept up the pretense of talking on my iPhone. I took a few steps and waved my ID badge next to the reader.

Nothing happened.

I touched the card to the reader, and again nothing happened.

I was stymied. I'd expected the cleaning guy's card to give me access to the entire seventh floor. But for some reason this one wasn't doing it.

Shit.

I knew the cloned card wasn't defective, since it had gotten me into the elevator and onto the seventh floor. But apparently there was another level of access. Maybe people who had offices on the seventh floor had a different series of numbers encoded in their ID badges. Higher access. Only for the company's top executives and their assistants.

But the cleaning crew also had to get onto the seventh floor, or it would never get cleaned. So at least someone on the crew had to have a badge that worked here. Unfortunately, I hadn't captured the right person's ID.

Behind me I heard the elevator machinery whirring to life as the elevator descended.

Someone had called it.

"Door's locked," I said into the phone, to no one. I inspected the wall-mounted ID card reader more closely.

The door was solid steel, a fire door. I wasn't going to be able to force it open. I was screwed. I thought for a moment. What the hell should I do now?

The elevator opened, and I spun around. A guy came out. He was dressed just like me. A security guard. He'd probably been watching the camera feed, seen me in the elevator, and wondered what I was doing here in the middle of the night.

What happened now was important. You always talk first. Initiate conversation. Take charge of the situation.

Still holding my phone to my left ear, I said to the guy, "Oh, man, I'm glad you're here."

"Can I help you, sir?" the guard said. He was tall, even taller than me, and had a pockmarked face and cauliflower ears. He looked like he used to box or prizefight.

I held up an index finger, telling him to wait a beat. "Hold on," I said into the phone, "you don't have to come all the way here. There's a gentleman right here who's gonna open the door for me."

I smiled at the guard. As if this was all some silly formality.

At this point, ninety percent of security guards would have relented and opened the door for me.

But not this guy.

"I'm sorry, what's this for?" he said, giving me a wary glance.

"Security audit," I said. "What's your name, please?"

"João Miguel," he said. "Jomi."

"Thanks, Jomi." I waited a moment for him to badge me in. But he was not a trusting soul.

"What's this security audit for, sir?"

I sighed with exasperation. "I'll call you back, Bill," I said into my phone. To Jomi I replied, "I've got the letter in my car, let me go get it. No, hold on. I have it right here." I took an iPad out of my messenger bag, tapped in my password to unlock it, and opened my email. The message I wanted came right up.

It was from the CEO of Phoenicia, authorizing a "security audit" to be conducted within the headquarters building from two A.M. to four A.M. *Please extend all cooperation* and so on. Dorothy had spoofed this email. It really looked like it came from the CEO himself.

And email is just as good as a letter to most people.

He squinted and leaned close to the iPad. Then he looked up. "Sorry, sir," he said. He waved his ID badge at the sensor and unlocked the door for me. He said he was sorry three times before he left.

I was now on the executive floor. I was inside.

# 49

The executive floor had mahogany paneling and thick carpeting. The halls were wide. Here and there were framed prints of sailing ships. I walked in near-darkness, waited for my eyes to acclimate, moved slowly and carefully. I figured out the arrangement as I walked. The leadership team—the chief executive officer, the chief financial officer, and the chief scientific officer—all had window offices on the south side of the building. They were all gathered in one spacious suite. The rest of the floor was the executive support team.

And when I reached the executive leadership suite, I realized it was separated from the rest of the floor by means of a large sliding glass door that was controlled, on the outside, by an RFID reader. I pulled out my card key and waved it at the gray square mounted on the wall.

And nothing happened.

So the cloned key card had gotten the elevator to move and did take me to the seventh floor. Once on the executive floor, though, it was functionally useless.

Did I dare call that guard—what was his name, Jomi? There was always the chance that he'd figured out there really was no security audit.

Best not to summon him if I could help it.

So I retraced my steps until I came to a supply closet I'd passed. Its door had been open, and I'd noticed reams of printing paper and shelves of office products. I flicked on the light and, in less than a minute, found what I was looking for: a can of compressed air. The sort of thing you use for dusting off keyboards and such. I flicked off the lights, returned to the hallway, and made my way back to the sliding glass door. This was a trick that my old friend Merlin had told me about. The security vulnerability here is that on the other side of the glass door is a passive infrared sensor. You didn't wave your key card. It sensed your approach, and it opened. They did that for fire safety reasons.

I turned the canister upside down and sprayed the air in the gap between the glass door and the doorjamb, pointing up at the motion detector.

The door slid right open, and I was in the executive suite.

More specifically, I was in an elegantly appointed waiting room with leather couches and chairs. At one end of the oval room were three assistants' desks. Each one was next to an office door.

The third door had a plaque on it that read:

### Dr. Arthur Scavolini
### Chief Scientific Officer

That door, I discovered at once, was locked. That surprised me. Given all the security measures, he sure didn't need to lock his door.

But he had. Dr. Scavolini took no chances. So I took out from a pocket in my messenger bag my Sparrows door bypass tool. It's called the Hall Pass. It's a funny-looking steel thing the size of a credit card, with a sort of beak at one end. I inserted it into the gap between the door and the jamb. Hooked the beak around the door latch. I had to lever the beak around the latch and pull it up before the door finally came open. It doesn't work on all locks, but it worked on this one.

The lights came right on. I quickly looked around, registering details. No CCTV cameras in here that I could see. I found the light switch and turned it off. My eyes adjusted quickly to the silvery moonlight. Pretty soon I could see just fine.

Arthur Scavolini's office was spacious and spare and modern and neat. One wall was all glass, floor to ceiling. Against the window was a table covered with silver-framed photographs, of Scavolini and his family. He and his wife and their three young kids. An eight-by-ten photograph of Scavolini with a familiar-looking black man with a large mustache. I'd seen him on TV a bunch but couldn't recall his name. He was a scientist and a celebrity. Next to him was a large telescope. Behind the two men was a black background with swirls of stars. It looked like the Milky Way. The photo was signed in blue ink, "to Art," then a big signature I couldn't read.

In front of the table was a large blond-wood desk, a simple slab of highly polished lumber topped with glass. The desk chair was a modernistic, ergonomic thing. The only items on the desk were a laptop and a couple of small placards with quotes on them.

I walked over to the desk and turned the laptop so I could see the ports at the back of the machine. I placed my messenger bag on the desk and took out the gizmo Devlin had given me. A four-port USB hub with two things already plugged into it: the black device called the Bash Bunny, and the credit-card-size computer drive that I was going to copy to.

I'm barely tech-savvy, but I knew enough to follow Devlin's instructions. Plug in the USB hub to a port at the back of the laptop. A blue light winked on. I looked at my watch, waited exactly thirteen seconds, and sure enough the blue light turned green. That meant it had done its thing, which was to crack the password on Dr. Arthur Scavolini's laptop. How it worked, I couldn't tell you. I just know that it worked on Windows workstations only.

I clicked the little switch down a notch, which put it in attack mode. The light went from green to red, which told me the thing was doing its next job: copying the contents of Dr. Scavolini's laptop to my little black credit-card-size hard drive.

Not everything, actually. But every file on the computer that ended in .pdf or .xls or .docx. Devlin told me he'd programmed it this way to cut down on the time it would take to steal the contents of the man's computer. I was looking for an old file on a clinical study. It might be a regular old word processing document, but it also might be a PDF file, or an Excel spreadsheet.

I've long ago come to the realization that I don't need to understand the technology to do the job, just as long as I can trust the people I hire. And I trusted Devlin and knew he was good at what he did.

Now I had to wait about ten minutes.

I sat in the ergonomic desk chair and looked at the two little wooden placards. Some executives place inspirational sayings on their desk. You know, like *Success is failure turned inside out* and *Don't worry about failure; you only have to be right once.*

Dr. Arthur Scavolini's placards—the words engraved in metal— were both science-related. One read, *The good thing about science is that it's true whether or not you believe in it.* The other read, *You are the result of 4.5 billion years of evolutionary success. Act like it.*

I waited impatiently for the Bash Bunny to complete its work. At any moment, I knew, the security guard might return. Or even the police, which would make my life far more complicated.

Ten minutes dragged on. I looked out of the window. Saw a few cars pass by on the highway in the distance. I checked his office for file drawers and didn't find any. He probably stored his files in cabinets outside his office.

I went out to his assistant's area and propped the door open. There were rows of cherrywood file drawers behind his administrative assistant's desk. I pulled at one. It was unlocked. I yanked it open. Glanced at them. These were personnel files. Nothing useful there.

I heard a *bing* and drew breath.

That was the sound of the elevator arriving on the seventh floor.

# 50

I froze.

Considered whether to go back into Dr. Scavolini's office, grab the Bash Bunny, yank it out of its USB strip in the middle of its data download, and close the office door. But I didn't know how much time I had. A few seconds? I didn't want to be caught inside the CSO's office. Actually, I could finesse that. I just didn't want to be caught with spy equipment in my hands, looking guilty.

But what if it wasn't the security guard from earlier? What if, instead, it was the Waltham police?

I had my answer about four seconds later, when the glass door slid open and a security guard hustled in. Not Jomi, a new one. He was holding a walkie-talkie in his left hand. This guard, unlike the last one, was armed. I could see the Glock in a holster on his left hip. He looked older, around fifty, and had a gray brush cut. Maybe he was a supervisor or a manager.

"Hey," he called out. "What're you doing here? Who are you?"

I'd left my iPad and my clipboard in Dr. Scavolini's office, but my badge was still hanging around my neck on a lanyard. I held it out to him. "Didn't Jomi fill you in?" I said.

"Who's your supervisor?" he asked.

I parried with my own question. "What's your name? I need it for my report."

But this guy would not be deterred. "I called the VP for operations, Mr. Thomas, and he never heard of no security audit."

That I hadn't counted on. Someone was doing their job. That rarely happened.

"Well done," I said. "I'll write you up with a commendation."

The guy hesitated, for just a moment. He wanted to believe me, but he'd made up his mind that I wasn't on the level. He'd come up to the seventh floor to kick me out.

Then he noticed that Scavolini's door was propped open.

"Hey, you're not supposed to be in there, I don't care who you are. Can I see your badge, please?"

I pointed to my ID key card on the lanyard around my neck.

"Your company badge."

I didn't have one. This guy was determined to break my balls. He was stubborn as a mule.

He pressed a button on his walkie-talkie and began to speak into it. "Omega six, this is Alpha twelve. I gotta run a check, do you copy?"

The guard was older than me and looked out of shape. He looked more like a back-office guy. But he did have a gun.

His radio crackled. "Roger, copy. Send traffic."

I took out my phone and swiped at it, touched the email app, and held it up for the guard to see. I approached, moving it closer to him.

He didn't even look at it. With his right hand he reached for his pistol. "Hold it right there," he said. "I'm shutting this down unless you have authorization."

Now he pointed the gun at me. One hand held the walkie-talkie, the other held the gun. He wasn't going to fire it. Not even close. But I couldn't take the chance of his flushing me out as a fake.

I shot out my left hand and grabbed his left sleeve, pulling him toward me suddenly, spinning him around clockwise. Now his body was between me and his gun. "Hey!" he shouted. His walkie-talkie fell to the carpet. I snaked my right hand behind him and grabbed his

202

wrist tightly. Then I yanked his right wrist up and back into a chicken wing. At the same time, with my left hand I shoved his head forward, cracking his forehead into the solid mahogany of the doorframe. Hard.

He sagged in my arms.

I took his gun and set him down on the carpet, facedown. He was out.

There were no security cameras in the executive suite, I'd noticed. For reasons of executive privacy, probably.

So his colleagues in the back office hadn't seen what I'd just done to the man.

I grabbed his walkie-talkie, pressed transmit, and said, "Disregard my last. The guy had the wrong building. He's leaving. Out."

Quickly, I went to Dr. Scavolini's desk. The light on the little device was still red, meaning it was in the middle of copying, but I couldn't wait here any longer. I unplugged it from Scavolini's laptop. Gathered the USB hub and the black credit-card-size drive, and put everything in my messenger bag.

Closing the door behind me, I raced for the elevator and punched the button.

The elevator doors opened on the freight entrance, the dark garage, lit dimly by low emergency lights. To my right was the entrance to the clinic. I glanced at my watch. No one would come into the clinic bedroom, I was sure, until six in the morning. Early, but not thumb-in-your-eye early. So no one would notice I was gone until then. Probably.

Then they'd find my discarded pH probe, slick with gel or whatever, and an empty bed. But by then I would be long gone. Maybe they'd conclude I had freaked out about that damn probe dangling down in my stomach and called it quits.

The best way out was through the loading dock exit, which was probably locked from the outside, not from the inside. Closed-circuit cameras in here, probably monitored by some security guy in another part of the building. Maybe they'd be watching, on alert. Maybe the guy who'd come to intercept me had informed the watchers in the monitoring station.

Or maybe not.

I walked through the gasoline-smelling loading dock, quickly but not too quickly, along the concrete apron to the right of the first vehicle bay, which was being used as a truck servicing area. The asphalt floor gleamed with motor oil. Past a pallet of wooden crates, five trash bins, a pile of cardboard boxes, past the closed door to the loading dock manager's office. A couple of dollies and a hand truck.

Down a short set of concrete steps. Past an electric forklift.

To the exit door, which opened easily, and I was outside in the cool air.

But I was not alone.

# 51

A couple of guys were running toward me. In the moonlight they were little more than jagged silhouettes. A third guy was walking behind them, taking his time.

"Whoa!" one of them called out to me, before I had a chance to say anything. He put his right hand out like a traffic cop. "Stop right there, buddy."

The first two stopped about ten feet away. As if they didn't want to come any closer. As if they were wary.

"Is there a problem, gentlemen?" I said.

"What are you doing?" the lead guy said. He was ruddy-faced, beefy. Next to him was the security guard who'd challenged me earlier. Jomi, his name was. With the pockmarked cheeks and the cauliflower ears.

"I advise you not to interfere with this audit," I said.

"The CEO doesn't know anything about a security audit," the lead guy said.

So someone had called the CEO. That was unexpected.

"Of course not," I said. "He's the suspect."

"What?"

"The audit was ordered by the board of directors in executive session," I said. "The CEO is not allowed to know about it. If you want to interfere with this, that's up to you, but I'm going to need all your names."

"Let me see your badge."

"Sure. It's in the car."

"Where's your car?"

I pointed toward the clinic parking area.

"You parked in the wrong lot," Jomi said.

"Oh dear," I said. "Gimme a ticket."

My mind was cranking away, trying to figure out some way out of the situation. The problem was, I didn't know what they knew or if anyone had seen anything on the security cameras.

"We'll go with you," Jomi said.

I shrugged. I started walking toward the Defender, and the three men fell in beside me. Two on my right, one on my left.

The left-hand guy said apologetically, "Sir, we've had a problem recently with volunteers in the clinic. Some of them enroll thinking they can steal meds. Last week one of them left the clinic and wandered around the building, breaking into pharmacy lockers."

The third guy, who hadn't spoken before, said, "We've had guys, they break into the dispensary, looking for amphetamines and opiates. These are lowlifes."

"I can see why you'd be suspicious," I said.

"You're not wearing a uniform, and you're not carrying your badge," Jomi complained. Not apologetic at all.

"You guys are doing a terrific job," I told him. "I'm going to report up the chain the high quality of your responses." I truly was impressed. They were ruthless.

The lead guy's radio crackled to life. "Broken arrow, broken arrow! We have an intruder. He just tried to take me down. Male, late thirties, six two, six four, dark hair. Gray pants, gray slacks. I stopped him at Dr. Scavolini's office."

Jomi had been looking at me the whole time, and now he stopped. We all stopped. He squared his shoulders. We were just about the same height.

"Let me see your wallet," he said.

"Sure," I said, and I feigned reaching for my right pocket, then jabbed my right elbow, hard, into his abdomen. Really sunk it in there. I must have connected with his solar plexus, because he gagged and staggered backward and collapsed to the ground. He was writhing in pain. Then one of them punched me in my kidney, and I saw stars.

With my left hand, I grabbed the nearest wrist of the guy to my right, then I bent my knees, which straightened out his left arm. Vising my right forearm behind his elbow, I pulled, hard. I had him in an arm bar, straining his elbow joint. At any point I could have broken his elbow. But I took pity on him. He was only doing his job. So I put on enough pressure to do some damage but let up before I heard the bone snap. He screamed. I used the levered arm to spin him counterclockwise into the guy who'd been on my left. They became momentarily entangled face-to-face. Almost intimate. I reached over with my left arm. Grabbed behind the neck of the guy who'd formerly been on my left side, pinning them together. At the same time I stomp-kicked the guy closest to me in the back of his right knee and then pulled. Both of them tumbled to the asphalt.

Behind me, Jomi was struggling to get up, and nearly succeeding, so I turned and drop-kicked him under his jaw, which put him out.

This wouldn't put an end to them, but it certainly slowed them down. I ran for the Defender and was out of that parking lot within a minute or two. Before any of them could recover quickly enough to find their camera phone and capture my license plate.

# 52

It was nearly six A.M. by the time I got home to my loft in the Leather District. I was bruised and battered and feeling some pain. Getting kicked around when you're twenty is one thing. But when you're older and a security guy lands a punch pretty well near your kidney, you do feel the pain. I took a few Advil, grabbed a power nap, showered and changed and felt a little better, and had just called Dorothy and asked her to meet me in the office when my mobile phone rang.

It was an admin from the clinic I'd just escaped from. She wanted to know what had happened. I told her I'd had a panic attack from having that probe down my stomach. I couldn't take it anymore, I'd had to leave. She told me that if I left the study at this point I was ineligible to receive any compensation. I told her that was fine with me.

Then the phone rang again, and this time it was Detective Goldman. He introduced himself, this time, as Detective Bill Goldman. Now he had a first name.

"I called you last night," he said.

"Sorry, I was occupied." I wasn't going to explain.

"You turn up anything yet?"

"Not me. What about Maggie's phone? Have you gotten her call record, at least?"

"Better than that: we have her geolocations."

It's amazing, and more than a little depressing, how much information law enforcement can find out about you. Not just the numbers you called but where you were when you did.

"Anything interesting?"

"Right before she went to Conrad Kimball's place, she was in the headquarters of a company in Waltham, Mass."

*Let me guess.* "Okay."

"A company called Phoenicia Life Sciences," he said. "Know anything about it?"

"Not enough."

"But why do you think she was there?"

So Maggie had been after more than Conrad's will after all. I smiled, shook my head. "Probably trying to get a copy of a clinical study that Kimball had buried."

"All right. One more thing. What's your read on Cameron?"

"The typical screw-up youngest son, is what I figured. He came with Maggie but left in the middle of the night, horny, on a booty call."

"Yeah, that didn't happen."

"I saw him arrive home at, like, four A.M."

"Big Boobs Betty didn't see him. No one at the Hole in the Wall saw him that night, and he's a frequent customer."


As I ended the call, I was thinking about Cameron Kimball and what he might have been doing in the middle of the night, that night. Whether he might have gone to meet, and murder, Maggie Benson. He'd been seriously drunk that evening. Did he even have the capacity to do it?

I had no idea.

I walked into my office, waved good morning to Dorothy. I wanted to sit in front of my computer for a couple of minutes.

209

Something tickled at the back of my mind about the quotes on Arthur Scavolini's desk. I'd taken pictures of them with my phone. The one about how science is true whether you believe in it or not. The other one about how you're the product of whatever billion years of evolution, act like it. I entered them into Google. The last one just pulled up a bunch of Pinterest quotes laid out nicely. The first quote turned out to be by Neil deGrasse Tyson, the astrophysicist who's the head of the Hayden Planetarium and is on TV a lot. To lots of science nerds, he's a rock star. A geek's Bruce Springsteen.

Then on my phone I pulled up the photo of Scavolini with the man with the black mustache and I knew right away that it was none other than Mr. Neil deGrasse Tyson himself. Clearly a peak moment in Dr. Scavolini's life, meeting such a celebrity.

I filed that away mentally, in case it meant anything.

Dorothy was impressed with the credit-card-size device, the solid-state drive onto which I'd copied—or at least hoped I'd copied—Dr. Scavolini's hard drive. I'd taken it out while the red light was still on and it had still been copying. Maybe that screwed something up; who knew, with computers.

She plugged it right in, looked at her monitor, and said, "Well, you got *something* here."

"Okay."

"Arthur Scavolini?"

"Right."

"Oh, there's a lot here. What am I looking for, Oxydone?"

"Or whatever its scientific name was before it was called that. And Conrad Kimball."

"Won't take long. I'll search and let you know." She didn't want me standing over her cubicle.

"Good. Let's hope there's a needle in the haystack."

210

"You know how you find a needle in a haystack?" she said.

"No, how?"

"Magnet. You got a magnet?"

"A rare-earth one. Neodymium."

"Well," she said, shaking her head, "maybe we'll get lucky. I'm impressed you got this—all on a physical penetration?"

"Right."

"Can I ask what you're going to do with whatever you find?"

"Me? Oh, I'm planning to bring Kimball Pharma down."

"Very funny, Nick." She smiled a sort of contorted smile and didn't look at my face. She would have seen that I wasn't laughing.


At first it seemed that we'd struck out. There was plenty of correspondence between Dr. Scavolini and top officers at Kimball Pharma, but none of it had to do with Oxydone. Other drugs, yes. In the meantime, I called the other scientist on my list, Dr. Sossong, the whistleblower.

His wife answered the phone, just like last time. I gave my name, again, as Ben Ellison, one of my cover names. I reminded her that I was writing a book. This time she put her hand over the phone, and I could hear muffled conversation. She came back on the phone and said, "I'm afraid Bill won't be able to speak with you."

"Tell him I have one last question, that's all. It's important."

Dorothy entered my office, and I put up an index finger to ask her to wait.

Dr. Sossong's wife put her hand over the phone again, and I could hear more muffled talk. Finally Dr. Sossong got on the line. Much less friendly than last time. "Listen, fella, I told you already, I can't talk to you. I *legally* can't talk. I shouldn't have talked to you the other day."

"This will be off the record," I said. "Your name won't be associated in any way with—"

211

"Don't call again," he said, and I heard a click. He'd hung up.

Dorothy said, "Are you interruptible?"

"Now I am." Before she could start, I said, "Could you do a social media search on Dr. William Sossong?"

She nodded, once. "Okay."

"That file I downloaded—I had to interrupt it before it was done copying. Is it okay?"

"It's okay. But I have a question for you. How could there be no documents that contain the word 'Oxydone' on his entire hard drive?"

"Maybe because the drive was only partially copied. Or maybe it's not under the trademark name."

She looked down. That morning she was wearing dark jeans and a lime-colored silk top and ridiculously high heels. Her usual look. "I have another possible answer to that question," she said.

"Yeah?"

"So I found this big PDF file among his documents, and I tried to open it. It said it was a corrupted file. Huge file, like a hundred gig. But I had a thought. What if it's an encrypted file?"

"Would they look the same?"

"At first, yes. And one of the documents I found on the doctor's hard drive was an instruction manual for VeraCrypt."

"Which is an encryption program?" I asked, because I wasn't sure.

"Right."

"Which is the program he used to encrypt the file," I guessed. "So can you decrypt it? Like brute-force it?"

"Nick, I used to work at the NSA, do you remember? Where I had access to basically the most powerful computers in the world? We couldn't crack it."

"So you can't?"

"Maybe the NSA can do it by now, who knows. But with the computing power I have, we're left with one option."

"Guess the password," I said.

"There you go."

"You try the usual suspects?"

"I got together a whole list. Date of birth, date of his wife's birth, his kids' birthdays, the names of his wife and his kids, the date of their wedding. I even tried Neil deGrasse Tyson."

"Nothing, huh?"

"Nothing."

"Do we know how long the password is? How many characters?"

"No idea. They recommend more than twenty characters."

"It could be any length?"

"That's right."

"That's discouraging. Why would he encrypt just one document?"

"It might turn out to be a folder. It could be a whole bunch of documents, all password-protected."

"Okay. So what are the odds of cracking this password?"

"The odds? Zero, Nick. The odds are zero."

"But you're not giving up."

"If you don't mind, I want to give it a go."

I smiled. She didn't give up easily. "Go for it."

# 53

Gabe's apartment was a dump. It was on the top floor of a shambling triple-decker on Putnam Ave. that had once been painted red. The paint had peeled so badly you could barely tell the color anymore. In front of the house the trash containers were tipped over. Half a bicycle was locked to a parking meter. What looked like a discarded baby stroller blocked the front door. His name wasn't on the bell, which read KOWALCZYK, the name of one of his roommates. It was around ten A.M., which meant Gabe was sleeping, but he wasn't answering his cell. So I rang the doorbell.

A few seconds later the front door buzzed open—no one asked who I was—and I took the splintering wooden stairs up two flights. The stairway stank of boiled cabbage.

The door to Gabe's apartment was marked with a cheap plastic gold-colored number three that had been nailed on with one nail. It rattled as I knocked.

The door came open, and some guy in his early twenties with a wild head of hair stuck his head out. The apartment behind him was dark. "Yeah?"

"Looking for Gabe."

"Hold on," he said, as unfriendly as possible, and he closed the door. I waited a beat. Gabe came to the door a minute or so later. Clearly he'd been asleep. "What's up, Uncle Nick?" He was blinking in the light. "What time is it?"

I could smell beer and cigarettes and a strong note of weed. His breath was bad.

"You done with the Camry?"

"Oh, yeah, hold on." He pushed the door closed.

"Am I not allowed to come in?" I said.

"It's gross, Uncle Nick," I heard him say behind the door. He came back a moment later with the car keys and dropped the ring in my outstretched palm. "Thanks again."

"Sorry to wake you up," I said. "Why did your grandfather want to talk to you?"

"Victor?" He put on an innocent look. "Because he's my grandpa."

"Did he want something from you?"

Gabe swallowed and looked away. He couldn't have looked guiltier. "No. He just wanted to see me."

"Victor wanted you to drive all the way from Boston because he wanted a visitor?"

"I'm not just a visitor. I'm his only grandchild. You know that."

"Gabe, what are you not telling me?"

"Nothing. He just said, you know, I'm his only grandchild, and you're never going to have kids, so I'm probably the only one he's ever gonna have."

"Yeah," I said, "okay. Listen. About Victor—just be careful of him. He'll ask you to do things; you've gotta be careful."

"He's behind bars, Uncle Nick. I mean, what can he do to me?"

I shook my head. "I just want you to be careful around Victor Heller."


It took me three and a half hours to drive to Port Chester, New York. I took the Mass. Turnpike to 84 and then 95. My mind kept returning to Maggie Benson's death. I realized I knew nothing about funeral plans for her or anything like that. I called Detective Goldman. "Did you find a next of kin for Maggie Benson?" I asked.

"She has a brother and a sister in Connecticut, along with her parents," Goldman said.

"I'm just wondering if a funeral's being planned."

"Sorry, don't know."

I asked if he had any updates on Maggie's murder, and he did not.

I thought about the houseful of suspects—the Agatha Christie aspect. I went through a mental list of Kimball siblings. Cameron? I remembered seeing him return to his room at four in the morning. The youngest Kimball kid seemed the most likely suspect in Maggie's murder, but for what motive? That stumped me. He also seemed so slight and physically unprepossessing, it was hard to imagine him shoving a strong woman like Maggie. Though I suppose anyone can shove anyone else off the edge of a cliff if it's done suddenly. Theoretically he could have pushed Maggie to her death. He just didn't fit the profile.

Paul, the eldest, didn't fit the profile either. He was a scholar, sort of a lost soul, and he seemed gentle. I wasn't sure whether he'd talked with Maggie that night. I didn't remember seeing them together. Hayden, the Broadway impresario—sure, she looked fit and maybe tough, but where was the motive? I couldn't think of one. Same with Megan.

I continued to suspect Fritz Heston and was frustrated by his alibi. There had to be a hole in it somewhere. But everyone had seen him leave, and the only way he could have gotten back to the house was by driving. So he would have shown up on the video cameras driving up to the house or entering it. But according to Detective Goldman, he hadn't. Whoever killed Maggie had to know how to work the video surveillance system, enough to switch off the rear-facing cameras in the house. Who else but Fritz Heston qualified?

Or one of his employees?

Simply put, Maggie had been killed by *someone* connected with Kimball Pharma. They'd done it for Conrad Kimball. In one way or another, Conrad Kimball now had killed two of the closest friends I'd had, Maggie and Sean. He'd just used different weapons.

And even if Sukie Kimball no longer required my services, I wasn't done with my work. I would take down the old man's company. If I managed to do that, I'd be making their deaths mean something.

# 54

The man I thought of as the whistle-blower, Dr. Bill Sossong, lived in the village of Port Chester, New York, which is part of the town of Rye and is right on the Connecticut border. Port Chester was about an hour from New York City on the Metro-North rail line, but more important, it was close to White Plains, where Kimball headquarters was located. Though it's right next to the wealthy town of Greenwich, Connecticut, Port Chester was not a particularly affluent place. Most people who lived there rented rather than owned. It looked like a working-class town that was struggling.

But Dr. Bill Sossong clearly was not. He lived in the Gray Rock neighborhood, in a big white colonial with black shutters, neatly trimmed hedges and bushes, and a beautiful green lawn that stretched all the way down to the water. Each house in the neighborhood had private waterfront access. I got there in the early afternoon and drove by the man's house a few times. We knew—Dorothy had filled me in—that he lived with his wife, had a couple of grown children, and that he was retired. His wife volunteered at a senior citizens' center four or five days a week. He'd been fired from Kimball Pharma, had given a number of outspoken interviews in which he criticized his former company, but then, after a few months, had fallen silent. Something had happened before he signed that NDA. I was curious.

I sat in my car, across the street and a few hundred feet down, pretending to read the *Wall Street Journal* but really keeping an eye on

Sossong's house. I wasn't going to just walk up to his front door and ring the bell and risk having him shut the door on me, which is what would likely result. After about an hour and a half, the front door opened, and a trim silver-haired man emerged with a Nike gym bag slung over one shoulder. He trotted out of the house to the driveway and got into a late-model Mercedes, throwing the bag into the back seat.

I started up the car and followed him.

I kept back a distance—there were no cars between us—until we got to the main road. There he made a left on a busy street, and several other cars zipped by before I was able to get there. But I maintained an eye on him. He turned right onto Boston Post Road, and I had no choice but to pull up right behind him. He drove a thousand . feet or so on the road and then turned into the parking lot of a strip mall that had a Marshall's and the Sports Club of Port Chester. He parked, and I parked in the next row. I watched him get out, grab his gym bag, and hustle into the sports club.

I was prepared to wait for him to emerge after his workout.

Then I had a better idea. I went into Marshall's, headed for the men's department, and quickly scooped up a cheap pair of sneakers, socks, a T-shirt, and gym shorts. With my purchases, I headed over to the sports club, which had a high-end look. A pretty young woman in a long-sleeved black SPORTS CLUB OF PORT CHESTER T-shirt greeted me.

"I'm not a member here, but I'd like to work out."

"Let me ask Ken, our member associate, to give you a tour."

"I'm not sure about joining just yet, so for now I'd like a day pass."

She sold me one for twenty-five bucks. Dr. Sossong had been there for twenty minutes. The locker room was empty. I changed, left my street clothes in a locker, and walked around the floor of the gym looking for Sossong. I found him on an elliptical trainer, already working up a sweat, watching TV. He was in the middle of a long row of empty machines, all a couple of feet away from one another.

I got on the machine next to him and started pumping away.

After a few minutes I turned to him and said, "This is the time of day to come in here, huh?"

He looked at me, smiled pleasantly. "Off hours, the place is deserted."

Then I said, "You knew Joan Chisholm." That was a name Dorothy had found. His former secretary/assistant.

Now he turned to me again, his eyebrows furrowed. "I did. Who are you?"

"What happened to her happened to a good friend of mine."

Sossong squinted at me, mopped away sweat from his face with the small white towel around his neck. "Do I know you?"

"No," I said. "But you helped me out with Phoenicia Health Sciences. You told me about Dr. Scavolini."

"Are you the writer?"

"Yeah," I said. "I'm the guy you talked to a couple of days ago."

He expelled a lungful of air. "I told you I can't talk to you."

"There's no one here to see us talk. Place is deserted."

He got down off the machine. "You're a persistent bastard, aren't you?" Shaking his head, he said, "I'm under an NDA. I legally can't talk to you."

I followed him down the aisle between rows of machines. "You already have," I pointed out. "Give me five minutes, and I'll leave you alone. You won't see me again. I promise."

He took a swig from his water bottle. "Five minutes. But don't come near me again. How did you find me here, anyway?"

"I heard you work out here," I said vaguely. "Your secretary, Joan Chisholm, got addicted to Oxydone. So did my friend Sean, a man who saved my life in wartime. For me this is personal."

We stood there, him sweating and me in my newly purchased cheap workout clothes from Marshall's.

"Mr. . . . What did you say your name was? Mr. Ellis?"

220

"Ellison." I'd used the name of a real journalist, in case he Googled me.

"Mr. Ellison, I don't know how I can help you. I've already told you more than I should have."

"It took real courage to become a whistle-blower," I said. "You did it because of Joan." I knew this from the dossier Dorothy had compiled, and he wasn't denying it.

"I'm not a whistle-blower."

"That's what all the news reports called you."

"Yeah, that's the fake news for you. Maybe I *should* have become a whistle-blower. Under the False Claims Act, you can make millions of dollars if the government successfully prosecutes. Some whistle-blowers have made a hundred million bucks. But I didn't do that."

"Why not?"

"Because I got fired before I had the chance. After Joan died, I just started doing interviews."

"And then stopped about a month later. You signed a nondisclosure agreement with Kimball Pharma."

"With the Kimball Family Trust, which owns Kimball Pharma."

"Why?"

"Why did I do it? Because I came to my senses."

"Because he offered you a lot of money to stop talking?"

"Something like that."

"Bought you a nice house in the Gray Rock area."

He looked at me in surprise. "How do you know that?"

"I do my homework."

"My income is dependent on keeping my trap shut. And my family's financial security is important to me."

"How would they know if you talked to journalists or not?"

"Conrad's security people are aggressive."

"Fritz."

"You know Fritz Heston?"

221

"We've met."

"Conrad runs Kimball Pharma like his own personal fiefdom. Fritz and his security officers are like his personal bodyguards."

"Did they ever threaten your life?"

"Obliquely."

"Would they—?"

"Harm me? If I started talking again? Sure."

"Why?"

"Why? Because of all the lawsuits. Billions of dollars are at stake here. That gets out, about the Estonia study, what they called the Tallinn file, and Kimball's going to go under. Go bankrupt." He mopped his face with the towel again. "Kimball is under huge pressure these days. All the protests. Conrad was always sort of paranoid, but he's gotten worse as he's gotten older. And Fritz does whatever Conrad says. But the company is vulnerable. I mean, their drug portfolio has always been too dependent on Oxydone. Their antidepressant never really caught on. There are better blood pressure drugs than the one they offer. Their migraine drug never made it to market. It's all about Oxydone. What is your book about, again?"

"I want to prove Kimball Pharma knowingly brought a drug to market that they knew was dangerous."

"Hey, some of the people who use Oxydone really need it. Cancer patients and such. But that doesn't account for most of its use. I mean, people inhale Oxydone like they're snorting cocaine."

"I'm talking about the Tallinn file."

"Art Scavolini wouldn't talk to you, huh? I'm not surprised. He probably got a nice payday too for keeping his mouth shut and making sure that study disappeared, and he doesn't want to screw it up."

"I haven't given up," I said.

"No. You don't seem like a guy who knows when to quit. You're not going to find that study. Kimball Pharma paid for it, and they own it, and it's under lock and key somewhere."

"But in a company the size of Kimball Pharma, there have to be others who got copies and held on to them."

He held up three fingers. His sweat dripped off his chin onto the floor mat. "Three people," he said. "Conrad killed that study, as soon as they heard about the addiction rate, and shut it down fast."

"Do you have a copy?"

"It was on a website you had to sign into. If I was smart, I would have downloaded a copy. But I didn't think."

"So who might have one?"

"The only people at Kimball who saw the study, who got copies, are Conrad and the PI and the CMO."

"The CMO?"

"Chief medical officer. Named Maurizio Zubiri. Brilliant guy. He's been at Kimball forever."

I made a mental note. "And who and what is the PI?"

"The principal investigator. The scientist who did the study. In Estonia."

"You don't happen to know his name, do you?"

"Come on. On a twenty-year-old study?"

"Could you find it?"

"Maybe."

"I'm sure there were plenty of studies done on Oxydone. So other trials didn't find the same rate of addiction?"

"The doctor in Estonia was a careful scientist. He designed a six-month study, and after only three days he noticed his subjects were going through withdrawal if they didn't get their Oxy. He wasn't looking for how addictive it was. He was looking for the right dose, basically. The addiction part came up as an unintended consequence. Every other study Kimball had done ignored that aspect. Shorter studies too."

"Ignored it?"

"Clinical trials involving addictive drugs like Oxydone are

extremely difficult to do. That's why there's so few of them. You have a high dropout rate, first of all. People in pain don't want to get the placebo. Then there's all the tricks a company can do. They can clean up the data. They show results only of those who complete the trial. The ones who got addicted? They get pushed out of the trial, so they don't show up in the final results."

"So how many people would have to be bribed to make this study go away?"

"At Phoenicia, just Art Scavolini. At Kimball, just Dr. Zubiri and the PI. Kimball Pharma is highly compartmentalized."

"And you don't know the name of the doctor in Estonia, so that just leaves Dr. Zubiri."

"Right. Wait . . . Cask. Like 'The Cask of Amontillado.'"

"Huh?"

"Mark—Marcus Kask. With a *k*. That was the Estonian's name."

"Unusual name."

"Not in Estonia."

"Why do the study in Estonia, of all places?"

"It's a lot easier to enroll people in studies in the old Eastern Bloc countries. Lots of them don't have health care, so they sign up for studies just to get covered. Also, Eastern Europe twenty years ago, it was the Wild West; you could do anything. You could massage the data. And if you didn't like the study, you just shut it down and put it in a drawer. Total freedom. Conrad knew if there was a problem, he could bury it."

I nodded.

"He probably knew this drug was more addictive than heroin, but he didn't want to have that scientifically confirmed," Sossong said.

"I see."

"Look," he said, "I'm talking to you because I feel bad for you. I know what it's like to lose a dear friend to opioids. But if you ever quote me, that will ruin me, do you understand that?"

"I do."

"Or worse."

"Understood."

"Now, if you don't mind, I have to get back to my workout. Don't let me hear from you again."

# 55

Leaving Port Chester, I stopped for a late lunch at a burger place. While I ate, I searched on my phone for "Markus Kask" or "Marcus Cask." I found plenty, in Sweden and Estonia, mostly. So that was a lost cause. I called Dorothy and asked her to search for a medical doctor and researcher in Estonia named Marcus Kask. Spelled however.

I'd paid and was on my way back to the Toyota when Dorothy called back. "I'm not sure I have the right one," she said. "This Professor Marcus Kask, spelled with a *k*, was a doctor at West Tallinn Central Hospital."

Tallinn. That had to be him. "Was?"

"Killed in a car accident on the Ring Road in Tallinn, seven years ago. Young guy too. Forty-three."

"Shit."

A man is killed in a car accident in a busy European city: there was nothing necessarily odd about that. But that left just the chief medical officer, Dr. Zubiri. And getting to him, a man who had worked for Kimball Pharma for years and was surely loyal, would not be easy.

Port Chester was only half an hour from Katonah and Kimball Hall, so I decided to take a drive to the Kimball house. I was thinking about Maggie. I took 684 into the Town of Bedford, and after a couple of turns found myself on the tree-lined Cantitoe Street, where Conrad Kimball lived. I slowed down when I recognized the stone gate booth and saw the street number. In the distance I could see the handsome brick gate house, which I had earlier mistaken for the main mansion. I didn't know what I was doing there, but I knew I shouldn't drive up to the house and call attention to myself. So I kept driving, along his property line, passing a clay tennis court near the road, and then taking a right onto Girdle Ridge Drive, which slashed through forest.

And I noticed something.

This was the end of Conrad's Katonah property, this road here. This was the property line. And it wasn't demarcated with a wooden fence or a chain-link one. The property was really too big to enclose with a running fence.

I pulled over when I saw an unmarked dirt road cutting through the trees on Conrad's side of Girdle Ridge Drive. I saw tire tracks from trucks.

This was a service entrance to Kimball's house.

I slowed and then turned onto the dirt road. It was narrow—the trees encroached close in—and the Toyota was scratched by branches.

The killer could have entered the property along this road. He, or she, wouldn't have been spotted on video.

Or would he?

I braked, reversed, and saw a discreet CCTV camera on a telephone pole at the entrance to the dirt road from Girdle Ridge. It wasn't exactly concealed, but it wasn't obvious at all.

There *was* video back here. I wondered if Detective Goldman had seen it.


The Town of Bedford Police Department was on Bedford Road, in a redbrick building with white dormers that looked like a suburban bank office. Inside I could see it had been recently renovated.

Goldman was at his desk. He didn't seem surprised to see me. But he didn't want to talk in the building. He drove us to a Dunkin' Donuts a mile or so down Bedford Road. As he drove I asked him about the dirt service entrance road and whether he'd seen the video from that camera from the night Maggie was killed.

He hadn't, and he seemed angry at himself about it.

"I asked my partner to inventory all video cameras," he said. "He must have missed it. Tunnel vision."

I didn't expect him to thank me, and he didn't. It went unspoken. We parked, and entered the Dunkin' Donuts. We both got coffee and sat at a table.

A guy in a black leather jacket entered, glanced over at us, and ordered something.

I went on. "Conrad must have an apartment in New York, right? A pied-à-terre?"

"Ten sixty Fifth Avenue," Goldman said. "Eighty-eighth Street. View of the park."

"Sounds about right. Are you any closer to finding out who killed Maggie?"

"The ME says the cause of death was blunt force trauma. She landed on her head and snapped her neck. And all the usual broken bones and contusions and lacerations."

"What about the manner of death?"

"ME won't conclude anything. She was probably shoved off the cliff. The ME is holding off pending further investigation."

"Do you have footprints from the ground?" I remembered standing on the pre-impregnated pad to create elimination prints, when Goldman questioned me back in Kimball Hall.

"We took several plaster casts of impressions in the soil. Someone appears to have scuffled with her on the ledge above the ravine."

"Male or female?"

"We can't ascertain that."

228

"You have casts of whatever shoes or boots Cameron had on."

"All the kids. But we're unable to establish a match."

"Because of the rain?"

"No, we've got some decent shoeprints despite the rain. Just not a match."

"Shit. If it was Fritz Heston, we know he's going to be careful with the forensic traces anyway," I said. "This is his business."

"He'd also know how to turn off any video cameras he wanted off."

"What about Maggie's iCloud account? She's got photos—"

"Way ahead of you there, chief. We got access to her iCloud account, but apparently she didn't back up her photos to the cloud. So we got no pics, and her phone was stolen."

"Have you been able to locate it?"

"Someone must have removed the battery or smashed it or something. So no, we haven't found it."

The guy in the black leather jacket was waiting for his order. He stood at the delivery counter and looked around but not at us this time. He had a medium-dark complexion, looked Middle Eastern. He had black hair shaved close to the scalp, a prominent jaw, and a thin scar cutting through his right eyebrow. He took his coffee and left the shop. So: nobody of concern. But I mentally clocked the face.

I turned back to Goldman.

"Right. So listen, uh, Bill, I need to ask you a favor. I want to take a look at Maggie's office."

"It's a home office, and it's sealed."

"Right, but could you get me in? With an escort, if you want, someone from the Manhattan PD?"

"What are you looking for?"

"To be honest, I don't know what I'm looking for," I said. "I know—knew her well, and I just might see something your people missed."

Goldman scratched his goatee. "I think that can be arranged."

# 56

Maggie Benson's apartment was on 126th Street in Harlem. This wasn't the Harlem I knew from when I was a kid. Now there were yoga studios and hip restaurants and a Whole Foods. Her building was kind of ugly, and run-down inside, with an elevator that didn't seem to be working. I walked up the six flights. The local NYPD guy was already there. He opened the door when I knocked. The crime scene tape around the door had been broken.

"You're from Westchester?" he said. He looked like he was twenty-two, though he had to be older.

I didn't correct him. Let him think I had something to do with the cops. I didn't need to talk to him. I said, "Is Crime Scene done with their work?"

"I think so, yes. They're done with the prints and the computers and all that. But you can wear these if you want." He handed me a pair of nitrile gloves as I entered.

I immediately smelled Maggie's delicate patchouli scent. Not the brash perfume she'd been wearing at Kimball's, when she was playing a role.

The apartment was immaculate, looked like it had just been cleaned and straightened out, but I knew that was just the way Maggie lived. She was an army girl through and through. On the left was a fairly big room that was clearly outfitted as her office. Framed things on the wall. Her state license. Diplomas. Certificates of attendance at training seminars—forensic analysis, debt investigations, public records searches. A small, spare home office. She didn't meet people here, I was pretty sure. On a simple metal desk was an open laptop next to a coffee mug. The laptop was a MacBook. It was plugged in, but it was dark. The police must have finished examining it.

I touched the trackpad with a gloved finger, and the screen came to life. A log-in screen with a blank for a password. The Bash Bunny wouldn't work here. It didn't work on Mac computers.

I looked at the screen and thought. Maggie was a pro. The password wasn't going to be "1234." Though I tried it, just to be sure, and I was right. It wasn't "1234." I had no idea what to try. It wasn't going to be the date that we met, that much I knew. Or "I ♥ Nick."

This was, I realized, a fool's errand. Going into Maggie's apartment and hoping to find some trace evidence she might have left behind—that was ridiculous. She was a pro and as careful as I am.

The laptop sat on a yellow legal pad. Maggie always had a legal pad. She always took notes on legal pads while she talked on the phone.

This one was blank. Which probably meant that she'd taken her notes with her, folded up into a small square—also something she used to do.

I switched on the desk lamp and looked at the yellow pad, then held it up to the light at an angle.

Yes. You could see the faint indentations of what she'd written on the top sheet, which she'd removed.

The cop who'd let me in had followed me into Maggie's office, but I could see he was losing interest. His radio blasted an indecipherable message; he picked up his handheld from his belt and spoke into it. As he did so, he walked out of the room and into the hall, and I took advantage of his absence. I grabbed a pencil from a jar of pens and pencils and did something that would make another professional groan. I shaded the surface of the paper lightly with the lead of a pencil, bringing out all the indentations in white.

231

The proper way to do this is to use an ESDA machine, an electrostatic detection apparatus, to lift indented writing off paper. It's nondestructive. But I didn't have that with me and I didn't have the time. And for my purposes, I didn't need it. The old-fashioned way worked just fine.

It brought up a constellation of notes in Maggie's bold handwriting:

**MEGAN KIMBALL**
**KIMBALL PHARM CONRAD K.**
**HK→$$$?**
**LAST WILL & TEST. REVISED???**
**COMMINGLING OF FUNDS???**

That last—*commingling of funds*—was underlined three times. Then there was a name, CONRAD BLACK, with a circle around it.

MEGAN KIMBALL—that was who had called her first, to hire her. And it was clear the call was all about Conrad, Megan's father. Megan was asking about her father's will, had it been revised? And something about HK and money. HK being Hong Kong? . . . Or Hayden Kimball?

*Conrad Black*: now, there was an interesting name. I didn't know the man, but my father did. A bright, scholarly guy. He's a Canadian financier, used to be called a "press baron," who was convicted on four counts of fraud. He used to own the *Jerusalem Post* and the *Daily Telegraph* but got in trouble and went to prison for embezzlement and such. What that really meant was putting his personal expenses— household staff, private chefs, private jets, chauffeurs—on the company tab. Even though it was a publicly traded company. Was another Conrad—Conrad Kimball—doing the same thing? And why was Maggie taking notes about it?

I grabbed the marked-up piece of paper and tore it off the pad. Folded it three times, like Maggie used to do.

232

I felt like I had something useful now. I looked around the rest of the apartment, her bedroom, and I felt a pang. More than a pang: it was outright painful to look around and see the neatly arranged detritus of her life. A poster of Santorini—she must have traveled to Greece after she left the service. A collection of snow globes from all the places she'd lived, which was a lot. Her drawer of panties.

But I knew Maggie was too careful to leave any unencrypted disks or hard drives lying around. There was nothing more here to find. I also, to be honest, wanted to leave. I couldn't bear to be there any longer.

# 57

Sukie Kimball was surprised to hear from me. I was vague, said that I had to talk to her, that it was "family business," and she gave me directions to her town house on Sullivan Street, in the Village.

I made a quick call and confirmed my plans: I was going to spend the night at a friend's pied-à-terre in the city. The friend was out of town, as usual. He was a trader in diamonds and precious stones, and he spent maybe twenty days a year in Manhattan. His apartment sat empty. I dropped off my car in one of those rip-off parking garages near Central Park South and took the subway.

It was early evening when I got there. Sukie's town house, between Houston and Bleecker, was a graceful four-story building—red brick with tall, original windows, black-painted lintels above them like eyebrows. Her studio and office was on the ground floor, the garden level, and it had a separate entrance. I rang the bell, and a young woman answered the door. Black-haired, early twenties, chunky tortoiseshell glasses. She seemed to be expecting me.

"Hey," she said, out of breath, "Sukie's in the editing room. Let me show you in."

I entered an empty sort of bullpen, a collection of desks set up in cubicles, which led to a narrow hallway. The young woman said, "Did you get hassled by any protesters out there?"

I told her I hadn't seen any.

"Oh, yeah, they've been here a lot in the last couple of weeks.

Someone figured out she's a Kimball, even though she's known as Susan Garber? And they got this address—I don't know how, but they did. I mean, she doesn't even work for the company or anything, right? She makes her documentaries, she stays out of the whole opioid thing, and she goes to all these *funerals*. I mean, she's one of the good guys!"

I told her I agreed.

She led me into the first room we came to, where Sukie was sitting at a desk with two very large monitors and a couple of expensive-looking speakers. The room was windowless and unadorned. A couch, a couple of chairs. One wall had a large corkboard covered with index cards. A rumpled middle-aged man was seated next to her. Sukie caught my eye and smiled. She was in the middle of a conversation with the rumpled guy. "Did you try Q?" she said to him.

"Yeah, it didn't work."

"Did you try moving Harold's fight up before the archival?"

"I did. I liked that."

"You think it works? Great. Okay, let me take a break, just a couple of minutes."

Sukie was wearing jeans and a black T-shirt and large gold hoop earrings. Her dark brown hair was up, tied back with a scrunchie. "Sorry," she said, "I've got my editor here and it's a little hectic. What's going on?"

"Couple minutes," I said. I didn't want to talk in front of the others.

"Let's go to my office."

Her office was the last room we came to, amber with low slanted light from the setting sun in a couple of large windows and French doors that opened onto a small, wild-looking yard. The yard connected to an expanse of lawn, a large communal garden shaded by old elms and sycamores and maples.

I pointed outside. "Open space in the middle of the city. I like it. Your neighbors okay?"

"They keep to themselves, mostly. Bob Dylan used to live on the garden. Anna Wintour still does."

My face was blank.

"Editor of *Vogue*," she helpfully explained. She sat behind a small, pretty antique desk made of fruitwood. I looked around, noticed a couple of paintings on the wall, good but no one famous, and a few statuettes tucked away on a bookshelf. No posters of her own documentaries. "Where are all the movie posters?" I said.

"You mean like in Hollywood? Tacky. Not my speed."

"But you're good." I'd read rave reviews of her documentary about white-collar criminals and another one about a strike at a chicken processing plant. She'd won awards.

"I'm not Barbara Kopple."

"Who's that?"

"Just one of the greatest documentary filmmakers of all time."

"Sorry. I'm ignorant. Why are so many documentary makers women, anyway? I don't get it."

"You want to know why? Because back in the seventies, there was this idea out there that women couldn't do fiction films—i.e., movies—but they could do documentaries. They could occupy themselves with this tiny, cheap thing."

"That's what documentaries are?"

"Compared to Hollywood movies. So what's going on?"

"Why did your sister Megan hire Maggie?"

"Maggie was Hildy, right?"

I nodded.

Outside, I could hear a male voice, tinnily amplified on a loudspeaker, shouting, *"The Kimballs are killers! The Kimballs are killers!"* and chants of something I couldn't quite make out. It sounded like "Blood money."

She looked stricken. "Shit, they're back."

The echoey amplified voice said, *"Say it loud, say it clear. Kimballs are not welcome here!"*

"This happen a lot?"

"Someone discovered this is where I live, a few months back, and since then there's been a protest weekly or more."

"They don't know you're the one member of the family who's doing something about it."

She nodded sadly and attempted a joke: "Maybe they don't like my docs."

We talked over the shouting, the amplified chanting, which had grown louder, closer. I repeated my question. "Why did your sister hire Maggie Benson?"

"I assume—I thought it was to get a copy of Dad's updated will. Isn't that what you told me?"

"That's only part of it. I think Megan is trying to unseat your father."

"You do?"

"Hear me out. I found notes from what I think is a conversation Maggie had with Megan. Presumably when Megan hired her. Yes, Megan wanted to get the will, but it seems her main focus was on your father's guilt. Crimes he's committing. Using company funds for personal purposes. Why else would she be looking into crimes her father has committed?"

Sukie looked directly at me. She didn't look surprised. "Because she's tired of waiting for him to die. She wants to force him out."

"She wants the iron throne."

She nodded, stood up. Walked to the door to the hallway and closed it. "She doesn't care about the truth coming out. But I thought you were stopping. I asked you to stop."

"I'm not charging you a cent. As for me stopping, that's up to me, and I don't want to. Not until I find out who killed Maggie."

She looked pensive. "You keep digging, you're going to get yourself killed."

I shrugged. I didn't believe that.

"Did you know Kimball Pharma has been losing money in the last few years?" she said.

"I didn't."

"I get regular debriefings from a guy in the family office. It seems my dad has been investing crazy amounts of money in research and development. He's founded subsidiary companies in South America and South Asia and Eastern Europe—labs working on developing new products."

"Do you have a say in this kind of stuff, or do you stay out of it?"

"I have a vote in the family trust, which owns Kimball Pharma. But we can all be outvoted by Dad. So, yeah, I stay out of it. I just think it's interesting that we're losing money because he's spending so much on research. I know Megan really hates what's going on."

"So maybe that's the reason, or maybe it's just plain old ambition, but I think Megan is trying to remove your father."

"This makes sense," she said. "It makes sense of a lot of things."

"Like?"

"We have an apartment in Paris. On the rue de Rivoli. Spectacular place. Legally it belongs to the company, it's for business use only, all that. But I lived there for a few years after I graduated from Oberlin. It was my apartment, and believe me, I did no business there." She smiled. "I know Dad has had mistresses, and he's always kept them in love nests around the world that the company paid for. Anyway, Megan and I had drinks a few weeks ago, and she was asking me for all the specifics of when I used the Paris apartment or the London town house. Like she was doing research. Now I get it. And I remember when Dad—"

There was a sudden explosion, a shattering of glass, and Sukie tumbled to the floor. Quick reflexes. A roar of shouts and screams outside. I leaped around the desk and saw that the left side of her face and her neck was bloody. Nearby on the floor were shards of glass and a brick that someone had thrown through her office window.

"You okay?" I said.

"Ow. I'm okay, I'm just—cut. The brick just missed my ear. Scraped me."

Once I saw that she was all right, I raced to the French doors, flung them open, and ran into the yard. Right away I saw the guy who'd thrown the brick. A large, fat man. He was trying to light a rag that had been jammed into a Coke can. Probably filled with gasoline. His intended follow-up to the brick.

He shouted, "Burn in hell, you goddamned bitch!"

I put on a burst of speed and caught up with him and slammed him to the ground. He squawked, "Fuck you, man!"

I had him in a half nelson, pinning him down with my knees. I kicked away the Coke can, could smell the gas. His lighter skittered away on the stone path.

He had tattoos on his neck and his arms. Probably on his obese belly too. "All right, asshole, shout all you want, but when you start hurting people, you're gonna get arrested." The man apparently had broken away from the organized protest and found a way into the communal garden.

With my left hand I fished out my phone, and as I was about to pull my right hand off the fat man to dial, I heard Sukie shouting, "Nick, no! Let him go!"

I turned, saw her standing in the middle of her small yard, a hand to the wound on her neck.

I said, "He could have burned down your house, Sukie."

"Let him go."

"Let me go, man!" the fat man bellowed. He flailed his arms and legs like an overturned cockroach.

"He's just going to come back after you."

She shook her head. "I mean it, Nick. Let him go."

239

Reluctantly, I eased up on the man, and he awkwardly got to his feet and stumbled away.

"You've got to hold these people responsible or they'll keep throwing bricks, they'll keep throwing Molotov cocktails," I said, approaching her. It was rapidly getting dark. I put an arm around her and walked her back into the house. "You've got to press charges."

"That's not me," she said. "I'm not that person."

"Well, maybe you should be."

"You don't understand," she said. "These people—they're on the right side. They've all suffered because of my family. All of them, there's a reason they're protesting. There's a reason they're throwing rocks and bricks. And bombs or whatever. Because they're in pain."

"Are *you* in pain?"

"It looks worse than it is," she said. "I just need to put some peroxide on it and a bandage."

She opened the interior office door. Her assistant, the young woman in the tortoiseshell glasses who'd let me in, was standing right there. "Oh, my God!" she said frantically. "What happened?"

"They're throwing bricks now," Sukie said.

"Your door was closed, so I didn't dare— Oh, my God, what can I do to help?"

"Get me a bag of frozen peas from the refrigerator upstairs, could you?" Sukie said. "And some peroxide and a couple of Band-Aids? And can you call Jeff to ask him to come over and board up the window?"

The young woman turned and ran down the hall toward the front room. Her editor, the rumpled guy, had stuck his head out of the editing room. "Was that a gun?" he said.

"A brick," Sukie said. "Glanced off me. I'm totally fine."

"You shouldn't stay here tonight," I said. "I should get you to a hotel."

She shook her head. "I don't want to go to a hotel."

"I don't want you staying here tonight."

"Where are *you* staying?" she said.

# 58

Sukie quickly went upstairs and packed a bag. I could hear scattered shouts of the protesters outside. A couple of organized chants: "Blood money! Blood money!"

She had a brief chat with her editor, who was staying there and working into the night. I grabbed her bag, and we went back out to the yard. I'd decided it was unsafe or at least unwise for her to leave via the front door. That was where the protesters were waiting for her. She said there was a way out through the back—probably the way the brick-throwing fat man had gotten in in the first place.

We crossed the community garden and went through a side gate on to Bleecker Street and flagged down a cab.

My friend's pied-à-terre was a one-bedroom on Central Park South, a high floor in a tower building. It had an amazing view of Central Park, spread out before you like a diorama, like a perfect little toy model. A big dark rectangle bordered by the lights of Fifth Avenue on the right and Central Park West on the left. A breathtaking sight.

When I emerged from the bathroom, I found Sukie sitting on the couch by the view of the park, weeping. She looked small and vulnerable curled up that way.

I came near and said, "Everything okay?" even though everything clearly wasn't okay.

After a beat she took a hand from her face.

"They don't know . . . They don't know that I'm fighting alongside them, that I'm fighting for them. They don't know."

"Not fair."

"You want to protest someone, go to Kimball Hall. Go to Chappaqua."

"Maybe they don't know where Megan lives," I said, sitting on the couch next to her.

"She's had some protests in front of her house. We've all been targeted. Everyone but Cameron, because he just flits around so much, he doesn't really have a fixed—" Sukie started shaking. "Oh, God, I think it's just hitting me."

"I know."

"I could have been burned alive. I was totally within range."

That was true, although I didn't confirm it. If I hadn't gotten to the fat man in time, he would have flung flaming gasoline at her.

She said, "I'm—Jesus, is no place safe for me?"

"You're safe," I said. Because she *was* safe, at the moment. I wanted to say, *I'll keep you safe*, but I knew I couldn't promise that.

She turned and put her arms around me, embracing me tightly. "Oh, God," she said. I could feel her hot breath on my neck. "This whole time I've been feeling so alone in this. But now—I don't know, I don't feel so alone. It's like . . . I guess I feel you're in it with me."

She moved her face in close and kissed me on the lips. I was surprised, but I responded. My heart began to thud. She kissed hungrily. I could smell her hair, something lavender and soapy.

There was something so exciting about how carnal she was—that she'd revealed herself to be. It was like she'd been unleashed.


When we were showering together afterward, she said—and I could tell she'd been waiting to say it—"Do you sleep with all your clients?"

I laughed. I thought of my last client, hangdog Mort Vallison.

"Seriously, do you?"

"It's not billable time, don't worry."

She lightly slapped my chest, laughed, and said, "You bill in increments of an hour?"

Then she noticed the ugly scar on my right thigh that started just above the knee and twisted toward my groin. She traced it with a finger—"Can I?"—and said, "I'm guessing there's a story."

For a quick moment I thought of what Sean had once said to me. He had been smoking a joint. "We get wounded, and we heal," he had said. "The wound repairs itself, right? But we're not the same. We take our scars with us. They make us who we are. And if we can't accept our scars, we haven't really healed."

But to Sukie, I said only, "A couple of bullet wounds and related damage. Happened a long time ago."

"What happened?"

I quickly recounted the incident in Afghanistan, made it sound as uninteresting as possible. I'm not very enthusiastic about telling war stories. When we were toweling each other off, I said, "You want to get some dinner?"

"Sure."

"Also, I want to talk to Hayden."

"Why?"

I'd been thinking of the note that Maggie had scrawled—"HK—>$$$?" Something about Hayden and money, right, but what did it refer to? I said, "I want to rule her out."

She got dressed in her jeans and a T-shirt and then grabbed her phone and looked at the time. "Knowing Hayden, she's probably in a rehearsal. Let me text her."

Her sister texted right back, and we had a date to see her in an hour.

The bar where we were meeting Hayden was located in a brownstone on West Forty-sixth Street, upstairs from a well-known theater watering hole. It had a name but no sign. No phone number. Tourists did not know about this place, and no New York theatergoer would ever find it. You had to know about it. As a result, it was full of famous Broadway types—stars, directors, producers, and so on. And the occasional tech billionaire.

At the top of the stairs the heavy blue curtains parted and I saw a dark bar with black-and-white photos on the wall, of Billie Holiday and Ella Fitzgerald and Louis Armstrong. But it was otherwise unadorned, undecorated, unchic, which of course made it chic.

Hayden was there, the center of a crowd. She was wearing black jeans and boots and a neatly pressed denim shirt, like she had been the last time I saw her. Branding, I figured. She was pressing cheeks with George Takei, Sandra Oh, B. D. Wong, and a couple of very good-looking actors from the movie *Crazy Rich Asians*. Maybe they were in her production of *Suddenly Last Summer*. Or maybe they were invited guests.

She saw us but kept chatting with people for another couple of minutes while we stood and waited. We sat at a table and ordered drinks—there was no cocktail menu. I got a vodka martini, and Sukie got a Negroni. Finally, Hayden came over, said, "Sorry, it's first preview—wait, what happened to you?" She kissed her older sister. "What the hell *happened*?"

"I'll tell you in a second. You remember Nick, right?"

She smiled perfunctorily at me and said, "You're the one who's in the dark arts, right? McKinsey?"

"That's right. Nick Brown."

Sukie told her about the brick-throwing and, worse, the guy with the Molotov cocktail. She cried as she relived it. Hayden looked terrified. I could see her realizing that the protests against her family *just got real.* I knew Hayden lived with her partner, a playwright who was semi-famous for having very long-term writer's block, in a huge loft in the West Village that looked out over the Hudson River. "Taylor and I have decent security in our building at home," she said, and then her voice got hushed. "But what if they—decide to target my theaters?"

"Not that I know anything about it, but if it were me, I'd be adding to my personal security detail," I said.

"I don't have a *security detail.*"

"You might want to think about getting one, for the time being. And you might want to change the name of your production company. But what do I know?"

Sukie excused herself, as we'd previously agreed on, and then Hayden said to me, marveling, "So you took down this Molotov cocktail guy?"

"He was a big target," I said. "Big fat target. Didn't require Superman."

She smiled.

I said, "So let me ask you something. Why aren't you Scott Rudin? Why aren't you Jordan Roth? Why aren't you Fred Zollo?" I named some big, successful Broadway producers whose names I knew from boning up in the last couple of days. People who did what she did but had a lot more success and visibility.

I couldn't interrogate her, because as far as she was concerned, I was just Sukie's boyfriend. Instead, I was a little aggressive. Right away, I saw that she wasn't expecting that. She was expecting deference. But she didn't wince or snap something back at me. She took a drink of her Scotch.

I thought of that scrawled note on Maggie's yellow pad: *HK—> $$$?* Meaning something about Hayden and money, but what?

"I can't finance all this myself," she said. "You hit a bit of a tender spot there, Nick."

"How so?"

"I mean, it's kind of an unfair comparison. Look at Jordan—and I love the guy, he's so talented—but we're talking deep pockets. His father is just a lot more generous than mine is. I kind of feel—well, first-world problems, right?—I mean, the things I've identified and had to miss out on! I think of the projects I developed off-Broadway that got taken away from me." She put her hand on my forearm. "You know, Nick, I would love to be in a position where I don't have to say no when I want to say yes. To not be constrained. I'm not my brother Paul. I'm not writing imaginary books about imaginary subjects, you know?"

That was not a dig I'd expected. But maybe she was just the blunt sort. I nodded, smiled. Made a mental note that I should also find a way to talk to Paul, up in Cambridge, Mass., and soon.

"I mean, this is real," she said. "It's theater, but it's real. It's as real as it gets." She took her hand off my forearm, took another big sip of her Scotch. "Sorry, just a tender spot. I'm not a complainer."

"Why do you think your dad won't open the floodgates a little?"

"Because of Big Sis. Megan." She said it liltingly, sarcastically.

"How so?" I remembered Hayden and Megan had pointedly avoided each other at their father's birthday dinner.

"Because she and Paul consider what I do a *hobby*, you got it? Let me give you an example—and I'm trusting you here, Nick, because you're with Sukie, so you gotta be okay. Megan once came to see a staged version of *Shoah* that I produced at the Long Wharf in New Haven, okay? And you want to know what she said afterward? She said, 'Kind of a bummer, no?' This is the type of sensitive soul we're talking about."

I sort of got what she meant. Megan didn't like the downbeat ending of a play about . . . the Holocaust. "So you would have received more support from Conrad if she hadn't been pouring poison in his ear?"

246

"Exactly."

"That makes sense," I said, and then I pushed further. "But Cameron doesn't do that, does he?"

She shook her head. "I mean, Cam's a bit of a lost soul. Never found his way, like the rest of us have. It's like there's something broken inside him that never got fixed. I've always thought of him as, like, the extra, the understudy. Waiting for a turn that may never come."

"I see. And as long as we're speaking frankly, I wonder how closely you guys have looked into Natalya's background."

She looked me straight in the eyes. "You're asking a very pointed question. We're concerned about it. *I'm* concerned about it."

I nodded. "I work with a lot of venture capitalists," I said, "and one of the most important things they do is due diligence. You're going to invest your fund's money, you want to get to know the people you're investing in. You fly over, you kick the tires, you talk to people, you check things out. I'm sure you do the same thing in the talent business."

"Sure."

"If your eighty-year-old father's not going to do it, one of you should. Hire someone to check her out. Get it done."

"You want to know what I wonder about," she said, so quietly I could barely hear her over the din in the bar. "Not 'Is she a gold digger?'—that's obvious. And common. No, I'm wondering if she's connected to some Russian oligarch, you know?"

"It's possible."

"I'm not saying she is. She could just be a gold digger with a heart of gold, right?"

"Where is she these days?"

"Oh, my God, it's the Westminster Dog Show, you didn't know that? She does not miss it. Why do you ask?"

Someone approached—a slender woman in her sixties with dark circles under her eyes—and said, "Are you Hayden Kimball?"

Hayden turned. "Who wants to know?"

The woman said, "Someone told me you're Hayden."

"That's right. And you are?"

The woman hissed, "Murderer!" She grabbed a glass of ice water from the table and dumped it on Hayden's head. "You killed my son!"

Hayden yelped, her hair wet and scraggly, water streaming down her face and blotching her shirt, and the woman fast-walked away. Her expression evolved from terrified to furious, but when I spotted Sukie across the room, she appeared to be suppressing a laugh.

# 59

We returned to my friend's apartment on Central Park South late that night. Sukie was exhausted and fell asleep before I did, but in the morning she woke me with her hand between my legs. Which I didn't mind.

Later, when we were debriefing about Megan, I said, "She sounds like a piece of work."

"She and Hayden hate each other like a couple of alley cats," Sukie said. "Have for years."

"But is either one of them a killer?"

She shrugged. "How could I possibly know?"

"You don't."

"If you told me that Natalya, who loves the outdoors and nature, shoved Maggie off the cliff in the middle of the night, that wouldn't surprise me."

"How can I get to her?"

"Natalya? She's always reaching out to me to get together in the city. Always emailing me invitations. She knows what I think of her, and she's campaigning. She's trying to bond with each of us, one by one."

"How about you accept her invitation?"

She smiled. "You like dogs?"

"I do," I said. One of the drawbacks to my constantly traveling life is that I'm gone too much to take care of a dog.

"Then I'll arrange it." She hesitated. "Uh, Nick—yesterday I said something I shouldn't have."

"Oh, yeah?"

"I said I no longer feel alone in this, this—what's going on. That I knew you were in it with me. That was totally presumptuous of me. I shouldn't have said it."

"What are you talking about?"

"I'm a client. A former client, anyway. I was in a business relationship with you. And when this gig is over, you're back to Boston."

"Come on," I said.

"It's presumptuous to think you could ever be committed the way I have to be. I am a Kimball. You're an outsider."

I wasn't sure how to respond, so I said, "We'll see this through together. I promise." Just then my phone rang. It was Dorothy. "Excuse me," I said, and I answered the call.

"I'm getting some interesting stuff on your favorite security director, Fritz," Dorothy said.

"Interesting how?"

"A sealed domestic abuse charge. From around twenty years ago. Around the time of his divorce. Allegations of physical cruelty. Sounds like a lovely man."

"Yep," I said. "Oh, I had a thought."

"About?"

"The encrypted folder. Try Neil D. Tyson. All one word." I remembered the photo of Tyson with Scavolini, the little stone quotes from Tyson on his desk. Scavolini clearly had a man crush on Neil deGrasse Tyson.

"Nope," she said, clackety-clacking away. "Not all one word, caps and smalls."

"Try all the variations. You know."

"Okay," she said. "But so far, nothing."

"Keep trying," I said. "Maybe we'll get lucky."

# 60

The Westminster Kennel Club Dog Show was going on at Piers 92 and 94 off the West Side Highway. We found Natalya just where she said, in the "benching" area. She kissed Sukie and gave me a firm handshake. She was dressed all in pink, her suit and her shoes. She was a very attractive woman. A forty-year-old Grace Kelly, but with one difference: up close you could see she'd had a lot of roadwork done.

Meanwhile, dogs by the dozens were walking by on leashes. I paid no attention to their owners. There were all sorts of breeds and sizes of dog, and they were yipping and barking. It was a cacophony. We walked past an area where people were showing off their dogs, and some were grooming them. I saw a big old English sheepdog with hair rakishly over his eyes. And then a huge Neapolitan mastiff, a homely dog but a fierce protector.

Natalya was grooming her Havanese, a small dog with long, silky black-and-white hair and button eyes, who was standing on a bench. She said she was entered in the show. The dog reminded me of Chewbacca, from the *Star Wars* movies. A Wookiee. But a very cute dog.

Sukie told Natalya about the brick and the Molotov cocktail guy. She looked at me and put a hand on my biceps, lightly squeezing. She hugged Sukie and told her how scary that must have been. The two seemed to get along just fine.

Then Sukie excused herself to go find the nearest restroom.

Every bench in the hall had a dog sitting on it. The dogs were all getting petted and groomed and primped. They were the celebrities, not their owners. The woman next to us was trimming the eyelashes of her cocker spaniel with a pair of scissors. A few benches away was a long-haired dachshund, which was getting lots of attention from visitors.

"How's your dog doing in the show?" I asked Natalya.

"Clara is select bitch," she said.

"Excuse me?"

She pulled out a ribbon affixed to a silver medallion from under the bench, a blue-and-white rosette, and showed it to me. It did say *Select Bitch* on it. I realized she was talking dog-show language. She kept brushing her dog, who responded by panting happily.

"Congratulations," I said.

"Winner of show always wire fox terrier."

"That right?"

She tilted her head and smiled. "You went after this bomber?"

I nodded.

"Yes, of course you did," she said. "You are sheepdog."

"I'm a sheepdog," I said dubiously.

"I read somewhere there are three kinds people—is sheep, is wolves, and is sheepdog. Most people sheep—just kind and gentle people. They never hurt others, except by accident. Then there is predators—the wolves. They prey on weak people. They feed on sheep. These are the bad people."

"Okay."

"And then is sheepdogs. They protect flock. They have drive to do this. They have gift of aggression."

I nodded.

She said, "You are not sheep. You are not wolf. You are sheepdog. You are guard dog, not attack dog."

"I see," I said. "And what are you, Natalya?"

She smiled. "I own guard dog. Dogs have owners, yes? Who owns you?"

"Maybe I'm a stray," I said.

She went back to brushing her dog, whose hair was so long I couldn't see her feet. "Clara," she said soothingly to her dog. Then, to me: "I think you are good man. Very observant. I have strong intuition, and I trust this intuition. And you are good for Sukie."

"Thank you."

"These children of Conrad—they are not sheep or wolves; they are scorpions."

"Is that right?"

"That's what he always says to me. His children see me as thief in night who comes to take their birthright away. Their greed makes them . . . it blinds them. I think it does not blind you. I think you see this."

I didn't want to agree with her, so I just nodded vaguely.

"Megan thinks she is very clever, what she is doing. But she is playing short game. Conrad, you see—he plays long game."

"He's eighty years old. That's a long game right there."

"I'm very sorry about what happened to Hildy." She said "Hildy" with a hard Russian *ch* sound, and she also said it with invisible quotation marks around it. As if she knew it was an alias. "I think she was someone special to you."

I concealed my surprise. "She was."

"No one else in family really sees you. Too blinded by greed. But I see you." She stroked the hairbrush over the long hair on the dog's face. "Clara, *dushenka*," she said to the dog. Probably a Russian word. To me, she said, "These are my private thoughts. I share them with no one. Not even Conrad. I like you, Nick."

"What's not to like?" I said.

"You know, Nick, when you grow up *extremely* poor like me, and then suddenly you have great wealth, you have maybe different perspective. You realize what is real wealth? Is other people. Is not dollars or rubles. Is what kind of person you are."

I paused for a moment. I hadn't expected this kind of directness from Conrad's fiancée. So I pushed a bit. "Tell me about Paul. He seems very gentle. Maybe a little out of it, but well meaning. Am I wrong?"

"Paul is more complicated than he seems."

*Who isn't?* I thought. "How so?" I said.

"Paul is Chow Chow. He has big fluffy coat and everyone thinks it is friendly dog. But Chow Chow can be very aggressive. They have jaws like lion. I had Chow Chow in Russia, big, fluffy, beautiful dog, but he can never stop biting. He jumps and bites people and digs holes." She paused and, after a meaningful glance, said, "We had to put him down."

"I'm sorry."

"Some breeds of dogs, like the Rottweiler and the pit bull, they are friendly and sweet and loving but very aggressive to other dogs."

"And what is Conrad?"

"He is my Chihuahua."

"But Chihuahuas are little."

"I once had a Chihuahua who is extremely loyal but if anyone else gets near me, he snarls and bites."

"Loyalty's a good thing," I said.

She looked lost in thought. "We had to put him down too."

We talked for a while, Natalya and I, until Sukie came back. She said to Natalya, "Looks like you two are hitting it off. I might wander around for a while."

"Sukie, my dear, I must go," said Natalya. "Clara and I. I have hairdresser appointment. Can I give you a ride anywhere?"

"Just back to my house."

"My car is outside. I will drop you two off."

We wandered through the halls of Pier 94 and took an elevator down to the ground level. Outside it was crowded with cars and cabs and a lot of people. When Natalya emerged, in her pink suit and holding Clara in the crook of her arm like a baby, a couple of shouts went up from the crowd. I heard "Kimball."

"Damn these people," Natalya said.

Some in the crowd started chanting, "Kimballs lie, people die!"

There were black signs that read GREED KILLS and KIMBALLS ARE KILLERS and a big red banner that read 200 DEAD EACH DAY. I immediately took the lead and ushered the two women across the bustling sidewalk to Natalya's car, a white Bentley limo. Someone threw an egg, which splatted on the sidewalk near her. The car pulled up to us just in time, and Natalya and her dog hustled over to the passenger's-side door. I opened the door for her. She climbed in, with Clara the dog, and then Sukie did.

When I was about to get in, I suddenly noticed something on the undercarriage of the car. Something had glinted at me. I said, "Hold on," then I closed the car door and knelt down on the pavement. I reached underneath, felt the hot metal next to the object I'd seen a few seconds earlier. I grabbed it. It easily came off.

It was a small, gray plastic box, around five inches long and two wide, with two big magnets on top. Inside, as I expected, was a GPS tracking device. Someone was tracking Natalya.

I shoved it into the pocket of my coat and jumped into the car. Once I closed the door it was quiet in there. The outside chants were muffled.

"What did you find?" Natalya said.

I pulled out the little gray box and showed it to her.

"What is it?"

"It's a tracker. A GPS tracker."

"I don't understand."

"It's for someone to follow you, track you down everywhere this car goes."

Her brows arched. She looked angry. "Who puts it there?"

"I don't know. I'll find out." I disconnected the battery from the GPS unit, disabling it.

She told the driver, "Please, Edward, get us out of here. Go very fast." The car slowly began to move. There were too many people around. Natalya began stroking Clara, in her lap.

Someone hit the car hard, or maybe kicked it. It made a hollow sound.

Suddenly the exterior of the Bentley was hit with dozens of what sounded at first like rocks. Splotches of paint covered the windshield and the side windows, yellow and pink. We'd been attacked by a couple of paintball guns. The protesters had come prepared with weapons. Yellow and pink paint streamed down the windows. They had known that Conrad Kimball's fiancée would be at the dog show.

Natalya was quietly crying as we drove away. But I kept staring out the window, because I had to double-check on something.

It took me a moment, but quickly I confirmed it. My stomach knotted as I recognized someone in the crowd. It was a swarthy man with a scar cut through his right eyebrow, and I knew for sure I had seen him before.

# 61

But where?

It wasn't in Boston that I'd seen the guy with the eyebrow. It had been recent, in the last couple of days. Then I called to mind the image of that same guy—close-shaved black hair, swarthy complexion, scarred right eyebrow—looking at Detective Goldman and me and ordering something at the Dunkin' Donuts, a mile or so from the Bedford police station yesterday. A fit man in his thirties who moved with athletic confidence.

He looked like private security to me. Ex-military, probably. There's a look the private security guys have—the watchful, distrustful eyes, visibly fit, short hair or a shaved head, clothing that attracts no attention. I assumed he worked for Fritz, but if he did, why was he in the middle of a crowd of anti-Kimball protesters? It didn't quite make sense.

Or maybe it did. Maybe Fritz planted his security people in the middle of protests against the company, as moles. Gathering intelligence on the protesters. But that wouldn't explain how his people had found me with Detective Goldman. I was being followed, but I couldn't quite figure out why. Or how.

Had Detective Goldman leaked my real identity to him? I doubted it. He said he wouldn't, and I trusted him.

That left a more disturbing explanation—that Fritz had checked out my cover and found a hole. That was possible.

Nothing's ever perfect.

. . .

I had to get back to Boston. I wanted to talk to the eldest brother, Paul, who lived in Cambridge. I said goodbye to Sukie, which was a lot less awkward than I expected, and grabbed a cab to the parking garage south of Central Park where I'd left the Toyota. I did a quick check for GPS trackers, didn't find any. I'd do a more exhaustive search later.

From New York to Boston the drive is around five hours. I wasn't followed, that I was certain of. I arrived in Boston in the early evening and checked in with Dorothy. No news.

Back at my loft, I disassembled the GPS tracker from Natalya's Bentley and took pictures of it with my phone and sent them to Merlin.

He called me that evening from his boat in Chesapeake Bay. "This is an interesting one," he said. "It's not domestic. Not US. It's made by Azur in Israel, for the Israeli army, the IDF, and Mossad and Aman, the Military Intelligence Directorate. Not for export."

"Why would someone use an Israeli device when you can have good old American, made-in-China products? You can buy whatever you want on the internet. Why Israeli?"

"Because it's what they're used to working with. And it's what they have."

"So we're talking Israelis who might have planted this?"

"Possibly. Are you doing something that would attract the interest of the Israeli government?"

"Not at all."

"There's always Israeli private security. One of their private intelligence firms."

But if that's what it was, who had hired them? To me, the most obvious culprit here was Fritz Heston, Conrad's protector. I could imagine Conrad pulling his security director aside and saying, "I want to know everywhere she goes. Is she cheating on me? Is she up to something?"

And in response the Israelis would put a tracker on her car. And maybe question the driver. Conrad would keep a close watch on the woman he was about to marry, because that was his way.

But why would Fritz outsource security to an Israeli firm? He had his own team. I didn't get it.


In the morning I called Paul Kimball, using the number Sukie had given me.

He sounded preoccupied when he answered the phone. "Nick Brown," I said. Then, to remind him, "Friend of Sukie's."

"Oh, God. She told me what happened. The arsonist. Like someone out of *Princess Casamassima*. She said you wrestled the guy to the ground. Thank you for doing that."

"I'm worried about Sukie and thought maybe we could have a chat."

"Of course," he said.

Cambridge, Massachusetts, is the home of a couple of great universities, Harvard and MIT. It's a city in its own right that happens to be next to Boston, a much larger city. It has its own character. Very fair-trade coffee, very quinoa grain bowl, and a wide range of wealth. It's a city of large, rambling houses off Brattle Street occupied by Harvard professors with trust funds, but also seedier places like Cambridgeport, where Gabe lived, and Central Square, where he worked.

I actually passed Paul's house several times, because I thought I'd somehow gotten the street number wrong. It was a modest brown shingled house on Franklin Street, just a few blocks from the main drag, Mass. Ave., which took you back to Boston. This house was a step up from the triple-decker where Gabe lived, a few blocks away—but not a big step.

It was not the house of a billionaire's son. But people with a lot of money don't always flaunt it. The founder of IKEA lives frugally and takes the bus everywhere and brings home salt and pepper packets from the store. Some who were raised in wealth sometimes prefer to live modestly. To not stick out from the crowd.

Still, for a very rich man who was raised in a mansion to live like a graduate student was . . . Well, something about it appealed to the contrarian in me. It made me like the man a little more.

Paul Kimball was Conrad's oldest child, the son of his first wife, Barb, a squat fireplug of a woman whom he divorced as soon as he started making real money. She had no interest in the family business and never remarried. But she was well taken care of by a generous settlement.

I checked the number again and rang the bell, and sure enough, Paul Kimball came to the door.

He had on horn-rimmed glasses and wore a loose-fitting gray cardigan sweater over a green polo shirt and ill-fitting ragged jeans and battered, unstylish sneakers. He could have been an adjunct professor at some local college. "Come on in," he said. "And thank you again for being so helpful to my sister."

Inside the house was dark and not just cluttered but jammed with books and magazines and papers. Sloppy piles of the *New York Review of Books*. In the center of the first room we came to was a long, beat-up, splintering wood dining table that was being used as a desk, covered with tall stacks of books interspersed with several laptops. I wondered if his brilliant MIT professor girlfriend lived here too. Some of the books appeared to be on something or someone called Adorno.

I reminded myself that I was Nick Brown to him, I worked for McKinsey, and all that. If he thought it was strange that a relatively new boyfriend of Sukie's was worried about her mental health, he didn't let on. He was probably worried himself about what might happen to him—all the Kimball kids had to be—so his safety was surely a subject that was very much at the front of his mind.

"I was about to make a pot of Lapsang souchong—can I pour you some?"

I accepted just to be agreeable. I followed him into the kitchen, which was low-ceilinged and had an old linoleum floor, spiderwebbed with cracks, and appliances that looked thirty or forty years old. The kitchen smelled faintly of cooking gas.

He poured water into a kettle and lit a gas burner by turning the knob. "It's terrible what happened to Sukie," he said, his back to me. "It could happen to any of us, I suppose. Though the protesters have left me alone so far, thank God."

"You've all got to be careful. The whole family." The kitchen window looked out onto a dark, small backyard surrounded by clapboard houses.

"Yeah, I take precautions," he said. "And after what happened to Maggie—I mean, Hildy. I'm so bad with names." He turned around.

I felt a little jolt. He knew Maggie's real name, somehow. I wondered who'd told him. Had Megan told him she'd hired a private investigator? Was that how he knew her name? Maybe Megan and Cameron and Paul all hired Maggie, together. Maybe Paul was in on it with his two siblings.

"Have they gotten any closer to finding out how she was killed?" I asked.

"Not that I know of. The police mostly wanted to talk to Layla and me about our whereabouts that evening. Our alibis." He pushed his glasses up his nose. "Let's sit in the other room."

We passed through an alcove where a large flat-screen was mounted to the wall. Nine panels on the screen showed different views of the exterior of the house, including the front porch and the backyard. It was a fairly sophisticated setup, especially for such a modest house as

261

this. He saw me glance at the screen and said, "Given the protesters, I have to be a little careful, you know."

I followed him into another small, dark, low-ceilinged room that was furnished with a few unmatched upholstered armchairs. He switched on a torchiere lamp, which shone a circle of light on the ceiling and gave the room a yellowish cast.

Then he sat in the high-backed chair, which looked like his favorite. I sat in a low-backed one near it.

"Dad was all about making money," he said. "I'm about making *meaning*. Maybe that's an old story. It's that line by Walter Benjamin"— he gave the name a German pronunciation—"about how every document of civilization is also a document of barbarism. The son wants to redeem the sins of the father but at the same time he's necessarily implicated in them, right? Not by choice but by the way we're subjects in, and of, history."

I suddenly remembered why I dropped out of Yale. "I see," I said, though I didn't.

"We all struggle with that. Sukie too, in her way."

"She's been through a lot," I said.

"She's very special," he said. "I think you know that."

"I do."

"I think life is hard for her. I just think she's still finding herself."

"Is she?"

He nodded, pushed up the bridge of his spectacles. "Make no mistake, I'm proud of her. I think her little documentaries are sweet. That one about the immigrants? I liked that a lot. It's such a great hobby for her."

"I think she considers it more than a hobby," I said.

Paul went on, ignoring me. "Did I say she was complicated?" He smiled. "She's so smart, you know that. She'll probably never tell you she got double eight hundreds on her SATs, but she did, and she chose to go to *Oberlin* because she really wanted the program in the arts.

262

The visual and environmental studies programs here—at Harvard, I mean—just aren't very strong."

This made me like him a little less.

He continued. "Where did you say you went to college? Tufts, right?"

"That's right."

"I was thinking Tufts. What a relief."

I hadn't said anything about Tufts University to Paul or anyone else. It appeared on the phony LinkedIn page for Nick Brown. So he had obviously Googled me.

"I've got friends in the comp lit department there."

"I was an econ major," I said.

"Of course you were. Sukie's very much her own person, though I think she's still figuring out who that person is. And I for one am eager to *meet* that person." He chuckled to himself. "She was so close to my father when she was a child. He was so proud of her then. He never missed one of her piano recitals."

"Nice."

"I gotta say, he never went to any of my debate-team tournaments, but he always made it to her piano recitals, and Father hates music."

"He must be proud of what she's accomplished."

"He couldn't be less interested. He finds her documentaries tedious, which really isn't fair."

"So that's a big change in their relationship."

"Something happened between them. I think they both disappointed each other in some way, but was there a moment? I don't remember."

"Huh."

"She's really Conrad's daughter. There's more Conrad in her than in any of the rest of us. On some level I've always felt they were two birds of a feather. The ones most alike."

The kettle whistled in the kitchen. He got up and excused himself.

He came back a couple of minutes later with two mugs, with teabag strings hanging over the lip of each. He set them down on the table next to me. "So, I don't know," he said. "If something happened. This is not someone who lets go of things easily."

"You mean Sukie?"

He nodded. "Or Father. Me, insults are like water off a duck's back. I don't remember insults, and I don't scar. Whereas you have Sukie, who remembers everything. She really does have an amazing memory. And she's a super-talented woman. But then, you know what the great Theodor Adorno said about talent, right?"

So Adorno was a person. "No," I said.

"'Talent is perhaps nothing other than successfully sublimated rage.' Do you take milk in your tea?"

"I'm good, thanks."

"I think that's how he put it. Come, let's Google the exact quote." He got up, waved me to accompany him, and went into the dining room, where all the books and laptops were set up on the table. He tapped a key on the nearest laptop, and the screen came to life. I glanced at it quickly and casually. It was dense with numbers, pulsing with charts and data. I realized I was looking at a stock trading screen. "Oh, that's IEX," he said. "Doesn't have the high exchange fees that the New York Stock Exchange does."

"Are you a trader?"

"I do a little forex trading, here and there." He tapped the keyboard, and Google appeared. He tapped some more, and now we were on some website dedicated to this Adorno guy. "Yep, I got it right," he said. "What a relief. *Begabung ist vielleicht überhaupt nichts anderes als glücklich sublimierte Wut. . . .*"

I followed him back to the sitting room. He said with a big smile, "Could you tell how relieved Dad was that Sukie brought you? You must have seen it. I gotta tell you, some of the guys she's been with before—I mean, they're all interesting people, but not Conrad's type. You know, sometimes I look at her, and she's got that Samson-in-the-temple look."

"Not sure what you mean."

"Didn't Samson bring down the temple of the Philistines?"

"You may be right."

"Yeah, he was like the first suicide bomber. Brought down the temple and himself with it. Is it hot in here?" He pulled off his cardigan, revealing his polo shirt and both arms covered with scratches.

He must have seen me glancing at his arms, because he said, "Damned rosebushes," gesturing outside.

"You were talking about Sukie," I reminded him, not sure what he was trying to say.

"Sometimes I wonder whether she's in the tent or outside it and about to torch it."

"Torch . . . what?"

"The house of Kimball," he said. "Kimball Pharma. You know, I look at these protesters, and believe me, I have so much sympathy. But with Sukie, it's like, she goes to all of these funerals, and I have to wonder whether she's crossed over. Whether she's playing for the other team. Oh, I don't mean that way. At Oberlin she had girlfriends and boyfriends both, but that's not what I'm talking about. I mean whether she's crossed the line between sympathy and revolt. Do you have a sense of that?"

"She's loyal to the family, if that's what you mean," I said. "But she's under a lot of pressure. You all are. What with the protests and now with Natalya."

He barked a bitter laugh. "Well, I'm not in the swing of things. My own path is very different from the others'. I'm not really a money person. But however uninterested in his world I may be, he's still my father and I'm loyal to him. You know, Father and I have a complicated

265

relationship. I'm sure I'm a disappointment to him. I'm not the Lach-lan Murdoch type he was hoping for." He chuckled.

"He's not really bookish, I take it."

"'Intolerance of ambiguity is the mark of an authoritarian personal-ity,'" he said, pushing again at the bridge of his glasses. "Adorno. I think you could fairly say that about my dad."

"Uh-huh."

"But I don't know, Nick, you're a man of the world—what do *you* make of Natalya?"

"She's smart. A sly one."

"Indeed."

Smiling, I said, "Think she's signed a prenup?"

"You get right to the point. Oh, yes. Oh my, yes. Dad tells me it's bulletproof, and she knows it. I don't know why my siblings are so agitated about her. If they're thinking she'll divorce him and take half the money, no, that's not going to happen."

"How old is he again?"

"Eighty. But longevity runs in the family. My only concern is mental—when he's going to develop signs of dementia. That will hap-pen to him too. Happened to both his parents, they got some kind of dementia in their nineties. By the time they died, they were gaga. Anyway, me, I just want to do my own thing. Publish my book, and publish it well."

"And when he dies?"

"Ah, that's the billion-dollar question, right? Well, you've met Me-gan, right?"

"I have."

"She needs to shoulder Father aside. You know, Megan, to her credit, I think she wants to make something. To help build a future. Again, that's totally not my path, but one thing I'll say about Megan, she is not a hobbyist. Unlike Hayden and Sukie. As they say, she's in it to win it."

"I got that sense too. And your brother?"

"Cameron is the most vulnerable of us all," Paul said. "You know, like Henry James's golden bowl with that invisible crack in it."

"Uh-huh."

"So we'll see. I just hope Megan remembers that old line—when you strike at the king, you must kill him."

# 62

When I left Paul Kimball's house, I decided to leave my car parked on Franklin and walk a couple of blocks up to Mass. Ave. and say hello to Gabe at his record store. The shop would just be opening.

The streets are narrow in this part of Cambridge, and there was no one else walking on the block. I made a right turn and went up Magazine Street, and I heard a car door open behind me somewhere down the street. I clocked it—basic situational awareness—and kept going the two blocks to Mass. Ave.

Paul's scratched arms had made me wonder. Had he really been wrestling with thorny rosebushes at this time of year? But why would he lie about it?

He was not the person I'd thought he was. He might have been uninvolved in running Kimball Pharma, but he sure wasn't uninterested. He wasn't the vague, out-of-it academic he seemed at first. He was sharp, and he was savvy.

But was he also a murderer?

I took a right onto Mass. Ave. The street was bustling with people.

Yet I had the sense that I was being followed. I felt a prickle at the back of my scalp. I passed a Thai restaurant and glanced at the menu, pausing for a moment as if I was considering whether to have lunch there. I looked in the reflection in the plate-glass window and saw a man half a block behind me who looked like a generic businessman. Short dark hair, steel-rimmed glasses, a suit and tie.

He passed me, which made me think I was just being paranoid, but after a few hundred feet, he stopped to look into the window of the Chinese restaurant where I often took Gabe.

He was looking to see whether I was going to turn around. He didn't want to lose me.

My stomach tightened.

The Chinese restaurant was closed. I'd noticed that when I was last in Central Square to see Gabe.

This was the sort of time when you want a cigarette. They're handy for giving you a reason to stop, pause, light up, and look around. But I didn't have any on me, since I don't smoke, and I hadn't come prepared.

I glanced at my watch. As if I was meeting someone. I looked back at the menu. Like I couldn't make up my mind whether to eat here. At this angle I could see enough of the man's face to know it wasn't the guy with the eyebrow. But he was around the same age—late twenties or early thirties—as the one who'd followed me from Westchester to Manhattan. He was evidently fit; he had the look. He was wearing a Bluetooth earpiece like lots of businesspeople do.

Maybe I *was* being paranoid. But I trust my instincts.

I turned and kept on walking past the guy. Past a yoga studio, past another Thai restaurant, past the record store, and I kept going.

The guy was following me.

Massachusetts Avenue is a heavily trafficked street in both directions, and there was no crosswalk nearby. But I stopped and turned and started trying to cross the street, which wasn't easy at that point. There was no stoplight. I wasn't able to look for my follower; I was intent on not getting killed. Finally I made it to the other side of the street, narrowly avoiding being hit by a speeding bicyclist.

This would flush him out. If he crossed the street now, I would know.

I entered the Santander bank on the corner and spotted an ATM.

Not that I needed one, but I wanted an excuse to look, to see how he responded. I inserted a bank card.

He was either window-shopping at the record store or pretending to. Then he turned around and began trying to cross the street, and I knew.

But I didn't want to let him know I knew.

I withdrew a hundred bucks, pocketed it and my card, and went back out onto the street. Kept going north up Mass. Ave. Sure enough, the guy fell in, following me at a distance of around half a block. He was good, but not good enough. He was following too closely.

I came up to a bicycle shop, stopped, and looked in the window.

The guy slowed his pace. Three college-age women in MIT sweat-shirts passed by, then an old guy, then a young guy in an MIT crew jacket, and I cut in to the flow of pedestrian traffic so that I was right in front of him.

I took a right at the next block, a small residential street, well-maintained old wooden triple-deckers on either side of the street, which was deserted. I got about halfway down the block and then began patting down my pants pockets as if I was looking for some-thing.

Abruptly I spun around. As I expected, the man had been follow-ing me closely, and now we faced each other.

"Excuse me," I called out. I drew closer. "Do you have a light?"

He said "Huh?," shook his head, and tried to pass me on my left. As we came abreast, I launched my right fist at the side of his head, targeting his ear with considerable force.

But before my fist reached his ear, his left hand came right up ex-pertly, striking my right wrist at the same time as he stepped back with his right foot. Triangular footwork. The guy was a pro. Trained in the martial arts. He'd hit me hard, and just in the right place.

My right arm went numb.

Shit.

I did the only thing I could: I whipped my left foot behind his left leg, trying to drop him to the ground with a hip throw.

But he was too good. He anticipated that move and lifted his left leg up, grabbed my right sleeve and left lapel, and quickly dropped to the ground, pulling me down with him. His Bluetooth headset clattered to the sidewalk.

I went down and over his prone body, my back smashing into the concrete pavement, and I felt the wind rush out of my lungs. Now he quickly rolled over and got on top of me. His full weight on me, he held me down by the right lapel with his left hand and immediately started raining blows on my head with his right.

I was in pain. I grunted. This was not going to be recoverable.

I groaned with pain, tasted blood.

I was in big trouble. I had only one option: I hugged his left arm to my chest, avoided the next blow by shifting my body to the right, and then hooked my left foot over his right ankle, hugging it to my left buttock.

Then I bridged up sharply using my right leg and levered him over my left shoulder. I rolled with his momentum and landed on top of him. I shot my right hand deep into the gap between the right side of his neck and his collar, then grabbed his left lapel with my left hand.

And I yanked hard.

My heart was hammering.

I had him in a classic cross-collar choke. He flailed and struggled, but I had him.

He lost consciousness in a matter of seconds.

A house door opened nearby and quickly shut again.

I was out of breath and needed to rest, but I couldn't afford the time. I grabbed his weapon from a holster on his left side. A Beretta. A semi-automatic pistol. I ground its muzzle into his left ear, and he came to.

# 63

But barely.

The man was groggy, punchy. He blinked slowly, his eyes searching. His nose was copiously bleeding.

"Name," I said.

He looked at me, and his eyes slowly came into focus. "Fuck you," he groaned. A trace of an accent of some kind?

"You're really going to make me do it?" I said, twisting the muzzle against the skin of his temple. "Because I will if I have to. Who are you working for?"

He stared defiantly.

I searched his pockets for a wallet, but all I found was a car key for a Hertz rental. I stuffed it in my own pocket.

"All right," I said, grinding the muzzle of the gun into his temple again. "I got no choice."

He was just about to say something, I could tell, when I caught a shimmer of movement in my peripheral vision. I looked up and over my shoulder and saw the man with the scarred eyebrow. He was holding a gun, and as I spun around and pointed the weapon, something hit me, hard, on the back of the head.

And everything went dark.

It might have been a minute later, or it could have been longer, but I came to and found both men gone. Fireflies swam in my field of vision. I got to my feet gingerly.

My head throbbed. It felt as fragile as an egg.

I looked around, oriented myself toward Mass. Ave., and began to walk, slowly and carefully. I stuck a hand in my pocket and found that the key to the rental car was still there.

The man with the scarred eyebrow had the opportunity to kill me but chose not to. I wondered why.

Slowly I crossed Mass. Ave., and I could hear a siren nearby. Someone on the block had seen the struggle and called the cops. By the time I reached the other side of the street, a police car was turning down the street where I'd taken down the Bluetooth guy. Since I was right near the record store, I decided to stop in and say hi to Gabe, as planned. I wanted to make sure he was okay.

He wasn't at his usual place at the back of the store. Sitting at the desk, instead of Gabe, was the guy I recognized as the owner, a heavy man with a close-shaved gray beard and thick glasses. "You all right?" he said to me.

"Yeah. I'm looking for Gabe."

"Not here," he said testily.

"Is he on break?"

"Gabe took his last break. He doesn't work here anymore."

"He doesn't? What happened?"

"Who's asking?"

"I'm his uncle."

"Well, Gabe misses too much work, that's the problem with Gabe. He's fired."

"I'm sorry to hear that."

"Look, I have two employees. I can't afford for one of them to keep taking sick days when he's not sick."

"Give him another chance," I said, but I could see he didn't want to argue about it.

On my way out of the store, I took out my phone and hit Gabe's number. It rang and rang. Finally his voicemail came on. I left a message: "Call me."

*Strange*, I thought when I'd hit End.


I retrieved the Defender, which was parked on Franklin Street, and drove over to Gabe's dilapidated house on Putnam. I rang the buzzer and waited.

Nothing.

I rang again, and a voice came over the intercom, faint and crackly.

"What?" Not Gabe.

"Gabe there?" I said.

"No."

"This is his uncle. Any idea where he is?"

A pause. "He left this morning."

"For where?"

"Hell do I know?"

"When?"

"Early. I don't know. He woke me up with all his noise."

"Tell him to call his uncle Nick, please."


Returning to my office, I tried Gabe's mobile phone several more times. No answer. Finally, I left a message sternly instructing him to call me immediately.

And I wondered: Could someone have gotten to Gabe—knowing that he was my vulnerability?

While I waited for him to answer, I called Hertz.

When I finally reached a human being, I said, "I'm calling to extend the rental period on my car. That's plate number—" And I read it off the plastic key fob.

A few seconds later, the woman said, falteringly, "Is this . . . Mr. Malka?"

"Yes, but don't mix up my account with my brother's again."

"Mr. Elad Malka?"

"Yes, it is." An Israeli name, it sounded like. "Where am I supposed to return it again?"

"That would be the Hertz office at Boston's Logan Airport."

The trick is to play the dunce. "Right, of course. I forget which credit card I have on file."

"Yes, sir, it looks like your corporate card, B. P. Strategy. Is that the one you wanted to use?"

"Which one is it, again? Can you repeat the name on the card, please?"

She did.

I wrote it down. *B. P. Strategy.* I had no idea what that was.

The man was named Elad Malka, somehow connected with a firm named B. P. Strategy.


Dorothy emerged from her cubicle after I hung up with Hertz. "My God, what happened to you?"

"How bad do I look?"

"Like someone beat you up."

"He certainly tried."

"More than tried. Looks like somebody took you down."

"Nearly, but not quite." I gave her a quick recap of what had happened.

Her eyes widened, and her mouth came open. "Good Lord, who did it?"

"Someone working for a company called B. P. Strategy. Can you look that up?"

"Be right back."

A few minutes later she stood at the threshold to my office. "B. P. Strategy is the trading name for Black Parallel," she said.

I'd heard of them. Black Parallel was a private Israeli intelligence firm with offices in Tel Aviv, London, and Paris. They liked to employ ex–Mossad agents. The guy, obviously a skilled professional, was likely an operative who'd once worked for Israeli intelligence. No wonder he was such a difficult opponent. Or at least such a persistent one. Also, they did Krav Maga.

"I think the guy who knocked me out might have been Black Parallel too."

"No doubt."

"To keep the first guy from talking to me, I assume. But why were they following me in the first place?"

"Working for Kimball, I bet."

"But for what?"

"Watching to see if you find the Tallinn file."

"Or to find out where I live."

"Could be."

"You haven't heard from Gabe, have you?"

"No," she said. "Why?"

"Because he just got fired from his job at the record store, and his roommate doesn't know where he is."

"What are you thinking?"

"I don't know what to think."

I looked up Black Parallel's website. It described itself as a "select

276

group of elite intelligence community veterans" that provided "tailored solutions" to "complex litigation challenges." This was all fancy language for the fact that they did dirty ops and provided not just muscle but smart muscle. They were spy mercenaries.

Black Parallel had probably put a watch on Paul Kimball's house in Cambridge, expecting me to show up there—as I did. Maybe they were trying to find out where my office was or where I live. Neither location was in any database under my real name.

A few hours later my cell phone rang. Gabe's number. I was relieved and, by now, angry.

"Thanks for bothering to call me back."

"Uncle Nick, what's the problem?"

"What's the *problem*? Where the hell have you been?"

"I can't work at home, so I went to the library."

"Why didn't you return my calls?"

"I had my phone switched off."

"Why haven't you been showing up at work? Do you know you got fired?"

"The guy's a jerk. A real asshole."

"How are you going to pay the rent?"

A pause. "Money's not a problem. I have some. Saved up."

"You just told me you're low on cash."

"I found some. Anyway, I can always get another job."

He was lucky to get a job at the record store. He didn't interview well.

"All right," I said. "I want you to stay in touch. I'm dealing with something sort of . . . volatile right now. I want to make sure you're okay. Check in with me regularly."

"Will do."

My phone beeped, and I saw it was Sukie. "Gotta go," I said, and I picked up Sukie's call.

"Where are you?" I asked.

"Indianapolis. Another funeral."

I had to give her credit. She didn't stop. No matter how busy she was on her documentary, no matter what else was going on, she kept going to funerals of Oxydone victims.

"Nick, I just got a call from Dad's office. His admin, Wendy. Dad is calling an emergency meeting of the family four days from now. At the house."

"Emergency? About what?"

"She said, 'The future of the company.'"

"What does that mean?"

"It means I need you to get that Tallinn file in the next four days. You're back on the clock."

"Why?"

"Because what if he declares bankruptcy? As a tricky way to get out of all the lawsuits, which he knows he's going to lose. Because bankruptcy freezes all lawsuits. And all those families that Kimball Pharma devastated, they get pennies on the dollar. They'll end up with nothing."

I thought of the encrypted folder, which might—or might not— contain the Tallinn file. And which was locked up forever unless we guessed the damned password. That seemed hopeless. Which left me with only the chief medical officer, Dr. Zubiri. He was one of the two people at Kimball who knew about the Tallinn study. Which meant he might well have retained a copy. If I could find a way to either steal it from him or force him to hand it over . . .

I just needed a few minutes alone with the man.

I called and told his administrative assistant that I was from Stat News, an industry news service, compiling a who's who in the pharmaceutical industry, and I needed just ten minutes of the doctor's time, in person. She apologized and said that Dr. Zubiri was "at sales conference."

"He is?" I said, surprised.

"At Kimball, the chief medical officer always goes to sales conferences, to update the sales reps on the products in the pipeline."

"Where is the sales conference taking place this year?"

"Anguilla," she said, adding huffily, "and no outsiders are allowed. I'm very sorry."

I called Sukie back and said, "I need to go to the Kimball sales conference in Anguilla. Which means I need you to go so I can accompany you. Only way I'll be able to get in."

"Why?"

"To talk to the CMO."

"He'll be there?"

"Yes."

"It's in Anguilla?"

"Right."

"Well, I've never gone to a sales conference. They sound awful. But gosh, I suppose I could go, sure, and take you with me."

"Anguilla. Maybe there's a direct flight from New York."

"Doubt it. But that's not an issue."

At first I didn't know what she meant.

# 64

I've flown on private planes before—it's one of the perks of my job—and have learned to act blasé about it. But I don't think I'll ever really get used to it. And it sure beats the slog that's travel for most people. Flying cross-country, for instance, can take more than eight hours, once you figure in the hour at each end you spend waiting at the airport. All that shuffling around, schlepping your bag, waiting in lines, taking off your shoes.

But fly private, you can drive right up to the jet, get on it, and leave minutes later. Flying New York to LA takes more like five or six hours, and it's all luxury. You can lie down and take a nap. The flight attendant will offer you lobster tail and champagne, or whatever you want to drink, while you watch *Trading Places* or whatever. First time I flew on a private jet I was, candidly, gobsmacked.

I drove the Defender to Logan Airport, to the Signature Aviation terminal, where I parked. Conrad Kimball's private plane was waiting, so I got right on it, handing my backpack to the flight attendant. The plane was a Gulfstream G550, which is a terrific aircraft. This one was kitted out with big comfortable-looking vanilla leather seats and walnut or mahogany paneling. You could stand up properly, which you can't in, say, the Citation.

I found Sukie sitting in a seat in the back of the plane, headphones on, working at a laptop. I gave her a kiss. Things felt different between us now, but confusing. She had originally been a client, then a lover; what was she now?

She was wearing a battered-looking pair of jeans that probably cost five hundred dollars, a gray-and-white T-shirt that looked vintage, a black blazer, and white sandals. No logos, no Gucci, no Fendi. Nothing that screamed new money. She was artsy. It worked.

When she saw me, her eyes widened and she slid off her headphones. "What the hell happened to you?"

I didn't want to scare her unnecessarily. "Cut myself shaving," I said.

"What really happened?"

"It looks a lot worse than it is." I'd put a small bandage over the cut in my cheek, but the whole right side of my face looked banged up, abraded from my hitting the sidewalk, bruised from being hit by the Black Parallel guy. It was hard to disguise.

"You're not going to tell me what happened."

"I was followed in Cambridge, got into a tussle, and got hit in the head. It could have been a lot worse."

She listened with her mouth slightly agape. "You could have gotten killed."

"I don't think that was their intention."

"Oh, *that's* a relief."

I changed the subject. "What's Anguilla like?"

"Never been there?"

"Never."

"Small island. Beautiful and unspoiled. Not too built up. But hard to get there."

"Maybe that's why it's unspoiled."

"To get to it, most people have to fly to St. Maarten and then catch a boat or a plane to Anguilla. Always a bit of hassle. Unless you have the use of your father's plane. We're going to fly directly in to the

281

Anguilla airport." The flight attendant handed Sukie a pink frozen drink. "She makes the best strawberry daiquiris. Want one?"

I ordered a Scotch on the rocks. I normally don't like to drink when I'm at work, but I figured this was a legitimate exception. She asked me what kind I wanted and reeled off a long list. I chose a Talisker 18.

After the flight attendant left us, I said, "Is this Kimball Pharma's plane?"

"This is Dad's. He took the BBJ—the Boeing Business Jet—to Anguilla with his top leadership team. He prefers the 737."

The flight attendant came back a minute later with my drink and a couple of plates of shrimp and lobster tail. I had a feeling there'd be lobster tail.

She was, by the way, extremely attractive and probably had an IQ of 150, because it's not an easy job being a flight attendant on a private plane. You're in charge of a million things at once—preparing the perfect cocktail, handling the food, making sure a car is waiting for your passenger at your destination, handling passports and customs and immigration, and taking care of the passenger who's vomiting. They're often recent college grads looking for some fun for a few years. I'm not sure how fun it is.

I leaned back and said, "I call this living."

"Yeah," Sukie said. "And thousands would call it dying. All this over-the-top luxury"—she waved her hands around, indicating the plane, the lobster tail, the whole thing—"to be honest, it's obscene."

"Harsh," I said.

The flight attendant was back. "Excuse me, sir, has the gentleman ever flown in a Gulfstream 550 before?"

I said no.

She launched into the safety briefing, pointing out the exits and the life vests, and Sukie put her headphones back on and ignored her.

When the flight attendant finished, she returned to the front of the plane and pulled a curtain, so we had privacy.

Sukie removed her headphones. I said, "Editing?"

She shook her head, turned her laptop around so I could see the screen: ten or twelve video windows. "No. It's the video feed from the security system at my town house in New York. I just want to know everything's okay while I'm gone. I need the peace of mind." It looked a lot like Paul Kimball's setup.

"Protesters still there?"

She shook her head. "They've been coming by in the late afternoon or early evening, five or six."

"I assume the Molotov cocktail guy never returned, right?"

"So far."

"Anyone try to break into the house? Any more violence?"

She shook her head. "Not yet. Did you ever figure out who put the GPS tracker on Natalya's Bentley?"

"Not yet."

"My father, I bet. Who's more suspicious than him?"

"I don't know who put it there," I said. It had been attached to the Bentley chassis in a place where you wouldn't put it if you had the time and opportunity to do it right. It was as if somebody came by, ducked down, and slapped the thing on quickly. If Conrad wanted his wife's car followed, he could simply ask Fritz, who'd have it done overnight, and done right.

So who could have slapped the thing into place? And using an *Israeli* device?

"Well, I think it was probably Conrad," she said, "and it tells me that he doesn't trust Natalya any more than the rest of us do. At least, that's what I want to think."

"Where on Anguilla is the sales conference taking place?"

"They're taking over a luxury resort." She told me the name.

283

"Am I cleared to be there?"

"You're my escort, so yeah."

"Didn't your dad wonder why you wanted to go to your first company sales conference?"

"I'm sure he suspects the worst. That I'm going to film it covertly, use it in a documentary. But he would never say no to me."

"Do you know Dr. Zubiri?"

"I've met him. But I don't really have a relationship to him. You're on your own there."

"I'll figure out a way. Will Megan be there?"

"Definitely."

"Then I want to find an excuse to talk with her too. What about Cameron?"

"Are you kidding? Hell no."

"How often do you see him?"

"Not very often. I'm afraid I'm just a little too mainstream for him. We all are."

"You make edgy documentaries, for God's sake."

"That no one sees. I'm unimportant in Cameron's eyes. I mean, don't get me wrong, he's perfectly nice to me."

"He seems to be a happy fuck-up, is that right?"

"He's more complicated than that. He's got a vein of anger in him. When he was in eleventh grade at Choate, he was institutionalized."

"Why?"

"For almost burning down the main school building. Hill House. He was kind of a fire bug."

"Are we talking a burning cigarette in a trash can? An accident?"

"Oh, no. He was trying to get out of final exams, so he made a trash-can fire with newspapers in the basement right underneath the dean's office. But it got out of control, and the Wallingford fire department had to be called. Extensive damages. Which Dad had to pay for. The fifth-form dean called Dad and told him to come that very night and pick up his son, because he was no longer welcome on campus."

"Doesn't sound very bright."

"He's plenty bright. Just crazy. When he gets drunk, which is often, he does crazy things. This was right after Dad announced he was divorcing Karen, his second wife. Cam couldn't concentrate at school, but more important, I think he was really angry. He knew Dad was playing around on our stepmother. On some level he was punishing Dad. He knew he'd be thrown out of school and that would embarrass Dad."

"Jesus. So he's a piece of work, huh?"

"It's more complicated than that. He always wanted to be his own person, to do something, but he just cares too much about what the family thinks of him. And Dad has always taken advantage of his vulnerability. Because Dad needs to dominate people. It makes him a man."

I flashed on Cameron at his father's birthday dinner, totally drunk. *He does crazy things.*

"So Conrad pretty much controls him," I said.

"Once, when Cam was really stoned, or maybe he was on Ecstasy, I don't know, he confided in me that Dad was holding something over his head. Something bad. Some piece of evidence Dad kept in his private files."

I remembered at once the folder Maggie had found in Conrad's safe. "Blackmail," I said.

She nodded.

"What do you think it was? What was the 'something bad'?"

"He killed a girl."

"Really."

"Right after Mom's funeral he got blind drunk and went out driving somewhere, and he hit and accidentally killed a teenage girl walking along the side of the road. Dad managed to pay off the right people. But he kept the file, the original police report and the related files."

"For what?"

"Keep him in line. There's a morality clause in the family trust. Anyone can be disqualified, excluded from voting, on the grounds of criminality. Dad's always threatening to pull out his files and get Cam disqualified if he doesn't stay in line. And he chafes at that, naturally. He holds on to this anger at Dad—he blames Dad for our mother's dying of cancer."

"Well, I need an excuse to talk to him."

"Next time I'll see him is at the family meeting, on Saturday. It's funny, he has an image of me in his head from childhood. That'll never change. Middle children always get overlooked or ignored. Or underestimated."

"Is that why you make documentaries?"

"I make documentaries because I have something to say."

"About white-collar criminals like my dad?"

She smiled.

"I saw *Gang Boss* on Netflix," I said. "Thought it was excellent." It was about two very different kinds of criminals. One was a man named Monster, the boss of a Los Angeles gang who did four years in Pelican Bay. Monster once stomped an older black man into extreme disfigurement. The other was Jeffrey Skilling, formerly the president of Enron, who was sentenced to twenty-four years but ended up serving only eleven. *Gang Boss* was about how similar the two really were. Gangbangers were basically no different from evil white-collar criminals who steal people's pensions and fire workers and ruin countless lives. If you're going to have sympathy for either of them, the documentary seemed to be saying, have sympathy for Monster. He had fewer choices in life. An interesting point, I thought. "I liked the look of it too," I added.

"Thanks. You know I shoot my own film, right?"

I'd missed that. Apparently that's pretty unusual. "I didn't."

"Yeah, in the late nineties I was a freelance assistant cameraperson. At a time when there were no female camerapeople at all."

"What do you shoot with?"

"You know cameras?"

"No."

"I mostly use the Sony FS7 and Zeiss Super Speed prime lenses."

"Well, you really captured the texture of prison. The feel of it. The squalor."

"You've been?"

"Only on visits."

"Well, that doc entailed spending a lot of time in maximum-security prisons talking to criminals and getting them to ignore the fact that there's a big camera pointed in their face."

"Huh." I paused for a moment. "So do you consider your father a criminal?"

She compressed her lips, nodded slowly. "He's not a good man," she said.

"Well, we have that in common," I said.

She hugged herself, a strange self-consoling gesture. There was something lovely about the woman, but at the same time, broken. She looked small and fragile, almost birdlike.

"But he's supposed to be a marketing genius," I said. "Right?"

"'Genius.'" She laughed. "He used to fly doctors to bogus 'seminars,' like golf trips to Pebble Beach. He flew doctors to parties in Cancun. And whenever he encountered holdouts—doctors who wouldn't prescribe Oxydone because they were worried about what it would do to people—he'd dangle the Kimball speaker's bureau in front of them. Which meant the doctor just had to give a fifteen-minute talk at dinner and he'd get a thousand bucks. Even if no one showed up. That's called graft. Kickbacks."

"That's a kind of genius."

"A twisted kind, yeah. But do you know what type of marketing my father really excels at? Marketing the Kimball name. Making it seem like we're all great philanthropists, lovers of truth and beauty. Which he does by spreading around money. Getting the Kimball name etched in stone. Notice it's mostly art museums and universities and hospitals that he gives to? That's because those places elevate us. Ennoble us."

The list of places to which the Conrad Kimball Foundation gave millions of dollars was impressive. The Victoria and Albert Museum, the Smithsonian, the Guggenheim, the Louvre. Mount Sinai Hospital in New York, Mass General in Boston. The Central Park Conservancy. There was the Kimball Library at Oxford, even the Kimball Escalator at the Tate Modern. "Come on," I said, thinking of my father. "Dirty money makes the art world go round. MoMA, the Met, Lincoln Center—they were all founded with dirty money. Rockefeller and Carnegie were robber barons. Your dad's just following a well-worn path."

"You know what I find fascinating? He's given hundreds of millions of dollars to art museums, claims to be a big lover of the arts, and in reality he has no interest in my documentaries."

I nodded. "That reminds me. I spent a little time with your older brother, Paul. Not what I expected." I hesitated for a moment. "I see what you mean about him not taking you seriously."

"Right? Paul was always a huge disappointment to me. You expect your older brother to be sort of nurturing, guiding you along—big brother, you know? Even being my half brother. But Paul was none of those things. He was absent. Went his own way. Lives in his own bizarro world."

"But could he have killed Maggie Benson? Does he have it in him?"

"I don't honestly know."

"He doesn't appear to be interested in Kimball Pharma. Like you."

"Like *me*? Oh, don't underestimate me, Nick. I get enough of that from my family. They dismiss me as some woolly-headed artist when the truth is, I know more about market share and prescription data and what debt load we're carrying than Megan does, I'll bet. We all get monthly board packets with the company's financials, and believe me, I always read all the materials. I know what the gross revenues are in South America to the dollar."

"Why?"

A smile. "You have to know your enemy."

"So why not go to sales conferences?"

"Unnecessary. A waste of time."

I hoped she was wrong.

She reclined her seat and a few minutes later drifted into a nap, while I worked on my laptop. The Wi-Fi was nice and fast. I looked up titles of books by Neil deGrasse Tyson, sent a list to Dorothy to try as many possible passwords on the encrypted folder. I called her to check in.

Then my phone rang. It was Gabe Heller's mom, Lauren, in DC.

"Have you talked to Gabe recently?" she asked.

"Yesterday. Why?"

"Because I got a statement addressed to him from Schwab, the discount stockbrokers? So naturally I opened it, and I almost freaked out. What the hell is he doing with an account worth four point six million dollars?"

"There it is," I said. "That's what's been going on."

"What do you mean?"

"Take a picture of that Schwab statement and email it to me, okay?" I hung up and explained no further, because I wanted to talk to Gabe right away.

I didn't even look at my watch. I called Gabe, got no response, and texted him, *Call me NOW.*

This time he called me right back.

"I want to know what stock tips my father has been giving you," I said.

There was a long, long pause.

Finally, he said, "Who told you?"

I explained about how his mother had opened his brokerage statement.

He was clearly not ready for this conversation. He hesitated and stumbled and eventually confessed that Victor had told him how to open an account with a stockbroker, and then gave him information on how to access an offshore account of his based in the Channel Islands that was worth half a million dollars.

Gabe had wired that half million to Schwab and bought what were called "put" options on the stock of a big telecom company that had been in the news a lot recently because of some accounting scandal. Apparently Victor had given Gabe a lesson on how to do this. Gabe is a quick study. When the public announcement came that the big telecom company's earnings were going to fall short, the stock dropped and Gabe Heller had netted $4.6 million.

I didn't have to ask Gabe where Victor got his inside information. I remembered reading that one of the white-collar criminals just confined to the same prison as Victor Heller was the CFO of that same telecom company.

I had no doubt that the two quickly became friends.

"I don't get what you're so upset about," Gabe said.

"Are you crazy?" I said. "That's insider trading."

"But . . . I'm not an insider!"

"You're a secondhand tippee, and the Supreme Court says that counts as insider trading. You could get caught, and you're old enough to go to prison like your dad."

"Grandpa said there was nothing illegal about it!"

"Victor has, shall we say, a loose understanding of the law. Do you know what insider trading is?"

"Not really."

I explained to him that buying stocks or even options on stocks with inside information was cheating and it was wrong. Also illegal. I told him about how the SEC watched for sneaky transactions like this. He could go to prison for twenty years. Victor was already there. To him, it would make no difference.

"But . . . But I'm going to buy Nana a house. She's always saying her condo is too small. And how about if I donate some of it to a non-profit that fights opioid addiction? I'm sure there's a bunch of those."

"Don't spend any of it," I said. "We have to figure out what to do about this. I don't want you going to prison like your father and your grandfather."

Gabe was silent for a long time. "You're scaring me, Uncle Nick."

"Maybe you should be a little scared," I said.


Three hours passed quickly, and we landed in Anguilla. As soon as we had landed, the flight attendant gathered our passports.

I did not have a US passport in the name of Nicholas Brown, so I gave her my real one. I had no choice. This was an international flight, and passports were required. I hadn't planned on traveling overseas under this identity, and I didn't have time to acquire a forged passport.

Would the Anguillan authorities compare the flight manifest with the passports they were given? Possibly; I didn't know how closely they looked. It's an island paradise; they're not trying to keep people out.

But would the *flight attendant* notice the discrepancy? For sure. Would she tell anyone? That I didn't know.

It worried me.

As it turned out, I was right to worry.

# 65

While we were waiting to disembark, I asked the flight attendant to come over.

"I'm working for Mr. Kimball," I said. "Doing some investigation on his behalf within the company. Mr. Kimball and I would appreciate it if you would keep my real name confidential."

"Of course, sir," the flight attendant said.

"What's your name?"

"Zoe Garcia."

"Zoe, I'm Nick. Very nice to meet you."

It was in the high eighties but dry when we emerged from the plane. We stepped right into a black SUV whose interior was air-conditioned to frigid. The driver had greeted Sukie by name, as "Ms. Kimball." Our bags were transferred from the plane to the back of the SUV without our having to retrieve them.

It was a short drive to the resort, which was ridiculously beautiful. The water was turquoise, the sand was white, the air was clear. There was steel-pan music playing. It was like being in a TV commercial.

The resort was modern and newly renovated, after the big hurricane of a few years ago, with bleached blond-wood floors and large glass windows. The check-in desk had been carved from knotty pieces of petrified wood. Outside was blond stone and white umbrellas and perfectly straight rows of palm trees.

Sukie checked us in and requested a king-size bed. I was her guest.

I didn't want to check in, in case they insisted on my passport and I'd have to give them the wrong name. A pretty young woman who was probably Anguillan—hair back in neat dreadlocks, a bright smile, an orange-sherbet blouse—greeted us and handed us a couple of key cards.

The bellboy escorted us to a suite on the third floor of the main resort building. All of the Kimball Pharma group was staying in the main hotel building, not in the separate bungalows some guests stayed in.

Awaiting us was a bottle of champagne on ice and a fruit basket. It was an endless suite, with great views of the ocean, which sparkled before us. From the windows, you could see no other part of the hotel, just beach and sea. The four-poster bed, with white linens and coverlet, looked out on the ocean through a huge floor-to-ceiling window.

Sukie had opened the champagne and offered me a flute. I decided to pass. I didn't have a lot of time, and I wasn't feeling relaxed. Plus I'd had that Scotch on the plane.

"You Kimballs live well," I said. "I guess you get used to it. Not sure I would."

"Yeah, well, it's blood money," she said. She poured herself a flute but didn't pick it up to drink. "I remember when I was filming in Haiti once, not long after that terrible earthquake, and this dreadful cholera epidemic had broken out? This one little girl—I had filmed her with her mother a week earlier, and her mother had died and the girl was in the hospital, terribly weak. And I went to visit her and she looked awful, her lips cracked and her eyes sunken, and she whispered to me, 'Can I have some water?' And of course I ran to the bathroom and filled up several glasses of water and gave them to her, and she gulped them all down, she was so thirsty.

"I knew the only way to fight cholera was to get as many people as possible clean, filtered drinking water. They needed cholera treatment centers. A two-hundred-bed center cost a million dollars for just three months. I donated three centers and enough money to keep them going for a couple of years. And when I went back to Haiti a couple weeks later, to see what was going on, I asked to see that little girl." Sukie looked at the ocean for a long time, then she turned back to me. "And she'd died, of course.

"And I realized that even if I had all the money in the world, there's only so much you can do. The need is so immense. And that was only one small part of one country at one particular moment in time."

Our doorbell rang. I assumed it was another gift from the hotel, but through the peephole I saw it was Megan Kimball.

I opened the door.

"Hello," she said to me hastily as she came into the suite, uninvited. "Sukie?" she called out.

Sukie emerged from the bedroom. "Right here," she said.

"I had no idea you were coming. I was only just told."

"I didn't need an engraved invitation, did I?" Sukie said. "I am an equal stakeholder, after all."

"Any reason you didn't tell me?"

"Last-minute decision," Sukie said. "Nick's never been to Anguilla."

"Oh, so you're here on vacation, right? Well, just to be clear, you don't have a role here."

"Nick may go to a few presentations."

Megan shook her head. "I heard from Stephanie that you've been requesting in-depth financial statements on the subsidiaries. Now you're at sales conference for the first time in your life. Why are you suddenly taking an interest in the company?"

"Because we're losing money," Sukie said. She'd clearly prepared an answer. "Maybe I don't have confidence in the leadership."

"This is my terrain, and you know it. I have worked my ass off trying to keep this company on track. Bring it into the twenty-first century. And protect against all the lawsuits at the same time. Meanwhile, you're making your silly documentaries."

"Have you ever seen a documentary I've made?"

"Sukie, grow up. Some of us have been pretty damned busy over the last decade. For me, Kimball Pharma is a challenge. It's hard work. For you it's . . . a piggybank, for your little projects."

Sukie flushed, looking like she'd just been slapped. "I'm here for support," she said.

"Bullshit," Megan said. "You're here to carve out a bigger share. You think you can suddenly helicopter yourself into the C-suite—well, baby, that ain't happening. What do you even know about this company? Do you actually care about it? While you're off making your nature documentaries?"

"White-collar crime isn't *nature*," Sukie snapped.

"Sorry, but I haven't had large swatches of free time to watch your little stories. I'm too concerned with saving what Dad built. We're facing the biggest crisis we've ever gone through, and the last thing we need is someone like you swanning in from your flower-child fields of heather. You're suddenly taking an interest?" She shook her head. "Sorry, but I'm not buying it. You think you can parachute in and Dad's going to make you executive chairman of the company? That's *not* going to happen."

Then she looked at me as if she'd forgotten I was standing there, and she stormed out of the suite.

Sukie stared with wide eyes and a nervous grin.

"Excuse me," I said. I followed Megan out and caught up with her by the elevator bank.

"I'm sorry," she said huffily, "but I'm on my way to a drink."

"I could use one myself. Mind if I join you?"

She gave me a hard look, and finally she shrugged.

# 66

I had an instinct about Megan. Everyone else thought she was this hard-shelled corporate storm trooper. But I knew better. All the vilification and all the threats had to take a toll, even on her.

At the tiki-themed bar she ordered a Cosmo and I ordered a Buffalo Trace. The bar was empty—it was early—and the drinks arrived quickly.

I took a sip of the bourbon and said, "So I'm just a management consultant, but the way you restructured the Czech operation? Hats off."

She turned to me, surprised, pleased. "I got a *hell* of a lot of push-back on that," she said, and swigged some more of her Cosmo.

I said, "It's like, you grab the wheel, you re-steer the boat, and everyone's howling, *You're off course, you're off course, you're off course!* And all you can say is, Did you notice I just steered us around a goddamned iceberg? You're *welcome*."

Megan snorted delightedly. "You're welcome, *assholes*," she added, setting down her drink a little harder than she probably meant to. "How long have you and Sukie been seeing each other?"

"Just a few weeks."

"Are you the reason she's been taking a sudden interest in the company?"

"Not at all."

"Because you McKinsey types—you have a tendency to go from

the hired hand to the boss. One day you're a consultant, the next day you're *hiring* consultants."

"Nah, I'm here strictly for support. You heard about how she was attacked at her house in the city, right?"

"Of course. We all heard."

"After what happened in Katonah, you have to take all these threats seriously. Margret Benson was a private investigator, I understand." She knew I knew.

"She was."

"And you hired her?"

She looked at me sharply, nodded.

"Where'd you find her?"

"She did some work for a friend. She came highly recommended."

"Did she get what you wanted her to get?"

She drew herself up. "I'm sorry, that's confidential." She poked her index finger in the air so the waitress would know she wanted another round.

I thought of Maggie's handwritten notes. The kind of information Megan had hired her to look for. "You must know your father well enough to know what he's about to do, right?"

"At the family meeting, you mean?"

I nodded. "He's going to declare bankruptcy, isn't he? Isn't the company in terrible financial shape?"

"Ha! Are you kidding?"

"Huh? Kimball Pharma has been losing money for years, hasn't it?"

She chortled silently. She looked at me, then at her empty Cosmo glass, resentfully. Her next Cosmo, her third, came quickly. She took a big sip and then confided, "My father has been expecting a catastrophe for quite some time. The one thing you can say for him, he's always a step ahead of everyone else."

"A catastrophe?"

"All these lawsuits over Oxydone. He knew the day of reckoning was bound to come sooner or later." She lowered her voice, stared at her glass. She sounded almost proud. "So he's been sweeping cash aside. Squirreling it away. Into shell companies offshore. And categorizing all that cash as investments in research. So Kimball Pharma has been investing all of its profits into what we're calling research. He started doing this eleven years ago."

"Clever," I said. "So when Kimball is forced to make huge legal settlements, it'll have no assets to pay out. That actually works?"

"It's not ethical, but it works. Not that ethics have ever stopped my father before. It's a clever scam."

I tried to probe further, but she got quiet. Gloomy, it seemed.

"What do you think happened to Maggie?" I said softly.

She tipped the nearly empty Cosmo glass to her lips and drained it. "Happened to her?" she murmured. "Got too close to the family. Too close to something she wasn't s'pposed to know."

"So you think she was murdered?"

She looked at me for a long time, then looked away. "Don't you think so?" she said.

# 67

When I got back to our suite, I found Sukie on her computer doing edits on her film remotely, exchanging text messages with her editor. She looked up and said, "Did she confess?"

She was being arch, but I decided to take her seriously. "So do you think she did it?"

"What do *you* think?"

I'd considered it. I answered her evasive question with my own question. "Would Maggie have had a reason to meet with Megan outside the house that night?"

"If Megan asked her to, sure. To discuss the job she'd hired her to do. They might not want to talk about it inside the house."

"And let's say Megan caught her by surprise back there—a sudden shove from behind at the right place in the woods is all it would take. She's a strong woman."

"But why would she do it?"

"I don't know. Unless Maggie turned up something she shouldn't have and told her about it."

She shook her head. "I don't see it."

I nodded slowly. When a private investigator works for an attorney, he or she is bound by confidentiality to the client. It's like an extension of attorney-client privilege. Under some state laws, there are penalties for divulging information. She'd have every reason to observe confidentiality.

But say Maggie found the Tallinn file, full of evidence that the company knew how dangerous its flagship drug was and buried the warnings. I could see her refusing to observe client secrecy like she was supposed to. You keep your client's secrets, yes—but she'd be outraged. Especially if Megan planned to keep the truth hidden. She'd do what she felt was the right thing, even if it caused her to lose a client and a payment. That was just who she was.

Sukie interrupted my thoughts. "You know, talking about the woods behind the house reminds me of something. I remember when I was maybe eleven or twelve, and there was a huge herd of deer, somewhere toward the back of the paddocks in Katonah. I ran at them, and of course, they scattered. As I knew they would. But there you had a couple thousand pounds of muscle, hoofs, and horns. And I was this shrimpy little thing. They could have charged me and trampled me to death."

"Good point."

"Well, my point is, there was some unwritten rule of nature saying which one of us was a danger to which. As long as everyone obeyed the rule, things would go on the way they always did. It's like with my father. He's a danger to us. He says what goes. He charges, we scatter. But maybe one day the script changes. We never know how much power we have until we use it. Who's the dangerous one? Who's the one in danger? It's like a belief system. And beliefs can change."

I nodded, smiled.

"What do you say we head out to the sales conference?" I said. "Establish our cover?"

She closed her laptop and got up to change. Since I didn't have to change, I worked on locating Dr. Zubiri.

According to the program we'd been given at check-in, we'd missed his presentation. That had been the day before. But I was certain he hadn't left. He'd want to enjoy a few days of ultra-luxury in the Caribbean. Anyone would.

The pre-dinner session was being held in an outdoor theater, open to the elements. It had squarish pillars and a swooping stone roof. This was not a thatched-roof kind of place. The theater's sunken rows of seats were nearly filled, the theater dark. We found a couple of seats at the back.

A rap video was playing on a giant movie screen, and I'd never seen anything like it. A giant Oxydone inhaler with purple arms and legs was dancing with a pair of white guys in black hoodies and gold chains and dark sunglasses who were making elaborate gang signs. The giant inhaler was rapping about how he "got a lotta doctors on speed dial" and something about "the last mile" and "clinical trial." We watched the screen, mesmerized.

When it ended, there was raucous cheering, and out of the darkness a white beam cut a small round spot. Over the loudspeaker a deep male radio announcer's voice said, "Ladies and gentlemen, we have with us this evening a special surprise guest." The spotlight moved up the dark curtains and stopped, and then the white circle of light gradually grew bigger and the curtains pulled back to reveal the old man himself, Conrad Kimball, standing there in his customary navy suit over black collared shirt. It was a look I'd seen in all of his publicity photos.

*"Doctor Conrad Kimball!"*

The extraordinary thing was how Kimball looked twenty or thirty years younger. The white hair cut short, the pale gray eyes, the suntan, or maybe it was makeup: he looked vigorous and healthy, a man in his prime, a man of power and prowess.

He smiled broadly. "My friends!" he said.

The crowd got to its feet, applauding their chairman, cheering the unexpected guest, the boss.

The spotlight drew in closer and then softened. "My fellow

warriors!" He extended his arms like a benediction. "With all the lies out there about Oxydone, all the propaganda, all the crazy protests and the vilification, all the fake news—I think it's worth stepping back for a moment and remembering what we are doing. What our mission is. And why I built this company."

He shifted his gaze from straight ahead to his left, looking directly at the sales reps seated right in front of him. "Hundreds of millions of people around the globe live with pain every single day. Right now. Pain that's untreated. Pain that's so bad that millions of them can't go to work. Or go to school."

Looking straight ahead now, he said, "I know a man named Jake. Jake has cancer, and he was living in unimaginable agony. Burning, stabbing torment. His life wasn't livable. His marriage had fallen apart, he'd lost his friendships. He told me that it was like being tortured every day, with no means of escape. Tortured! He was on suicide hotlines several times. Because chronic pain drives people to suicide. He saw five practitioners before he finally got help. And then a wise doctor prescribed Oxydone." He paused. "It was a godsend. For Jake, Oxydone was a miracle. *He was given his life back.*" He raised his arms in the benediction pose again.

"Now, has Oxydone been abused in the substance-use community? Undoubtedly. Just like they abused opium a hundred years ago and still do. Just as some people are allergic to penicillin, some have these susceptibilities to opioids. But penicillin has spared multitudes. And so has Oxydone."

He turned to face another segment of the audience. "But that must never stop us from bringing the miracle of pain relief to the lives of millions of sufferers. People like Jake. People with arthritis or migraines, with neuropathic pain or fibromyalgia or back pain or any other chronic discomfort." He bowed his head, and after a beat, he looked up. "What I want you all to remember is that we're not the villains here. *We're the ones who treat the pain.* We're the ones who do so much to alleviate suffering around the world.

"This medicine that's derived from poppies, it's a gift from nature. A gift that we bestow upon the hundreds of millions of afflicted people who need it so desperately. Ultimately, that is what we are giving the world. A gift."

The spotlight faded, and the house lights came up, and everyone had gotten to their feet to cheer the old man.

"My friends," he said over their cheers, "let's go out there and *save lives.*"

I applauded, along with everyone else, and meanwhile I was thinking. The fact that Conrad Kimball was here had suddenly changed everything.

# 68

By the time the session had broken for dinner, I had located Dr. Zubiri. He was a tall, spindly man of around sixty, with silver hair and wire-framed glasses with thick lenses. He was wearing an aquamarine polo shirt and neatly pressed chinos, and he was seated up front, in what I realized was the VIP section.

"Excuse me, Dr. Zubiri?" I said.

"Yes?"

"A moment?"

Wary. "What's this about?"

I lowered my voice. "It's about the lovely country of Estonia and its beautiful capital, Tallinn."

He blinked a few times. "Do I know you?"

"No, but you might want to. Why don't we talk in private?" I pointed to an unoccupied spot off the path by the amphitheater wall.

"Who are you?"

"Just a guy who's doing some investigation into Oxydone."

"Get the hell out of here. I don't have to talk to you!"

"You're right, you don't have to talk to me," I said. "You don't have to. You *want* to. You want to talk to me the way a drowning man wants a life preserver. Look, you want me to walk away from you right now, I'm gone. And then you're going to have fifteen to twenty years in federal to think about whether you made the right call. Because you're the one person the family is going to hang out to dry."

"The—family?"

"The Kimballs. Let me assure you of one thing: the family will look after its own. And that means that you, my friend, are going down."

"If you're some kind of activist shareholder or something, you can forget it. I am absolutely loyal to this company."

"Oh, I respect your loyalty. And they're *banking* on it. You are taking the fall for the Tallinn study."

Zubiri's expression was frozen, but I could see the facial muscles twitching, a blood vessel pulsing. He said nothing.

I went on. "Is it too late for you? I'm not sure. There might be a play."

"What exactly do you want from me?" he said feebly.

# 69

I want the Tallinn study," I said.

"I don't— That was on a portal that's been shut down. I never kept a copy. I wasn't allowed to."

I was afraid he'd say that. Another strikeout.

But I wasn't done with him. "One more thing," I said.


A quick stroll through the hotel confirmed that Conrad Kimball was staying, of course, in the presidential suite, on the third floor. Room 322. Which was on the other side of the building from the suite Sukie and I were in. I walked along the third-floor corridors, noted the room numbers on either side of the presidential suite, outside of which a security guard was sitting, even when the old man wasn't there. In short order I had a fairly good mental map of the main resort building.

I glanced at my watch. I had to keep track of time, because I didn't have much of it. I had until Conrad Kimball finished his dinner. Which could be forty-five minutes, or it could be longer. Or it could be less.

Back in Sukie's suite, I called room service.

"Yes Mr.—Kimball?"

"I'm doing a surprise birthday celebration for Megan Kimball. I'm going to want a bottle of Dom Pérignon, if you have it, delivered to her room—actually, I forgot her room number, I believe it was room three oh—"

"Ms. Megan is in room two-twenty," the woman said.

"Two-twenty, right. One bottle of Dom Pérignon to— No, actually, you know what, deliver it to my room and we'll bring it to her directly. Yeah, let's do that. Thank you."

Room 220 was, unfortunately, on the floor below the presidential suite. But I could work with that. It was directly below, which was useful. Now all I needed was a key to 220. I changed into a pair of jeans and sneakers, a small backpack slung over my shoulder, and went down to the front desk, where I noticed with relief that the shift had changed. The woman with the dreadlocks and the orange-sherbet blouse from this afternoon was gone. In her place was another woman, chubby with a spray of freckles across her dark face.

"Excuse me," I said. "I'm such an idiot, but I left my key in my room. It's under my wife's name, Megan Kimball in Room 220?"

"Yes, sir," she said. "Could I bother you for a driver's license?"

I patted the side pockets of my jeans. Shook my head.

She smiled. "No worries."

She tapped at her keyboard and put a plastic blank into the machine, then handed it to me.

"Thank you," I said.

I knew that Megan Kimball was at dinner in the restaurant, sitting at her father's table. That meant there was no one in her room. I took the elevator to the second floor and found 220. Stood for a moment outside the door, listening. Then I tapped my key card against the sensor. The green light clicked on, and I pushed open the door.

Room 220 was a suite, the same size as Sukie's. I knew its layout already. I noted the sliding glass doors to the balcony off the living room. The floor-length drapes were half drawn. A crescent moon suspended in the dark sky shone watery light into the room.

307

And then I heard an electronic beep and the room door coming open.

I slipped behind the drapes and tucked my body in against the glass of the window. Was it housekeeping, with the evening turndown service? At night they would probably draw the drapes all the way. I stood there breathing silently and then heard a woman's voice saying, "Lactaid, Lactaid, Lactaid."

It was Megan. She'd forgotten something.

I waited. If she decided to pull open the drapes, or close them, I'd be caught. It would not be easy for me to explain what I was doing in her room. Hiding behind the drapery.

About another minute went by, and then I heard the door shut again. She had probably just left, though I couldn't be sure. I waited for another full minute and then emerged from behind the drapes.

She wasn't there.

I'd left the black backpack on the floor a few feet away. Had she come into the living room she would surely have noticed it.

I grabbed the backpack, slung it over my right shoulder, and returned to the balcony. Slid open the glass doors. The air outside was noticeably warmer than the air-cooled inside. The water was a thousand feet away, down a gentle sandy slope, but at night it seemed closer. A soft breeze was blowing. Then I looked up and saw the balcony of the room directly above: the presidential suite.

Less than ten feet above my head, but more than I could reach, even if I jumped. From the backpack I took out a nylon rappelling rope and all the rest of the equipment: some carabiners, a waist harness, and a titanium overhead anchor, proof tested to twenty-two hundred pounds. I'd set it all up in advance in Sukie's suite. I tossed the anchor up, and on the second try it hooked over the steel railing on the balcony above with a metallic clang.

I waited a moment, just to make sure that sound hadn't been heard within the presidential suite—if anyone was in there, which I doubted. Conrad, I knew, was downstairs in the restaurant.

Sliding the ascender up the rope, I stood up and then moved the second ascender. With two healthy pulls, I was hanging on the rope, dangling up in the air, nearly level with the balcony railing. Now I was looking directly into the presidential suite, into a room with a large table. I grabbed the railing and swung my legs over, landing on the balcony.

As far as I could tell, I hadn't been seen by anyone on the ground. I decided to leave the rope in place. It was risky, but it was my only way out of there. I couldn't leave the presidential suite through its front door, outside of which sat the security guard.

There was a good chance, I knew, that the sliding doors here might be locked. That would have been unfortunate.

I would have had to climb down and abandon the plan.

But they weren't; they slid smoothly open, and I was inside.

# 70

The room was dark and quiet.

I stood listening for a moment. I heard no one in the suite, just the breeze from outside, some distant music from down the beach. The slight hum of the honor-bar refrigerator. I pulled the glass doors closed, and it got even quieter. Most of this room was taken up by a coffin-shaped conference table. Would Conrad sit in here? Or elsewhere in the suite? I had to assume this room was one possibility. I had enough devices.

Walking around the room, I selected the device I wanted to plant on the ceiling above the conference table. It looked like a smoke detector, but it contained a GSM bug. So as soon as it detected sound, it recorded and stored it, compressed it, and then sent it out in a burst every thirty minutes. I climbed onto the conference table, squeezed a little Superglue, and the thing stuck firmly to the ceiling, right above the head of the table. Underneath the table I plugged in a power strip that also contained a GSM bug. The strip looked like it belonged there.

I paused, listened again. Conrad was downstairs at dinner. Was there anyone here? Did he travel alone, or had Natalya accompanied him? What if she was asleep in the master bedroom? Was there security inside the suite as well as out?

I had no idea what to expect: I saw only the deep darkness of a hotel suite. I switched on my little Maglite and ventured farther down the corridor and came upon a living room with a large TV. This looked like a comfortable place to have a conversation. Another spot where Conrad might confer, either on the phone or in person. Here I planted two devices, the fake smoke detector on the ceiling and an electrical plug converter, a white cube, the kind you see in Europe. This too had a SIM card inside, was powered by the electrical current it was connected to, and worked the same way as the fake smoke detector: triggered by ambient sound, it would start recording and would send compressed sound files every half hour. I plugged that in between the lamp plug and the wall outlet. It was unobtrusive and looked like it belonged there, even though the lamp plug, of course, didn't actually need a converter.

When I was finished, I switched off my flashlight, stopped, and listened. I heard a cart pass by in the outside hallway, and I froze.

I waited, listening.

Then a doorbell chimed, a knock at the door and a voice: "Housekeeping!"

She was here for turndown service, which meant turning down the bed linen and preparing the bed, maybe leaving a chocolate on the pillow. I almost called out, "Not now, please," until I realized that the security guard outside the room would take notice that someone was inside a suite that was supposed to be unoccupied. And that would not be good.

But the door she was knocking on was thirty feet from where I was standing, and she was about to open it.

Noiselessly, I raced across the carpet out of the room, down the hall, toward the conference room that opened onto the balcony. I pulled closed the drapes, then slid open the glass doors behind them and slipped out to the balcony, closing the door behind me.

I looked out, looked down and to either side. I didn't see anyone out there. Not yet. Nobody had seen me climbing up the rope from the second floor. Probably no one would see me climb down the same rope. Kimball Pharma had taken over the hotel, and nearly everyone associated with the company was downstairs at dinner.

The problem was that I couldn't leave the ropes and titanium anchor and carabiners in place once I returned to Megan's balcony. If I did, they'd be spotted by hotel security and/or management at some point in the night. In the morning light, for sure. That would raise questions about the security in the presidential suite. It would send up an alarm. And rappelling down, using the rope, necessarily meant leaving the rig in place. So I had to take the rope with me, in the backpack, and climb down some other way.

The ground floor of the hotel had high ceilings, so I estimated the height at three stories to be around forty-five feet. Directly below was hard stone. Would I survive if I jumped? Probably, if I rolled right. But I'd probably also break some bones. Which I preferred not to do.

I unfastened the anchor from the railing and put it with the rope and all the other gear into my backpack. Then, grasping the steel pipe, I swung my legs up and over. Climbing down the railing, my feet dangling, I swung my feet around and then touched down on the steel rail of the floor below. Megan's balcony. I gripped the bottom rung of the third-floor railing as I swung my feet again, torqueing in toward the glass doors, and then I let go, landed on the second-floor balcony.

The drapes were drawn—I'd drawn them myself—and I could see that the lights in the room were on.

I'd left them off.

Someone was in Megan's suite. Turndown service? Or was it Megan herself?

For at least the time being, I was trapped outside. I went over to the sliding doors and gently, slowly, tried to pull them open.

They were locked. I definitely hadn't done that. Either the housekeeper had done it or Megan had returned early from dinner again because the Lactaid hadn't done the trick, and for some reason she had locked the balcony doors. And now I was definitely stuck here.

I'd known this was a possibility, so I'd thought it through, the worst-case scenario.

I looked out the balcony, eyeballed the drop at fifteen to twenty feet. Onto hard stone. Maybe fifteen feet from the bottom of the second-floor balcony. Definitely doable. To parkour champions, this was nothing.

I didn't have time to overthink it. I swung my legs outside the railing, grabbed the top rung, then dropped rung by rung until my feet were dangling in the air—and then I let go. Spun and crouched and dropped, landing, hard.

I sprang to my feet, wincing a bit. I did a survey: legs okay, knees relatively okay.

A minute later, I pulled out a mobile phone and called Dr. Zubiri. "Ready," I said.

# 71

I was fairly certain no one had seen me climb or descend the hotel's exterior. Hotel security was what I worried most about, and I hadn't seen any of them. But as I was stuffing the ropes and carabiners and such back into my backpack, a florid-faced, thick-set guy strolled past. He didn't seem to notice me, but something about him got my attention. He looked like a retired soldier.

I made a mental note.

I was hungry by then—I hadn't eaten since the lobster tail at lunch—and was planning to order room service when I got back to the suite and saw that Sukie was gone. There was only a note, on hotel letterhead—*Join me at dinner downstairs xx.* I found her sitting alone at a table set for two. She was drinking coffee and looking at her phone. She was wearing a white blazer over a white T-shirt and white pants with sandals.

I called over the waiter and ordered a New York strip steak, medium rare.

When the waiter had left, she said, "Want to tell me what you've been up to?"

I smiled. "Better for you if I don't."

She furrowed her brow, shook her head. "Really?"

I looked around the dining room, saw her father sitting at a big round table with Megan and Fritz. The others were probably big shots in the sales department. This was their event. They were hosting the CEO.

Then someone approached Conrad Kimball. Dr. Zubiri was saying something urgent. Kimball looked receptive. He was nodding, almost rhythmically. Then he appeared to ask something, and Zubiri replied.

I had a fairly good idea of what they were talking about. If Zubiri was doing what we'd agreed upon, he was telling Conrad that a reporter had called him, asking about the suppressed Tallinn study. That the reporter had a copy.

Conrad leaned to his left and muttered something to Fritz. Then the two men stood up and left the dining room.

If I had figured out Conrad Kimball correctly, he would be heading directly to his hotel suite to confer with Fritz. Zubiri had provoked a crisis; now Conrad would be huddling with his security chief in his suite. Talking aloud, near one of my recording/transmitting devices, about the Tallinn study. I wouldn't have to return to retrieve the devices; they would broadcast out compressed files every thirty minutes, send them via text message.

I'd be electronically eavesdropping on Conrad Kimball.

Sukie and I returned to the suite, and about thirty-five minutes later, my iPhone lit up. I'd just received a text containing a compressed audio file.

The crisis conversation was under way.

People really do generally behave in predictable ways. Conrad and his security chief were talking, and I was capturing their words. I listened to a moment of the audio file through my AirPods to make sure the recording was working:

VOICE 1 (CLEARLY CONRAD KIMBALL): The Tallinn study? I thought the only copy left was in Katonah, and I burned the goddamn thing!

VOICE 2 (PROBABLY FRITZ): Could someone have found it in Estonia? Could the scientist in Estonia be talking, after all this time?

CONRAD: Dr. Kask? Not very easily. We took care of him years ago.

FRITZ: You think Megan's behind this?

CONRAD: She's ruthless. She'll do anything.

FRITZ: True.

CONRAD: I want this weekend to go off without a hitch. I don't want trouble from her. I don't want her getting in the way.

FRITZ: Understood.

CONRAD: Why is Sukie here?

FRITZ: I'm working on that. I can't figure it out yet.

Sukie passed through the sitting area where I was listening with my AirPods, right around the moment when her father spoke her name on the recording. It was disorienting.

I took out my earphones. "I think I have what I need," I said.

I noticed that a red blinking light on the room phone had just come on. I pointed out to Sukie that one of us had a message. I called the front desk.

"Yes, Mr.—Brown?"

"Yes."

"You have a message from a Mr. Heston. He left his mobile number."

# 72

It was a few minutes before nine, but Fritz Heston had left his message just five minutes earlier. I called his number.

"This is Fritz," he said by way of answering the phone.

"Nick Brown," I said. "You wanted to talk."

"Mr. Brown, I'm terribly sorry to trouble you after dinner. It can certainly wait until morning if you prefer."

"Let's talk right now," I said. "What's this about?"

"I'd rather talk in person. Would that work for you?"

We arranged to meet in five minutes in the lobby. Sukie was watching a documentary about Beyoncé. "I'm off to meet Fritz," I said.

"Really? For what?"

"No idea. He wants to meet me."

She looked alarmed. "What do you think he wants?"

I shook my head. Actually, I had a pretty good idea what he wanted.

"I'll be back soon." I left her watching the documentary and went downstairs.

Fritz Heston was sitting in an easy chair in the lobby, dressed, as he was at dinner, in resort attire. A muted, vaguely Hawaiian shirt and chinos.

He got right up as soon as he saw me. Extended his hand and shook firmly. "Mr. Brown," he said.

"I didn't expect to see you here. Is security a concern in Anguilla?"

Anguilla was a small island; cruise ships didn't stop there, and its only flights went to other Caribbean islands. There was only minor crime. It was safe.

"Security's a concern everywhere these days," he said. He gestured to another chair close to his, and we both sat down. The lobby was empty. There was no one around.

"What are we talking, snorkeling accidents?" I said. "You can't be expecting protesters down here. They couldn't afford it."

"Not all the threats are from outside the firm."

"What does that mean?"

"Why are you here?" he said.

"Never been to Anguilla before."

"And why is Sukie here?"

"Ask her."

"I'm asking you. And how long did you think you'd get away with the fake name? Do you think I'm an idiot?"

So the flight attendant must have told him about my US passport, the different names. "I'm sure you're excellent at what you do," I said.

"Quite a legend you put together."

He meant my alias, Nick Brown. "I always keep a few workable legends around in case I need them."

"And why did you need it?"

"Sukie thought the family would be uncomfortable if they knew she was dating her security guy."

"Is that what you are, a private security guy?"

I evaded his question. "With all the anti-Kimball stuff going on out there, it's not safe to be a Kimball. You know that as well as anyone. And I doubt she's the only family member who's hiring their own security."

"I didn't know you did private security, Mr. Heller. I had the sense you were more in the private spy trade."

"If you've done your homework on me, you know my background."

"Okay." Meaning he'd done his homework.

"So when a client has a security need, I can provide it."

"You're a little overqualified to be a security guard."

"No such thing as overqualified. Not when you're a Kimball and you can afford to hire the best." I smiled.

"I guess women fall in love with their bodyguards fairly often, huh? Dating the client?"

"Look, I know it's a big no-no in our line of work," I said. "But screw it. We fell for each other, okay? Believe me, I'm the last person who wanted this to happen. Because I know what everyone's going to think."

"What's that?"

"That I'm some kind of gold digger, of course. But this is real. We're in love. Not that I expect anyone to believe that." I was confessing to a lie, of course. It made me look bad, which made it all the more plausible. "Anyway, you wanted to see me?"

# 73

Of course, Fritz had wanted to ask me about my real identity, and I'd dealt with the issue head-on. He had nothing more to say to me except to apologize for bringing up the matter.

By the time I got back to the room, Sukie was asleep. We hadn't made love since that time in New York. In the morning we had a room service breakfast.

I had an omelet and a lot of coffee, and she had French toast and fresh-squeezed orange juice.

I told her I needed to get back to Boston as soon as possible. "Can you order up the jet?" I said. "I have a lot to do before the family meeting."

I had what I needed on Conrad Kimball: I had evidence indicating the guy had ordered a hit on an Estonian scientist. But I still needed to get the damned Tallinn file.

Maggie knew about the file. She had been killed to keep it secret. And if it remained secret, Maggie would have died in vain.

*I just handed you the baton, sergeant,* she'd said. *Your only job is to run like hell and bring it home.*

I wanted to run the baton home. For Maggie's sake.

"Are you listening to me, Nick?" Sukie said. "I wanted to tell you last night, but I fell asleep. I just got big-footed by my sister."

"Big-footed how?"

"She just made a move on me. She's announced she's taking the jet this afternoon."

"You mean you're going to have to fly commercial?"

"You don't get it, Nick. She's up to something. And it's nothing good."

"So can we fly with her?"

"If you want."

"I'm fine with that."

"Listen, I broke my shoe. Broke the heel on my sandal."

"Okay," I said. "Didn't you pack other shoes?"

"Just the sandals. I'm not exactly a fashion model, in case you haven't figured that out. I have, I think, maybe ten pairs of shoes. So this morning I need to leave the resort and buy a new pair."

She told me the hotel's shop didn't have much selection, so the concierge had recommended a boutique on the cliffside road at South Hill, one of the districts of Anguilla.

"Then I'm going with you. You're not going by yourself."

"That would be nice," she said.

My mobile phone rang. Detective Goldman. I took the call on the balcony.

"I'm sending you a couple of video files. From the CCTV in the foyer on the night of Conrad Kimball's birthday."

"Images of the guests," I said. "The family."

"Yeah. Take a close look."

"Will do," I said.

An hour later we were picked up in front of the hotel by a black Suburban. The driver appeared to be a local, a hotel employee, but I always assumed the worst. That he was paid a little extra by Fritz to keep his ears open, report what he heard.

So on the way we didn't talk much. It was about a fifteen-minute drive from the hotel, along Route 1, the major thoroughfare on the island.

Periodically I looked at the road behind us. I was fairly sure the Audi following us had been doing so since the resort. The car had pulled up right behind us as soon as we left the gates of the hotel. It had the Anguillan light blue license plate, and it ended with an R, meaning the car was rented.

Now our driver signaled for a right-hand turn. I looked around. As we turned into the driveway for the boutique, the Audi passed us. I felt a moment of relief. I'd been overly suspicious. I got out and walked with Sukie into the shop, which smelled of leather and coconut.

The store manager, a large woman in a muumuu, had clearly been alerted to Sukie's visit—a quick heads-up call from the concierge at the hotel, I bet—and fell all over herself trying to be helpful. There was no one else in the shop.

Looking at the rows of shoes on display on their shelves, I suddenly had a thought. I called Goldman back, and he picked right up.

"Do me a favor," I said. "Can you find me a specific shot from the security cameras in the foyer from that night?"

"What shot?"

"I want to see their feet. Their footwear."

"Their footwear."

"What they were wearing that night. Does the camera angle pick that up?"

"I'll take a look. Send you what we got."

A video clip arrived on my phone seven minutes later. It wasn't easy to see details on the small screen, but I pinched-to-zoom and swiped and double-tapped and managed to move in close enough to confirm a theory of mine.

I stepped over to the front window of the shop to call Goldman back and explain.

As I peered out through the slats in the blinds that hung down in front of the floor-to-ceiling window, I saw the same Audi, with the Anguilla plates, coming from the opposite direction, pull into the boutique's narrow parking lot.

So now it was obvious he was following us, but the question was, who was he working for? Certainly Fritz Heston distrusted me, no matter how polite he was about it. What was I doing with Sukie, what was Sukie up to? It wouldn't surprise me if the Audi driver was one of Heston's employees.

I returned to the women's shoe department, where the manager was saying to Sukie, "Madame, I have the cutest pair of Jimmy Choo sandals with fascinator bows."

"Bows?" Sukie said. "No thanks, not for me. Just something simple in white."

The front door opened, and a *bing* sounded, and a man entered.

The florid-faced man I'd seen at the hotel earlier. The man driving the Audi. Would he be a Kimball employee brought down to the island for security? I didn't think so. He was too unprepossessing physically. He was chunky. Maybe, instead, he was a local working for Kimball. That made sense.

The manager excused herself and went up to the newcomer. He spoke to her in a low voice, something about "looking around," and she returned to Sukie.

I decided to go up to the guy and confront him directly. When he saw me approaching, his eyes narrowed. He didn't expect his quarry to approach him. It wasn't in the handbook.

He said, "Yes?"

"If you're trying to let us know we're being followed, congratulations, you've succeeded. But if you're trying to be subtle, well, your technique needs a little work."

"Do I know you?" He sounded South African.

"Nick," I said. I stuck out my hand to shake, and he instinctively flinched. When he realized he'd overreacted, he glowered. It all happened in about two seconds.

He didn't tell me his name. But I could tell he was pissed off. I'd called him out, insulted his competence. No one likes that.

# 74

Sukie bought a pair of simple white sandals, Christian Louboutins; I told her she looked nice in them, and we got back into the hotel's Suburban. But instead of returning to the hotel and packing up to fly out, she told me she wanted to have lunch at a place she'd found previously on the far eastern end of the island.

I made a private deal with the hotel driver, dropped him off at the hotel, and drove the car myself. It took a half hour to get there, and when we did, I was surprised at how modest it was—a beach shack, right on the beach and not in one of the resorts. We were early for lunch and got a table by the water.

It should have been relaxing—it felt like a tropical island cliché, nearly like a film set, the sand and the water and the beach umbrella— but I was feeling the immense press of time. I wanted to get back to Boston and prepare for the Kimball family meeting. I didn't want to be sitting there having lunch. I sneaked a glance at my watch. If I didn't somehow end up with the Tallinn file, none of my plans stood a chance of working.

"I found this place when I was here a couple years ago," Sukie said. "I know it doesn't look promising, but they have the best conch fritters. And johnny cakes."

I ordered a Jamaican beer, a Red Stripe, and she asked for a frozen margarita. We were the only customers there.

"The real reason I wanted to get out of the resort," she said, "was so we can talk openly. Knowing my father, and Fritz, our suite might be bugged."

I nodded. Anything was possible.

"I saw you talking to that guy in the store," she said. "You know him?"

"I know the type," I said.

"What do you mean?"

"A local guy, a retired mercenary, I bet. From South Africa, I'm guessing. The kind who takes the occasional freelance job. Local talent."

"But hired by who?"

"That's the question."

"Fritz?"

"Not likely. He'd use his own company employees."

She began absently, straightening the sugar packets in the holder on the table. "Then who?"

I shook my head. Shrugged. "What do you know about the meeting on Saturday?" I asked.

"Just that we have to take a vote on 'the future of the company.' So it's a big deal."

"Any guess what that means?"

She shook her head. "Like I said, maybe he wants to file for bankruptcy."

"He sounded very gung-ho at the sales conference."

"He was defending his legacy, his honor. Of course he was. But if he does file for bankruptcy, I lose. That Tallinn study will do me no good anymore. Basically I need to have it, like, yesterday."

"If Kimball files for bankruptcy, what really happens to all the lawsuits against them?"

"They all get frozen. That means the company gets to escape its reckoning. Instead of paying damages to families it destroyed, it gets away scot-free. If Kimball goes bankrupt, all these people around the country who are suing them will get pennies."

"Why would your father need a family meeting to declare bankruptcy?"

"Because we each sit on the board of the Kimball Family Trust, which in turn owns Kimball Pharma." The sugar packets were now perfectly aligned.

"You each get an equal vote?"

"Hell no. Dad gets fifty-one percent, and the rest of us get a total of forty-nine percent. But a vote to declare bankruptcy requires a supermajority. Which means he needs two of us to go along with his plan. And I'll bet Megan won't agree to it. Or Paul. And obviously I won't."

"That still leaves two, Hayden and Cameron."

"Wild cards," she said. "You're not going to get that Tallinn file in time, are you?"

"Unlikely," I admitted. "But now I have a recording of Conrad and Fritz talking about it and whether it leaked. They also talk about 'getting rid of' a scientist in Estonia. But tell me something: What if I do get the file? What will you do with it?"

"You've asked me that before."

"Humor me."

"I trigger an inquest and criminal investigation, and families of victims will get compensated. And, yes, justice is done."

"Okay."

"I just know," she said, "that if we don't dig up a copy of the Tallinn study, my father will be unstoppable."

"We still have two days. Anything can happen."

"That's what I'm afraid of." She paused, looked at me. "Why do I get the feeling there's stuff you're not telling me?"

"I'm not?"

"Like what you're up to. What you're doing. What's going on."

"That's not part of the deal," I said.

"But I hired you."

326

"And fired me and hired me again. But you asked me to get you a particular file. Not to tell you how I was going to do it."

"Do you not trust me?"

"Of course I do. I'm protecting you. There are things I don't want you to know because it's better for you if you don't. Let's just leave it at that."

Our drinks arrived. She took a sip of her margarita and then said, "I'm not—how do I say this?—I'm not great about trusting other people, as you've probably surmised. I'm starting to feel close to you, and warning sirens are going off in my head, *Danger, danger.* Because I don't want to get burned. Again. So if you're going to betray me, let me know now."

"Betray you?"

"Everyone has an agenda."

"And what do you imagine mine is?"

After a moment, she shook her head. She didn't know, and she didn't answer.

The sun was bright on the beach, and the interior of the shack, a hundred feet away, was shadowed. I was able to see a hulking figure enter the shack and talk to the bartender.

"I need to know I can trust you," she said. "It's so hard for me." She hesitated. "You're not like anyone else I've known."

"Let me ask you something. Sort of difficult. Paul talked about something that happened between you and your father, when you were in your teens."

"I can't—I can't—I need to be strong. I need to do what I need to do. I can't go there." Tears were flooding her eyes.

I had to ask her. "Did your father—"

She closed her eyes and replied in something close to a monotone. "Maybe he was drunk. Maybe he was, I don't know, drunk with success. He'd just turned down a huge offer from Pfizer, and . . . He felt like he could have anything and anybody."

327

"And he did something."

She nodded mutely, tears in her eyes. "I still can't talk about it," she said very quietly.

I took her hand. "A guy I knew in the Forces once told me we all get wounded," I said, "and we all take our scars with us. And if we don't accept our scars, we haven't really healed."

We sat in silence for a minute or so, waiting for our food, neither of us hungry. They were taking their time. I asked the waiter for a second Red Stripe, and then I happened to notice the Audi I'd seen earlier, parked on the side of the road not far from where I'd parked the Suburban. "Stay here," I said.

"Where are you—?"

"I'll be right back."

I went into the shack, which was a large kitchen next to a bar and a few small tables—most people sat on the beach—and when my eyes got adjusted to the dark interior, I didn't see the South African there anymore. A young male bartender at the blender, and two sweaty-looking workers in a small, hot kitchen.

When I exited the shack onto the road, I saw the red-faced, chubby retired mercenary standing near his Audi, smoking a cigarette. The guy from the shoe store. He was wearing a white ball cap and sun-glasses and talking to another guy. Younger, slimmer, tougher-looking.

I went up to them. "Thought I'd make it easy for you," I said. "You want to follow me, here I am."

"*Jy was deur jou ma se gat gebore want haar poes was te besig!*" the chubby mercenary said.

I had no idea what he was saying, but I could tell it was some sort of obscenity. "I thought I made myself clear," I said, and suddenly I kneed him in the balls. I heard the air leave his lungs—*oof*—and he crumpled, toppled, onto the sand, clutching himself. "*Cuiter!*" he gasped. "*Fok!*"

"They should have given you more information on who you're following," I said.

I first saw something glinting in the sun and then saw that the second guy had pulled out a nasty-looking knife with a serious blade. I was, of course, unarmed. Weren't they always saying Anguilla was extremely safe?

Disarming a guy bearing a knife is always a problem, no matter what you see on YouTube videos. Quickly, I looked around for some kind of weapon of opportunity but saw nothing. Asphalt, sand, the concrete walls of the beach shack, a couple of parked cars. Maybe a rock I could use as a bludgeon. But I didn't see anything else.

I stuck my left arm out toward the guy to goad him into taking a slash at me. Because when he did, he'd move in close enough for me to do something to him. If I was really lucky, I'd be able to snatch his hand away right as he lunged and not get cut.

But sometimes you have to make a sacrifice. That's called *sutemi*, a Japanese word in the martial arts meaning to sacrifice something in order to gain a tactical advantage. Or so I remember from training.

He whipped out his right hand, the knife slashing at me. I managed to grab his hand, but not before he sliced the back of mine.

The pain was intense, but the adrenaline was pumping and I was hyper-focused. I saw the serrating on the blade. The talon in the knife's logo. The hair on the back of his knuckles. I pivoted to my left and slammed the edge of my right hand down onto his arm in a knife-hand strike. I could hear the bone snap, and his knife clattered to the ground as he roared in pain. I was pretty sure I'd broken his ulna. That's the thinner long bone in the forearm. I know people who have broken half-inch boards with a knife-hand blow. I wasn't that good, but I was clearly good enough to inflict pain on the guy. And a broken arm.

Both men were writhing on the ground now, howling. I glanced at my right hand, saw that the cut was deep and bleeding copiously. Sukie raced up to me, gasped when she saw the wound. "Get in the car!" I shouted.

I swooped down and grabbed the guy's knife, but then I realized that I wasn't done here. The first guy, the chunky mercenary, had gotten to his feet and was now pointing a gun at me.

# 75

S ukie screamed, and one of the waiters shouted, "No, man!"
And I thought about my options. There weren't many. Normal situational logic didn't apply here. Whoever they were, they surely weren't tasked with killing me. They were local guys, local cutaways, and they'd been humiliated, and now they wanted to take me out.

These guys were blunt instruments; they didn't do microvascular surgery. Their idea of subtle was Thor's hammer. I know people like this, and they can be deadly, in their blunderbuss way. When you get them mad, they're going after you, and they don't give a shit. That's the danger.

The second guy, with the broken arm, was sitting on the ground, dazed with pain. But that wouldn't last long. He would recover too.

"Drop the knife," the chubby guy said. He might have still been weak from the blow to the balls, but the gun he pointed at me—a semi-automatic pistol, large and black, a SIG Sauer—looked pretty steady.

"What?" I said, just to piss him off.

"You heard me. *Drop the knife.*"

I had no choice. I dropped the knife.

"Now kick it away."

"What?"

"*Now!*"

I kicked it away. "Sukie," I shouted, "get in the car now!"

The mercenary came closer to me. "Now turn around."

"What?" I said, and he finally lost patience. He shoved my right shoulder with his left hand to spin me around.

I'd been waiting for a moment like that.

I spun to my right, but I kept going until I was next to him, my left shoulder up against his right. He tried to adjust and re-point the gun at me, but he was too late.

I wrapped my left arm over his right arm at the biceps and tucked it under my left, hugging it tight to my body so he couldn't really use it. Then I grabbed the barrel of the pistol and wrenched it around and pointed it back at his face. His wrist was hyperextended, so to stop the pain he let go of the weapon. He had to.

I backed up a step, the gun pointed at center mass. "On your knees, my friend, or I'll kneecap you right here."

He knelt. He didn't have a choice.

When I noticed the second guy starting to get to his feet as well, I wagged the barrel at him and said, "On your knees too."

The second guy got to his knees.

"Who are you working for?" I said.

Neither man replied.

"I'll ask you again," I said. "Who are you working for?"

The thinner man replied first. "Black Parallel." He pronounced it "Bleck." He was South African too.

"And who are *they* working for? Who's the client?"

The thicker man said, "Hell do I know? We're just doin' our *fokken* job."

I had a good idea who these people were all of a sudden. Probably Afrikaners, refugees from justice from the apartheid era. They probably didn't feel safe in South Africa anymore. Maybe they did some bad things back in the day when they were in the South African police. And some things people don't forget. When your son has had his arms ripped out by the police, it's hard to forgive. Chickens come home to roost.

"All right," I said, knowing there was nothing more useful I could get from them. "Get out of here now, unless you want to deal with the police. Go." I sure didn't want to face the Anguillan police and the hours of bureaucracy that would entail.

I backed up until I was at the Suburban. I got behind the wheel. "Come on," I said, "we'll get lunch back at the hotel."

But I wasn't hungry, and I had a feeling she wasn't either.

# 76

I was fairly sure we were safe as long as we remained within the resort, which had its own security. They wouldn't come after me as
long as I was there. And I had no doubt that Sukie was not a target.
But she was, of course, shaken up.

I wondered at first why Black Parallel had hired these subpar op-
eratives to go after me. They must have been alerted to my presence
in Anguilla and scrambled to find local talent.

I got some bandages from the front desk and spoke briefly in the
elevator, which seemed safer than talking in the room.

"I need to get back to Boston," I said. "Now."

I called a local taxi company directly instead of asking the
concierge—I didn't want the hotel to know I was leaving. I didn't know
how plugged-in Black Parallel was, but I assumed someone at the hotel,
or several people, had been paid to keep track of my whereabouts.

My cell phone rang. It was Natalya Aksyonova, Conrad Kimball's
fiancée. In New York I'd given her my number.

I took the call on the balcony. I had a favor to ask her.


I had a dilemma over what to do with the pistol I'd confiscated. The
SIG Sauer P226 was an excellent weapon, extremely accurate. Nine
millimeter. It was loaded, which meant sixteen rounds, if it was full—
one in the chamber and fifteen in the magazine.

I decided I'd throw it into the ocean on the way to the airport. So I had it with me, stuck in the waistband of my pants and concealed by my untucked shirt, when my cab arrived: a dented, rusty-looking Hyundai.

Sukie hugged me tight. "Are you going to be okay?"

"Don't worry about me," I said. But she looked awfully worried. I kissed her and told her I'd see her again in two days.

The driver, an affable islander, had on some kind of talk radio, a call-in show. A young woman was complaining about her boyfriend. The road was deserted. I watched the countryside go by. The island had been badly damaged by Hurricane Irma a few years before, and here and there you could still see wreckage on either side of the road, broken buildings and bent palm trees.

I was about to ask the driver to pull over so I could toss the gun into the ocean, when suddenly he shouted and slammed on the brakes, which squealed loudly. "Shit!" he screamed. The cab swerved to the left and then to the right and then fishtailed before slamming to a stop.

"Look on the road," the driver croaked, pointing. "Bastards!"

Someone had placed a spike strip across the narrow road, a portable tire-deflation device that folded out, baring rows of spikes. Despite the driver's quick reaction, the tires had been punctured and were hissing.

Then a bullet blew a hole in the cab's windshield.

And then a second shot.

The cabdriver opened his door and leaped onto the road, screaming in terror. He ran back in the direction from which we'd come. I was sitting in the back seat on the passenger's side, and I immediately ducked down, lowering my head. I was being fired at from the right side of the road. Keeping my head down, I opened the driver's-side door and climbed out, using the door as a shield. I needed to get down behind the wheel well of the front left tire, because I remembered from my training that the best protection would come from the

335

engine block. Bullets could go through the windows or even the trunk of the car, but nothing would penetrate the engine block. I had to stay near the hood.

Now I yanked the SIG Sauer out of my waistband and raised my head just enough to see a couple of shooters across the street. I recognized the bulky mercenary from before, the one whose weapon I'd confiscated.

He was probably even angrier and now determined to kill me. It was like when I was a kid and accidentally kicked an underground yellow-jacket nest and they emerged in a terrifying cloud coming at me.

Or maybe the Afrikaners' orders had changed. Maybe they were instructed to take me out.

Now he was back, with someone else. He fired a shot, which went high and wide, hitting an abandoned building across the street behind me.

At the same time another round hit the right side of the car, spider-webbing the right-hand window. There were at least two of them, I knew, maybe three. I couldn't be sure. Because they were using handguns, they had to be relatively close. Handguns are only accurate up to around fifty yards; beyond that the aim degrades significantly.

Two or three of them against me, with one handgun and sixteen rounds, if the magazine was full. I had to make each of my shots count.

Trained police hit their targets less than half the time. A fifty percent hit rate is considered good. So sixteen rounds wasn't much when you're outnumbered that badly.

I squeezed off three shots, aiming directly at where I'd seen the assailants seconds before. I heard a scream, and I was fairly certain I had taken one down.

Then I saw one of the men cross the street toward me, toward my side of the taxi. He was coming up on my flank, and when I tried to stick my head up and take aim, a volley of shots came at me, preventing me from moving.

I desperately needed to change my position. I was about to be exposed, as soon as the guy came around the hood of the car. I spun around, saw the abandoned building, realized it was probably my best cover. I fired straight ahead, a few shots, and then squeezed off another two to my left, covering myself as I raced to the deserted building. A wood-and-drywall building like that would serve as poor cover from the gunfire, I knew, but it was decent concealment at least.

I needed all I could get. At least half of the magazine was empty now. But I was glad I hadn't yet tossed it.

Gunfire echoed in the street as they—the two remaining shooters, I guessed—fired at me.

The building was some sort of abandoned restaurant. I raced through the front area, which looked like it had once been the dining room, and then farther in until I found a tiled space that once must have been the kitchen. Most of the major appliances were gone. The front dining room offered only one wall of protection, and that was made of plasterboard. The kitchen offered me three walls of protection. The more walls between me and the shooters, the more walls the bullets had to go through, the more the velocity of the bullets would degrade. The safer I'd be.

But one of them raced into the building just moments after me. I saw him in my peripheral vision as I stood in the abandoned kitchen and fired off a shot. He kept coming at me, firing wildly. I fired off three more rounds in quick succession, right at his chest, and finally he stumbled and fell. I saw in an instant that he was a young, fit guy, wearing a Kevlar vest. So they were professionals. The rounds had hit him in the chest, and he was knocked out, though probably not dead.

I briefly considered stopping to steal his vest, but there really wasn't time. So I backed up into the kitchen and looked for the exit to the jungle-like vegetation behind the building. Just one shooter remained now, and he was somewhere inside. I weighed my options. I could run out of the building, into the jungle, and be pursued by the remaining attacker, or I could stay in the kitchen and fight.

But I didn't know where the other one was.

In the adrenaline rush, I'd lost count of how many rounds I had left. I estimated three or four.

Suddenly a couple of bullets punched through the drywall and tile. He was on the other side of the wall.

I aimed at the hole that had just been made, and I heard a scream. I'd got him.

A few more shots came through the tile, and then the shooter came hobbling out of the front dining room, grabbing his leg in agony, firing at me. I ducked behind the metallic hulk of an old stove hood and fired my last couple of shots at him without aiming.

The silence, after the deafening shots, was thick. It vibrated. My ears rang.

I was now as certain as I could be that the three of them were down. I ran out of the rear door and into the underbrush, and no gunfire followed me.

Meanwhile, another car had been caught on the spike strip, its horn sounding. I could see it back there. And I kept on running north.


I got to Anguilla's airport on foot, after walking and running for about a mile and a half, looking pretty banged up but in fact feeling okay. Mostly enduring that jittery post-adrenaline letdown. Feeling grateful that nothing had gone against me on the roadside. My three attackers, at least one of whom was probably dead, were not nice guys. I didn't feel bad about what I'd had to do to them. I dumped the SIG Sauer in a drainage ditch outside the airport, and then I bought a ticket on the next flight to St. Maarten.

On the plane I found myself thinking about the last time, before the Conrad Kimball dinner, that I saw Maggie Benson.

We'd met for lunch at a Turkish restaurant she liked a lot on the East Side of Manhattan. I hadn't seen her for a few years, but out of the blue she'd reached out to me, asking to meet. She was even more beautiful than when we were going out. She'd let her hair grow, and she'd put on a little weight, which looked good on her. She seemed happy.

She had a lot of questions about what I did for a living, and it became clear that she was thinking seriously of becoming a private investigator herself. I remembered her saying, "It's safe, right?"

"Safe how?"

"I mean your personal safety. Like, I don't need a weapon, do I?"

"Better if you have one," I said.

"Oh, really?"

"I've used mine a couple of times," I said. "But I think that's the exception. It's mostly safe. Boring, sometimes, but safe. Hey, listen. About what happened—"

"Water. Bridge."

"Seriously, I didn't get it at first. I think I do now, and . . ."

She gave me a long look. There was a lot of sadness in her eyes. "Licensing," she said. "How does that work, state by state?"

She hadn't wanted to talk about it, what I'd done with General Moore, but I knew it was still there between us.

I thought back to happier times. When she'd slapped a pile of folders down on my desk. And the words kept echoing in my mind:

*I just handed you the baton.*

*Your only job is to run like hell and bring it home.*

And I knew I wasn't going to let Maggie down. I wasn't going to let her death be for nothing.

I had to make it right.

# 77

I arrived in Boston in the late evening. By the morning, I was running on empty. I got to my office and made some coffee and found a profoundly discouraged Dorothy Duval.

She had tried every password cracker program she knew of. Nothing worked. Dr. Scavolini's encrypted folder remained encrypted. It was a huge folder too—one hundred gigabytes.

Dorothy is very good at what she does. I had no doubt she had done everything she could think of. But without proof of the Tallinn file, I would lose. Conrad Kimball would escape justice. The recording in Anguilla wouldn't be enough.

This happens. The bad guys win sometimes. You move on.

Then my phone rang, and it was Detective Goldman from Bedford. "Did you have a chance to talk to Cameron?" he said.

"No, not yet."

"Well, I did. I talked to him about that alleged 'booty call' he made in the middle of the night. I told you, he didn't make any booty call. The kid went to score some fentanyl from a dealer in Newburgh, New York. So it couldn't have been him."

Stunned, I said, "You got that out of him?"

"Not easily, but yes."

"What about the cameras at Fritz Heston's house? Have you had a chance to check them out?"

"I did. They confirm that his car didn't leave his house until he got the call from Conrad, in the morning."

I nodded to myself. "Okay," I said. "I'll call you when I know more."

Half an hour later Gabe sauntered into the office. He dropped the key to my Toyota on my desk. Then he came around behind me to peek at what was on my computer monitor. "Why are you Googling Neil deGrasse Tyson?" he said. "Is he a client? Cool."

"No. Trying to figure out a password."

"His?"

"No. A fan of his. But I might be barking up the wrong tree. I have no idea. It's worth trying."

"How long is the password?"

"No idea. We don't know."

"Letters and numbers?"

"Could be. Or catchphrases."

"Huh," he said. He was mimicking me but probably wasn't aware of it. "Could be anything."

"Pretty much."

"The good thing about science is that it's true whether or not you believe in it."

"Okay," I said. Apparently he knew the Tyson quote too.

"I mean, that's a quote. Something he says. Neil deGrasse Tyson. It's a meme."

I squinted at him, tilted my head. "A meme."

"A meme, you know? A meme. You know what a meme is?"

"Sure." My understanding was that a meme was basically a saying, maybe a catchphrase, a caption on a photograph passed around the internet. Usually clever and funny, but not always.

"So it's a meme. Something like that. It's something he said once. Google it."

I did, without understanding fully what he was talking about, along

341

with Tyson's name. A bunch of cartoons of Tyson came up, and some YouTube windows. I read aloud, "'The good thing about science is that it's true whether or not you believe in it.'" It looked to be a more popular phrase than I'd thought.

"That's it. You got it."

I IM'd Dorothy and asked her to come in. She arrived a few seconds later. "Yes? Oh, hello, Gabe," she said frostily.

"Hello," he replied neutrally.

"Gabe here has a passphrase to suggest. For the encrypted folder."

"Okay."

Gabe said, "The good thing about science is that it's true whether or not you believe in it."

She looked at him. "That's a passphrase?"

He explained.

Dorothy shrugged, then said, "Can I use your chair?"

I got up and let her sit at my keyboard. Gabe looked over her shoulder. She tapped for a while and then repeated the sentence. She typed it in. Looked back at Gabe with satisfaction on her face. "With spaces," she said. "Nothing. Doesn't work."

"Now try it without any spaces," Gabe said. "All one word."

Dorothy nodded. She tapped away at the keyboard. "Nope."

"Shit," Gabe said.

Then Dorothy said, "Watch out, guys, we're dealing with a badass over here."

"Who, Gabe?" I said, ready to defend him.

"Try it!" said Gabe.

"Try what?" I said.

"'Watch out, we got a badass over here.' It's another Tyson meme," said Gabe.

Dorothy tapped some more. "Nope. Let me try it without the comma. No spaces."

She hit a couple of keys. Blinked a few times, inhaled sharply.

"Lord, that did it!" she said. "That did it. That worked. Oh, my Jesus God."

"It worked?" I said, stupidly.

"*Watchoutwegotabadassoverhere*," she said, beaming. "All one word, no comma."

"Well done, guys," I said. Dorothy shrugged, and then Gabe did too.

"It's not just one document," she said. "It's a separate drive full of documents. There's a folder labeled OXYDONE ESTONIAN STUDY, 1999."

"That's it," I said, my heart thudding.

"And a lot of correspondence about it, looks like," Dorothy said. She tapped at the keyboard some more. "Here's one from Conrad Kimball. Wait, a bunch from Conrad Kimball. To and from him." She chuckled, nearly giggled. "It's all here, Nick."

Gabe looked at me, and I winked at him, unseen by Dorothy, to let him know I knew the score. That he deserved some credit too, not just Dorothy.

She said, "You want to Dropbox it or something to the client?"

"Can you put it on a thumb drive?" I said. "And I need to see Devlin as soon as possible. I'm going to Katonah tomorrow. And you, Gabe. When I'm done, you and I have to talk."

# 78

I was tense about returning to Kimball Hall. Too many things had to go right. And there were too many variables. For one thing I really had no idea what Conrad Kimball was planning, and that made a difference. Nor what Sukie was going to do.

Early in the morning I picked up a couple of large black coffees from Dunkin' Donuts and set out for Katonah in my old Toyota.

My cell phone rang, an unknown number.

"Heller!" a man's voice barked.

In just two syllables I recognized the man's Israeli accent.

"Shlomo," I said. "Been a while."

Shlomo Avishai was a colonel in the Israeli Military Intelligence Directorate, the Aman. We'd once worked together, coordinating an operation in Barcelona.

"Heller, I don't know if you heard the gossip, but I went private, just like you. You might know of the firm I work for now."

"Black Parallel, by any chance?"

He chuckled.

"You doing a job?"

"For professional reasons I can't tell you the name of my client. But I should tell you that you have a reputation in certain quarters," Shlomo said.

"Good or bad?"

"Heller, if your reputation was lousy we wouldn't waste our time following you. You are known to be a formidable investigator. And our client wanted to know everything and anything you might find on Kimball. They figured if anyone would dig up the dirt, it would be you."

"Anguilla—" I began.

"I'd love to tell you those incompetents in Anguilla have been punished," he said, "but you seem to have taken on that task yourself."

South of Hartford I hit traffic on 84 but shortly thereafter took the exit for the Saw Mill River Parkway. In a few minutes I arrived at the Inn at Katonah, where I'd met Sukie before.

I was half an hour early, which was good.

It was time I needed.


A black town car pulled into the inn's parking lot, right on time at nine o'clock.

I slung the small backpack over my right shoulder and climbed into the back of the limo. Sukie was there. She gave me a kiss.

"Do you have it?" she said.

I'd called her the night before and told her I'd bring it with me. I'd also told her it was too big a file to email.

"Here it is," I said, handing her a small metal flash drive bar, a tiny thing, a mere twist of metal. "It's dynamite. A very compact weapon of mass destruction." Then I pulled out my phone and showed her the folders of documents.

"Which one is the study itself?"

I dabbed at the phone's face and scrolled, and then I showed her.

She stared for a long time. Finally she shook her head and smiled. "I knew you'd find it."

I shrugged modestly.

"I don't want any copies going anywhere," she said. "We're clear on that, right?"

"Clear," I said. "Where's the meeting? The library?"

"No. The map room, on the second floor, because he likes the big round boardroom table when things are serious. Whenever a meeting's called for the map room, you know it's dire."

I had seen pictures of the room in an *Architectural Digest* spread on Kimball Hall. A graceful, round room whose curved bookshelves were lined with leather-bound volumes. A big round mahogany table that seated twelve. The floor made from reclaimed Ponderosa pine. Several antique standing globes, and framed maps on the curved walls.

"Will you be able to get me in?"

"Probably. You count as a significant other by now."

"I thought it was family only."

"Well, Conrad likes you."

I just smiled. I knew better.

A few minutes later, the big old house jutted into view, castle-like. Kimball Hall was no longer the beautiful, elegant mansion, the stately home with a million rooms. Now it seemed gray and cold, looming ominously like a haunted house. A house of death. I kept flashing on that morning, the police lights in the sky, the cops in their Windbreakers. Maggie's body, with the broken neck, the head twisted.

The white sneakers.

Just ahead of us was another town car, which stopped on the circular drive right at the front door to discharge its passenger, Hayden Kimball, in a black leather jacket.

We got out a minute later. "Here we go," Sukie muttered to me as we entered.

A butler at the front door offered to take my backpack, but I kept it slung on my left shoulder. He greeted Sukie—"Miss Kimball"—and escorted us into yet another room, a dining room, one I hadn't seen before. Like all the others at Kimball Hall, it was formal and stuffy, with unmemorable seascapes on the wall in ornate gold frames. A sideboard was heaped with breakfast pastries and a silver coffee urn.

Conrad was seated at the head of the dining table, wearing a navy suit and tie, while Natalya, elegant in a white suit, greeted arrivals like the hostess at a dinner party.

Paul was already there, without his beautiful Moroccan girlfriend. He was standing next to Hayden, chatting uncomfortably. Servants were bustling around serving coffee.

When Paul saw me he stiffened and said loudly, "Hey, what's he doing here?"

"As you know, he's my significant other," Sukie said.

"It's family only, isn't that right?" Paul said to his father. "Otherwise, I would have brought Layla."

"I don't mind if he's here," Hayden said.

Megan entered the room, in a navy suit like her father. She'd overheard the exchange. She said, "Well, I do. Only family. I'm sorry, Nick."

I said nothing.

"It's up to Dad," Sukie said.

"Ah, our meeting this morning is for family only," Conrad said, looking at me. "Family plus Fritz and the stenographer. And Natalya. Spouses and our, what is your term, *significant others* can wait in the library. I'm sorry about that, Nicholas." He cleared his throat. "Anyone know the whereabouts of my ne'er-do-well son?" He did not sound amused. Cameron was the only one I hadn't yet talked with. Maybe today there'd be an opportunity.

"He knows about the meeting," said Paul. "If he doesn't show, he can't vote; it's simple."

Natalya caught my eye and smiled and gave a small, almost undetectable nod. I doubted anyone noticed.

I smiled back.

Suddenly I heard a great crash from somewhere inside the house nearby, and Cameron entered the dining room. He was weaving from side to side, apparently drunk. He was wearing jeans and some kind

347

of bowling shirt, lime green and soiled. On his feet was a pair of Abloh Off-White high-tops.

"Oh, for God's sake," his father spat. "What the hell is wrong with you? Get some coffee into you and sober up. However you do it."

Cameron glanced around the room and saw me. "I remember you," he said quickly. "Nick something. The gold digger. Oh, did I say that?" He put a hand over his mouth. "Mouths of babes, right?" He was talking unusually fast. He had to have been on some sort of upper, something speedy. It was in his rapid speech, his shallow breathing. His movements were jagged and strange.

"Hello, Cameron," I said.

"You know how I can tell you're a fortune hunter? It's the way you look. You're like a catalog model. Not Armani or anything. More like—Lands' End. I can picture you in a gray ribbed Henley. And if I clicked on a button, it would turn *heather*." He laughed nastily.

From the head of the table Conrad said, "Jesus Christ, drunk again, at ten in the morning. I need your vote."

"He's on speed, Dad," said Paul.

"Well, you're not getting my vote," Cameron said. "Not feeling it, sorry."

"You and I need to have a little private chat, now," Conrad said, rising stiffly from the table. "Let's go."


Conrad led Cameron out of the dining room and into the room next door. After a minute or two I excused myself, ostensibly to use the bathroom, and went out into the hall outside the room where the two were arguing. Loitering outside the open door, I listened.

"—an alcoholic like your mother," Conrad was saying. He didn't seem to understand that his son was on meth at the moment, not booze.

Cameron's voice boomed, "You drove her to drink. Way you went

348

around screwing everything in a dress. Blatantly cheating on her. Lied to her face."

"Aren't you the moral authority," his father said. "You, who killed a young girl!"

"You know damned well that was right after Mom's funeral. I was out of my mind."

"That could have ruined your life. You should be grateful I knew who to pay off."

"And you hold it over my head? What kind of sick person does that?"

"Don't make me do it," Conrad said.

"Fuck you, Dad," Cameron said. A few seconds later he burst out into the hall and stormed out of the house.

# 79

When I returned, the family was arguing about me, about whether I should be allowed into the family meeting.

Sukie spoke calmly. "If you're going to have a vote at all today, you're going to let him in."

Conrad was seated again at his place at the head of the table. "I told you already, it's family only."

"You know damned well that, per the articles of incorporation, you can't hold a meeting with two missing principals. So if you don't let Nick in, I'm going to bail, and you won't have a meeting. Take your choice."

I didn't expect to be allowed into the family meeting in the map room, so I'd made other arrangements.

With Natalya, who believed Megan was leading a cabal to oust Conrad and keep Natalya's hands off of Conrad's fortune.

I'd asked Natalya to put a book on the shelves. It was a leather-bound edition of *The Late George Apley* by John P. Marquand. I'd selected the book from an antiquarian bookstore in downtown Boston, based entirely on the color of its binding. Which was based on reviewing the *Architectural Digest* piece on Kimball Hall.

The thing about rich men's libraries is, the books are rarely opened.

Inside the book George Devlin had cleverly inserted a miniature video bug.

But as it turned out, I didn't need it.

The meeting started promptly at ten. I sat next to Sukie at the round table. Minutes of the last meeting were read by a stenographer I hadn't seen before, a mousy woman of around forty with thick glasses and short brown hair who showed up just before the meeting began.

Then Conrad Kimball cleared his throat. He began to speak in a hoarse but loud baritone, his West Texas accent as leathery as a worn rodeo saddle.

"We have a decision to make today," he began. "Whether or not to be acquired by Tova Pharmaceuticals of Haifa. Which I think is a no-brainer. This way we'll get to escape all these crazy lawsuits."

Hayden interrupted. "You want to give away your legacy, Dad? You started Kimball Pharma. It's your baby. You want it to just . . . disappear into some corporate behemoth?"

"If we do nothing, we're going to get sued into oblivion," Conrad said. "There'll be nothing left. Now we have this Israeli pharmaceutical company that wants to acquire our portfolio of drugs. And they're willing to assume our legal liabilities? To me, it's an easy decision to make."

An Israeli pharmaceutical company, I thought. That's who would hire Black Parallel, an Israeli private intelligence firm. Of course they were interested in me, in what I was investigating, what I had. Because I represented a huge potential threat to their deal.

I was a threat to Tova Pharmaceuticals.

They knew who I was—or they'd found out—and they knew that as an investigator I was relentless. If there was something to be found out about Kimball, some kind of dirt, they wanted it. There were probably all sorts of clauses in their offer that would allow them to withdraw if they discovered anything bad, any illegality, any false information.

Hayden said acidly, "A division of a giant Israeli pharma company. Our name will disappear. We'll be ordered around by some megalomaniac in Haifa. I for one think it's a serious mistake. A really bad move."

"Let me remind you," her father said, "that you'll have plenty of dough to blow on your all-Japanese production of *Raisin in the Sun*."

"And what happens to me in your little scenario?" said Megan. "If and when Tova takes us over? I don't see my name anywhere on this."

"Megan, my dear," Conrad said, "we know all about your schemes. Trying to have me declared incompetent. Yes, we know all about them."

"That's not true," she protested indignantly.

"Fritz has some recordings to refresh your memory. Girl, I started this company before you were born, and I intend to run it until I can't anymore, and I'll be the judge of when that is."

"Are you actually firing me?" she said.

"As the mother of four lovely children—my heirs, let us not forget—who doesn't want for money, you have nothing to worry about. I'm sure you're highly employable."

"Untouchable, more like! You think anyone's going to hire a Kimball these days? Paul, say something! This is an outrage!"

"You're wasting your time," Conrad said. "I think you'll find Paul did some valuable work on the valuation of the Tova deal."

"Well, I'm not going to sign this—I don't see why I should."

"Let me make your decision easy for you. If you don't, I'm going to cut you out of the goddamned will. You too, Hayden. Your distribution will be a nice round number: zero. You people are a sport of nature, I tell you. It never ceases to mystify me how two human beings could have given birth to a brood of scorpions. What about you, Sukie? Any questions?"

Sukie nodded and looked around. "Yeah, I got one," she finally said.

"Let's hear it."

She drew herself up. "Are you going to give interviews from your prison cell, Dad?" she said.

A long, stunned silence, and then Conrad laughed. Everyone else was watching them, their eyes moving from Sukie to Conrad and back.

She opened her laptop on the table in front of her. "This is the famous Tallinn study and all of the correspondence surrounding it— hold on, right here—"

"That's an invention out of whole—" Conrad began.

"All the documentation, right here," she said. "Proof."

"What— How the hell did you get that?" Conrad said. "Who gave it to you?"

Sukie was looking at her laptop, tapping a few keys. The folder wasn't opening. Her laptop looked frozen. She looked at me, then looked back at the keyboard, faltering for a moment. "As soon—as soon as this is released, Dad, you will face criminal charges for providing the government with false and misleading information about Oxydone. You lied and covered up and you had the study buried, and this folder of documents nails down every last damned detail. You will go to prison for the rest of your life." Her face was flushed, her eyes glittering.

"What the hell do you want all of a sudden, Susan?" Conrad said flatly.

"I want the keys to the car."

A long pause. "The what?"

From a leather portfolio she pulled out a sheet of paper and slid it across the table toward her father.

"I want you all to sign this piece of paper, turning over the management of the company to me and the professional team of managers I'm going to bring in."

"What?" Conrad nearly shouted.

"She's got to be kidding," Megan said. "Sukie, you have got—"

"And if you don't," Sukie went on, "the Tallinn file will be front-page news in the *Times*."

Hayden said, "You would do that to us, Sukie?"

But Sukie continued, ignoring the question. "This right here is a legal instrument that transfers all executive rights and responsibilities in your name over to SKG Enterprises. And that includes ownership of the hundred billion dollars in cash you've squirreled away offshore. That's right. I know about that too."

"What cash is she talking about?" Hayden said to the others.

Sukie looked at Hayden now. "For the last eleven years, Kimball Pharmaceuticals has been secretly siphoning out its cash. All the cash we could afford. Transferred to shell companies in offshore locations around the world that are supposed to look like R-and-D companies. Totaling over a hundred billion in cash, right, Paul?"

"A hundred and eleven point five billion, if memory serves," said Paul. "Wait a sec—let me double-check. Yes, I remembered right. What a relief."

"And what if we don't all sign this 'legal instrument'?" Megan said.

"Then the Tallinn study gets released," Sukie said, "and Dad goes to prison."

Megan shouted, "You'd be tearing down our own house, you idiot!"

Hayden said, "And if we do all sign it, it stays buried, is that what you're saying?"

"And then what?" said Megan.

"Oh, it's going to be a beautiful narrative," Sukie said. "The reformer daughter takes over the company. Undoes the sins of the father. Wall Street's going to love it."

"This is absurd," Conrad said, folding his arms across his chest.

Megan said, "And how does the reformer daughter undo these . . . sins?"

"We're going to transform Kimball Pharma into a company that makes anti-opiate drugs," Sukie said.

I tried to suppress a smile.

"Where's the profit in that?" Megan said.

354

"Where's the *profit?*" Sukie said. "Look at Vivitrol—on its way to being a billion-dollar drug. Same with Narcan. And generic naloxone nasal spray. You don't know how big the market is? The CDC is calling for millions of new anti-opiate prescriptions. The US government has allocated billions and billions to fight the opioid epidemic. So are countries all over the world. The potential is mind-boggling."

She paused, and for a moment no one else spoke.

"That's insane," Megan said.

"Actually, it's kind of brilliant," Hayden said.

"I think it's genius," Paul said.

"You see," Sukie went on, "the only way to save the company is to change it. Look, Motorola used to make car radios, right? Now they make cell phones and computer chips. There's a great metaphor I read once. If you leave a white fence post alone it becomes a black fence post. So if you want it to stay white, you have to keep painting it white. You want something to stay the same, you've got to constantly change it."

I felt cold. A tingle began at the base of my neck.

*If you leave a white post alone* . . . Victor, my father, had said that exact thing to me a week ago.

But when had Sukie met with Victor?

And then I remembered: Victor was the reason she came to me in the first place. He'd told her about me. She'd met him while she was doing research for her documentary about white-collar criminals.

Was this whole thing his idea in the first place?

But Sukie wasn't done talking.

"So those billions in cash are going to found a corporation called Kimball Wellness Worldwide, Inc. And I'm going to be the CEO. A pharmaceutical firm that's developing a new line of drugs that save people from opiates. Help people break through addictions."

Conrad, who'd been staring at Sukie, finally spoke. "*Anti*-opiate? What the hell do you know about that?"

"Let's cut the bullshit," Sukie said. "The opioid market is stagnant. The anti-opioid industry? Surging. Daddy, your day is over. You made a fortune selling knives. I'm going to make an even bigger fortune selling Band-Aids."

"You—you know nothing about the pharmaceutical business," Conrad sputtered. "What do you know about running a multibillion-dollar corporation? The biggest thing you've run is a shabby little film company with three employees and seven part-timers. Smaller than most hometown accounting firms."

"You've always underestimated me, Dad. You all have. But now you don't have a lot of options. You give me the keys to the car or I blow it all sky high, with you in it."

"I don't believe you'd do that," Megan said.

"Try me and see," Sukie said. "We'll go bankrupt."

"You'd really let that happen?" Megan said. "Why are you trying to destroy Daddy?"

"Destroy? I don't need to destroy him. Daddy's done. Time to retire to your yacht, Dad."

"So you don't give a damn about all the victims you're always talking about?" said Megan.

"Of course I do," Sukie replied. "But these lawsuits? Please. Most of the money goes to those greedy legal eagles anyway. And what do you think the families intend to do with their winnings? Buy a couple of double-wides? You think lawsuits are the answer? Forget it."

Sukie had lied to me all along. She wanted the Tallinn file as leverage, yes. But really as blackmail to force her father to turn the company over to her.

As I listened, I realized that I smelled smoke. I'd been aware of it for the last few moments, while Sukie was talking, but now it was unmistakable. I noticed a slight haze in the air.

"There's a fire," I said, standing. "We have to move."

Paul got up from his seat, as did Fritz.

"Fire!" Fritz shouted.

I rushed over to the door and felt it.

It was hot. The doorknob was scalding.

I knew immediately what had happened. Cameron and gasoline, two combustible substances.

By now everyone in the room had leapt up from the table. "Get down!" I shouted.

Black smoke was seeping under the door.

It seemed counterintuitive to get down, to sit on the floor, I knew, with the smoke coming in at floor level. But hot smoke rises, and the good, cooler, breathable air settles down.

"Oh, my God!" Megan cried.

Now a fire alarm upstairs began to clang. I thought of the century-old wood, dry as tinder, going right up in flames. And I knew the Ponderosa pine floor of the map room would go up soon, maybe in seconds; it was highly flammable.

"Megan, get down," I said.

"I am not going to get trapped in here," Megan said, racing to the door.

I saw what she was trying to do. She wanted to get the hell out of there, so she was going to open the door to run into the hallway and down the stairs. It was nearly an involuntary reaction.

And it would be a serious mistake.

"No!" I shouted. "Stop. Don't open that door. The only safe way out is through the window."

Natalya was waving her hands around. "My puppy! She's in my bedroom! Somebody get her!"

"I will not get trapped in here!" Megan repeated.

"Don't open the door!" I told her. I found it hard to stop coughing.

Fritz was helping Conrad out of his chair. The old man looked sick, sleepy. I shouted to Fritz, "Get him down on the ground!" Most people who die in fires are overcome by smoke, deprived of oxygen.

I was watching the Kimball family go into panic mode. I knew what was about to happen. I knew what the family was going to do.

Most people would react the same way.

When they're surrounded by a fire, most people get tunnel vision. The ancient fight-or-flight instinct kicks in. They rely on muscle memory all of a sudden—they're driven to follow old familiar pathways. In house fires, children will hide under a bed or in a closet. When people panic on airplanes, they inevitably run toward the front of the plane, where they entered. People become irrationally fixated on going out the way they came in.

So Megan and Sukie and the others wanted to open the door to the hallway, which would be a great mistake. That would pull the fire into the room. Then they would try to rush into the hall, toward the stairway, which had probably become a chimney by now.

Absolutely the wrong way to run. This fire was too fast-moving.

Instead, I ran to the window. It looked out over the rear terrace. Directly below were paving stones. A drop of approximately twenty-five feet onto stone would break bones. I thought of Anguilla and reassured myself that I'd done it before.

But then I remembered that in Anguilla the drop had been far less.

I unlocked the window and pulled it open, and immediately I felt an inrush of air. I heard a shout.

I yelled, "Over here!"

Then the door to the room came open and a pillar of black smoke billowed into the room. Now the thick, dark fog was everywhere. I gasped for breath and could feel the heat scorching my lungs, my throat. Everyone was coughing now, bent over.

I shoved a standing globe aside and clambered out the window, holding on to the frame. Directly below me was the patio stone, but maybe ten feet away from the house was a patch of evergreen shrubs, what looked like boxwood or arborvitae. My eyes were watering from the smoke; I could barely make out the shapes. I knew that if I was able to leap out of the window to a distance of ten feet from the house, my fall would be broken by the shrubbery. If I fell short of that, my neck would be broken.

"Over here!" I shouted again.

Finally I could hear distant sirens. The driveway was half a mile long; it would take a few minutes before the firemen were able to get out the ladders. And longer till they found us.

I decided to jump.

I lowered myself out the window, grasping on to the windowsill, down an arm's length, and pushed off against the exterior wall of the house.

Then I let go.

Kept my feet down, my legs and feet pressed tightly together.

My knees slightly bent for the impact.

Feet down.

I crashed into the thicker branches of the taller shrub, which jabbed painfully, like knives, into my ankles and thighs. I let out a yell. I was hurt. But I had landed, and without any broken bones, as far as I could tell.

I took a few uncertain steps. Then, limping a little, I forced myself to run across the patio past another ornamental shrub, over to the garden shed. There I found a ladder, as I'd hoped I would. I lifted it off its hooks, ran with it back to the window to the map room.

Fully extended, it was a little too long, but that was better than too short.

The first one to climb out and onto the ladder was Sukie.

# 80

Within twenty minutes, all of the Kimball family had been rescued from the second story. The fire department arrived by the time the third person was coming down the ladder. Eventually a few of the firefighters came around to the back of the house, where we were all gathered on the lawn, looking back as the flames ravaged Kimball Hall.

Conrad looked agitated, even furious, but not scared. He was issuing instructions to Fritz.

Cameron stood by himself, looking up at his handiwork. I heard him say, "Burn, baby, burn."

His face was strange, his eyes darting around frantically, and there were tears streaming down his cheeks. A couple of policemen flanked him. He wasn't going anywhere.

We stood back, watching the water jets douse the flames on the second story. My eyes smarted, and my throat was sore. I was waiting for Detective-Sergeant William Goldman of the Bedford Police Department, whom I'd texted in the meeting.

"How the hell did you know about all this corporate finance?" I asked Sukie.

"I learned from the best," she said. She met my eyes. I knew she meant Victor.

My stomach twisted. "Was it his idea?"

She shrugged. Her eyes looked off somewhere into the distance.

I knew that meant yes.

"He told me you were a sucker for the bird with the broken wing," she said.

I felt the air go out of me. Finally, I said, in a cool voice, "Why did you do it?"

She looked at me as if she didn't understand.

"I saw the video," I said. "You didn't disable *all* the cameras."

I could see a change in her gaze. It dawned on her what I meant. My scalp prickled.

I said, "I know *how* it happened. Maggie, I mean. You said you had something to tell her, and you took her over there"—I pointed to the stone wall, the ledge—"and all it took was one big heave. Doesn't matter how skilled she was, it just took one surprise push when her back was turned. No, my question is *why* the hell did you have to kill her?"

I was bluffing about having seen the video, of course, but Sukie didn't know that. She stared at me, her eyes widening.

"I had no choice," she whispered, almost inaudibly.

She'd recruited me at the funeral of my friend Sean, who'd succumbed to the very drug she wanted investigated. That was no coincidence. She knew what she was doing.

Which meant she had access to people deeply in the know. She was a woman on a mission, who claimed she'd been radicalized by the death of a close friend who'd been addicted to Oxydone.

That's what she claimed.

But I knew it was something else. Over the years, greed must have overtaken her. A greed for power. I thought of what Paul had said, that there was more Conrad in her than in any of the rest of the siblings.

That they were two birds of a feather.

Who was the one member of the family expert in video? The filmmaker, of course.

Who knew how to disable the cameras remotely?

The answer had been right in front of my face the whole time.

Oddly enough, it was her shoes that had first tipped me off, set something spinning in my mind.

The morning after Maggie was killed, Detective Goldman had asked everyone to wear the shoes they'd worn the night before, so the police evidence unit could take footwear impressions.

Sukie was wearing something different, I noticed.

At dinner the night before, she'd been wearing a pair of suede pumps with an ankle strap. Jimmy Choo, I was later told. The next morning, she was wearing a pair of suede Prada sandals that criss-crossed at the toe. The brands I didn't know.

But I could see the difference.

My recollection was confirmed in Anguilla, when Detective Gold-man sent me video taken in the foyer of Kimball Hall on the night of Conrad's birthday dinner. I pointed out to him that the shoes Sukie was wearing in the video were the pumps with the ankle strap. Not what she wore for the footwear impressions for the police the next morning, to mislead them.

Then Goldman found the exact same pair of Jimmy Choos at the back of the closet in Sukie's old room at Kimball Hall. They matched the impressions taken on the ground at the back of the house where Sukie had pushed Maggie.


It had taken me a while to figure Sukie out.

At first I'd wondered why she was so insistent on letting the pro-tester in her backyard with the gasoline cocktail go. Until I realized she'd probably hired him in the first place. To make her seem imper-iled. And to keep me on board.

Thanks to Victor, she knew I had a soft spot for the damaged bird. She read me right.

Victor had told her where my vulnerabilities lay.

The rag was soaked in gasoline, but I bet the can was filled with water. She was probably never actually in danger.

"Maggie wouldn't cooperate, would she?" I said. "I knew that woman, and I knew her code of ethics. She always wanted to do the right thing, even if it was the hard thing. She didn't find the Tallinn file, but she had dirt. Not the study, but a folder that proved the study existed. And she was going to break her confidentiality agreement with you and turn the documents over to law enforcement. To get the facts out there."

"We're talking about millions of lives," Sukie said, her eyes sparking. "Hundreds of thousands of deaths. This is a war. Don't you see the war going on in this country?"

I watched her, impressed. She was good.

"Oh, sure, our government sends thousands of young people to fight wars in foreign countries," she went on, "and gives guys like you medals for killing the enemy. But if one person has to die—"

"Maggie wanted to hand the file over to the FBI," I said. "You needed it kept secret. So you could use it as leverage against your father."

How, I wondered, would she keep *me* from turning a copy over to the FBI? Or some newspaper? Did she think that because we were lovers, I wouldn't turn against her?

She turned and saw Detective Goldman coming across the lawn.

"How many people did *you* kill, Nick? The next question is, why? Because at least I know why I did what I did." In a smaller voice she said, "I'm sorry she had to die."

My eyes filled. I felt more sadness than anger. Sukie was a sociopathic manipulator who needed to keep me on the trail. She'd researched me. And played me, skillfully. At one point she even pretended to want me to stop, feigning worry about my well-being, so I wouldn't suspect her. Instead, I'd redoubled my efforts.

Telling me to stop was like waving a red flag in front of a bull. And she knew that.

"You didn't really go to all those funerals, did you?" I said. "You told me you did, sure. And you went to Sean Lenehan's because you knew I'd be there."

She stared at me with some combination of resentment and indignation. "Maybe not as many as I said, but I'll be making a doc about the horrors of this epidemic, and I'm going to win a goddamned Peabody Award."

"From your prison cell?" I said, deliberately echoing her words.

She just looked at me for a long moment.

Detective Goldman nodded in my direction and said, "Susan Kimball, you have the right to remain silent."

I couldn't look her in the eye.

# Epilogue

A few days later, after the arrests of Conrad Kimball, Cameron Kimball, and Sukie Kimball, Gabe called me, sounding desperate. I told him to come by my office. He came in a half hour later, visibly upset, and showed me the Schwab app on his phone.

"I called Schwab and they said it's too late, there's nothing they can do about it," he said.

The balance in his account was zero.

Four point six million dollars had disappeared.

He was stunned and angry and despondent. "They said an authorized wire transfer was requested, and the funds have been moved to an offshore account."

I nodded, because I wasn't surprised. It was Victor, after all. He'd siphoned the $4.6 million away, as he'd always planned to.

"He played you, Gabe, just like he plays everyone," I said gently. *Like Sukie played me*, I thought.

"You know the old story about the little boy and the rattlesnake?" Gabe shook his head.

"A little boy's walking one day when he sees a rattlesnake on the ground in front of him, shivering," I said. "And the snake says, 'I'm old and freezing and about to die. Please pick me up.' And the boy says, 'But you're a rattlesnake. You'll bite me.' The snake says, 'No, if you pick me up, I'll be nice. We'll be friends.'"

"So the boy picks up the snake," Gabe said, impatient.

"Exactly. And of course the snake bites him. And the boy says, 'I trusted you! You promised me! Now I'm going to die!' And the snake says, 'Yeah, but you knew what I was when you picked me up.'"

Gabe nodded.

"Victor took advantage of you," I said, putting my arm around his shoulders. "I'm sorry it happened. But you knew he was a snake. I told you so."

My phone buzzed. I picked it up. It was one of the *New York Times*'s health reporters. I'd gotten her name from a friend.

"Excuse me," I said to Gabe.

Into the phone I said to the reporter, "I wanted to give you a heads-up. I'm about to email you a very large file of documents that I think you'll find interesting."


Later, Cameron told the police that he meant only to burn his father's evidence files, in the home office. He hadn't intended for the fire to spread to the rest of house.

He didn't know the files were in fireproof safes and cabinets anyway.

Sukie needed me to understand why she had had to do what she'd done. In her mind, the brilliant ends—her *anti*-opiate corporation—plainly justified the brutal means: Maggie's death.

She didn't know that I knew the woman and cared about her.

She also didn't know until later that the flash drive I'd given her, ostensibly with the Tallinn files on it, actually contained the same bug I'd used at Phoenicia headquarters. It had copied the contents of her computer and emailed everything to me.

I had plenty of evidence to give Detective Goldman.


Maggie Benson's parents were still alive, so sadly enough they had to bury their younger daughter. Maggie had also left a brother and a sister. There were a lot of family at her funeral in Madison, Connecticut, in a fine old Gothic Revival Episcopal church.

I was surprised to see Patty Lenehan, Sean's widow, there. She'd driven all the way from Westham, on Cape Cod, a good four-hour drive. She wanted to pay her respects.

After the funeral service, she and I talked for a bit outside the church. We talked about Sukie Kimball and why she'd done what she'd done. She told me that Brendan was starting to do better.

Then she told me she'd gone to see the funeral home director in Westham who was trying to rip her off. She told him that if he insisted on billing her eighteen thousand dollars, she'd go to the VA and the local newspaper.

He quickly backed down.

"Well done," I said. I knew I couldn't have done any better.

"Don't be a stranger, okay?" she said, her gaze lingering.

We drove together to the cemetery, a big and beautifully landscaped place right outside of Madison. Maggie's parents had arranged for a military honor guard detail, a couple of young army guys from the local recruiting office. They folded and presented the flag, from over her casket, to Maggie's parents. They played taps, again using a boom box.

It was a beautiful fall day, crisp and clear, almost cold. The trees were red and orange and gold, and leaves swirled around us. The wind was strong. My eyes watered.

After the casket was lowered into the grave, I found Maggie's parents. Her mother was small, like Maggie had been, and had the same beautiful eyes. The same liveliness. Her father was a big man in a wheelchair, bald and square-jawed and powerful looking, even in his old age.

"Maggie told me about you," her mother said. "She said you were one of the good ones."

I shook my head modestly. "I wish I was as good as she thought I was," I said.

367

She tilted her head, but before she could ask me to explain, her son put his arms around her.

Maggie's father took my hand warmly. His big hand was leathery and dry and cracked. He was looking around at his gathered tribe, his surviving son and daughter and their spouses and kids.

"Family," he said to me. "It's a powerful thing, isn't it? End of the day, it's what holds us together."

I swallowed hard. I didn't know how to reply. The sun was glittering, dancing on the autumn leaves. Finally I said, "I'd like to think so."

# Acknowledgments

The Kimball family isn't based on any real-life family. Long before I decided their money derived from pharmaceuticals, I was drawn to the terrain of great family wealth, dynastic ambitions, and shame. For legal assistance I'm indebted to Joe Teig of Reed Smith, Christopher Lynch of Reed Smith, David Sheldon, George Warshaw, Mark Batten of Proskauer, Jay Waxenberg of Proskauer, Jay Shapiro of White and Williams, Lori Smith of White and Williams, and particularly Celeste Letourneau of Reed Smith.

On the byways of the Pentagon, thanks to Lieutenant Colonel Richard (Rick) Drew. On Nick Heller's Special Forces background, my thanks to Sean Parnell, retired Staff Sergeant Kevin Flike (an American hero), and especially retired U.S. Army Special Forces Command Chief Warrant Officer John Friberg. For the Spanish translation, thanks to Oscar De Muriel.

The *New York Times*'s Barry Meier wrote an excellent book on the opioid crisis, *Pain Killer*, and helped me make sense of the business pressures behind it. Ed Silverman, of the invaluable *STAT*, was a terrific source on the pharmaceutical industry. On the development of drugs and clinical trials, I was helped by Dr. Maurizio Fava, the chairman of the department of psychiatry at Massachusetts General Hospital; and Professor David Armstrong of the Division of Gastroenterology at McMaster University Medical Centre. Dr. Amy Cohen helped me understand grieving children and families.

On Broadway, I got some sage insider advice from Evangeline Morphos. On documentary filmmaking, thanks to David Schisgall. My fashion gurus were Ashley Segal, Lucia Baldwin Rotelli, and Jillian Stein. Thanks to Wake Smith for details on the Choate school. On house fires and procedures, my thanks to Tim Simkins. A big thanks to a very astute hacker, Jayson Street. I'm grateful to Nick's trainer, Jack Hoban, and to my unindicted co-conspirator, Giles McNamee. I'm grateful as well to Detective Jeremiah Benton of the Boston Police, and my own team, Clair Lamb, Karen Louie-Joyce, and Marilyn Saks Goldstein. In the UK, I'm grateful to Laura Palmer and the team at Head of Zeus for their support; and especially Clare Alexander of Aitken Alexander.

Finally, my deepest thanks to the team at Dutton: John Parsley, Christine Ball, Amanda Walker, Elina Vaysbeyn, and Cassidy Sachs; and to my terrific agent, Dan Conaway of Writers House. Thanks once again to Emma J. S. Finder and Michele Souda, for their steadfast, loving encouragement. Most of all, for help above and beyond, I thank my brother, Henry.

# About the Author

**Joseph Finder** is the *New York Times* bestselling author of fifteen previous novels, including *The Switch, Guilty Minds, The Fixer, Suspicion, Vanished,* and *Buried Secrets.* Finder's international bestseller *Killer Instinct* won the International Thriller Writers' Thriller Award for Best Novel. *Guilty Minds* and *Company Man* won the Barry Award for Best Thriller, and *Buried Secrets* won the Strand Critics Award for Best Novel. Other bestselling titles include *Paranoia* and *High Crimes,* which both became major motion pictures. He lives in Boston.